REMNANTS OF THE FIRE

JEANENE COOPER

This book is a work of fiction.
References to real people, events, organizations, or locales are intended
only to provide a sense of authenticity and are used fictitiously. All other
characters, establishments, and incidents are products of the author's
imagination and are not to be construed as real.

Published in the United States of America

First Printing: July 2011

ISBN: 0-9833-4140-0
ISBN-13: 978-0-9833-4140-6
LCCN: 2011929562

Inquiries should be addressed to:
Purple Ditto Publishing
P.O. Box 11
Mullett Lake, Michigan 49761

For Janna,

my steadfast guardian since the day I was born...

⚜

ALSO BY JEANENE COOPER

"If I Should Never Wake"

The Northern Region of Michigan's Lower Peninsula,

also known as "The Tip of the Mitt"

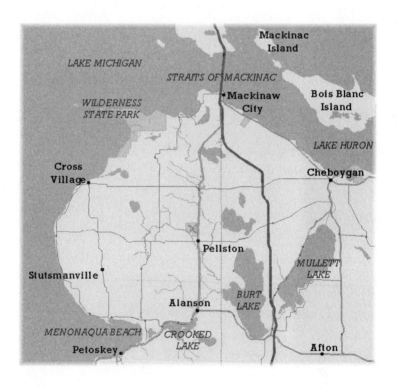

REMNANTS OF THE FIRE

"Everything we hear is an opinion, not a fact.

Everything we see is a perspective, not the truth."

— *Marcus Aurelius*

❖

Prologue

Despite completing her mission later than anticipated, Magdala felt no sense of urgency. On the contrary, she chose to linger in the sprawling forest of Wilderness State Park, wading through golden leaves scattered by Lake Michigan's gusty winds as she pondered all that had happened, and all there was left to do.

Wandering beyond the dense stands of poplars, birches, and maples, Magdala made her way along a narrow path of sand that wound between weathered cedars and pines, guided by the scent of damp stone. As the trees thinned and more of the late afternoon sun trickled through, she finally arrived at what she longed for — a place that would return her to the idyllic childhood she had left behind two decades ago.

She continued beyond the marsh grass that marked where the waters had receded, kneeling down in the sand and grasping a fistful of the damp gravel washed ashore by the waves tumbling in from Lake Michigan. Grinding the pebbles in one palm, she reached up with her free hand to tuck a dark ringlet of hair behind her ear. Then closing her eyes, she allowed the warmth of the Indian summer sun to take her back.

A faint vision formed in her mind, of teenaged brothers wrestling, the elder tugging at the scarf wrapped around the younger one's neck. Father in a long nightshirt enters the fray, separating the two with pats to their backs before embracing them both in his burly arms. Mother is there, too, her smile warm and assuring as she looks on with loving eyes. But in an instant, they are all taken from her, consumed by a sudden burst of flames.

The memory of the abrupt explosion shook Magdala from her daydream. Although the blast was now merely an image in her mind, it was still as real as the day it had happened… long

ago, when they took her home and her family away from her
forever.

Standing with a start, Magdala dashed the fistful of gravel against the shoreline, wiping the remnants from her hands.
She took notice once again of the brisk breeze blowing in from
the northeast, straightening her shoulders and pulling her wrap
tightly about her head and neck. With her determination now
rekindled by the painful memories of all she had lost, Magdala
considered what still needed to be accomplished, now certain
she would never waver until her revenge was complete.

"Hey, what are you doing out here?"

Startled by the voice yelling from behind her, Magdala
turned to see a tall conservation officer approach from the
wooded pathway, striding quickly through the marsh grass toward her.

"I spotted a truck that must be yours back in the woods,"
the unfamiliar man in uniform told her as he held up a large
piece of fine netting. "And I found this in the pickup bed. Is it
your net?"

"You tangled it," she replied as she took the net from his
hands and began to untangle the bundle.

The man brushed the net's grime from his hands, rubbing
them together for warmth. "You're aware that you can't use gill
nets in this area, aren't you?"

"Gill nets?" Magdala asked, confused.

"Gill nets... for catching fish." He pointed at the netting in
her hands. "Native Americans can use them in some waters, but
not here."

"Oh." She nodded, amused that her dark complexion cou-
pled with a bit of netting had brought him to misconstrue her
ethnic background.

"Ma'am, I'm not sure you understand. I'm a conservation
officer with the DNR," he told her, pointing at the identifying
patch stitched to the sleeve of his brown jacket. "It's my responsibility to enforce our state's environmental regulations, and that
includes any Native American agreements."

"I see." Magdala responded even though she didn't get his point.

"So, do you even have a card for using one of those?" the officer asked, his hands now on his hips.

"A card?"

"A native card..." He scowled. "I thought you were a tribe member. Aren't you?"

"Oh, yes." Reaching into her pants pocket, she pulled out the Odawa-Ojibwe tribal card they had made for her to use — just in case.

"Let's see," the man said, taking the card from her. "So you're with the Menonaqua Beach Band. I was just at your casino the other night," he noted with a grin. "Played the one-armed bandit, but didn't do so well."

Magdala did not know of this bandit, so she said nothing.

The officer glanced at the card once more. "Says here your name's Magdala Dawani. Now that's a new one — Dawani." He smiled. "I can't say I've heard that name around here before." He handed back the card. "So, as I was saying, Magdala, you're not allowed to use gill nets in any coastal areas zoned for—"

"Harp net," she interrupted, watching him through narrowed eyes as she tucked her card back into her pocket.

"Well, whatever your people want to call them, you just can't fish with them around here, okay?"

"I don't." She shook her head, glancing at the ruined net.

"Well then, that's good." He glanced at the netting. "That's a strange net, anyway. I've never seen one like that for fishing — doesn't seem strong enough, especially in the big lakes."

"I don't fish."

"Okay, then..." The man tilted his head and furrowed his brow. "So, what *do* you do, then? I mean, you've got these nets here and some unusual contraptions back in your truck... all of it making me wonder what you're up to here."

Magdala raised an eyebrow. "Why wonder?"

The officer raised his brow in return. "Why? Because it's my job to watch over this area and make sure it's not disturbed. See all of this property?" He motioned with his arm along the length of the beach and then toward the trees. "It's habitat for the piping plover, an endangered bird that only nests here and nowhere else in the world, so we're really protective of this land."

"Protective..." She paused, smirking at the irony.

The man tightened his jaw. "Well, I thought you might be more cooperative if I just explained what we're trying to accomplish, but I guess I was wrong." He shifted his weight. "I still need some answers here, Miss Dawani, so why don't you just tell me what it is you're doing out here all alone with all that stuff you've got in your truck?"

She raised her head, the wind picking up as it blew her wrap about her chin and shoulders. Unintimidated by the man's temper, she answered, "Waiting."

"Waiting?" His eyes narrowed. "So, who are you waiting for?"

Magdala reached into a fanny pack she had strapped just above her hip and removed a fistful of celluloid capsules, each shaped much like a tube of lipstick but a bit smaller. She handed the objects to the man.

"And what are these?" He rolled the tubes back and forth between his hands. "More gizmos?"

"I am waiting... for them," Magdala said, turning away and walking toward the edge of where the waves lapped at the shore.

"You're waiting... for these things?" He held one between his thumb and finger, tilting it to study it from all angles. "I don't understand."

"Do you know poems?" she asked him, still walking.

"Poems?" He shook his head. "Can you just tell me what these things are?"

Slowly walking the shoreline, Magdala glanced to the south, gazing at the forest to her side as she quoted from a Frost poem that Brother Rami had taught her years ago in the orphanage: *"The woods are lovely, dark and deep..."*

"Magdala, come on back so we can talk about this," He yelled to her, fisting the capsules in both hands as he motioned for her to return. "Hey, Magdala, are you okay?"

She continued walking the water's edge, the waves washing over her shoes and pant legs.

"Hey, I'm not going to hurt you, and whatever's bothering you, we can talk about it." Heading toward the waves, the officer kept calling to her. "I can help you, Magdala, so why don't you just come back here and—"

"I am done waiting," Magdala interrupted, reaching into her fanny pack and squeezing the detonator's trigger.

In a sudden explosion of fire, the capsules erupted, flames igniting the man's face and upper torso in an intense fireball. Screaming in a staccato of horrendous shrieks, the man scuttled about the shore, beating his face and chest with flaming hands as the fire spread by way of the combustible substance now adhering to his body.

Magdala stared at the blaze engulfing the man, listening to the familiar crackle and pop - the hideous sounds of human life afire. The smell of smoldering flesh pierced her nostrils, bringing with it an onslaught of recollections — inescapable memories of all the times when she had seen others die by fire. Her mother and cousin, the little girl, the nun, the soldier, the nurse... they all had looked the same at this point, when the fire had taken its grip, refusing to relent.

In the man's chaotic frenzy he fell to the ground, rolling about the gravel as he should, yet still unable to squash the flames. He tumbled to the shoreline where the waves lapped at the flames, diminishing what was left of the momentary inferno until it was extinguished. In the end, only a hint of smoke rose from the man, his body now still but for its ever so slight rise and fall with the motion of the waves.

The increasing winds dissipated the grisly stench, taking with it all of Magdala's recollections as she returned to the present. Turning toward the forest, Magdala reached into her fanny pack once more.

"The woods are lovely, dark and deep..." she repeated. Then with the squeeze of the second trigger, she watched in awe as a multitude of small firecrackers erupted, sending sparks flying through the trees. With simultaneous pops and bangs, the dry trees began to smolder, smoke trickling out from limbs that swayed in the lake breeze.

Magdala kept her eyes on the trees, noticing some flames popping to life as she stepped from the waves back to shore. *"But I have promises to keep..."* she continued Frost aloud as she walked toward the path that led back to her truck, leaving the body and fire behind her.

"...And miles to go before I sleep."

Chapter 1

"How's my driving?" Bridger Klein scowled as he read aloud the words adhered to the back of the slow-moving semi. "We've been staring at that sign for the last ten miles. Can't you get around this guy?"

"Are you *really* going to ask me that?" Neon Kashkari clenched the steering wheel even tighter, his knuckles white as he leaned his head left and drifted slightly across the center line for another look. Darting back into his lane, Neon cringed as an SUV hurtled past them. "An Escalade! Did you see that? A freakin' Cadi Escalade almost hits us head on, and *you* want me to pass – is that right?"

"Forget it." Bridger shook his head, acknowledging the futility in attempting to pass an eighteen-wheeler while stuck in a steady stream of two-lane traffic. Their best chance to get around this guy would come further up M-31 in a spot where the highway temporarily widened to accommodate a passing lane.

"No, how about I try again? Yeah, I'll give it another shot, right when there's another enormous, armored Humvee-wannabe bearing down on us." Catching a pothole with the left front wheel, Neon over compensated, grazing the gravel shoulder of the road.

"Whoa!" Bridger braced against the dashboard.

"I got it! I got it!" With hands at ten and two, Neon swerved their compact hybrid back into the lane.

"Not so sure you do!" Bridger lowered his hand from the dash. "Good God, man! After all that time working security with the Indian Embassy, driving people all over the place... didn't anyone *ever* teach you how to drive?"

"Of course they did!" Grabbing his Burger King cup from the center console, Neon slurped his lukewarm coffee. "I'll get us there, dude. Have I ever let you down?"

"No, but there's a first time for everything."

Neon smiled. "Oh, ye of little faith…" Taking one more swig from his coffee, he returned his cup to the console. "At least I can drive better than you."

"Yeah, that you can," Bridger had to admit. Since he had grown up on historic Mackinac Island where cars were not allowed, he had not learned to drive until he was in his mid-twenties. In the ten-plus years since, he had found even riding in a car to be somewhat disconcerting and so he avoided the task of driving whenever possible.

Neon pressed his head against the frame of his door. "I can see a little of the smoke in the sky off in the distance, but this guy's in the way — can't get a full view yet."

"I can't see much — just looks like a haze from my side. With our luck, it's probably no big deal."

"No, we've still got a ways to go, so don't worry. If it's been burning all night and they still don't have it contained, then it's got to be a big story this time. I can feel it in my gut." Neon slapped his taut stomach. "And if we need to spread out when we get there, you just go ahead and get your background scoop with the first responders while I get some action footage we can dub in later." Slapping his stomach a few more times, he added, "But first, I need sustenance. Hand me another Croissanwich."

"There's one left." Bridger reached to the backseat, retrieving a cold breakfast sandwich wrapped in grease-soaked paper.

"What? And no more tots?" Neon snatched the sandwich, ripping away the wrapper and shoving half into his mouth.

"You're such a pig. Just keep your eyes on the road so we get there in one piece."

Still chewing, Neon muttered, "Oh, I'm on it, BK!" With the back of his hand, he rubbed crumbs and grease from the dark stubble on his chin.

Bridger tossed the empty bag into the back seat and cracked open his window. As the odor of fast food and scalded coffee dissipated, the cool air of autumn filtered in, bringing with it the distinct scent of burning wood and leaves. To Bridger's right, the sun had risen high enough that it now cleared the tops of the tall evergreens lining the highway, pouring light into the car from the hazy sky above them.

Stuffing another large bite of sandwich into his mouth, Neon accelerated up closer to the bumper of the semi. "Come on, you moron. Move!" A piece of chewed sausage flew from his mouth and hit the windshield. "Oops," he added, wiping away the sausage with his shirt sleeve as he stayed tight to the truck's tail.

"Okay, you've made your point on the passing thing, so just back off this guy, will ya?" Hunkering down in his seat, Bridger closed his eyes and savored the warmth. "I don't care how long it takes us to get there, anyway."

"You don't?" Neon stayed tight to the semi. "Because I thought we were in some big hurry, like there was a fire or something. Oh, wait a minute... there *is* a fire, isn't there? Yeah, that's where we're headed in the first place!"

Bridger winced at the mention of fire, an involuntary reflex he had not yet overcome in the twenty-nine and a half years since the accident. "There's *always* something burning, Kashkari. Just wake me up when we get there."

"No, not true, comrade. There's *not* always a fire; it just *seems* like that because whenever there *is* a fire, Al always sends *us* to cover it."

Bridger cringed again, his eyes still closed as he reached back and scratched at the enormous scar carved into his right shoulder blade.

"Yeah, I think the boss-man has us pegged as his official WHAM-News firemen," Neon continued as he wadded up the last of his sandwich in its wrapper and tossed it over his shoulder. "Whenever there's even a chance that something's burning, you can count on ol' Alphonse Rainier to call on the same reporter — that would be you — and the same trusty cameraman — that, of course, would be me — for every fire story, thus creating an *illusion* of constant fire that can't—"

"Okay, enough with the illusion stuff!" Bridger snapped, sitting upright.

"Wow! Just clarifying the facts, man — didn't mean for you to get your boxers pinched in a knot!"

"Well… you're right! Al *does* always send us to cover the same old stupid, insignificant…" He paused, unwilling to use what he considered an even worse four-letter f-word — the one that rhymed with ire. "Well, just look at this!" Retrieving his disheveled notebook from between the seats, he flipped through them. "It's just car wrecks and accidents and… the names are different, but it's always the same, repetitive bullshit." He tossed his notes aside. "When are we going to get a *real* story?"

"But I think this *is* a real one!" Neon clicked on the radio that hissed as he switched it to AM. "Local radio's already reporting major acreage burned overnight, so maybe we'll catch a break on this one and come up with some amazing story about…"

"About what?" Bridger asked as he rubbed the patch of reddish stubble on his chin, anticipating another one of Neon's preposterous notions of what was newsworthy.

"Well, I don't know yet. Maybe like… like rescuing an animal or something. Yeah, like a whole den of wolverines — a mamma and her babies, caught in the blazing forest inferno!"

"A forest rescue…" Bridger twisted in his seat. "Some cutesy little human interest story is *not* what I had in mind."

"Cutesy?" Neon smirked. "Uh… have you ever tried to rescue wolverines? *Not* pretty."

Bridger smirked. "Yeah, funny, but it's not humor I'm after, and not gore either. You of all people should know that."

Neon ran his fingers through his unruly hair, grasping a dark brown tuft in his fist and pulling his head back and forth in a nod of agreement.

"I just want a chance to do some *real* investigative work — and I don't mean like asking the cops who ran the stop sign. I want to dig deeper — show people something they need to know that isn't so obvious... because the truth never is."

"Oh, I get it." Neon clicked his tongue. "So, now we're back to the old 'truth quest' thing, are we?"

"Always on it, dude. I'm always on it." Bridger picked up his Blackberry, scrolling down through his already answered emails.

"Well, I'm not so sure that the whole 'the truth shall set you free' business is all it promises to be."

"Yeah, well it's got to be better than the status quo." Bridger stared at the last email, another rejection from a regional network he had applied to. "But it's not just about this stupid, dead end job. It's Uncle Silas, too."

"Again with that?" Neon rolled his eyes. "So, what's the Professor done to piss you off this time?"

"Nothing. That's the problem," Bridger answered, still disturbed by his most recent argument with his uncle. In the years since the deaths of his parents, Bridger had grown ever more curious about the circumstances that had taken his mother and father from him, and so for answers he had turned to the man who had raised him — his father's brother, Professor Silas Klein. But Uncle Silas was a man of few words outside of the lecture hall, and so Bridger knew little more than what he'd been told since childhood: that his mother had died from a brain aneurism just before his father had been killed in a fiery crash that had almost taken Bridger's life, as well. But his uncle's continual unwillingness to share any further details regarding his parents' untimely deaths had, over time, led Bridger to suspect there was more to the story... and to harbor an ever-increasing resentment toward his guardian — the sole remnant of his lost family.

"So, you and Professor Sy don't see things eye to eye?" Neon chuckled at his feeble rhyme. "That's nothing new, so just give it a rest, bro. Besides, you need to be thinking about *this* story. Time to get your game on, BK. We need to hit the ground running with one of those creative angles you're so good at masterminding. So, what's the plan? What're your instincts telling you?"

"My instincts are telling me that Uncle Silas is a bald-faced liar." Bridger thumbed through the papers scattered between the seats. "He keeps telling me he has no idea where my folks were born. But I still remember when I was young, he took me to visit one of his professor buddies down at U of M and I overheard the guy telling him how much he liked my parents and how sad he was about what happened. When I asked Uncle Silas later how the guy knew my folks, he told me that both were born and raised in Ann Arbor and that his friend knew them through the university there."

"There, you see? Then he *did* tell you something. So now you can get back to being Mr. Happy Bridger and we can get back to the news reporting business — that is, as soon as we can pass these eighteen wheels." Neon gritted his teeth, yelling, "Come on, you idiot! It's a semi, not a school bus!"

"Yeah, but now Uncle Sy swears he never said my parents were born in Ann Arbor. He must have figured I'd forget what he said... just like I've forgotten so much else. But I remembered." Bridger paused, gathering up a few sheets of paper that he rattled in the air. "So, I checked the records in Washtenaw County and all of the surrounding counties, as well — and in all those searches, I didn't find one single birth certificate from anytime even close to the early nineteen-fifties that matched either an Elliott Bridger Klein or a Roslyn Udele Ellsworth-Klein. They're nowhere to be found." He slapped the papers in his lap. "So, I called up Dr. Klein and asked how it was that a professor with a background in Communications and Archaeology and, no less, a Ph.D. in American Studies, can't manage to direct me to a couple of birth certificates, one of which is for his own brother who he—"

"All right! One more mile to the passing lane!" Neon interrupted, nodding at the highway sign as they passed it by.

"Stop changing the subject, will ya!" Bridger snapped. "I really want your opinion on this because you know him as well as I do, and I think you'd have to agree that he's hiding something."

"Okay, maybe he is, but I don't want to get into this. Besides, I headed off to DC for that job he got me at the Indian Embassy nearly twenty years ago, and I haven't seen that much of him since I've been back in Michigan — doubt I still know him as well as you think I do."

"The man pretty much raised you, just like he did me, so you know him well enough to see how obvious it is that he's not telling me everything there is to know about my folks... or the accident."

Neon raised his eyebrows, glancing at his friend. "But you lived with your folks until kindergarten, BK, and you were right there *in* the accident." He bit his lip. "I just don't get you, dude — What more is there to tell?"

Bridger crossed his arms. "You *know* I can't remember what happened, so why do you always put that back in my face?" Turning his face away from Neon and into the breeze blowing in through the open window, he stared at the pines and poplars racing past the moving car. "And it's not like I haven't tried to remember. What, with all that therapy and hypnosis crap they've put me through, you'd think my uncle would want to help me remember. But no, he seems to think it's best that I keep it suppressed... and I suppose you do, too."

"Hey, I have never said that!" Neon objected.

"Then why change the subject?"

"Because every time you bring this up, you end up getting all pissed off at me like it's somehow my fault — just like you are right now!"

Bridger hated to admit it, but he knew his friend was right. "Yeah, well... I'm sorry about that. Guess I just wish somebody could fill in the blanks for me."

"Finally!" Neon exclaimed as he pressed the accelerator, veering left as the semi stayed right, the one lane widening into two. Holding his fist to his mouth, he simulated chatting on a CB radio. "Breaker-breaker one-nine, let me know 'How's *my* driving' while I'm passing you, good buddy!" Then extending his fist into the air, he tugged it down twice, motioning for the truck driver to blare his horn.

As the trucker obliged, Bridger turned his attention from the side window to the open road ahead. There he set eyes upon the full magnitude of the situation, staring at the enormous swathe of gray smoke angling across the horizon in the distance. "Oh, my God, Neon! Look at how big that—"

"That's crazy!" Neon's eyes widened at the sight of the vast plume now altogether visible in the northern sky. "We've never covered anything like this. Maybe this *is* our big break."

"Maybe..." Bridger furrowed his brow, appraising the potential significance of the story ahead of them. "Yeah, it's huge compared to others, but it's still pretty rural, far from any towns." He removed the Michigan map from the glove compartment, folding it so that only the northwestern portion of the Lower Peninsula was visible. "We've got wildlife, recreational, and environmental angles to cover if it stays in the park. There'll be a little more interest because of its size, but not much with the locals if it just burns trees and doesn't threaten anyone's personal property."

"Brutally true, BK. You've got that journalist's instinct, always cutting to the—"

"Wait a minute," Bridger interrupted as he noticed a curious variation in the smoke. A darker plume was now rising further to the west, drifting easterly to meet with the gray. "That's not the same..." Pausing short of his least favorite word, he waved his hand at the massive gray cloud. "With so much acreage burning, this whole patch of smoke must have a lot of depth to it, and yet notice how it's not quite as dark as that band rising up on the western edge," he added, pointing left toward the darker strip of smoke. "That smoke's a lot more dense — maybe a Ringelmann four, whereas the big cloud is more of a Ringelmann three."

Neon tilted his head. "A Ringel-what?"

"Ringelmann — you know the scale for measuring smoke density? I looked into it a few years back — figured we should know a thing or two about smoke if we were going to be in this business." Bridger rustled the map. "That smoke's thicker with debris, and it's coming from a different place."

"A different place?" Neon's eyes scanned the horizon. "What? Are you sure?"

"Positive," Bridger answered, pointing at the map. "You need to turn left past the Pellston Airport and head toward Lake Michigan."

"But the fire's more north. Why are we going west?"

"Northwest…" He pointed to Wilderness Park on the map, "Here's where the big clouds are coming from…" Drawing his finger southwest along the edge of Lake Michigan, he traced the shoreline until he reached the first small town on the map. "… and here's where the new plume's rising."

Neon glanced at where his friend's finger had stopped. "Cross Village? But it couldn't jump all those miles from the park."

"I know, so it's got to be a separate burn, and by the looks of that smoke, I don't think it's just trees." Bridger folded up the map. "It may not be as big in size, but I've got a feeling it's the bigger story, so let's check it out."

"Then we go with the Bridger instincts!" Neon accelerated, passing another car before the road narrowed back into one lane. "Call it in to the station."

"Uh… maybe we should wait on that. Better see if I'm right before Al gets a chance to tell me I'm wrong."

"Oh, so we'll do this as one of our *covert* missions, the kind that always pisses off our pal Alphonse?" Neon lowered his brow into a devious expression, his grin widening. "I like it!"

"It's just a detour, and I'll text Kelli Sue when we get there — let her break it to Al."

"So, dump the unpleasant task on sweet Miss Llewellyn, the unsuspecting receptionist?" Neon shook his head. "Man, when you sniff a story, you're not above exploiting the little people, are you?"

"Who, K-Sue? She may be young and inexperienced, but she's tougher than you might think." Bridger retrieved his

Blackberry, scanning for any breaking news on the fires. "She's a great little researcher in a pinch, too — should come in handy if we need some last minute background on this." He glanced up just in time to see their turn approaching. "Hey! Slow down, dude! That's our turn!"

Taking the corner, Neon swerved left, wheels squealing as he cut in front of oncoming traffic. "Like that? Just one of many moves I learned when I drove for the embassy."

Bridger pushed himself away from the side door where he'd landed on the turn. "Didn't they teach you anything valuable there — like how to stay alive?"

"Hey, I've told you before, BK…" Neon lowered his voice as if someone else were listening. "I can't tell you any of my secret-agent-man stuff, 'cause if I did…" He glanced left and right with an exaggerated expression of paranoia. "…well then, I'd have to kill you."

Bridger laughed. "Yeah, everybody thinks they've got something worth hiding, don't they." He rolled his eyes. "All right, so enough with the secrecy crap. Just get us there in one piece so we can have a shot at reporting something people might actually need to know."

⚜

Chapter 2

B ridger stared out his open window at bloated black clouds billowing into the northern sky, their point of origin close at hand.

"It's got to be just around this corner — turn up here at Oak Road." Bridger pointed to his right while checking their current location on his Blackberry's GPS application. "Looks like it's on the outskirts of town."

"Are you sure?" Neon barely slowed for the turn. "I thought it'd be on the main drag — maybe that new weaving place with all those looms, or more likely that Polish restaurant everybody's always talking about."

"Legs Inn? Naw." Bridger shook his head, still staring at the dot moving across the GPS application. "No, it's right here, I'm telling you. Make the turn!"

Neon braked hard, swerving onto the unmarked path of pavement, his eyes now staring north. "Whoa! Look at that!"

Bridger glanced up to see tall, deciduous trees lining the narrow road, their varying tones of gold and auburn outlined by the black torrent of smoke racing skyward beyond them. He rolled up his window as the smell of smoke intensified, rekindling in him some unpleasant reminiscence that remained just out of his mind's reach.

"Guess you're right," Neon admitted. "So, if it *did* miss downtown, then what's burning?"

"On this map, it looks like farmland and maybe some greenhouses, but I can't be sure. There's also some place marked the Vineyard B&B that might be involved. I'll text K-Sue now — see if she can get us some background."

"Yeah, while Al's yelling at her because we didn't go where we were supposed to..." Neon smirked. "I can see him now with those bloodshot eyes bulging, beads of sweat dripping off that black eight-ball skull of his while he's puffing air like a bull about to charge…" He glanced in his rear view mirror. "Hey, looks like the cavalry's coming."

Bridger turned around to see a pickup and an SUV gaining on them, each topped with a single, flashing red light. "This must be exciting stuff for volunteers," he commented. Turning back to face forward just as their car topped a hill, Bridger saw strobes of red, blue, and yellow flashing ahead of them. "And looks like the pros got here first. That's good — some authorities to quote."

Now approaching ground zero, Bridger caught his first glimpse of the flames, his heart racing and stomach turning as they always did at the initial sighting of a wildfire. His saving grace was that he knew from experience this feeling would pass once he jumped into the story, but for that brief moment every time, he would suffer a sense of anguish so powerful that his eyes would well with tears.

"Smoke getting to you again?" Neon handed him a napkin left over from breakfast.

"Always does," Bridger replied, taking the napkin and wiping his eyes.

"Yeah, it's burning the hell out of my eyes, too. Can't let a little smoke stop us now, though — got to buck up and get ready to go!"

Bridger smiled, grateful that his best friend was never critical or disparaging about his anxiety; Neon always knew the best way to get him through it.

Approaching a pair of sheriff and state trooper cars parked amid the fire trucks, Neon pulled off in the dry weeds along the shoulder of the road, well out of the way of emergency vehicles. "Best stay back here. I'll get my gear." Popping the trunk, he jumped out and hurried to the back of the car.

Closing his eyes and taking a deep breath, Bridger whispered to himself: "Do this right, BK, and maybe you won't have to do it again." Then exhaling, he opened his eyes wide and stared at the flames flickering just up ahead. "Okay, let's do this," he added, grabbing his Blackberry and papers before exiting the car and heading without hesitation toward the inferno.

"Right with you, pal." Neon jogged up next to him, bearing his camera and video gear under his arms.

Striding ever closer to the scene, Bridger felt the heat intensify as familiar crackles and snaps emerged from the rumble of combustion. But he refused to be intimidated, ignoring the twinge of recollection stirring within him. "Looks like all of the greenhouses caught fire." Pressing on, he glanced at the rolling smoke, noticing the purplish-green hue that ebbed and flowed through the blackness as the menacing clouds hurtled skyward. "All of that plastic, peat moss, fertilizer – it must intensify the smoke."

"I'll get some angle shots that show both fire and smoke." Neon withdrew his tripod, popping up the legs. "Maybe I'll do a slow pan up from the flames to the sky. What do you think?"

"Whatever – I trust you." Bridger stopped a moment, pointing toward a small group of firefighters. "Hey, I think I see Trooper Ward over there talking to those guys."

"Oh, yeah," Neon nodded as he coughed, choking a bit on the smoky air. "Holly's always good to you, BK. I think she's got a thing for you, pal," he added with a wink.

"She's old enough to be my mother."

"Hey, age never stops a cougar. Rrr-oww!" Neon clawed in jest.

"Just hurry up and get some footage, smartass, and then meet me over there." Turning away, Bridger hustled toward the group while removing his Blackberry from his pocket. Glancing at the screen, he noticed a text message waiting for him from Kelli Sue. Saving it for later, he scanned through the apps, turning on the one for voice recording just as he stepped up to Detective/ Sergeant Holly Ward.

"Thanks for the update, guys," Holly remarked to the departing firemen, turning to meet eyes with Bridger. "Didn't expect you here quite yet — thought you'd be off covering Wilderness Park."

"We saw the smoke coming from here and thought we'd check this out first — maybe get the latest info from my most trusted source." Bridger smiled, raising his Blackberry toward her as he started his voice recording app.

"I just got here a short time ago, so I don't know too much yet."

"Well, what'd the guys have to say?" Bridger asked, nodding toward the group of firefighters as they pulled gear from a nearby truck.

Holly tilted her head, tucking stray strands of her gray hair back into her trooper's cap. "You know I can't say much yet, Bridger. It's all very preliminary." She pointed toward the fire. "I can tell you that these greenhouses and surrounding farmland are all a part of the Village Plant and Fruit Farm."

"And where's the Vineyard B&B?"

"Further down, and up in flames." She shook her head. "I don't know how they all got out of there without anyone getting hurt, or worse."

"Really?" Bridger found it a curious statement. "Did it spread fast?"

"You might want your own eye-witness accounts on that, Bridger, and I've got to get back to my own investigating so—"

"Just a lead, and I won't quote you." Bridger shut off the Blackberry, sliding it back into his pocket.

"They described popping sounds, like fireworks or multiple cap bursts, and then the attic and roof burst into flames."

Just then, Neon jogged up from behind carrying his camera still attached to the tripod. "Got that done, so now I need a little footage of you, Detective Ward, if you don't mind…" Without waiting for a response, he set up.

Ignoring Neon, Bridger asked her, "So all of the guests just ran out of the place before the fire spread?"

"Yeah, the innkeeper — nice lady — she said she quickly checked the rooms and accounted for all the guests, so we're pretty confident they're all safe."

"And so the B&B must be where the fire started." Bridger made a note on paper.

"Not so sure about that," Holly noted. "The innkeeper and all the others say the same thing; that when they ran out, they saw some of the greenhouses and trees already in flames — looks like spontaneous combustion in multiple locations."

Bridger kept writing. "And can I quote you on that?"

"No." Her answer was terse. "I'm only telling you this so you don't go incorrectly reporting that the fire all started with the B&B."

"Oh, come on!" Neon complained as he stepped behind his camera, ready to film. "That'd be great info on camera!"

"And you're not going to get it, Neon," she reiterated. "Now hurry up and start rolling because I haven't got all day — got to get going here."

"Yes ma'am!" Neon obliged as he framed an image with both Holly and Bridger in the picture. "Ready when you are."

"Thanks." Bridger nodded toward Holly. "Start with your usual stats." He didn't need to tell her anything more.

"At approximately nine this morning, the Emmett County Sheriff and Fire Departments were alerted to a fire at the Vineyard Bed and Breakfast as well as the neighboring Village Plant ånd Fruit Farm. Fire, police, and rescue units were dispatched from area communities while others were diverted from their current positions at the Wilderness State Park."

"Has that left you shorthanded for containing the Wilderness Park fire?"

"Officials assure us that they still have enough units to deal with the park blaze while contending with this fire, as well."

"Do you or other officials have reason to believe these incidents might be connected?"

"There's no reason to believe that at this time, but we remain open to that possibility as we continue to pursue any and all leads as to what may have caused either of these fires."

Bridger couldn't resist trying to get something extra. "Where do you believe this fire started?"

"Oh, it's still too early to tell, but I have no doubt our experts will be able to piece that together." Holly grinned at him, unwilling to budge.

"Have there been any reports of injuries or fatalities in either of the fires?"

"Our preliminary findings indicate that everyone safely evacuated the bed and breakfast, and the owner of the farm has accounted for all of his employees, so we currently believe this incident was free of casualties." Holly paused, a glint in her eyes. "However, we've received word that a Wilderness Park conservation officer hasn't reported in and is now considered missing. The officer's name has not yet been released."

Bridger nodded with appreciation for the new information given on camera. Certain he should not press this topic any further at the moment, he asked, "What about containment? Do you feel you have control of these fires?"

"Authorities at Wilderness Park are saying the fire is seventy to eighty percent contained and predict they'll have a full handle on it by noon, barring any unforeseen changes in the weather. As for here in Cross Village, the firefighters have done a tremendous job of assessing the fire and directing units to deal with hot spots, so we should have this location under control shortly, as well."

"Has the fire jumped at all? Do you have—

"I think you've got a good start, guys," Holly told them both as she stepped back from the camera. "I've got a lot to get to, so better end it there."

"Thanks for the leads," Bridger replied. "Is there someone at the DNR I could follow-up with on the—"

Interrupting Bridger mid-thought, a clean-cut man in a windbreaker bearing a state park patch cut in on them. "Did you see this one?" Pointing toward what once was the B&B, he spoke to Holly. "It's just like the copper I told you about at Wilderness!"

"Copper? Like the metal?" Bridger asked Holly.

Holly stopped. "Bridger, this is Dawson Rivard, a historian with the state parks. He's the one who brought news of the missing officer just before you got here."

Rivard extended a firm handshake to Bridger, adding, "Yeah, and I also came here to tell the detective about this Native American artifact — a copper shield — we found at Wilderness. It's something we never see around here!"

"And I promise we will take a look at it," Holly assured him. "Once we—"

Rivard ignored her, now speaking to Bridger. "I was just wandering back to my car, staying on the road so I wouldn't get too close to where it's still burning, and bam! I spot another copper almost exactly like the one I already found! It's just crazy, huh?"

"Let's get this," Bridger said to Neon while spinning his finger in the air to indicate filming.

"Already rolling," Neon answered as he held his eye to the camera.

"So, Mr. Rivard, who did you say you're with?"

"It's Doctor Rivard, Ph.D. in Anthropology. I do work for the Michigan Park Services."

"Okay, and I understand you've brought news from the fire at Wilderness Park. First, what do you know of a missing DNR officer?"

"Uh, I was informed that Kent Blackburn of the DNR was on duty at the time the fire started last night and that he hasn't been heard from since."

Bridger caught a peripheral glance of Holly rolling her head in disgust over the revelation of the officer's name. Turning from the camera for just a moment, he assured her, "We won't include that until you say it's okay."

Holly crossed her arms. "You better not."

Turning back to Rivard, Bridger continued. "Tell us about your other discovery."

"Well, at dawn this morning, I joined a group at Wilderness Park that was assessing areas where the fire had been put out, and that's when we discovered something we've never seen in this area – a Native American copper!"

"Can you explain what that is?"

"A copper? Well, when referred to in Native American terms, that would be a large flat sheet of metal – copper, obviously – shaped into what we'd call a flared shield that has a T-shaped ridge beaten into the lower half."

"A shield?" Bridger questioned. "You mean, like one used in fighting?"

"No, they're not for defense; they're for trade, and prestige. Some are quite small, with the largest ones ever discovered measuring no more than thirty inches high – which is about the size of these two!"

"Meaning that you've now found another one?"

"Yes, there's one at this fire site, as well!"

"And are you saying these coppers aren't typically found in this part of Michigan?" Bridger asked for clarification.

"I'm saying they're not found at all in Michigan, or in the Midwest, for that matter," Rivard expounded, shaking his head and waving his hands with both palms down for emphasis. "Sheet copper was prized by the northwestern tribes found along the Canadian Pacific coastline, but never here. Even though the Great Lakes' indigenous people heavily mined the vast ore deposits in the Keweenaw Peninsula of Michigan's UP, you would never see hammered copper shields like this anywhere around here!"

"And coincidentally, you found them at the scenes of two separate yet somewhat similar fires–"

"A little premature on assuming similarities, aren't you, Bridger?" Holly interjected. "I prefer to see this for myself, Dr. Rivard; that guarantees that I make *educated* assertions with the evidence. So, come on – let's see what you've got."

"Well, okay!" Rivard obliged, leading the two away from where the fire continued to rage, toward what remained of the B&B.

"I'll catch up!" Neon assured his partner, detaching the tripod and collapsing it into his bag before shouldering his camera to chase after the three.

"It's past here a little further." Rivard directed them down the road toward a tan Chevy Malibu with official state plates parked near a guard rail.

"The guy's an eager one," Holly noted under her breath as she walked along side of Bridger. "I know you're an eager one, too, Mr. Klein. Just make sure you stick to the facts and don't get ahead of yourself."

"You know I always do," Bridger replied as his cell phone vibrated in his pocket. He ignored it, feeling quite sure he knew who it was — a call that had to wait just a little bit longer.

"Hey, hold up," Holly yelled to Rivard. "We don't have this area roped off and I don't want you going in where we haven't had a chance to—"

"Don't worry. I won't go where the fire's been," Rivard promised her. "There's no need to anyway. You can see it right from here." Now standing at the guard rail, he pointed downward at the ravine below him. "This stream running through here must've stopped the fire from spreading."

"Wait before you say any more!" Neon panted as he jogged past Holly and Bridger, propping up his camera on his shoulder and pointing it at Rivard. "Okay, Doc... Let's show and tell."

"Uh, yeah..." Thrown for a moment, Rivard's enthusiasm returned. "I was looking down here at this stream, noticing how the water must have stopped the fire from spreading, and that's when I just happened to see that glimmer on the other side."

Neon panned the camera along Rivard's pointing arm, continuing downward into the ravine before coming to a halt. Holding the camera still and steady, he continued to roll a bit longer before stopping.

Bridger came up behind him, asking, "Did you get it?"

"Oh, yeah! Can you see it over there?" Neon pointed to the tarnished shield. "When the one bank burned away, it must have opened up this area enough to let in light — made it easier to spot the thing."

Bridger stared at the copper as it reflected back flecks of light from the sunshine breaking through the smoky haze. "It doesn't look like I thought it would... for something old," Bridger admitted.

"Who said it was old?" Rivard replied.

Bridger gazed at him, confused. "Well, from what you said... I just assumed these were relics."

"Assumed..." Holly smirked.

"Hey, I never said they were authentic!" Rivard's forehead tightened, his gray eyes narrowed. "Quite the contrary, I told you that Native Americans in this region never had these." He shrugged his broad shoulders. "But I still think it's strange that they'd show up like this, and at both fires. Don't you?"

"Yes, I do," Holly admitted as she jumped the guard rail and headed down the steep gradient toward the copper.

Bridger was right on her tail, racing down the mossy embankment littered with leaves. Distracted by his cell phone vibrating once more, he failed to notice a protruding tree root. Catching it with his toe, he tripped and slid, stumbling his way through loose leaves and gravel to where he almost collided with Holly.

"Watch it, Bridger!" she scolded him. "There's spots still smoldering on this side, so be careful where you step."

"I'm fine, I'm fine," Bridger insisted, brushing himself off as he reached the copper before her. "Look at that! It's got some kind of symbols hammered into the thing."

"They're probably syllabics," Rivard told them as he skillfully descended the bank to join them. "The copper at Wilderness was marked with Aboriginal syllabics, so if this one's like that one..." He paused, studying the markings. "Yeah, these are the same."

Holly knelt down, grasping each side of the copper with her gloved hands. "So, you're sure this thing's the same as the one at Wilderness?"

"Similar, but not identical," Rivard answered. "Same shape, about the same condition, both with First Nation markings... but the syllabics on this one look a little different. I think the two of them must each say something different."

"So, can you translate them?" Bridger asked as his phone vibrated once more.

"I can try." Rivard rubbed the dark stubble on his buzz-cut head. "I already took a shot at deciphering the other one, but it didn't make any sense — it's like the syllabics don't match up with a true Aboriginal language. But I can keep trying until—"

"Hold on," Holly interrupted, releasing one side of the copper so she could turn up the volume on her two-way radio.

The speaker crackled. "...10-70, possible 10-80 reported at Beacon Hill Retirement Village at Stutsmanville. Multiple condo units engaged with reports of four... no, five injuries. Ambulances have been dispatched. Calling for additional police and firefighting units to respond from other scenes..."

Holly grabbed the copper in both gloved hands, yanking it from the ground. "I've got to go, and this is going with me." Tucking the shield under her arm, she hurried back up the embankment.

"It's another fire, isn't it?" Bridger was right behind her in hot pursuit.

"I don't have time for this, Bridger!" Holly yelled back at him as she drew her two-way from her belt, depressing the side button to speak. "This is 78-19, will respond to Beacon Hill. Recommend implementing a Type 4 county-wide IMT with Lieutenant Varney as Incident Commander, over."

Rivard caught up to them. "An IMT? What's going on?"

"That's an Incident Management Team — something they put together when they need to coordinate a wider response," Bridger explained. "Sounds like there's another fire."

"And I don't need you fanning it!" Holly snapped at him as they made it back to where Neon was still filming. "I hope you two will practice some restraint with the public. We don't need people panicking on top of everything else." With that, she jogged past them and back toward the pack of emergency vehicles.

Neon lowered his camera. "Did you say another fire?"

"Yeah, and we've got to get to it!" Bridger answered, turning to Rivard to hand him a business card. "I want to follow up on this copper thing – maybe get them both translated. Can you text me with your contact info?"

"Uh, sure, and I'll send you the photo I took earlier of the copper Detective Ward has, plus I'll take one of the other copper I took from the park."

"You have the other copper? Well, that's great!" Bridger smiled, shaking his hand before backing away. "Thanks a lot, Dawson."

"Sure. So, let me know if you find one at the next fire." Rivard unlocked his car. "We'll be in touch."

"Absolutely."

"Hey, let's go!" Neon yelled as he took off for the car. "Just tell me where we're headed."

"It's that gated retirement place with the golf courses they built north of Harbor Springs," Bridger told him while withdrawing his phone from his pocket, taking note of the three missed calls from Kelli Sue.

"Oh, man! That place is practically brand new!" Neon maintained his stride as he glanced at the phone in Bridger's hand. "But you know you've got to call the station."

Almost to the car, Bridger punched the call back button and pressed the Blackberry to his ear. "Yeah, it's me."

"Oh my God, Bridger!" Kelli Sue blurted loudly in his ear. "Al is *so* mad at you two!"

"I'm sure, but we've got the real deal going here, so he's just going to have to hold off on the Wilderness Park thing while we go to another fire that—"

"I know, Beacon Hill. It's just nuts, isn't it?"

Bridger paused. "How did you already know about the—"

"The Beacon Hill fire? Are you kidding? It's all over the news! Even the cable networks are picking it up! And Al said you'd call and want to go there, and he said to tell you absolutely no."

"What? But this is huge! We have to go!"

"Yeah, and Al told me you'd say that, too, so he already sent somebody else. Sorry about that," Kelli Sue lamented.

"You can't be serious! Who did he send?"

Kelli Sue hesitated. "Sonny Dais."

"Al sent the weathergirl?" Bridger shut his eyes in total disbelief, unable to visualize how the dainty red-head with her cosmetically whitened smile could ever convey the ominous nature of this mounting threat to the public.

Neon shook his head as he pushed the remote to unlock the car. "Sorry, but I'm not surprised."

Opening his eyes, Bridger went off on Kelli Sue. "Well, you tell that SOB he can just forget about us going to Wilderness! I'm not going to be his little errand boy going to all the stale stories while I've got great leads to follow up on!"

Kelli Sue was slow to reply. "He doesn't want you to go the Wilderness."

Bridger scowled. "He doesn't?"

"No, he wants you back here... right now."

Opening the passenger-side door, Bridger climbed in. "Half the state's on fire and he wants us to come back there?"

From the driver's seat, Neon frowned, looking puzzled.

"Yeah, and Al said immediately — no questions." Lowering her voice, Kelli Sue added, "He's really upset, Bridger. I overheard him on the phone talking about something to do with that protest still going on over at the Menonaqua Beach Indian Casino — how he thinks it could end up causing more trouble than the fires."

"Really..." The Indian reference connected with Bridger, reminding him of the coppers. "I need some quick research from you, K-Sue. Put together a history of these shield-like things called Native American coppers. Then figure out which of their languages are most common in this region and see if there's a cipher that can make sense out of something called Aboriginal syllabics. You got all that?"

"Still… writing… got it!"

"And most important, find out what's got Al so upset. Can you do all that for me?"

"I'm on it!" she answered.

"You're the best, K-Sue. Tell Al we're on our way." With that, Bridger pressed end on his cell, tossing it aside as he looked to Neon. "Head back to base, partner."

"Really?" Neon steered out of the weeds, pulling a U-turn. "I'm surprised. It's not like you to give up on a story without a fight."

"Who says I'm giving up?" Bridger poked at his Blackberry, opening an email from Rivard that included a photo of the copper. "As far as I'm concerned, we're just getting started."

⚜

Chapter 3

"You people are a nuisance!" Naomi Drummond grumbled under her breath as she navigated her way through the steady stream of protesters marching to and fro in front of the Menonaqua Beach Casino.

"Save – our – homes! Save – our – homes!" the crowd of locals chanted, waving signs that read *It's OUR Native Land* and *Eminent Domain is an Imminent Threat.*

"Why don't you give ours back," she muttered as she scampered in stiletto heels up the casino's front steps, gripping her leather brief case at her side.

A security guard greeted her with a smile. "Good morning, Ms. Drummond," he said, holding the door open for her.

"Morning," she replied to the familiar man whose name she could not recall. "You make sure all the guests get through this mob without a problem," she added, passing through the door.

"I always do."

"Good," she said to herself, pausing long enough to glance up at the casino's spectacular centerpiece – an enormous clock fashioned with stripped timbers and natural gemstones to resemble a Native American medicine wheel. Scanning the vast clock face, its first quadrant composed of amber citrine, the second of dark red garnet, and the third of black onyx, Naomi's eyes came to rest on the fourth quadrant of colorless rock crystal backlit with white light. There she saw the copper hands of the clock, the minute hand overlapping the hour hand where they hovered at the left edge of eleven.

"Yes!" she breathed to herself, relieved to know she had arrived in time for this obligatory meeting. With not a moment to spare, she headed to the left of the clock where she darted around a wall and down an obscured hallway. Pressing her free hand to the side of her up-do to make sure every brunette hair was in place, she advanced toward the closed doors of the secluded conference room.

"You made it, and in record time." Bill Granger greeted Naomi by opening one door for her, turning on his good leg to extend his free hand as he balanced on his carved walking stick, his long braid of white hair dangling to his side.

Naomi tried to catch her breath, hindered by the offensive scent of tobacco smoke mixed with lemon furniture polish emanating from the conference room. "Yes, I suppose that might be a record." She shook his hand reluctantly, not because of the skin graph scars they bore but because she knew what had caused his injuries. Naomi wanted nothing to do with a man who had been nicknamed 'Butane Bill' due to his earlier years of pyromania. He had nearly killed himself when he burned his own house to the ground, and she continued to wonder why the band's chairperson would hire such a man to be his personal assistant.

"Can I get you a coffee?" Bill offered.

"No, I'm fine — just in a hurry to get down to business." Naomi patted her briefcase.

"Well, Chief Weatherwax is waiting for you." Bill motioned for her to enter. "There's ice water on the table, so let me know if you need something else. I'll be just outside the door."

"I'm sure we'll be fine," she replied as she entered the dim, mahogany-paneled room to find Takota Weatherwax, Chairman of the Menonaqua Beach Band of Odawa and Ojibwe Indians, seated at the opposite end of a long conference table. "Oh, and I see that Chepi's here, too," she added, both surprised and concerned to see the chief's daughter seated at his side. She strode toward them, putting on a smile as she extended her hand. "Good to see you both!"

"Welcome, Naomi." Takota put out his cigarette and rose to his feet, straightening his arthritic back as he reached out with leathered hands to clasp hers, shaking it. "You said this was urgent, so I took the liberty of inviting Chepi since I often seek her advice on important issues. I hope you don't mind."

"Not at all," she lied, reaching across the table to shake hands with Chepi, as well. "It's good to see you again."

"You, too." Chepi nodded and shook hands, a chunk of her blunt cut, jet-black hair tumbling over her narrowed, dark eyes. "My father says you've got documents that might help our tribe settle this land dispute."

"And we're eager to see them," Takota added. "You know how I feel about that marina and all those homes between our casino and the water's edge; we've never wanted to remove those people from the land of their ancestors, even though it's the land of our ancestors, as well."

"Of course," Naomi replied. "And United Tribal Consortium appreciates your compassion for the people who currently hold the deeds to land that's rightfully yours."

"But they aren't false deeds." Takota took his seat, lifting his hands with weathered palms upturned. "Those people may have bought their land from thieves, but they still paid for it. They were tricked, too, so taking the land from them would be wrong. We'd gladly settle this if we were given a comparable parcel, so I'm hoping that's what you've brought us."

Naomi frowned, shaking her head. "No, the UTC Council remains adamantly against such concessions, especially now that we have evidence that further substantiates our claim."

"Meaning *your* claim," Chepi said. "Although our band remains a member of the UTC, you as the Council Chairwoman must know that the Menonaqua Beach Band does not agree with *your* desire to take these waterfront properties from their current owners."

"And *you* must be aware that the Council has to pursue what is in the best interest of *all* the member tribes, which means we can't ignore what's come to our attention." Naomi removed papers from her briefcase. "I have here copies of the recently discovered Treaty of L'Arbre Croche and Michilimackinac, a document signed on March 20, 1841, by Petoskey's founding father Chief Neyas Petosegay and then President of the United States, William Henry Harrison." Handing one copy to Takota, she disregarded Chepi as she continued. "In brief summation, the treaty refers back to articles in the Treaty of Washington, a document signed in 1836 by a handful of Odawa and Ojibwe who betrayed their people by surrendering northern Michigan and the Upper Peninsula for money."

"…while they selfishly kept large parcels of land for themselves," Chepi added. "We know all this, Naomi. The people who signed away our land were killed for their betrayal, but you and the Council continue to fight for this land around the marina and along the Little Traverse Bay, and I don't understand how—"

"Let's hear her out, Chepi," Takota interjected, handing his copy of the document to his daughter before extending his hand to Naomi for another.

"Thank you." Naomi turned to the second page before handing over the document. "You'll see I've highlighted in this Treaty of 1841 where it mentions Articles Two and Three of the Treaty of 1836. Both articles indicate that large tracts of land were intended for tribal use, and that these lands were to be reserved for five years from the date of the treaty's ratification, which could be construed to be as early as the date it was signed — March 28, 1836."

"Reserved for five years, and no longer." Takota added. "I'm familiar with what's written in the Treaty of Washington."

Naomi smiled. "Well, then you must know that there's an exception in Articles Two and Three; both articles say that the land will be reserved for no longer than five years *unless* the United States grants permission for the tribes to remain on said lands for a longer period… which is exactly what President Harrison granted at the request of Chief Petoskey."

"What?" Takota stared at the document, frowning. "I'm not following you."

"Don't you see?" Naomi grabbed her pen and pointed to the area highlighted on the chief's copy. "Right here, it refers to those tracts granted to the tribes. You could probably read this better if we opened the blinds," she added, motioning toward the windows.

"Keep them closed," Chepi insisted. "It just antagonizes the protestors when they see us in here from just outside the window. Can't you hear them out there?"

"No," Naomi answered, pausing negligible moments to catch a hint of the muffled, rhythmic mantra from those she considered her immoral adversaries. "I hadn't noticed," she added, her resolve intensified as she continued to explain the treaty. "Anyway, here's where it lists our rights to Beaver Island and Round Island, and a thousand acres on the Thunder Bay River, another thousand on the Big Sail of the Cheboygan River, and my favorite... fifty thousand acres along Little Traverse Bay — the land we're reclaiming!"

Takota shook his head. "But all of this was settled with land grants given to establish new locations for the tribes and casinos and–"

"This is far from settled!" Naomi insisted. "This newly discovered treaty extended the rights to these lands indefinitely, which would mean permanently!"

"And where did you get this?" Chepi asked.

Naomi was losing her patience. "It's on page two where I showed your father that–"

"No, I mean where did you get *this*?" Chepi waved her copy of the treaty in the air. "How can you know this is even authentic? Chances are–"

"Chances are it's real!" Naomi snapped. "Professionals have worked all through the night to give us their best preliminary assessment which indicates that this is a legitimate document."

"Harrison was known as Old Tippecanoe from his battle with Tecumseh," Takota recollected from history. "The two fought over the Fort Wayne Treaty, with Tecumseh saying it was illegitimate because only one tribe agreed to it without the consent of others, while Harrison argued it was binding and was willing to kill to enforce it. If that was the case, then why would a warmonger like Harrison sign this peace treaty?"

"Our historian addressed this in his findings." Naomi retrieved more papers from her briefcase, disbursing them to the others. "He points out that Harrison served as an Indian Agent under President James Madison, traveling to the Northwest where he negotiated treaties with the tribes of that region."

"He also writes here that Harrison died shortly after he supposedly signed this treaty," Chepi noted as she perused the historian's report. "The man only served thirty-two days in office, the shortest presidential term in history."

"Which the historian believes may explain why this treaty fell through the cracks." Naomi tugged at her jacket lapels, adjusting her shoulders as she stiffened her back. "Nonetheless, once we prove its authenticity, then the UTC can take this before the courts and legislature as we—"

"Continue to fight with our neighbors over these lands?" Takota shook his head, tightening his arms across his chest. "No, we're not in favor of this."

"Besides, this treaty was never ratified by congress." Chepi slid her copy back across the table. "It's not even legally binding... and I'd still like to know where you got it from."

"It doesn't matter how we got it!" Naomi retorted, not surprised to find the chief's most loyal advocate to be as outspoken as ever. "All that matters right now is that we have this copy to work from while we continue to track down the person holding the original."

"You mean you don't even have the original?" Chepi rolled her eyes. "Oh, this is ridiculous! You're just going to cause more trouble for our people while you trot out this bogus treaty and make a joke of us!"

"You may not believe in this document, Chepi, but it is quite credible — enough so that it will strengthen our position." Naomi grabbed Chepi's copy, slipping it back into her briefcase. "This treaty says those lands should never have been taken from us, and now that the people of this state are paying the price for all of this pent up outrage, then maybe they'll finally listen."

Takota scowled. "What do you mean?"

"Well, the fires, of course! Do you think they're just a coincidence?" Naomi slid her hand into the exterior pocket of her briefcase, gripping the yet unrevealed note she had been hesitant to share... until now. "You should know what this conflict is doing to the people you are supposed to represent." Withdrawing the paper, she handed it to Takota.

He studied the paper with an expression of mounting distress, his bronzed complexion losing its ruddiness until he looked pale.

"What's wrong?" Chepi asked him. "What does it say?"

Takota read aloud from the copy of a handwritten note. "Return our land or revive the time of fire."

"And it's written on tribal letterhead." Naomi snatched the note back from the chief. "Menonaqua Beach letterhead, that is. I found that threat along with the copy of the treaty in an unmarked envelope stuck inside my screen door when I made it home last night." She clasped her hands, rubbing them together as she tried to steady her nerves. "I must admit it's a bit upsetting to think some pyromaniac decided to hone in on my address, of all places."

"That's an understandable concern." Takota furrowed his brow. "Please allow us to arrange security for you. I'll have Bill keep an eye on your place until the situation's dealt with."

"No need," Naomi insisted, indignant over the absolute absurdity of offering Butane Bill as protection against a would-be arsonist. "I'm taking care of that, but it's not me I'm worried about. It's *your* people, Takota — *our* people." She frowned, attempting to look distressed. "When this letter hits the media, it will reflect poorly on the Menonaqua Beach Band."

"Nonsense." Chepi reached across the table and retrieved the note, staring at the heading. "So what if this is our letterhead? That doesn't mean someone from the tribe wrote it." She put the note back. "It could just as easily be someone framing us, trying to make it look like these fires were started by someone from our tribe so they can discredit us in this whole legal battle."

"That's exactly what I thought!" Naomi jumped at the chance to make her argument. "If someone from the Menonaqua Beach Band was behind these fires, it would be stupid for him to narrow the field of suspects by connecting himself with the tribe. That's why I think this is a ploy — a way to make us look bad so we lose any legal standing. So, I plan to beat them at their own game by talking to the media first." Standing up, Naomi handed them both the last paper she had planned to give them. "This is a chance for the public to see that it's the Native Americans who are under attack here — that these picketers are trying to stifle our livelihood while denying us our claim to what is rightfully ours."

Takota scanned the press release he held in his hand. "You've scheduled a news conference?"

"And it's here?" Chepi added with a tone of outrage in her voice.

"For one o'clock," Naomi replied. "That means we have less than two hours to prepare, so I *will* need help from your people, Takota." Grabbing her briefcase, she stepped back toward the door. "If I may still take you up on your offer of help from Bill, I'd like him to get a podium set up outside right where the pick-eters are marching."

"You want to publicize the picketing?" Chepi stood up, waving her arm toward the shades drawn to block the view of the disgruntled crowd. "That's not the P.R. image we want out there! These demonstrations have hurt us enough already."

"And that's why we're going to turn this around on them." Naomi reached the door, opening it to address Bill who still stood in the hallway. "We need you to get a podium placed out-side the front doors of the casino, right at the top of the stairs. It's for a press conference at one, so do it right away; the media might arrive within the hour to set up their microphones. Can you handle that, Bill?"

"Uh, yeah, I'll get going on that." Bill turned, almost trip-ping before he hobbled off with his marching orders.

"What do you think you're doing?" Chepi raised her voice to Naomi as she advanced toward her. "This is *our* facility! You don't call the shots around here. My father's the one who—"

"Yes, I'm the one, Chepi." Takota reminded her of her place. "And this action's already been taken, so like it or not, the media's now on its way. Just like the waters flowing to the ocean, we can't stop it — we can only make sure it flows smoothly without any big waves that could cause destruction." He turned his dark eyes to Naomi. "I wish to speak at the news conference, as well — right after you. Can we agree on that?"

"Of course," Naomi answered, realizing she would need to word her initial statement so as to prevent the chief from stopping what she planned to put in motion. "I think it would be most appropriate for you to have the final word... and given that, let me leave you with Chepi for just a moment while you two consider what you might want to say. I have to step out to make a quick phone call, but I'll be right back so we can coordinate our statements."

"That'd be best." Takota nodded. "And I want to make a quick call to the police."

"What?" Naomi halted. "But why do you need to call them?"

"We need to tell them about this threat." Takota withdrew his cell phone from his pocket. "It's best for your protection and others, too — that is, unless you've already told them yourself."

"Uh, no... but they'll know soon enough, from the press conference."

"You got this letter last night but never called the police?" Chepi's tone was judgmental.

"You know, hindsight's always twenty-twenty, Chepi," Naomi snapped back. "Last night there was only one fire burning, and I figured this guy who left the envelope was just some crackpot taking advantage of the opportunity to make an idle threat. I didn't know the other fires were going to happen, and it's just been a couple of hours since they were even reported, so we'll get the word out soon."

"But we should let the authorities know now." Takota opened his cell phone.

"Well, I suppose we should," Naomi pretended to agree. "And since I'm the one who received the note and the treaty, I guess I should be the one to call it in." She again tugged at her jacket, buttoning it to keep everything in place. "I'll do that right now before I even make my other call, so don't worry — You two just focus on your statement and I'll handle the police." With that, she marched out of the room and into the hallway, closing the door before they could inundate her with anymore of their annoying opinions.

The phone vibrated in Naomi's hand, just as it had been for the last five minutes. Staring at the words *Private Caller*, she pressed accept, annoyed with the Consortium's PR man who felt the need to block his caller ID. "I told you I'd get back with you when I knew who sent this stuff to me, but I don't know yet! So, why are you bothering me?"

"Because *I* know," the voice said on the other end.

"Who is this?"

"The one who sent it."

"Really." Naomi shuddered, almost dropping her phone. "Uh... and who would that be?"

"Someone trying to help — just call me Thoreau."

"Thoreau... yes, and so..." She took a breath. "Why are you calling me?"

"To assure you that the treaty is real, and that the original is forthcoming."

"Well, that would be helpful. So, when can I get it?"

"All in due time."

"Okay." Naomi steadied herself. "And what about... the fires?"

"I would assume they'll continue, which should help your cause."

"I see..." She went speechless, unable to further probe the circumstances she found so alarming.

"You're not a target of the Firekeeper, Naomi, so don't concern yourself with that," Thoreau assured her.

"The Firekeeper... and that's not you?"

"Oh, no!" Thoreau laughed. "I'm just a guide, Naomi, and I want to get you focused on the threat you ought to be concerned with... the one from your people's greatest enemy."

"What?" Naomi struggled to balance her phone with her shoulder while removing a folded paper from her briefcase – the one paper from the unmarked envelope she had chosen not to show the others. "You mean this typed one that threatens to kill trespassers? No signature – just a medicine wheel with hash marks along the–"

"That is not a medicine wheel." Thoreau's voice was almost a whisper. "It's crosshairs..."

"Crosshairs?" Naomi unfolded the paper and studied the symbol. "Well, I guess it could be." She swallowed hard. "Someone must've put that on there thinking it would scare us."

"It should scare you," Thoreau told her. "Those people mean what they've written – they *will* kill anyone who tries to take their land."

"Really..." Naomi tightened her grip on her phone. "And who are *they*?"

"The crosshairs gives it away – it's a Mil-Dot Reticle, and there's just one prominent group that uses it for their logo – the Michigan Battalion."

"Militia," Naomi whispered, tugging her collar up around her neck.

"They don't like it when people try to take their lands, or the guns they've buried in them."

Naomi trembled, her heart racing. "I'm sure... they... don't."

"Turn the letter over to the authorities, Naomi. They'll keep you safe while you tell the media what cowards these militia people are for threatening you and your people."

"The news conference..." she muttered as it dawned on her how vulnerable she would be. "You know about it... and they might know..."

"Keep your head and stick to your guns. The original treaty will show up by tomorrow – I promise," Thoreau said and then hung up.

"Hello! Hello!" Naomi yelled at the phone.

Chepi must have heard her as she swung open the door. "Is everything all right?" she asked Naomi.

"Oh, just great!" she answered as she poked at her phone, dialing 9-I-I.

Chapter 4

"This is an ONUS News Alert from our breaking news desk where we have a report of a serious fire involving multiple homes at a gated retirement community in northern Michigan," announced cable news anchor Kate Stoneham as she appeared on one of the WHAM newsroom monitors. "For details, we go to our correspondent at the scene, Sonny Dais, who is with our ONUS Network affiliate WHAM-TV out of Burt Lake, Michigan. Sonny..."

Bridger stared at the monitor, his mouth gaping as he saw Sonny's image appear on the screen.

"Yes, Katie, it's quite a scene here at the Beacon Hill Golf Community just north of Harbor Springs..."

"Did she just call her Katie?" Kelli Sue asked as she, too, stared at the monitor from her desk far across the open room, a location closest to the office's front door.

Bridger shook his head. "Yes... she did."

"...and the fire has now moved, sweeping its way from this condo unit to the clubhouse just across the way," Sonny noted with an ill-considered smile, wielding her hand in a broad circular motion as if the fire were a weather pattern on a green screen.

"Finally... a chance at a serious network segment, and she acts as if it's the daily forecast," Bridger griped.

"It should be you covering this," Kelli Sue replied, her pale blue eyes narrowed as she glared at the screen. "That ditzy girl can't hold a candle to you, Bridger."

"At least a dozen people have been transferred to the nearest hospital, some with quite severe injuries, Katie!" Sonny smiled as she reported with an enthusiasm more appropriate for cheerleading at a ballgame.

Bridger threw up his hands. "I cannot believe this!"

"I'll turn it down." Kelli Sue grabbed one of the control-lers from a box on her desk, muting the volume so that only the faint drone of elevator music from the neighboring office could be heard. "I would just turn it off, but you know how Al wants an eye kept on the network, and I don't want to get in trouble."

"Al…" Bridger grumbled as he turned away from the muted travesty playing out on the screen to look through the panel of glass windows that lined his boss' office. "What the hell is tak-ing him so long?" he complained as he watched Al nodding at whatever he was being told by his boss, Pennelope Wirth, Vice President of Mission Broadcasting. "He wants me back here pronto, and for what! So I can watch him talk to some boss-lady from corporate? Must be nice to be important."

"Yeah, that woman always shows up at the worst times, and Al's got to deal with her, but in the meantime…" Kelli Sue rose from her desk, heading Bridger's way. "…I did get some more info on that Anishinaabe language."

"Thanks, K. Did you figure out what those coppers say?"

"Oh my God, no! Those syllabic things are tricky!" Snapping her gum, she tossed some papers on his desk. "That's the rest of my research on the area tribes."

He looked at the top page. "So, the Odawa and Chippewa of the area are all considered part of what they call the Anishinaabe peoples?"

"Also known as the First Nations peoples — it says so right here." She reached toward him, wafting hints of citrus perfume and spearmint gum as she pointed out details in her notes. "And I found out that Chippewa can be another name for Ojibwe — guess the two are kind of interchangeable, but some prefer one over the other."

"Hmm…" Bridger slipped on his new reading glasses so he could make out the tiniest details in the photos of the cop-pers he'd received from Rivard. "But you couldn't find anything about coppers native to Michigan."

"Nothing for the plural *coppers*, but plenty on the singular *copper*. I gave you all of that over an hour ago. Didn't you read it?"

"I scanned it." Failing to recall the report's details, he shuffled papers about his cluttered desktop, unable to find it.

"It just says that Michigan's Keweenaw Peninsula is where they've got the biggest deposits of native copper in the whole world, and that they think Native Americans mined it because archeologists found copper along the trading routes around here — copper they could prove came from those mines because it had this special isotopic kind of makeup that's only found in that one place, and nowhere else in the world." Kelli Sue reclined against the edge of the desk across from Bridger, stretching out her long, slender legs in front of her. "You'd know all this if you'd just read what I gave you."

"I know. I'm sorry." Bridger continued searching his desk until he almost tipped his dirty coffee mug off the edge. "I'll look into that later. Maybe we could even send in a copper for testing — see if it's from around here. But for now, let's just focus on figuring out what both of them say."

"Well, that'll be tough enough," Kelli Sue told him as she reached for the nape of her willowy neck, twirling her crimped blonde hair with her fingers. "I thought it'd be like playing *Wheel of Fortune*, but trust me — it's not."

"So, it wouldn't help if I bought you a vowel?" Bridger smirked.

"You have no idea. You can't just match up those syllabic things to individual letters. It's more like translating Chinese, but this language has these consonant-vowel pairings called *abugidas* where the symbol always represents the same consonant but the position of the symbol decides the vowel."

"So, you're saying the symbol means the same consonant no matter which way it's pointing, but if it's pointing left, it has a different vowel following it than if it's pointing right?"

"For the most part... like the V-shape represents *p* — which I think is confusing enough." She smirked. "So, if it's a normal V-shape pointing down, that means the *p* is followed by *e*. If it points up, that's *pi*. Then pointing left is *pa* and right is *po*."

Bridger reclined in his chair. "Okay, so it's challenging, but we should be able to figure that out."

"I've already done that much," Kelli Sue told him as she reached further across his desk and pulled a paper from the bottom of her latest stack. "There are also some triangle shapes that don't have a consonant, and there's a sideways-S that stands for *sha*. With all of that, this is what I came up with." She handed him the paper.

Pressing his drooping glasses back up his nose, Bridger compared the chart to Kelli Sue's handwritten deciphering of the two Anishinaabe phrases.

ᖧ ᐊᑫᕐᕫ ᑳᣉ ᐱᒀᑎ ᐃᔆᣀ᜶ᣀ ᕤᕭᕫ ᕓᐱᐅᐊᕫᑎ ᕫᕫᕫᣀ
NA ANACITA KA SHA PIME TI ISA SOSOSACA YAMITA CIP ITEATA TI CIMITASISI

ᖧᖧ ᐱ ᔔᣀᒪ ᔔᣀᐊᕤ ᕤᣉ ᣉᣀᖧᕤ ᕤᕫᕫ ᒪᣀᒪ
NANA PI YESA MA YESAAME YASA SHASANA MEYA YAMITA CAPIMA

"So, this must still be in the Anishinaabe language," Bridger said to Kelli Sue as he handed her back the paper. "Now all you have to do is just translate that to English."

"Just…" She laughed. "I've searched all the translation sites I can find, plus I also called NMU's Native American Department, and I keep coming up with the same answer — this isn't translatable."

Bridger frowned. "But it has to be, or why go to all the trouble of writing this?"

"Well, maybe it's just a diversion to throw off the authorities." Kelli Sue cracked her gum. "The only thing I've picked up on so far is a grouping of a three syllabic pattern. It shows up one time on the Wilderness copper, then again on the B&B copper, and it deciphers to *yamita* — which doesn't translate to a darn thing…" She hesitated before continuing. "You know, I thought of someone else who might be able to help us. This guy's studied the history of local tribes and, as a matter of fact, he's helping fix up the old Indian Dormitory over on Mackinac Island, making it into a museum for—"

"No, I don't need help from Silas." Bridger cut her off once he realized she was alluding to his estranged uncle. "I've still got plenty of sources of my own to turn to." He reached in his pocket, pulling out his Blackberry. "I'll check back with this Dawson guy – see if he's getting anywhere with—"

Al's office door burst open, stopping Bridger mid-thought as his attention turned to the large man and slender woman now stepping into the newsroom.

"I appreciate your help, Alphonse," Pennelope Wirth said with her hand extended.

"And yours, Penne," Al replied with a vigorous handshake.

Bridger glanced at Kelli Sue. "Penne?"

"Yeah, like the pasta," she whispered back. "Weird, I know."

With her chin held high, Penne strode toward the newsroom's front door, her creased gray slacks swinging gracefully with each step as she buttoned the front of her matching suit jacket. "Be in touch, Alphonse," she added, offering a glancing smile to Bridger and Kelli Sue. Then reaching beneath her blunt-cut wisps of whitish-blonde hair, she found her Bluetooth and pressed it, commanding it to call a number as she went out the door.

Al said nothing more to his boss as she departed, instead turning his somber gaze toward Bridger. "And now, I need to see you."

Bridger raised his eyebrows, feigning a look of surprise. "Me? You've got time to see me?"

"Come on, funny guy." Turning back toward his office, Al motioned with his beefy hand for Bridger to follow him, adding, "And K-Sue, I need you to send in the other funny guy, too."

She jumped off the desk. "He's in the editing room – I'll get him."

"And once you get him, could you keep working on those translations?" Bridger asked her as he headed for Al's office.

"You know I won't give up that easily," she answered, already striding off to find Neon.

"I owe you big time," he yelled after her as he stepped into Al's office, then turning to his boss. "So, why'd you call us back here when we were right in the middle of a story?"

"Have a seat," Al directed him while dropping into his own leather chair behind his desk. "I've got something more important for you and Neon to cover."

"Really?" Bridger planted himself in a side chair. "Because I thought we were already covering something pretty important when you pulled us back in and then sent Little Miss Sunshiny Dais out to do what *I* should have been doing!"

Al cocked his head, crossing his burly arms across his broad chest. "Now son, what makes you think you can just come in here and talk to me like that? Sometimes I think you forget that I'm your boss."

"Oh no, you do plenty of things that keep me well aware of that fact." Bridger reclined back, tucking his hands in his pants pockets. "But you know, sometimes you act more like a dad than a boss — or better, a friend."

Al took a deep breath. "You know I like you Bridger, no matter how hard you may make it sometimes. I try to look out for you, and everyone else around here, so I'm sorry if that comes off as coddling to you." He turned to look at the sky outside his window, staring at the ominous smoke billowing upward in the west. "But I've also got a business to run, and some tough decisions to make, and if you don't agree with the way I make those decisions, then I'm afraid you're just going to have to deal with that."

Neon burst through the door. "Am I missing the party?" He grinned as he plopped down in a spare seat. "Bet you're celebrating my great video footage I dubbed into Sonny's network segment. That shot — the one where I started on the fire and panned up through the smoke all the way into the sky… Beautiful! Just freakin' beautiful!"

"Hope you get an Emmy," Bridger quipped as his eyes rolled upward to stare at the ceiling.

"Hey, maybe I will!" Bridger lightheartedly punched his partner in the arm before turning to his boss. "So, what's our next mission, Alphonse?"

"I'm sending you two over to Menonaqua Beach to cover a press conference scheduled for one o'clock." Al picked up the press release from his desk, passing it to Bridger. "A woman named Naomi Drummond who heads up the United Tribal Consortium is presenting some new document the UTC thinks will solidify their tribal claim to that big parcel they've been trying to seize — you know, that land between the beach and casino, including the Menonaqua Marina."

Bridger glanced at the press release. "This woman sure picked a bad time for a presser." He looked up from the paper. "With all these fires burning, this doesn't seem all that important... if you ask me."

"Well, I've decided it *is* important," Al responded. "People around here want to know how that conflict's going to play out — if eminent domain trumps individual rights. Besides, she's talking on the front steps of the casino, right where all the landowners are picketing, so I thought you'd want to cover this. Protests, confrontation, lots of controversy..." Al smirked. "I thought it sounded like your kind of story."

Neon's eyes widened. "Yeah, dude! And while we're at it, let's do one of those detailed color pieces you're so good at putting together. We'll get some average Joe interviews — you know, like first person accounts from people on both sides. And then you can add some analysis, some of the history..."

Bridger's thoughts remained elsewhere. "I'm also going to keep looking into these fires. I've got some leads Kelli Sue's helping me with that—"

"Yeah, I know about the coppers — saw the pictures on K-Sue's desk before you two even got back here." Al stood up from his desk. "She can keep working on those for you while you're gone — *if* you promise not to go traipsing off on your own again without my permission."

Bridger was hesitant to make a promise he wasn't sure he wanted to keep. "But what if we stumble onto a lead? Can't we follow up?"

"It's a simple request, Bridger; you call me and ask — *first*." Al looked over at Neon, pointing at him. "And *you*... You keep him on a tight leash. I don't want him wandering off like some dog smelling somebody else's garbage just put out down the street."

"Aye-aye, sir!" Neon snapped a weak salute, still slouching in his chair.

Bridger rose from his seat. "Hey, you don't need him to keep me in check. I'll keep the deal." He extended his hand. "And if you know me at all, then you know my word is my bond."

Al shook his hand, nodding. "Yes, it is, son. So promise me you'll stay focused on this — get all the details and sources for this woman's claims and bring them back here for me before you go off on some other tangent. Okay?"

"I promise."

"Good." Al approached Bridger, giving him a pat on the shoulder. "And if you boys get there early, you can get your interviews, but make sure you just cover the story — don't *become* it."

"Who us?" Neon protested as he hopped out of his seat, heading for the door. "Have we ever done that?"

"Yes, you have," Al answered as he walked Bridger out of the office. "I don't have time to be bailing you boys out of another one of your mishaps, so just stay on track and get back here ASAP. There's a lot still to be done by the six news."

"Look what I've got!" Kelli Sue greeted the three just outside of Al's office, holding up a photo on printer paper.

"What is it?" Bridger asked as he took the paper from her.

"Another copper," she answered

"Another!" Bridger's mind was racing. "Where did you get this?"

"Cody Ackerman... you know, Sonny's cameraman?"

"The Kodak." Neon interjected his counterpart's nick-name "Way to go, Kodak man!"

Kelli Sue nodded. "Yeah, I told him to look around for another one while he was covering Beacon Hill, and he just sent this to me — said he found it by the burned down community center." She grinned. "Guess my suggestion paid off."

"Miss Kelli Sue Llewellyn, you are amazing!" Bridger exclaimed, giving her a fist bump.

Al sighed. "And so much for promises."

Neon slapped Al on the back, assuring him, "No, it's all right. We're still on our mission, big guy!" He strutted toward the main door. "Come on, compadre. We have mucho work to do!"

Bridger pointed at Kelli Sue. "See what you can do while I'm gone."

"Isn't that what I always do?" she answered before heading for her desk.

Bridger looked at Al. "Those three coppers are on the K-Sue shelf until I get back — I promise." Grabbing his gear from his desk, he followed Neon. "We've got this covered, so don't worry."

"But I will worry..." Al replied as the two headed out the door. "I always do."

⚜

Chapter 5

Most of the casino's parking spaces were filled by the time Pastor Rodney Creighton drove his Ford Edge into the lot, dry leaves whirling about the pavement as he backed his four-wheel drive crossover into a corner space in the back row. He preferred a distant parking spot anyway since he had arranged the rendezvous for an inconspicuous location by a cluster of white pines in the back of the lot, a place he chose to provide the best cover for their brief meet-up before the news conference.

He only had to wait minutes before Air National Guard Captain Ted Laski wheeled his refurbished Plymouth 'Cuda nose first into the space next to Creighton. Taking a last drag on his cigarette, Laski flicked the butt out the window before turning his piercing blue eyes on the pastor, snapping him a salute.

Creighton clicked the key in the ignition so he could lower his own window to speak. "Hope you've got our young men with you," he said to Laski.

"One had a last minute conflict, but the other two are here." Laski motioned toward the backseat. "Got anything to say, gentlemen?" he asked the young men behind him, revving his muscle car one last time before shutting it off and getting out.

Dylan Granger leaned forward from the rear passenger seat, a swathe of his ashen brown bangs falling in front of his bronze-framed glasses. "Hey there, Pastor Creighton." He flicked his hand with a quick wave, then drew his bangs back behind one ear, grinning.

On the driver's side, Dylan's childhood friend, J Paul Tamarack, popped the rear door. "Yeah, we've got your back, Pastor — ready to defend," he responded as he climbed out between the two vehicles, hiking his tattered, baggy jeans back onto his hips before they sagged to the ground.

Creighton opened his own door, rolling up the window and then removing the key before he exited. "Glad you men were willing to meet today." An abrupt burst of wind caught hold of Creighton's comb-over, revealing the pastor's bald patch as his graying blond hair whipped about in the pine-scented air. "I appreciate your dedication to the cause," he said to J Paul as he zipped up his windbreaker and adjusted his clerical collar, then combing his hair back in place with his fingers.

Climbing out of the 'Cuda, Dylan schlepped with long, gangly legs around past the car's trunk. "Well, Captain Ted told us you needed numbers in the crowd, so we got a couple of guys to cover our shifts at the marina... and here we are," he said, rolling up the sleeves on his oil-stained jean jacket.

"And you know these boys are loyal minutemen," Captain Laski noted once out of the driver's seat. "As Scout Master, I could always count on these two to do their duty, and they're no different now that they've graduated from high school." Slamming his car door, Laski slapped his hands down on the backside of J Paul's broad shoulders, maneuvering him forward until he stood next to his friend, Dylan.

Creighton met them, extending each an admirable smile. "Well, in the short time I've known you two – ever since I transferred here to become Pastor at Burt Lake Revival – you boys have shown yourself devout to both God and country." He reached toward his favorite, J Paul, patting at the patchwork of stubble on his cheek. "You've given us hope that the next generation will follow in our footsteps – protect and defend."

"Oh, and we will, sir!" J Paul nodded. "Me and Dylan here – we thought about enlisting, but we know from all Captain Ted's taught us over the years how the government keeps wiping out good men on foreign wars when the real fight's coming here – and sooner than you'd think!"

"No doubt, son," Laski agreed, turning to Creighton. "I told these boys I didn't want to lose them over other people's fights. There's no need for them to be shipped off to some God-forsaken desert like I was in Gulf One." He turned his gaze back to the boys. "Yeah, I may still be stuck teaching combat readiness for the Air Guard, but I won't have that for you boys. I don't want you trapped in that poor excuse for a military that they might as well call the Foreign Legion — not when you're needed right here to deal with our own, damn government, all hell-bent on taking us over."

"Well, we'll do what we can," Dylan told his old troop master. "What's the plan here?"

"Just listen," Creighton answered, holding his finger to his lips as he motioned for silence.

Over the rustle of dry leaves skidding across the pavement, the sound of nearby protestors rose in the distance. As the wind diminished, each word became intelligible. They chanted, "This — land — is — *our* — land," their tone almost sing-song as it echoed across the parking lot.

"This land *is* our land," Creighton told them as he motioned toward the marina and surrounding property. "Unfortunately, these casino owners understand the value of waterfront and the potential war chest they could amass by developing it for their own purposes, so they're determined to take it — at any price." He scanned the northwestern skyline until he found the distant plume of smoke, pointing at it. "Including that price..."

Dylan glanced toward the smoke, scowling. "You mean the fires? They wouldn't do that, would they?"

The pastor nodded. "Oh, yes... they would."

"Like the old burnout," Laski added, lifting his tightened jaw. "They think it's their pay-back time."

"God damn bastards," J Paul grumbled, his brow furrowed.

"Burnout?" Dylan asked. "What burnout?"

"The burnout of 1900 at Burt Lake's Colonial Point," Creighton replied. "I figured your card-carrying Grandpa Bill must've told you that story long ago, Dylan. Isn't he part Odawa or something?"

"And part pyro," Laski added. "No shame on you, though. That's your grandpa's past — not yours."

"I know," Dylan nodded, pushing his hands deep in his jeans' pockets.

"Well, Colonial Point was one of many settlements where Indians lived after they'd sold their land to the government," Creighton told them. "They'd been allowed some time to continue living there without any taxes, but then they were supposed to start paying after a while — just like the rest of us responsible citizens have to." He sighed. "Well... they didn't pay — or they paid sometimes when they felt like it, but not every year. And it went on like that for decades until people got fed up and sold the property to a guy who *would* pay his taxes."

"Sold it..." Dylan cocked his head. "But who sold it? The Indians?"

"No, they didn't own it anymore, son," Laski argued with emphasis. "If you don't pay your taxes, then the government can foreclose — an extreme reality we've all had to learn to live with."

"But the Indians wouldn't get off the land," Creighton continued. "So, the new owner got Sheriff Ling of Cheboygan County to enforce their eviction. Guess they didn't want a big confrontation, so the sheriff and his men waited until the Indian men had gone to their lumbering jobs in town and then they moved the rest of the Indians and their belongings out of the houses and burned them down."

"They burned down all their homes?" Dylan asked with eyes wide.

J Paul shook his head. "No, Dylan... Didn't you hear what Ted said? Those houses weren't theirs anymore. They belonged to the new guy — the one who bought the land. Remember?"

"But those people were still living there, weren't they?" Dylan's voice was raised, sounding a bit troubled.

"Yes, but no one was hurt in the fire," Creighton guaranteed him. "I know your heart, Dylan — how much you love your neighbor as yourself." The pastor patted his young parishioner's arm. "They were able to go live with their people in Cross

Village — something they should have done a long time before all this…" He paused, pondering the more imminent conflict. "But now it would seem these Indian's ancestors have decided the best way to deal with us is in kind."

Dylan ran his fingers through his windblown mop of hair, turning to gaze at the distant smoke. "And that's why you think Native Americans are the ones who started these fires?"

"We don't *think* it, son — we *know* it!" Laski barked. "Show them what you've got there, Pastor."

Reaching into his windbreaker pocket, Creighton removed a folded piece of paper. "I received this along with some fake treaty these people are trying to pass off as proof of their ownership. Of course the email was anonymous so there's no way to trace it back to any particular band member, but the general source is obvious." He handed it over for the two young men to read.

"Return our land or revive the time of fire," J Paul read aloud from the letter, his expression one of indignation. "And look — it's got Menonaqua Band info printed on the top!"

Dylan frowned. "If you think my grandpa's involved with this—"

"Despite old Butane Bill's shady past, we'd never jump to that assumption about your grandfather," Creighton interrupted to assure the young man. "So, is this going to be a problem for you? Can you still help us out here?"

Dylan looked down, grinding the toe of his tattered hiking boots against the pavement. "No, there's no problem — I'm in."

"Good…" Creighton grinned. "…because I think it's safe to say *someone* is trying to intimidate these people into surrendering their God-given right to live on their own land, so it's up to us to confront them if we hope to live here in peace."

"And thank the good Lord we've got Pastor Rod to lead us in this righteous cause," Laski proclaimed, wrapping his arm around Creighton's back to give his opposing shoulder a few slaps of approval in tough-guy fashion. "With all of his previous militia experience and connections, he's got the know-how and the means to push back against any federal takeover of our private property. Don't you, Pastor?"

"Well, I hope so, Captain," he replied. "So, this is where it begins, men — this is where the UTC plans to tell the media about this trumped-up treaty, but this is also where *we* will show the media that God-fearing Americans will not surrender."

"Oo-rah!" J Paul bellowed.

"Yes, and we'll want to hear your voice out there today," Creighton assured the young devotee. "So, time to split up to our tasks. J Paul, I'll have you stay with me."

"And you're with me, son," Laski told Dylan as he stepped back to the side door of the 'Cuda. "I've got your marching orders — you're going to help me spread the word to the crowd." Opening the door, Laski removed a ream of printed flyers and handed them to his new assistant. "First, we're going to pass these out to the friendlies in the mob — get them on board for our organizational meeting at the church tonight." Reaching into the old car, he locked up before exiting. "Then when that lady starts talking about this treaty crap, we're going to tell her what she can do with it." Walking back to Dylan, Laski smiled at him as he asked, "So, are you ready to raise a ruckus?"

"I guess so."

"Well, then we're out of here," Laski told the others as he turned with Dylan and headed toward the casino.

"We'll meet you back here afterward," Creighton yelled to them as they headed into the sea of cars in the lot, disappearing from his view.

"And what do we get to do?" J Paul asked.

"You..." Creighton paused for dramatic effect as he stepped between the two parked vehicles, heading for his back hatch. "Come on, and I'll show you."

J Paul followed, jogging to the back. "What've you got for me?"

"Something befitting the son of a long-time militia member," Creighton answered, popping the hatch. "I have no doubt that your dad, John Paul Sr., would be right here with us if it weren't for his emphysema, and so today... we'll make him proud." He took out his keys and unlocked his portable gun case, revealing a pair of nine-millimeter Berettas.

"Sweet!" J Paul picked one up, weighing it between his hands. "Where'd you get them?"

"That's loaded, but the safety is on," Creighton advised him as he picked up the other pistol, studying its underside with admiration. "The government has no right to control gun ownership, so we got these like most of our stockpile — free of bureaucratic interference, through our militia channels."

J Paul flipped his gun, rubbing his finger along the frame just below the slide. "The serial number's filed off — smooth as a baby's bottom."

"That's right. There's no sense in licensing our property with a government determined to either tax it or take it." Checking the safety, Creighton tucked his Beretta into his pants at his side, draping his windbreaker over it. "What we own is our business, not theirs... and today we're keeping it with us, just in case."

"So, I get to carry this one?" J Paul asked.

"Yes, you do. I've seen how much you've matured — how ready and willing you are to act as a protector of liberty. So, for this operation, you are assigned the duty of defender — someone entrusted with one of our weapons to be used in our defense."

J Paul gripped the pistol, swallowing hard. "So, I'm supposed to hide this, right? And I only pull it out if things get crazy, like if some Indian pulls a gun or something. Is that what you want me to do?"

"That's a good way to put it." Creighton nodded, grateful for the young man's willingness to follow instructions. "Only two other minutemen are packing along with you and me, so we need to take up positions away from each other." He motioned with his head toward the casino "Let's get going so I can show you where you need to be when this thing gets started."

"And I'll be good and ready when it does," J Paul replied as he reached toward the base of his spine, tucking his pistol on his backside between his boxers and baggy jeans while leaving his camouflage T-shirt untucked to cover it.

"No doubt, you will be." Creighton locked up the gun case before slamming shut the Ford's back hatch and locking it, as well. "Just keep to yourself and don't let anyone know you're a part of this mission; that includes the cops, the protesters, and even other minutemen." He stared into J Paul's eyes. "Are you all right with that?"

"Hell, yeah! The gun, the secrets... they're all safe with me!" J Paul tightened his belt, making sure the gun was secured at his back. "I won't let you down."

"Of course, you won't," Creighton replied, smiling at the determination he could see in J Paul's expression. "Now let's go get into position so we're ready to respond — that is, if we have to," he added, despite knowing full well that a confrontation was exactly what he was looking for.

❧

Chapter 6

"I can't believe there are this many people here," Bridger remarked as he walked through another row of vehicles. "The property owners and tribe members must've gotten the word out that this presser was going down."

"And you didn't think this was a big story," Neon responded as he appeared from the other side of a minivan, striding with Bridger toward the next row of cars ahead of them. "It looks like Big Al was right – this could be even bigger than the fires."

"All depends on what we make of it." Bridger held his hand up to his forehead, blocking the high-noon sun so he could better see the mob gathering a couple more parking rows ahead. "Looks like there are plenty of people we can talk to – maybe get a couple of quick interviews in before Drummond speaks."

"I'm with you, pal," Neon agreed as he emerged from another row of cars. "Let's get one of each – a homeowner and a tribe member."

As Bridger came out from between another set of cars, he finally caught a glimpse of the podium located at the top of the stairs, a couple of microphones already attached to it. "Yeah, but let's talk to people who are already near that podium. I want to be in position before this mob gets too tight."

"Good plan," Neon replied before plunging into the final row of cars.

Bridger had worked in crowds before. He'd covered festivals and other celebrations around the region where people would linger near the camera in hopes of being seen on television, but he was sure this would be different. The people gathered here had an agenda to promote, and Bridger was determined to avoid being used as a conduit for either side's propaganda.

Walking across the mulch of a landscaped island, Bridger stepped off the curb into the crowd milling about the edge of the casino's main driveway, a four-lane stretch of pavement that had been blocked off at the far ends with reflective orange cones. From where he stood, he could not see a clear path to the main staircase as the crowd ahead of him was packed with protestors resting their picket signs on their shoulders, holding their positions in the lull before the storm.

Neon pinched his thumb and finger together in his mouth, whistling. "Found the ramp – this way." He tossed his disheveled hair to one side, motioning toward the handicap entrance.

"Right behind you," Bridger answered as he negotiated the outer edges of crowd, hurrying to catch up.

Neon looked back long enough to yell, "Find your mark – I'll set up topside." Already on the ramp, he jogged upward, rounding a brick wall that blocked him from Bridger's view.

"Get good position!" Bridger yelled after him as he continued his own forward momentum, plowing into a weathered-looking man standing like a sentinel at the foot of the ramp. "Sorry, mister!" Bridger stepped back as the man righted himself, his scowl deepening the creases that ran down his jowls toward a scar on his neck.

"Don't worry about it," the man said, brushing off his bomber-style leather jacket as he walked away.

Bridger continued his dash upward while looking back at the man, nearly bumping into another person who gave him a dirty look. "Press," he yelled back as he banked the ramp's curve, nearly plowing into a white-haired woman walking ahead of him.

"Oh, dear!" she shrieked, almost losing control of the wheel-chair she was pushing with an elderly man cradled in its seat.

"Whoa!" Bridger rolled to one side, grazing the woman as he went down on one knee to avoid her. "I'm so sorry! I didn't see you."

"Well, you need to slow down, young man." She stopped, regaining her balance as she scolded him.

"Yeah, I'm with the media and have to get to. . ." He paused, realizing his reasons were insignificant to these two people he'd nearly injured. "Here, let me help you with that." He reached toward the wheelchair, offering to push it the rest of the way up.

"Oh, well, yes. . . that would be helpful," the woman replied, scuffling to the side as Bridger took hold of the grips.

"No, no, no," the elderly man protested. "You know I *don't* want other people pushing me around, Dixie."

"Just let the man help me, Gus," she insisted as she shuffled up the slight incline.

"It's the least I can do after I almost plowed into you," Bridger added as he pushed the man upward at Dixie's side.

"Well, I don't need a pity push," Gus told Bridger, adjusting the black cap on his head. "We take care of ourselves — aren't beholding to anyone."

"Oh, stop your complaining, Gus. It's me he's helping." Dixie continued to take small steps forward, reaching over to brush something from her husband's shoulder before adjusting her own jacket.

"So, I take it your names are Gus and Dixie?" Bridger asked, hoping they might be his first mark for an interview.

"Mr. and Mrs. August Levering. . . but you can call me Dixie."

"No he can't," Gus grumbled.

"My name's Bridger — Bridger Klein."

"I thought so," she replied with a smile. "I've seen you before on television. Are you doing a story on the protest?"

Bridger nodded. "Yes, and the news conference."

"It's not news!" Gus argued. "It's a bunch of horse shit!"

"Gus!" Dixie blushed.

"Well, it is!" Gus took off his cap and slapped it in his lap, revealing what was left of his white hair. "The government's got all sorts of land they could give to these people, but they'd rather steal mine because they know it's worth a lot more." Rubbing the edges of his cap, he turned it to reveal the letters NRA emblazoned in red above the curved brim. "That's the real story here, Mr. Bridger Klein, if you're man enough to tell it."

"What I'd prefer is that you tell it," Bridger replied as they reached the top of the ramp. "If you're willing, I'd like to take you and your wife over a little closer to my cameraman over there." He pointed toward where he could see Bridger setting up his tripod. "I'd like to interview the two of you for my story."

"Really?" Dixie grinned broadly. "That would be wonderful!"

Gus returned his cap to his head. "Oh, yeah, your girlfriends would love that!" His voice was thick with sarcasm.

Dixie bent at the waist so she could look her husband in the eyes. "But it would also help our side if people heard what this fight is doing to us." She glanced up at Bridger, asking, "Wouldn't it?"

"I would think so," Bridger replied as he glanced at his watch, concerned that he was running out of time. "Let's just give it a try and see how it goes. Okay?" He pushed Gus forward, not waiting for his reply.

"Yes, that's a good idea." Dixie scuttled along at their side.

Gus gripped the armrests on his wheelchair. "But I'm warning you now, I'm going to speak my mind on this."

"That's what I want you to do," Bridger told him as he parked his chair just a few yards to the side of the podium. "Just maybe without the colorful adjectives, but we can even bleep those out afterward if you still drop one."

Neon headed toward them. "Well, look at the lovely couple we have here!"

"Yes," Bridger agreed with a nod. "Mr. and Mrs. Levering, this is my cameraman, Neon Kashkari."

Gus scowled. "Neon? What in the hell kind of name is Neon?"

Bridger chuckled. "Yeah, it's actually spelled N-y-h-a-n, so we call him Neon. It's Indian."

"Odawa? Chippewa?" Gus asked.

Neon smirked. "Hindi... you know, like New Delhi?"

"What?" Gus held his hand to his ear. "A new deli?"

"He's from India, Gus." Dixie patted her husband's arm. "They call him Neon – like the color."

"Actually, it's a gas." Neon grinned before turning and heading back to where he'd nearly finished setting up his camera.

"Yeah, and he's going to be behind that camera, so you don't need to worry about him," Bridger told them. "Now, I won't introduce you because I'll add your names in my voiceover later. I'm just going to ask you a few questions and all you have to do is speak up when you answer. Okay?"

Dixie patted her hair and smoothed out the front of her blouse. "I have to admit I'm a little nervous."

Gus tilted his head, looking up at his wife. "Oh, for Pete's sake, it's just a—"

"Hey, you can't be up here." A man with a long braid of white hair gimped toward them, leaning against his walking stick in one hand as he waved at them with the other. "We're having a news conference up here, so you'll have to stay on the lower level."

"Says who?" Gus snapped at the man.

"Says me," the man argued.

"I'm Bridger Klein with WHAM." Holding up his press card, he motioned toward Neon. "That's my cameraman set up for the presser, and I'm just going to talk to these people real quick before your event gets started."

The man extended his scarred hand to shake. "I'm Bill Granger, in charge of the set up."

"Good to meet you," Bridger replied, noting a hint of alcohol intermingled with the overpowering scent of tobacco on the man's breath.

"Same." Bill nodded. "So, you can stay, but they've got to go."

"What!" Gus straightened up in his seat. "I'm here for the speech, too, and I'd say that since I'm in this chair due to an old war injury, then these wheels are *my* press pass – they *entitle* me to be up here."

"He can't see from down there," Dixie added. "And we might get hurt in that pushy crowd."

"Look, I don't want to cause a problem for you, but I'm only supposed to let the press up here." Bill shook his head. "The UTC's running this show and my hands are tied."

"So, you're with tribe, aren't you?" Gus looked at Bill with narrowed eyes. "Dixie, he's one of the people trying to take our home away from us."

"Hey, I'm not trying to take anyone's home, mister. I'm just trying to get you off the upper level."

"Yeah, and that's because you don't want to let me speak — you don't want people to know what's really going on here."

Bridger motioned for Neon to record. "And what is it you want people to know, Mr. Levering?"

"I want them to know that there's a conspiracy — a conspiracy between the Indians and the federal government to seize our most valuable lands. None of them care who it belongs to. They don't care that I've lived in my house since I was a born, and that my daddy grew up in it before me. They don't care that my wife and I have lived there since we were married fifty-two years ago, and that we raised our kids there…" He seemed to be choking up, but gathered himself to continue. "They think it's okay to do this to us homeowners because they've gotten this notion that the land was somehow stolen from their distant ancestors."

"But it *was* stolen," Bill interjected, shifting his weight as he placed his walking stick in his other hand for support.

"So, you disagree with Gus?" Bridger asked, bringing Bill into the interview.

"Of course, I do." Bill pointed toward the marina in the distance. "All that property was taken over nearly a century ago by white investors, and that wrong has never been righted."

Dixie looked concerned. "But I thought you were interviewing us, Bridger."

"Oh, I am," he tried to assure her. "Got to get both sides, but to you, Dixie… What do you think? Is there a past wrong here that hasn't been corrected?"

"Oh, well I…" She paused. "Well, I suppose some people were wronged way back when."

"Dixie!" Gus blurted. "What the—"

"Now, just let me finish before you get your blood pressure up." She patted her husband's shoulder. "Yes, some Native Americans lost their land a long time ago, but the government's already given land back to try to fix things... I mean, look at this place." She motioned toward the casino. "We've given the Natives land, and the government has a lot more land they could give them. But we shouldn't have to give them land the individual people already own free and clear, because that would be wrong, too... and you know what they say: two wrongs don't make a right."

"Okay, enough with this... you people can't stay up here." Bill reiterated. "You have to go back down to the driveway."

"Oh, I see!" Gus replied. "Now that you've taken *this* property for your little casino here, then you think you can control whoever's on this land, as well. God forbid you'd have any dissenters on your stage — might look bad when you bring out the big shots." Gus reached down, tightening the brake on his chair. "Well, I'm not going anywhere, fella, so if you want me to move, you're just going to have to drag me!"

Bill gimped closer to the man. "What... do you think you've cornered the market on disabilities, buddy?

"Hey, let's take it easy, guys," Bridger intervened.

"Think you're the only one who's ever had anything bad happen to him?" Bill continued.

Bridger held up his hands toward the two men. "Emotions are running high today, but there's no need—"

"You have no idea!" Gus squeezed his fists. "I've sacrificed so much for this country, and for what? ...to have you and your tribe take my home?"

"I don't want your God damn home!" Bill yelled, spit spraying from his lips. "I just want you to get your sorry ass off the—"

"Bill!" a woman's voice sternly addressed him from behind. "What are you doing?"

Bridger turned to see a striking woman striding toward them, her cropped, black hair glistening in the sunshine as it bounced with her feathered earrings about her head. She wore a fitted tunic decorated with bright beads that had been stitched into a floral pattern, a short dress she complimented with a tall pair of slouchy suede boots she had pulled up over her black tights.

"These two people aren't press," Bill told her, motioning toward the man in the wheelchair and his wife at his side. "They're not supposed to be up here – got to move them back down with the crowd."

"They're with me," Bridger vouched for them. "I brought them up here for an interview."

"And who are you?" she asked.

He held up his press card. "WHAM News – Bridger Klein."

"I'm Chepi Weatherwax, an assistant of sorts to the Menonaqua Beach Band Chairman," she replied as she extended her hand, shaking his. "And these people are..."

"A couple I was interviewing," Bridger replied.

"They're homeowners from the beach," Bill added. "And they're causing trouble already."

"We don't want any trouble, Miss." Dixie pleaded. "I just brought my husband up here so he could see better, and we wouldn't get bumped around in the crowd."

"And exercising our freedom of speech," Gus added. "That is, if we still have that right."

"What?" Chepi tilted her head, looking confused.

"Listen, buddy..." Bill spoke through gritted teeth. "You can exercise all the rights you've got, but you've got to do it down there with everyone else."

"Are you kidding, Bill? What's wrong with you?" Chepi's expression was one of astonishment. "These people aren't a threat – you let them stay up here."

"No, they can't," Bill argued. "It's not our call, Chepi. UTC told me not to let anybody up here but news people."

"Well, I'm overriding that order, and if someone has a problem with it, you tell them to see me." Chepi turned to the

Leverings. "I'm sorry if there's been some misunderstanding. You're welcome to stay up here for as long as you like."

Gus sneered. "So, can we stay in our home for as long as we want, too?"

"Stop it, Gus!" Dixie scolded her husband, then producing a smile for Chepi. "Thank you, Miss Weatherwax."

Bill scowled. "But Naomi said that—"

"Mr. Granger will make sure no one tries to remove you," Chepi assured the couple. "You'll just need to stay at least this far from the podium to leave room for people from the media, like Mr. Klein here."

Bridger grinned at her. "And we appreciate that."

She smiled back. "No problem. Now, I need to go find the chairman before this all gets started in a few minutes, so if you'll excuse me…" With a tip of her head, she backed away from the group.

Bridger followed her. "I've got just one other request, Chepi. Could I speak with you after the press conference?"

She tilted her head, studying him through narrowed eyes.

"I mean, on camera," he clarified with an awkward chuckle. "I'd like to get your perspective on the events happening here, and elsewhere, if you could spare me a few minutes."

Her sleek lips curled into a smile. "Yes, I'd be happy to speak with you afterward… on camera." As she stepped away, she added, "But I hope you'll have more than a few minutes because when this event is over, there's going to be a lot more I'll want to say."

❦

Chapter 7

Magdala hurried about the vacant women's shower room at the Menonaqua Beach Marina, choking as the overpowering aroma of lemon cleaning products caught in her throat. Her coughs echoed in the empty space, accompanied by the shuffling sound made by the soles of her shiny black shoes scuffing against the tile floor. Turning on the sink faucet, she cupped icy water in her hand and brought it to her mouth, drinking enough to control her coughing.

Stretching out her back, Magdala's muscles still ached from a morning of less than adequate rest. When she had parked along side the other overnight vehicles in the marina lot just before dawn, she had found it hard to sleep in the cranked-back driver's seat of her truck, especially while hiding herself beneath a blanket. But with the sun now high in the sky, she knew there was no more time to rest for her work was far from finished.

The chill still lingering in the unheated bathroom helped to wake Magdala, causing goose bumps to form on her arms as she slipped them into a dark navy shirt. Buttoning up to the neck, she attached a clip-on tie before twisting her curly hair into a large comb-clip, completing the look with a security guard cap pressed onto her head. She then tucked her shirttails into her dark pants and slipped on a navy windbreaker, double checking the trigger mechanism tucked in one pocket and her chrome nine-millimeter Baby Eagle hidden in the other. With one last glance in the mirror, she found everything to be in place.

Stepping out of the bathroom and into the glare of the sun, she removed a pair of Ray-Bans from her pack. Glancing down to slip them on, she didn't notice the young man coming around the corner of the building, almost walking right into him.

"Whoa there, lady!" The scruffy-faced man dodged her, his arms outstretched like an eagle's wings as he maneuvered about her side.

Magdala only glanced at him from behind her sunglasses, continuing on as if nothing had happened.

"Didn't know anyone was around this morning," The man said, following her.

Magdala rolled her eyes behind the dark lenses, frustrated that she would now have to deal with this encounter. "Yes?" she said, turning back toward the man.

The man wiped grease off his hands with a filthy rag. "You know, we're pretty much closed up here for the season. Was there something you needed?"

She faked a smile, trying to back away. "No, thank you."

"You sure?" He followed her. "I just work in the shop – filling in for a friend today so it's not my normal shift. Maybe that's why I never seen you around here before."

"I am okay," she replied, continuing her sideways shuffle away from him.

"Nice uniform – you work at the casino?"

"Yes, I work."

"Don't we all!" He chuckled. "So, I can get in the boat shop if there was something you were after – pop or a beer..." He laughed again. "Well, guess you can't have a beer on duty – maybe later."

"Maybe," she smiled again, trying to hide her agitation. "I must go now."

"Okay, well just watch out there." He pointed at the upper corner of an alcove in the side of the building, a spot where more than a half-dozen bats were clinging together, overlapping one another. "Don't know what brought them back around – I seen a bunch all around the building today."

Magdala cocked her head, studying the bats and then him. "Do they worry you?" she asked.

"Awe, no, but thought they might spook you!" He laughed. "Just showed up this morning – hadn't seen any in a while. I wondered if they might be rabid."

"Rabid?" She didn't understand.

"Yeah, you know, sick with rabies? Wouldn't want them to bite you or something, so stay clear of them... if you know what I mean."

"Yes... I do," she answered with growing concern that this pest was taking notice of her limited understanding. Tucking her hands in her coat pockets, she took a hold of the Baby Eagle. "I will go... before they bite."

"Yeah, well, *they* might bite, but *I* don't." He chuckled, seeming a bit unsure of himself. "Man, you're in a hurry to get going, aren't you? So, what's the deal?" He leaned against the exterior wall of the marina. "Going to a fire or something?"

Her eyes went wide behind her Ray-Bans. "The fire?"

"Oh, no, not those fires." He laughed, still ill at ease. "No, I was just kidding, you know, like..." He paused, his expression changing. "Oh, wait... I get it now. You *do* have to go — got to get over there for that big press conference they're having, I bet." He smiled, looking a bit relieved. "Man, I thought you were just trying to avoid me or something."

Magdala cocked her head the other way, still gripping the Baby Eagle as she weighed the threat this man posed.

"Hey, Dale!" a deep voice yelled from inside the marina. "You want to get back to work now?"

"Uh, that's the other guy — thinks he owns the place," Dale remarked, smirking as he pointed his thumb in the direction of the voice. "So, I'll be around all afternoon if you get a chance to come back by after you're done over there." He stood up straight, tucking his thumbs through his front belt loops.

"You work inside?" Magdala asked him, pointing at the building.

"Yeah, right in there." Dale winked at her.

"That will do," she muttered, removing her hands from her pockets as she turned toward her truck.

"Well, good enough!" he exclaimed from behind her. "Just come on in and find me."

Magdala ignored him, hurrying so she would have enough time to plant the next copper before the start of the press conference.

"See you around, then," Dale yelled from a distance.

"No," she quietly answered. "You... will not."

Chapter 8

"There's more to this story than meets the eye," Bridger said as he stood next to Neon and the camera, awaiting the start of the presser.

Neon narrowed his eyes and grinned with an expression suggesting he'd just eaten a canary. "I'd say whatever more there is to this story already met your eye." He laughed. "Oh, you got it bad for that pretty little spit-fire, don't you?"

"What are you talking about?"

"Don't give me that, BK. I was filming the whole thing." Neon placed both hands on his camera. "Want a playback to refresh your memory?"

Bridger couldn't help but smirk.

"No, you don't need a playback – it's all still fresh in your mind." Neon nudged him with his elbow, adding, "You dog..."

Bridger rolled he eyes. "All right, enough with that... I still say there's more going on here, and that girl is ready to talk about it. I just have to get in position – be near her when this thing gets over so I can talk to her."

"Oh, yeah, you better be near her... so you can talk." Neon winked.

"I'm not kidding, Neon! I can tell she's not happy about whatever's going on here, and I'm going to get to the bottom..." Bridger paused, interrupted by the vibration of his phone. "Now what?" he muttered, withdrawing it to find an urgent text.

"Is that Al again? Man, if he's dragging our butts back to–"

"No, it's this Dr. Rivard guy again." Bridger looked at the photo sent to him. "It's another copper... Yeah, but it's the same one Kodak already sent us." Bridger tucked his phone back in his pocket. "Looks like this guy really wants us to figure these things out."

"Probably so he can take all the credit," Neon suggested. "But don't get distracted by those coppers again – keep your eyes on the prize…" Neon raised his arm, pointing toward the front doors of the casino. "…and here comes the prize right now."

Bridger turned to see Chepi emerge from the building, her arm entwined with that of an elder man whose leathered skin had a golden hue in contrast to the crisp white shirt he was wearing.

"Pretty tight with the old man," Neon remarked as he looked through the camera lens. "I thought you said she works for him."

"I did," Bridger replied as he watched the two sidestep the podium, further studying the band's chairman. "What's the guy wearing?"

"You mean that great big silver buckle tied to his neck. It's a bolo tie. Haven't you ever seen one before?"

"No, not that – I mean that scarf-like thing hanging from his shoulders…" Bridger pointed at the woven band of tubular shells Takota wore like a religious stole, its intricate pattern of purple and ivory shimmering with a pearlesque luster.

"That's a wampum belt," Neon answered, still looking into the camera as he pushed the record button. "I remember your Uncle Silas showed us one at Fort Michilimackinac – told us it's for ceremonies, and that the pattern's supposed to be some kind of message stitched together by the tribal peacemaker."

"Really…" Bridger nodded despite his lack of recollection.

"And the individual beads, they're made from the tube part that runs through the middle of those… those… Oh, what do they call those shells? Gastropod shells, I think – you know, the ones that look like the swirled ice cream you get at Dairy Queen?" Neon paused, the expression of enthusiasm fading from his face. "Silas even broke open a shell and showed us… Don't you remember?"

"Guess not," Bridger admitted, still bitter about Silas.

"Man, that's too bad," Neon said, glancing at his friend. "He taught us a lot – about history and science, and life… Maybe you should try listening more and remembering more."

Bridger scowled at him. "Remembering is still a bit of a problem for me — don't *you* remember?"

"Whatever, dude," Neon scoffed, returning his eyes to the camera's view of the people gathered around the podium.

Bridger turned his eyes back to center stage, as well, where he watched Chepi release her escort's arm and move a couple of steps away from him. "I need to get over by her," he told Neon, still watching in case she moved further.

"Are you sure you want to be to the side of this thing? I mean, you usually face the speaker head-on, ready to ask questions if you get the chance. And that Chepi girl, she's not more than twenty feet away from us, if you stay right here."

"I'm not letting this angle get away from me," Bridger replied as he leaned over, reaching into Neon's bag and pulling out a couple of ear pieces. "These have mikes, don't they?"

Neon nodded, being careful not to jar the camera.

"Wear this so we can communicate if needed." Bridger handed over an ear piece. "When the presser's done, be ready to move if we need to go elsewhere."

Neon turned his ear piece on and slipped it over his ear, furrowing his brow. "I'm always *way* ahead of you, so don't nag, Mom!"

"Fine," Bridger mumbled, turning away with little concern over Neon's momentary bout of pouting. Negotiating the muddle of media personnel and their equipment, he made his way to Chepi's side.

At that same moment, the band's chairman stepped over to her other side. "It would be best if you stood with me." He spoke loud enough to be heard over the chatter of the crowd.

"I'm sorry, Dad, but I can't do that," she answered.

"Dad?" Bridger mumbled, flabbergasted.

"Oh, yes," Chepi replied, taking notice of Bridger at her side. "This is my father, Takota Weatherwax, Chairman of the Menonaqua Beach Band."

"And you are...?" Takota asked, extending his hand.

"Bridger Klein, sir." He took a firm grasp of Takota's hand, shaking it. "I'm a reporter for WHAM-TV."

"Thank you for coming," he replied before turning back to his daughter. "Chepi has some different opinions about today's announcement so—"

"And you do, too, Dad," she interjected. "I don't know why you're going to stand there with that woman when she doesn't—"

"But I have to, Chepi," he insisted. "She's representing our people when she speaks, and I need to be ready to step up and say something, as well — try to keep the peace."

"That's going to be impossible when she's done talking."

"Maybe, but I still have to try and you should try, too."

"I *am* trying, but I won't stand by while..." Chepi stopped mid-thought, distracted by the sudden outburst of cheering and jeering from the crowd.

Glancing momentarily at the mob, Bridger looked back in time to see a woman dressed in professional attire prance to the podium.

"She has protection, and you don't?" Chepi spoke with a tone of outrage, apparently taking notice of the bulky state trooper stationed tightly at the speaker's side. "You've seen the threats, Dad."

"Threats?" Bridger's eyes narrowed as he wondered what she meant.

"We have our own security," Takota assured his daughter, stepping slowly away from her. "I'll be safe, and you will be, too..."

Chepi looked glumly at her father. "But I just *can't* stand by that woman."

Lowering his eyes, Takota turned and moved closer to the podium, taking up his place along side of Naomi.

Bridger rubbed his chin, unsure if he should ask or say anything.

Chepi continued to watch her father's every move. "He wants me to be more... like him."

Just then, Naomi began to speak. "It's my pleasure to be here today to announce a historic finding," she said into the multiple microphones attached to the podium. "But first, I'd like to thank Chairman Weatherwax for hosting this news conference on such short notice."

Bridger heard dispersed applause interspersed with a couple of boos before the crowd noise diminished. All eyes were now focused on Naomi Drummond.

"As many of you know, the Menonaqua Beach Band of Odawa and Ojibwe Indians has been seeking for some time now to rectify a past injustice caused when lands were unlawfully seized from our members' ancestors."

"They didn't pay their taxes!" a man yelled from the foot of the steps, supported by a couple of whoops from behind him.

Naomi ignored them, continuing. "Although an isolated parcel of undeveloped property was offered as consolation for this acknowledged wrongdoing, it proved inadequate in comparison to the lands that were taken."

"Bought!" a woman yelled.

"Bought and paid for!" another chimed in.

"Yes, we have heard the arguments," Naomi answered. "For the people who today live and work on this stolen land, whose predecessors were duped into paying for a false bill of sale — I feel badly for the angst this has caused you and your loved ones. But I also feel the pain of the people I am sworn to serve."

"No, she doesn't," Chepi whispered toward Bridger. "She only feels for one person... herself."

"As Chairman of the United Tribal Council, I am most concerned about maintaining and strengthening the tribes throughout Michigan."

Chepi bristled, crossing her arms snuggly across her chest. "What she's most concerned about is strengthening her own position," she grumbled to Bridger. "That woman will pick any fight she thinks she can win, just to make herself look good."

Bridger tilted his head, gazing at her inquisitively. "So, what makes her so sure she can win?"

Chepi leaned toward him, whispering in his ear. "The treaty."

"What treaty?"

Naomi waived a large document she held in her hand. "And this document proves that the land between here and Menonaqua Beach has always belonged to, and continues to belong to, the First Nation Peoples..." She pointed at the signature at the bottom of the paper. "...a right granted by the man who signed this agreement made in 1841, the then President of the United States of America!"

"Whoa!" Neon's voice transmitted loudly in Bridger's ear.

The crowd conveyed a collective gasp, as well, followed by a groundswell of chatter.

"You knew about this?" Bridger asked Chepi.

"The woman stuck it in front of us a couple hours ago."

Naomi attempted to continue. "In 1836, the Treaty of Washington deeded this property to us for five years. This 1841 treaty extended the deed... indefinitely."

"They didn't pay for it!" a woman yelled from the lower level, waving a sign that read *End Government Tyranny!*

From his wheelchair on the upper level, Gus chimed in. "They never paid the taxes — we always pay!"

More voices rose up from below, one man yelling, "The land was ours!"

A woman countered, "We bought it!"

Another screamed, "It wasn't for sale!"

Signs waved as the chanting resumed. "Stop — this — now! Stop — this — now! Stop — this—"

"Give — it — back!" a lone voice countered, others quickly chiming in. "Give — it — back! Give — it—"

Naomi waved her arms. "Please... if I could just finish—"

"Yeah, it's ours, not yours!"

"You can't take my home!"

"It's my home!"

"No, it's not!"

A sign was swung, a punch thrown, a man pushed, a woman fell, the crowd swayed...

Shoving Naomi aside, the trooper leapt down the steps, disappearing in the expanding brawl. Naomi tripped in the commotion, falling into Takota's arms.

Chepi cringed. "I knew this would happen!"

"Film the crowd, Neon!" Bridger yelled in his mike.

"Already am," Neon's voice came back. "No one's winning this one, dude. These people are just grocery shopping!"

"Just keep rolling!" Bridger told him as he focused helplessly on the hostile mob pushing inward, more people joining the fray.

"Dad should have cancelled this," Chepi lamented.

Bridger watched the few people emerging from the battle's perimeter, some running while others staggered in their escape. "Is the treaty real?" Bridger pressed.

A rock was thrown, a woman fell, a man bled, the cameras rolled...

"No! Well..." Chepi looked beside herself. "...maybe. I don't know!"

Bridger pressed her. "Where'd she get it? Who's it from?" He took notice of a young man beyond the crowd, his camo T-shirt, his restless stance, his edgy glances about the mob...

"I told you, I don't know!" Chepi snapped, leaning away from him. "I've got to get to my dad!"

Bridger noticed the man in camo neither fled nor joined the fight, shifting his weight with hands behind his back. Then something glimmered, a blinding reflection off metal like the flash of a camera, right by the boy in camo.

"Zoom on camo-boy!" Bridger commanded in his mike, but it was too late. He watched as the light disappeared, the young man dropping to his knees. Now realizing what was happening, Bridger yelled, "Gun!"

"Get down!" Neon yelled in his mike, diving in the direction of his friend but unable to reach him.

Bridger turned to shield Chepi, shoving her aside as he heard the sharp bang.

"No!" she screamed, her hands outstretched as she tumbled toward the cement pavement.

Bridger held tightly to Chepi's shoulders, his momentum forcing her toward the ground. Rolling to break his own fall, his back smacked against the pavement, whipping his head backward. The loud crack of his head hitting the cement was the last sound he heard before all went dark and silent.

Chapter 9

Magdala pounced on the young man she had just pistol-whipped to make it look as if she brought him down when in fact he had already been collapsing to the ground. Continuing the act, she grabbed the unconscious man's wrists with her gloved hands and wrestled with him, faking a struggle in case any of the frantic people screaming and fleeing the scene took notice. Slamming one of his hands against the pavement, she hastily wrapped his limp fingers around the still smoking Baby Eagle, smacking his fist against the cement once more for good measure. With the second strike, the gun slid from the unconscious man's hand, striking the curb beside him. Climbing off from her victim, she quickly grabbed the loose gun, gingerly holding it by the trigger guard so it could be kept as evidence.

Just then, a bulky trooper with his gun drawn charged from the crowd. "I've got him covered!" he assured Magdala, running over to take charge. "Man, looks like you really nailed him!" He cautiously approached the suspect, tucking his gun away and reaching down to check his pulse.

"His gun," Magdala said, handing over the weapon that, only moments ago, she had fired over the young man's shoulder as he had tumbled to the ground.

The trooper used a handkerchief to take the gun from her, tucking it carefully in his coat pocket. "He seems okay, except for the head-butt you gave him." Quickly cuffing his captive, the trooper patted him down. "Good thing you stopped him before he squeezed off anymore shots…" Lifting the back of the suspect's camouflage T-shirt, the trooper removed a nine-millimeter Beretta. "Looks like he planned to do some serious damage."

"That's J Paul!" a young man in a dirty denim jacket abruptly yelled at them from a distance. "What're you doing to him?"

"Hey, do you know this guy?" the trooper yelled back.

"What're you doing!" The young man scowled as he approached them, his arms flailing.

"Are you with this guy?" The trooper asked Dylan again as he lowered his hand toward his holstered gun. "Come over here. I need to talk to you, kid."

"What – the…?" J Paul muttered as he cracked open one eye. "What – is…?" He tugged at his restraints.

Magdala took notice of J Paul regaining consciousness, a sure signal that it was time for her to leave. "You come here!" she yelled at Dylan, intentionally sounding as threatening as possible. "I have him!" she then told the trooper as she dashed from his side, running toward Dylan.

"Hey, wait!" the trooper yelled after Magdala, but she ignored him and kept running, knowing he would have to stay with the suspect now in his custody.

Dylan ran, as well. "But I… I…" he yelled incoherently, fleeing Magdala's feigned pursuit.

She continued the chase, allowing her target to keep his distance until he finally eluded her in the fleeing mob. Having shirked the trooper, as well, Magdala now had only one last task to complete – one that should allow her to flee the chaotic casino scene without calling attention to her departure.

Turning for the casino parking lot, she tucked her gloved hands into her jacket pockets, her gait resolute as she moved with the chaotic crowd. Firmly grasping the trigger device, she considered what was about to happen, and all that had happened before. She thought of others who had already burned – her family, friends, enemies, strangers – found the rhythm in her memories, in her stride, in her poetry – remembered lines of solace, lines of reason, lines of wisdom… Brother Rami had taught her poems when she was most vulnerable, and they lingered with her, gifts of insight and consolation that she called upon when she needed them most.

Magdala had not forgotten the flirtatious advances of the marina mechanic — a loose end in need of resolution. She found her rationale in another quote from Frost, whispering, "From what I've tasted of desire, I hold with those who favor fire." Ever mindful of the consequences of her actions, she still did not hesitate, continuing her stride as she pulled the trigger.

With pops and bangs, flames erupted in the distance, halting the fleeing crowd. Some screamed and dropped to the ground, fearing further gunfire. Others staggered about, pushing and tripping over one another as they rushed the parking lot, recklessly pursuing their quickest path of escape. Doors slammed, engines revved, and tires squealed as cars moved haphazardly through the lot, muscling their way through the expanding traffic jam.

Seizing her chance for escape, Magdala hustled through the casino parking lot, attempting to appear as a fearless security guard hurrying toward the marina to help others. With the wail of sirens growing in the distance, she made her way past scurrying people and haphazardly angled cars, determined to reach the street where her truck was parked before the emergency vehicles arrived.

Still jogging, she gazed at the marina workshop, satisfied to see its weathered wood exterior already fully engulfed in flames. With her truck within sight, she heard the tell-tale rumbles and bangs of combustibles igniting. Clicking her keyless remote, she reached for her truck door just as the combustibles erupted. Paints and oil, resin and solvents... all of it exploded in a fireball that blew through the workshop's rooftop, taking with it anything that had remained inside — all the boats and equipment and, of course, the people.

As the plume of fire raced skyward, Magdala leapt into her truck and turned the key. With a quick glance, she felt confident no one had paid her any attention. People were now fleeing the fireball's smoky residue, a dark cloud of scorched oil and burning rubber that choked those around her. Coughing herself, Magdala closed the air vents before shifting the truck into drive and pulling away from the curb. Already on the street, she avoided the mass exodus from the parking lot, taking a quick turn east at the traffic light to head toward the next task she needed to complete. Then she would go north to the rendezvous point where she would meet with Thoreau and Brother Rami. They would help her restock and give her more assignments, work she would need to complete yet tonight to keep the fires burning.

Chapter 10

The explosion jolted Bridger to consciousness. Cracking open his eyes, he found himself staring upward into the blinding sun, the back of his head still resting against the cold, hard cement.

"Holy crap!" Neon yelled, kneeling by his friend to pat his face. "Come out of it, Bridger!"

"What... the..." Bridger moaned, rolling onto his side where he could see the black smoke racing into the sky. "More... fire?" He shuddered at the sight.

"We need to get you out of here!" Neon scanned the panicked mob, noticing the trooper lifting up a man in handcuffs. "Al will have my head for this."

"What... happened?" Bridger asked as he reached for the back of his head, finding it damp. He grimaced, pain piercing through the back of his head. Removing his hand, he found it smeared with blood.

"Shit! Are you hit?" Neon sounded terrified as he pushed Bridger further to his side, searching through his bloodied hair for a wound.

"Ouch!" Bridger yelled through Neon's harsh examination. "I'm not shot!" he added, still trying to gather his wits.

"No, you're not," Neon agreed. "Must've smacked the pavement, hard-head." Neon rubbed his hands on his jeans, wiping off Bridger's blood. "It's not as bad as it looks – shouldn't even need stitches. Can you get up?"

"Yeah..." Bridger eased himself up, his head throbbing and ears ringing as he noticed the commotion around him. "Where is... where's Chepi?" Looking to his other side, he spotted her next to him, face down on the pavement.

"I'll get her!" Neon insisted, jumping across Bridger to where he could reach her.

Warding off the pain in his head, Bridger redirected his instincts toward helping Chepi. "Hey, you okay?" He stroked her hair away from her face, noticing a bloody scrape on her cheek bone just below her closed eyes. "Come on, Chepi! Wake up!"

Neon rolled her on her side, putting his ear to her nose. "She's breathing." Prying her eyes open with his fingers, he gazed at her pupils. "Yeah, she just hit the ground hard, too," he tried to assure Bridger as he made a fist and pushed it between her breasts.

"She doesn't need CPR." Bridger grabbed his arm. "What are you doing?"

"Well, I'm not groping her, if that's what you think! Just knuckles in the sternum – it always wakes them if you–"

"Ow-ow! It – hurts!" Chepi panted between words.

"Always does," Neon replied, removing his hand.

Bridger looked into her open eyes. "Hey, you're okay."

"Oh, my God, it hurts!" she cried out as she reached with her left hand and pulled the other out from underneath her hip, revealing the ripped, red flesh of her right palm that was oozing blood.

"Shit!" Bridger ripped off his jacket and white button-down, feeling the cool breeze against his bare skin as he wrapped the shirt around her hand."

"Let me look at it." Neon grasped the sleeve of the shirt, using it to sop up enough blood from her palm so he could see the wound.

"That hurts! That hurts!" Chepi cried out.

"Shot went through her hand – blew out her palm." Neon glanced behind them. "Bullet stopped there," he added, pointing at a waist-high chip in a cement wall behind them, what remained of the flattened bullet lying on the ground below it.

Bridger pulled his shirt from the wound, ripping it with his teeth so he could tear away a piece long enough for a tourniquet. "I'm just going to tie this around her arm to stop the bleeding."

"No, they don't do tourniquets anymore," Neon told him as he supported her arm. "I'll wrap the rest of the shirt back around her hand and you tie it off with that strip for pressure."

"Is it... going to be okay?" Chepi gasped through gritted teeth.

"You'll be fine." Bridger tried to sound more certain than he was as he looped a knot.

"Yeah, help's coming," Neon added as sirens wailed in the distance.

Tugging hard, Bridger tightened the rag. "We'll get you out of here."

Chepi winced, biting her lip.

"Sorry," Bridger added. "And we'll get you something for the pain."

"Chepi!" Takota yelled as he worked his way to his daughter's side. "They shot her!"

"She'll be okay, but you need to keep calm for her," Neon advised him. "Let's get her inside — and you, too, Bridger!" he added, sounding equally concerned for his friend.

"I promised she'd be safe, and then..." Takota eyes went wide as he studied Bridger's back. "You're bleeding, too, son!"

"I'm fine, and I can get her." Bridger grunted, trying to suppress the throbbing pain in his head while struggling to lift Chepi.

"No, I'll carry her — you just follow," Neon insisted, slipping his arms under Chepi and lifting her.

"Okay, then..." Still dazed, Bridger heard the approaching sirens grow louder. He glanced about the chaotic scene, taking notice of two cameramen from rival stations with their cameras still rolling. "Hey, I'll get your camera, Neon — still got a job to do."

"Are you kidding me?" Neon snapped at him. "You stay with us — let's go!"

"And I've got you," Takota insisted as he offered Bridger his arm, guiding him to his feet. "You could use some help, too."

"It's just a scrape." Bridger repressed thoughts of the pain as he walked at Takota's side, following Neon toward the casino doors. "Head wounds – always look worse – a lot of blood."

"Looks like your back's cut up, too," Takota remarked as he guided Bridger through the front doors. "Did you hit it on something?"

"Maybe…" Bridger reached for his bare back, finding just a bit of dampness along the bumps and grooves of his old scar.

"His back?" Neon positioned Chepi on an oversized leather couch, then turning to Bridger. "What else did you do?"

"I don't know." Bridger looked at his hand, finding it smeared with more blood.

"Looks more like a scrape shaped like the number four." Takota motioned with his hands, replicating the size and shape of the wound. "Two scrapes come down and one across, but I don't know how he could have done that."

Neon tugged off his hooded sweatshirt and used it to wipe away the blood on his friend's neck and back. "It's just blood from your head that's smeared on your old scar, so you're fine." He cautiously tugged the hoodie over Bridger's head. "This'll keep you covered so the competition can't make you a part of tonight's news," he added, pointing at a cameraman whose lens was directed at them.

"Thanks." Bridger slipped his arms into the sweatshirt, then grabbing the hood and pressing it firmly against his head wound as he hissed in pain. "Damn those guys! They're getting this story, and we're getting nothing!"

"Give it a rest, BK," Neon told him, motioning for him to sit in the chair beside them.

"No, I'm fine," Bridger insisted as the paramedics rushed into the building. One came toward him, but he waved him off. "Not me – the girl needs help."

"And I need help over this way!" Naomi Drummond yelled from across the room where she reclined in a chair, her foot propped up on a coffee table.

"First my daughter — she's been shot." Takota insisted, waving his arms at the paramedics until they came to Chepi's side.

"But I'm in a lot of pain over here!" Naomi continued as another paramedic entered the room, rushing toward her.

"Hey, you should take a number, lady!" Neon yelled.

Bridger grabbed Neon's arm. "Don't get in her face about it. I still want to interview her."

"Well, not right now, you're not!"

"No, but if we follow her to the hospital, then we'd probably be first to interview her, and we could get Takota on—"

"No, no, no!" Neon told him. "We are not chasing this! You promised Al you'd go back right after the presser, and I have to say by the look of things, it's over!"

"But Al didn't know that—"

"—that this would happen?" Neon finished. "Of course, he didn't! And just after I promised him I'd keep you out of trouble, look at what happened! Man, he's going to be so pissed at me." Neon headed for the door. "I'm grabbing my equipment and then we're getting out of here." He pointed out the casino's windows at two state troopers talking to witnesses just outside on the front steps. "We don't want to get caught up in this with a bunch of questions from the troops."

"Well… okay." Bridger reluctantly agreed as he realized Neon was right; if the troopers started questioning them, then they'd wind up stuck at the casino, unable to keep working the story.

"I've got to go," Bridger told Takota. "But I'll be in touch… to see how she's doing." He reached between the paramedics, gently grasping Chepi's shoulder. "You're going to be fine. Just hang in there."

"Thanks," she muttered through parched lips.

"Yes, thank you, Bridger, and you must take care of yourself, as well," Takota added as he reached with both hands behind his own neck.

"You mean this thing?" Bridger gently patted his hood against the tender patch on the back of his head. "It'll be fine."

"Not your head, but the scar on your back…" Takota removed a long cord from behind his neck, pulling it over his head and upward until a small leather pouch emerged from the collar of his shirt. "Something tells me you're still in need of healing."

"No, like Neon said, it's just an old scar."

"Wear this," Takota insisted, handing the leather pouch to Bridger. "It'll help."

Glancing to his side, Bridger noticed Detective Holly Ward entering the building, so he took the pouch and backed away. "Thanks."

"Old wounds run deep, my friend," Takota said after him. "They can take a long time to heal."

"Yeah, it's worth a try," Bridger replied despite having no intentions of wearing the thing.

"Hey, Klein?" Holly shouted at him. "And what do you think *you're* doing here?"

"Just following up on the news, detective." He gave her a sheepish grin.

She tilted her head, her hands on her hips. "Now don't you go giving me any more trouble than I've already got with this situation, Bridger."

Still clutching the pouch in his hand, Bridger winked at her. "Aw, you know me, Holly." Heading out the door, he yelled back, "I wouldn't dream of it!"

⚜

Chapter 11

"It's never easy when I have to make this call," Al bemoaned in a voice just loud enough to be heard on the speaker phone in his office. "I just got word that your nephew found his way into another incident."

"Don't tell me he was at that casino?" Silas Klein sounded alarmed on the other end of the line.

"He wasn't shot, Silas," Al told him. "Neon called to say he's fine. He just got a little banged up hitting the pavement, but he's okay."

Silas sighed into the phone. "I thought you were going to keep him out of this mess."

"Well, I thought I was, too, but you know how bull-headed he gets when he smells a big story. The kid is one determined son-of-a-bitch."

"Just like his father," Silas added.

I thought if I sent him to the casino, then he'd be *away* from the fires — not in the center of this whole mess!"

"I understand... all too well. So, where have you got him now?"

"They're headed back to the office as we speak. I figure I'll keep them here working on the story until I can come up with something else to do with them."

"I see," Silas replied. "Well... thanks for trying to keep him reigned in."

"It's what I do, old friend. I just wish I could do it better." Al tilted back in his leather chair, looking out his window at the smoke in the sky. "So, when Bridger gets back here, he's going to be hell-bent on pursuing this story, and I think that's a bad idea. I have no doubt that all of this trouble is part of our problem resurfacing."

"I hear you, and I agree," Silas replied. "With more fires and now this treaty threatening the landowners, we're certain the Cadre is somehow involved — and that's why Bridger has to stay far away from this."

"I know, but I'm just not sure how I'm going to stop him this time." Al leaned forward, jostling his computer mouse until his screen came to life. "You know, he's all over those coppers I told you about. Maybe I can get him focused on deciphering them here at the office — or even send him to you on the island for some help with them."

Silas laughed. "Good luck getting him to come here. He doesn't want anything to do with me, so he'd have to be pretty desperate to make that trip."

"Well, I figure it's worth a try." Al scanned a web search. "In the meantime, I want to get a look at what happened at the casino — see if I spot any of our old acquaintances." He clicked on a source. "I'm already finding video of the incident online, compliments of our friendly news competitors."

"I'm looking at it here, too," Silas informed him. "Do you know anything on the shooter yet?"

"Just preliminary info — he's a twenty-year-old, card-carrying member of the Michigan Battalion."

"So, if the militias weren't interested in this before, then they sure as hell will be now," Silas speculated.

"You don't see the shooter on video," Al commented as he scanned another download. "I guess that's no surprise since everyone was focused on that Drummond woman standing at the podium."

"Yeah, I'm just looking at video of her ducking when the shot went off, and I'm happy to say I don't see Bridger in this frame."

"Wait... I just found one where the camera pans to the crowd." Al searched the hectic scene for signs of the shooter but saw nothing more than some pushing and shoving. "It's just a big brawl until the gun goes off. Then everybody crouches and looks around before mass panic takes over." Al continued to watch. "This camera jostles a lot, anyway – guess I can't blame the camera guy for panicking, too."

"Look at the channel seven webpage. They've already put up a tease for their six o'clock broadcast."

Al clicked on the competitor's site, bringing up a page that included a video box labeled *Update at 6* under their breaking news banner. "So, what are they peddling?" he wondered aloud as he clicked play on the video.

"Oh, no!" Silas erupted on the other end of the line. "Are you seeing this?"

Al watched as the video focused on the injured woman at the scene. "Yeah, I just see Neon moving toward the girl – oh, and that must be the back of Bridger's head," he added as he noticed the bloodied blond curls in the foreground.

"Keep watching..."

Al watched as the woman revealed her bloodied hand, the cameraman then zooming in on the image. "More sensationalism – they've always got to include that." He continued to watch as hands wrapped white fabric around her hand, the cameraman then pulling back to reveal the broader scene once more.

"Do you see it now?" Silas asked.

"Dear God..." Al clenched the edge of his desk as he continued to watch, the cameraman zooming once again – this time, on the indelible scar Bridger bore on his back.

"All this time we've been able to hide it, and now it's out for the world – including them – to see."

Al took a deep breath. "This is my fault, Silas. I let you down."

"No," Silas insisted. "You've done more than I ever could have – more than any of us could have. Maybe we'll get lucky and it won't be seen."

"Are you kidding?" Al replayed the video, pausing it once the image of Bridger's scar was clearly visible on the screen. "The Cadre's *going* to see this video."

"And then they'll know who Bridger really is... *very* dangerous business."

Al shook his head. "What the hell are we going to do?"

"We need to call Penne – get her involved right away," Silas answered.

"She was just here this morning – came by to discuss how the Cadre might be using these fires toward their cause," Al recalled from his earlier visit with his boss. "She's going to be so pissed at me for how I handled Bridger."

"No – just worried how this information might be used."

Al folded his hands. "You mean… against the other."

"Yes," Silas answered. "So, I'm going to call her right now and fill her in, and then I'm heading over to talk with Bridger. I know he won't be happy to see me but we have to talk."

"And what are you going to tell him this time?"

"This time?" Silas paused. "Well, I guess I'm finally going to have to tell him the truth, Alphonse, because we just can't hide it anymore. It's out, and so the day's finally come when we have to tell him about Benedict."

⚜

Chapter 12

Ignoring his aching head, Bridger instinctively reached toward the scar on his back as he stared through the car windshield at the inferno raging across the road, his vision beginning to blur with tears. "Damn, that's intense – burns the sinuses." He squinted as teardrops fell down his cheeks, wiping them away and pinched his nose with one hand while rubbing his shoulder blade with the other.

Neon drove erratically, weaving around slower vehicles as he pressed his cell phone to his ear. "Well, we're still trying to get out of the parking lot, Al, so we'll get there as soon as we can!" he yelled into the phone. "I already told you, his hard head is just fine! Oh, and by the way, I'm okay, too, in case you were wondering about me, thank you very much." He tapped the brakes, avoiding another car.

"Watch it," Bridger shouted.

"I'm trying!" Neon yelled back as he snapped his phone shut and tossed it in the back seat. "He hung up on me! I can't please any of you whiners!" Hitting the accelerator, Neon whipped around a couple of cars and squeezed between two more before finally banking a quick right out of the lot.

"Hey, turn in here!" Bridger pointed at a driveway across the street.

"What?" Wheels squealing, Neon followed his directive, turning into another parking lot before Bridger had a chance to answer. "This isn't a short cut, dude; it just goes around back of the marina – you know, the one that's on fire?"

"Yeah, I realize that!" Bridger scanned the landscaped grounds that stood between them and the fire. "But there's got to be one around here somewhere."

"One what?"

"Another copper..."

"Are you kidding me?" Neon slammed on the brakes. "I just told Al we're headed back, and I told *you* we weren't doing this, and then you go and—"

"I bet that's it!" Bridger pointed at an object over by the marina's dumpster.

"You don't know that's—"

"It's got to be!" Popping his door handle, Bridger jumped from the car and dashed along a gravel path that led to the dumpster.

Throwing the car into park, Neon was right behind him. "Dude, don't do this to me!" he yelled, his voice barely audible over the commotion of shouts and sirens, hoses hissing and flames roaring.

"Hey, don't go over there!" A nearby fireman yelled at Bridger. "Another truck's coming any second to work that side."

Bridger ignored the warning, continuing to dash forward on his mission.

"Got it covered!" Neon waved off the fireman. "I'll pull him back," he added, continuing his pursuit.

Bridger was just a few steps short of the dumpster when the inferno's intense heat caught up with his memories. He suddenly collapsed to his knees in the gravel, squeezing his eyes closed as he tried to block out the sudden vision of a red-hot branding iron hovering before him. The fiery glow grew larger, its heat intensifying as the smoldering iron seemed to approach him. With his hands tightened into fists, he pushed his inner wrists against his eyes, trying to force the image from his thoughts.

"What are you doing!" Neon yelled as he grabbed hold of his friend's arm.

"No!" Bridger screamed, lowering his fists as he jerked away his arm. "I'm not leaving 'til I get that copper!"

Neon grunted with fists in the air, then ran the few last steps to the metal sheet and pulled it from the ground. "It's hot, damn it!"

"Both of you, get out there!" the fireman yelled as a fire engine wheeled onto the nearby lawn, its siren blaring as the truck approached us.

Neon blurted expletives as he dashed back with the copper in one hand, grabbing Bridger again with his other. "Snap out of it! Come on!"

Bridger rose from his knees and ran with Neon back to the car, crawling into the passenger seat as Neon climbed in on the other side.

"Here's your stupid copper!" Neon yelled, shoving the copper at Bridger and rubbed his palms against his jeans. "Hope you're happy!" Dropping the car into reverse, he wheeled it backward just far enough to avoid the curb, then throwing it into drive and speeding his way out of the lot, onto the road.

"Crap, this thing *is* hot!" Bridger complained as he tilted the shield against the dashboard, running his fingers tentatively over the embossed syllabics scrawled in rows across the copper. "I knew there'd be another one... and look!" He pointed back and forth between two groupings of syllabics. "That's *yamita*, the one Kelli Sue found in the first two coppers, and it's in this one — twice! So, maybe this one will be enough to help us finally break the code!"

"Yeah, well, why don't you leave the solving to the cops, partner? I mean, you're supposed to be a reporter — not a detective!"

Bridger looked at his friend. "And, so what's got your panties all bunched in a knot?"

"You!" Neon jabbed his finger at Bridger. "You're getting all crazy obsessed with solving this stuff when your job is to report the story — not *be* it!"

"Good God, now you sound like Al!" Bridger shook his head in disbelief. "That's just the kind of thinking that keeps us stuck in this dead end job. We've *got* to do more investigative work if we're ever going to get noticed by some metro or national people!" He paused, looking down. "But if you're not interested, then—"

"You know I've always been game for that stuff," Neon insisted. "But not when it's this dangerous!"

"Yeah, listen to you talk," Bridger scoffed. "I know you've always been a risk-taker."

Neon kept his eyes on the road, staring straight ahead. "Maybe I have been, with myself... but I've never put you at risk."

Bridger mulled over his comment, realizing it was true. "Well, you don't need to be my mom, or my personal bodyguard or anything like that."

"Really? And what was that back there?" With his thumb extended, Neon shook his fist in the air, motioning like a hitchhiker toward the smoke and fire behind them. "You have another one of your freak-outs because you're on top of a fire, but you don't think you need my help getting you out of that?"

Bridger shook his head, embarrassed that Neon recognized why he had collapsed.

"And that shooting..." Neon continued. "I *didn't* help you there, because I couldn't get to you in time." He shook his head. "You know, if something happened to you, Al's not the only one who wouldn't forgive me!"

Bridger turned from his friend and stared at the ominous smoke billowing in the afternoon sky. "Yeah, I know... Silas has always expected you to be like a big brother to me, counting on you to look out for me when—"

"I wasn't talking about Silas..."

Bridger looked back at Neon to find him blinking back tears.

"You *are* like a brother to me — the only brother I've ever known." Neon reached up to his visor and pulled out his sunglasses. "I don't watch over you just because I'm asked to." He slipped on the glasses, pushing them up his nose. "Don't you realize? It's me I'd never forgive."

❖

Chapter 13

Pastor Creighton took the back roads, weaving his way north and then east as he hurried toward the Christmas tree farm owned by young J Paul Tamarack's parents. He had already initiated the militia's phone tree, imparting the command for all available members to gather at Tamaracks' home where they were to support the family and wait for further instructions. There was no doubt in his mind that they were following his directive at this very moment, and equally no doubt that they would expect him to arrive with a plan of action already in hand.

Creighton used the road time to call his Battalion comrades across the state, informing them of the shooting incident and suggesting they prepare for potential repercussions from Michigan's Governor Ella Thompson, a progressive liberal hell-bent on undermining the Second Amendment. He further recommended a proactive call to arms, requesting that all the militias assemble at the Battalion's Northern Michigan compound to prepare their defenses as well as a joint preemptive strike should one be deemed necessary. All leaders agreed to the emergency meet-up, planning to converge at the compound with all available members and weaponry by noon tomorrow.

Tossing his phone aside, Creighton glanced at the distant eastern sky where a crop-duster gained altitude above the evergreens. Banking to its side, the plane then headed toward him, its whirling props droning loudly as it flew low overhead and headed westward toward the fires behind him. The plane must have taken off from the Cheboygan airport up ahead, a landmark that indicated he was nearing his turn.

He tapped his brakes at the sight of Grangers' Gourd and Pumpkin Patch, a sizeable family farm run by the children and grandchildren of Butane Bill. Just past Grangers' place, he turned left onto an unmarked dirt road, wheels skidding through loose gravel that clattered beneath his car as he sped along side countless rows of Blue Spruce, Concolor Fir, and Scotch Pines. Slowing as he neared the farmhouse, he weaved between cars and trucks parked haphazardly along both sides of the road, squeezing past more vehicles in the driveway to take the liberty of parking his Ford on the Tamaracks' side lawn. He then leapt from his car, noticing the scent of pine and burning leaves as he jogged to the side screen door and gave it an obligatory tap before letting himself in.

"Hey, Pastor Rod's here!" A beer-bellied man tilted his Pabst Blue Ribbon can toward Creighton, acknowledging the pastor as he entered the packed kitchen.

A raspy-voiced woman shouted, "Praise God!" She waved her Camel cigarette through the smoke-filled air, ashes flying as she pointed toward the packed hallway across the room. "Captain Laski and the Granger boy are that way somewhere, too. They just finished telling us what happened."

"Those damn Indians must've provoked John Paul's boy," insisted an elderly man wearing a camo cap and vest. He patted Creighton on the shoulder. "He's a good kid, Pastor. What can we do to help?"

"Well, you already helped by coming so quickly." Creighton grinned at the sizable turnout. "It's important for you to be here... for John Paul, and for Millie."

With these few words, Creighton watched all eyes turn toward the far corner table where John Paul Tamarack stood. Stepping toward the man, he took notice of John Paul's determined demeanor; his graying eyebrows furrowed tightly below his receding hairline, his jaw set and chapped lips pursed, his hands pressed deeply into the front pockets of his dirt-stained canvas workpants.

"John Paul." Creighton reached toward him, his hand outstretched as he moved forward to shake.

The crowd parted to let Creighton pass, revealing John Paul's wife Millie seated at the Formica-topped table, her face pale and blotchy. She clenched wads of tissue in her hands.

Millie rose from her seat. "Good. Now you're here so now we can go." She spoke rapidly, turning swiftly toward her husband to continue. "See, he's here now John so we can go. You said we'd see J Paul when Pastor got here and now he's here so let's go." Reaching across the table, she grabbed her purse.

"Now, hold on, Mill." John Paul held a hand up to his wife. "First we've got to hear what Pastor has to say."

"But..." She dabbed at her puffy eyes and straightened her untucked blouse. "...but you said we'd go when he got here and he's here and—"

"I said we *wouldn't* go 'til Pastor got here and filled us in! Now let's hear what the man's got to say!" He turned away from his wife, his head held high as he looked to Creighton. "What do you think, Pastor?"

"Millie, I'm sure J Paul's safe in custody." Creighton tried to assure her.

Millie lowered herself back to her seat, quietly burying her face in her tissues.

"I contacted our best militia attorney, and he's headed to the jail right now to represent your son." Creighton looked at his watch. "Why, I bet he's already there, Millie, so you can rest assured he's in good hands, and that our guy will advise J Paul to remain silent until we can sort this out."

"Which we will do," added Captain Laski as he swaggered from an attached hallway into the kitchen. "Like I told you when I got here, that boy was provoked!"

"Yeah, and he... he didn't shoot the girl, either," Dylan Granger stammered from the hallway.

Laski glanced back at Dylan. "Now son, I know you're still upset over this and that it probably all seems a blur, but you can't cower at times like these."

"But I'm… I'm not cowering!" Dylan insisted. "J Paul wouldn't take a random shot like that one – not from that far away… and sure not while my grandpa was standing there!"

Laski scowled. "But Dylan, we were there. We all saw it."

Millie began to sob.

Creighton shook his head. "Don't do this, Dylan. You've got to stand behind your friend and be proud of him, just like the rest of us. You shouldn't take that away from his parents."

Millie lifted her face, running her fingers through her bleach-streaked hair. "No one's taking away my pride in my son…" Still sniffling, she paused to catch her breath.

"And no one's going to, Millie," Creighton told her.

"…and *no* one can make me believe my son shot that Indian girl!" Millie rose to her feet once again. "I know my son, and he just… he wouldn't do that!"

Creighton reached out and placed his hand on Millie's shoulder. "Of course, it's hard for you to imagine, Millie. And it could be that he just meant to fire a warning shot – something to stop that evil UTC woman was spewing all of her hateful rhetoric."

The crowd muttered words of agreement.

"No, that doesn't make sense!" Dylan shouted above the crowd noise. "I mean, where'd he get that gun anyway? We didn't bring it with–"

"You don't see a concealed weapon, son." Laski reached beneath his shirt and quickly drew his Glock 25, flaunting it before Dylan's wide eyes. "That's supposed to be the idea."

"And all of this speculation is unproductive, anyway," Creighton added. "What we need to do right now is figure out where we go from here, and not just for J Paul's sake but for the sake of us all."

"What do you mean?" Millie scowled. "It's my son who's in trouble here!"

Creighton looked into her eyes. "Actually, this could mean a lot of trouble for all of us, Millie, so I need for everyone to hear me out on this."

Millie blotted her eyes. "Well, you go ahead and do that, Pastor Rod, but I've got to go to my son now." With all eyes on her, she stepped through the parted crowd, heading toward the door. "You all make your plans and then see yourselves out when you're done." And with that, she was gone.

John Paul was right behind her. "I'll take care of this," he grumbled as he left the house as well, the screen door slamming behind him.

"Well, their response is certainly understandable under the circumstances," Creighton tried to assure the crowd.

"Of course, it is." Raspy girl tapped out her cigarette in an ashtray. "The boy's got troubles, Pastor, but what's that got to do with us?"

"Well, I've been in contact with other militia leaders across the state, and they're hearing what I'm hearing – that Governor 'No-Guns' Thompson plans to use this incident to further her gun control agenda."

"What?" Camo man blurted.

"Yeah, and that means she'll want to shut down concealed carries!" Laski snarled. "Next she'll be trying again to compile that gun registry database thing she's always wanted, but this time she'll get away with it; that is, if she can manage to scare enough of the public over this shooting thing."

"And that's why the other militias agree that we've got to stop her before she reaches her real objective, which is taking away all the guns."

"She'd take our guns?" Beer guy asked.

"Of course, she'll take them, if she can find them," Laski replied. "And if she gets that database, she can locate everything that's registered... easy."

"And then there's still that Drummond woman trying to take our land, and we know she's in cahoots with the Governor," Creighton added. "That means they're trying to take our guns *and* our land!"

"You mean, taking our guns *so* they can take our land!" Laski grimaced. "Yeah, from my cold, dead hands!"

The crowd grew boisterous, seething with hostile language.

"Well, we got to stop these hoodlums, Pastor!" camo man insisted. "What do *you* say?"

"I say I agree, and rest assured, our fellow militias from across the state agree. They'll be headed for the Tip of the Mitt for a meet-up we'll be organizing at our Michilimackinac Compound by noon tomorrow."

"Oo-rah!" Beer guy bellowed, raising his can high as the crowd whooped along with him.

"But we need to get this planned tonight so we'll be ready to run this operation tomorrow." Creighton headed for the door. "I've still got a lot to do to get ready, so that's why I need you all to make some calls. Use the phone tree to reach all the members. Then get a hold of some property owners from the shooting today to see if they're ready to defend themselves, too. Tell them all to be at the church by seven tonight so we can get organized."

Raspy girl flicked her Bic lighter. "And what's the plan from there?"

"Defending our rights by any means necessary — that's the plan!" Laski shouted. "Now let's get those calls out, people, because the time's come to fight fire with fire!"

⚜

Chapter 14

Slipping into the WHAM newsroom through the emergency exit door, Bridger hoped he and Neon could sneak to their seats unnoticed. But once the door clicked shut behind him, he turned to find Kelli Sue already heading their way.

"Honey? I'm home!" Neon held out an arm, grinning.

"Oh, my God! They said you're hurt! Are you okay?" She grabbed Bridger by the shoulders, closely inspecting him.

"Well, I'm a little banged up, but I'll be all right," Neon mocked.

"And you've got blood on your shirt!" She set about searching his neck for his injury.

"*My* shirt," Neon clarified. "And really, I'm okay."

Bridger pulled away from her. "Don't touch it, K. It's fine now – just a bump on the head."

Her hands went to her hips. "Fine, my foot!" Chomping her gum, she raised one hand to point under Bridger's arm. "And what's that?"

"It's another copper."

"Give it to me," she demanded, taking the copper away from him and pointing toward Bridger's desk. "And you go sit down while I get you an ice pack."

"And I'll take a coffee, extra sugar." Neon winked.

Kelli Sue glowered at him. "Just get him to his seat, funny guy." Turning away, she took the copper with her as she headed for the office kitchen.

"I don't need any help," Bridger insisted as he walked to his desk.

"Good, because you're not getting any," Neon replied, following him.

"But I do need you to start editing so I can see what you got at the shooting. Maybe there's enough footage for us to—"

"I'll get to it — right after Al's done chewing on our asses."

Bridger looked through Al's office windows, finding his boss absent. "But he's not even here right now."

"Oh, he's here somewhere, no doubt." Neon sat down in the chair next to Bridger's desk. "The guy's a blood hound — it's like he can smell us when we come back to the office."

"Well, I can't wait around if we want to be first to..." Bridger paused, turning his attention to the television as a quick jingle trumpeted the top of the news hour on WHAM's cable network affiliate. With the ONUS News logo filling the screen, Bridger thought he saw the words *Michigan Shooting* scrolling along the banner at the bottom.

"Committed to responsible journalism..." the deep voice-over announced. "This... is ONUS News."

"Where the onus... is on us," Neon quipped as he slouched in his chair.

"...always is." Bridger nodded, chewing at his thumbnail while his eyes remained on the monitor.

"Occurring Now, United States..." the network talking-head in a suit and tie announced, the same words blazoned across the large box hovering next to his left shoulder. "... Senator Westinghouse says he will not resign despite allegations by the Justice Department that he—"

"No more coverage of the fires." Bridger stared at the television, still biting at a hangnail. "Guess they're just going to talk about the same old DC news."

"Hey, it beats another report from Sonny." Neon cleared his throat, raising his voice an octave to say, "And this fire thingy..." Waving his arms in circles, he exaggerated the weatherwoman's hand gestures. "...it's kind of like a big cold front, except this one's hot!"

"Don't remind me." Bridger shook his head, his eyes never leaving the screen. "Just get that film together while K-Sue and

I get these coppers solved. If ONUS isn't reporting anything more on the fires yet, then we still have a chance at being first with this angle." He continued to gnaw at his nail.

"Are you going to eat that thing?" Neon pointed at Bridger's thumb. "You know, biting your nails is a disgusting habit – you can't do that when you become a big time reporter."

Bridger stared at Neon. "Shut up." He laughed. "And you should talk about disgusting habits."

Kelli Sue returned, handing Bridger an ice pack wrapped in a towel. "Keep this pressed on that bump, and you'll thank me tomorrow,"

"Thanks K." Bridger placed the cold compress against his head, grimacing.

With a ring from the office phone on the reception desk, Kelli Sue headed for it. "Sorry if it hurts, Bridge," she yelled back to him, then answering the phone. "WHAM News…"

"Guess there's no coffee." Neon smirked.

"Yes, Mr. Klein is fine," Kelli Sue said into the receiver. "No, that's an old wound from years ago."

"What's she doing?" Bridger asked Neon.

"Yes, I'll let him know that, thank you." Kelli Sue hung up, rolling her eyes as she turned to Bridger. "Another female fan wants to know if you're okay."

"Aw, isn't' that sweet?" Neon smirked. "Didn't know getting hurt would make you a chick magnet, did you?"

"But how do they know I got hurt?" Bridger asked her.

"Well, they saw the video."

"What video?" Bridger snapped.

"The video of *you!*" Al answered as he approached from behind them, seeming to have come from nowhere. "Don't you know, Klein? You're an internet sensation!" Al scowled, his jowls tightening. "In my office… now." He went ahead of them, taking a seat in his office chair where he waited.

Kelli Sue lifted the copper to her desk, "I'll get to work on deciphering this."

"Thanks K," Bridger replied as he headed with Neon toward Al's office door. "And would you call Detective Ward, too, to let her know we have it?"

"Yeah, I will, but we'll be in trouble for taking this thing, won't we?"

"You won't be, but she'll be ticked at me – might as well get everyone mad while I'm at it," Bridger answered before entering the office, closing the door behind him.

Without saying a word, Al turned his computer around so the two could see the screen as he played the entire video of Bridger revealing his scar.

"Shit," Bridger muttered. "That makes me look like an idiot."

Neon shook his head. "I tried to cover it..." he looked at the ceiling. "...and I thought I'd blocked all the camera angles."

Al stood up, tucking his hands in his pockets. "Well, you didn't, son, and now this has gone viral – for *everyone* to see."

"Okay, well it's just some sensational video... but it doesn't have any information on the background or the aftermath, so we can use this!" Bridger eyes were wide with new found enthusiasm. "All we have to do is figure out how to connect this with our news coverage so people can get the full details of–"

"No," Al told Bridger, then looking to Neon. "It's over."

Bridger glared at Al. "What do you mean, it's over?"

"This is my fault," Neon said, his eyes meeting Al's.

"No, it's not anybody's fault!" Bridger insisted. "The girl was hurt, Al! So, what were we supposed to do? Just leave her there bleeding so we could stay out of the story? Hell, we were already neck-deep in it!"

"And I shouldn't have let that happen," Neon said to Al. "I let you down."

"Well, it doesn't matter now," Al replied. "We'll just have to make some changes."

"What are you talking about?" Bridger questioned. "I just want to get to work on this story, and we're losing precious time while we sit here and argue over whose fault it is that I ended up in somebody's video!"

"Just hold on," Al told Bridger, turning again to Neon. "I do need something on tonight's broadcast, so give all your footage to Kodak and he'll put it together with a Sonny voiceover."

"Are you kidding me?" Bridger raised his hands in outrage.

"But I know what I've got in the can, Al, so maybe I should do the edit," Neon suggested.

"No, I'll need you for another meeting in a few minutes, so get Kodak started and then come right back here."

Neon sighed, looking at Bridger. "Sorry, dude," he said as he left.

"What the hell!" Bridger glared at Al. "You think that I can't be objective because I was at—"

"No, you can't!" Al snapped back. "You're not satisfied reporting facts and letting the viewers draw their own conclusions. Instead, you want to put the pieces together for them — tell them what they should think. You want to turn everything into some giant conspiracy that'll land you a network job, and *that's* why you're not objective."

Bridger stood with lips parted, eyes wide, staring at Al. "You really think that? But that's not true! I base everything on the facts, and just because I'm willing to dig a little deeper—"

"And that's how people can play you! They just plant the clues, like those damn copper things you're chasing after, and you play along, never considering that maybe that's what the bad guys *want* you to do."

"That's insane! Who's going to go to all that trouble to—"

"But they *did* go to all that trouble, Bridger, and you *are* playing along. Seems like some damn arsonist's trying to pull our chain, and I'm telling you right now, we are not going to be yanked!" He crossed his arms tightly across his broad chest. "No, we will not be a party to fueling the real fire that arsonists desire: the power to scare people into a mass irrational reaction."

"What are you, an authority on arsons now?" Bridger rolled his eyes in utter frustration.

"No, but I do have a different perspective on this, Bridger —
one that comes from years of experience, and one I've got to show
you today."

"Fine, whatever… but will you still just let me figure out
what the coppers say before you make a final decision on whether
or not they're newsworthy?"

Al took a deep breath. "Okay, you and Kelli can keep playing Suduko with the damn things for now; but if you figure
them out, I'm the first to know. Got it?"

"I got it." Bridger reached for the door.

"Oh, and we both know someone who could probably help
you get those things solved in no time. He's an authority and a
relative of yours who's—"

"I don't need to talk to Uncle Silas about this — I can solve
them myself."

"Fine — solve them yourself, but you still need to talk with
your uncle."

"Well, sorry Al, but I'm not going to the island." Turning
the doorknob, Bridger stepped out of the office.

Al followed him out. "You don't have to go to the island.
He's here."

Bridger wheeled around. "What!"

Al motioned down the long, windowless hallway, pointing
past the office restrooms toward the far end wall where a large
door always stood, closed and locked… except for today. Now
it was wide open, and Uncle Silas stood framed in the doorway.

"Sorry for the unplanned visit," he said as he stepped into
the dim light of the hallway.

Bridger stared at him, speechless.

"I just…" Silas shifted from one foot to the other. "I saw
the video on the internet, and I talked to Alphonse about what
happened today…"

Bridger glared at Al. "Is *this* why you want me off the story?"

"No, Bridger," Silas insisted, stepping closer. "It's much
more than that, and I'm here to explain — to tell you things
you've wanted to know but I couldn't—"

"Really? You picked today for the truth tour?"

"I picked today because I had to — because you're in danger now, and I have to explain."

"Danger? What are you talking about?"

"I'm talking about your past and about that horrible scar on your back." Silas gazed at Bridger, his weathered skin taut as he grimaced with a terrified expression. "When they see that mark on your back, Bridger, they will know who you are, and you will be dragged into this mess in ways you can't imagine."

Chapter 15

For the past years of Bridger's stay at WHAM News, he had always assumed the locked office was used merely as a storage room. In a way, it was; but instead of supplies, the room contained a cache of information. One wall was lined with file cabinets while the opposite wall held floor-to-ceiling cabinetry divided into multiple work stations, each equipped with a state-of-the-art computer. Screen-savers whirled and the network hummed, ready for operation.

"What is this?" Bridger wondered aloud as he took a seat at one end of the room's central conference table.

"It's a substation of sorts," Al answered from the doorway. "I'll let Silas explain," he added before exiting, shutting the door behind him.

"So..." Bridger stared at the bank of computers, "Never knew this was in here... but apparently you did." He pursed his lips. "Guess it's just another secret — something else I was left out of the loop on."

Silas tugged up his khakis as he sat on the edge of the conference table. "Yes, another secret, I suppose..." He looked down, twirling one of his loafers from the ankle as he pointed his toes, forming a circle in the air. "But you were never out of the loop, Bridger; no, you were always right smack in the middle of it."

"Really..." Bridger reclined in his chair. "So, would you mind explaining that?"

Silas sighed, relaxing his foot as he looked to Bridger. "I'll try. It's just that... this is going to be difficult for you to hear."

Bridger stared back at his uncle, taking note of how much the man had aged. "Well, it can't be any worse than *not* knowing."

"I'm not so sure about that, but I guess we'll see..." Silas tugged at his gray goatee. "So, I should begin by telling you that quite a few years ago, when you were quite young, you were used as a pawn in a very serious game."

"A game?" Bridger questioned.

"Like I said, a very *serious* game — not for amusement, but in a competition, nonetheless — one with far-reaching consequences for our country and even abroad.

"Oh, for God's sake! You *always* do this — talking in these broad, sweeping generalizations that tell me *nothing*! Just get to the point! What kind of game are we talking about here?"

"A political game — one intended to undermine the Union."

"*The* Union..." Bridger furrowed his brow. "...as in the Union and the Confederacy? Like civil war stuff?"

"Not necessarily with a north and south divide, but a division just the same."

Bridger laughed. "So, you're telling me that there are people who are trying to split up the country, and they're trying to use *me* to do it? Wow!" He snickered. "Now there's a story! And you thought this crazy fiction would actually satisfy me?" Pressing his palms to the tabletop, he shook his head.

"Hear me out on this," Silas said as he pulled out a chair and sat in it, rolling himself closer to Bridger. "All of these fires, and the treaty and the shootings... these people *want* to trigger civil unrest."

"And how do you even know who's behind this?"

"Comparisons to past attempts to do the same. These incidents have raised a lot of red flags that are still being looked into, even as we speak."

"Looked into by whom? Is this some project you're doing with students at Mission U? And is your project tied into all of this?" He motioned toward the computers and file cabinets. "Because I could look into this from the bureau and—"

"No!" Silas held up his hand. "You can't be involved in this anymore — not now with that video of your scar out there for the whole world to see!"

"Oh – my – God!" Bridger rubbed his face in his hands. "I don't understand this! So what if I've got a scar on my back from an accident! Who cares?"

"The Cadre cares, because..." Silas paused, unable to finish.

"Who?"

"The Cadre – the ones who..." Silas took a deep breath. "...who branded your back."

Bridger gasped, the memory of the branding iron flashing before his eyes once again.

Silas reached for his nephew's shoulder. "That's what these people did to you, Bridger, and that's why we had to protect you."

"What?" Bridger stammered. "But... it was... an accident." His stomach churned, a gut feeling telling him it was not.

"There was no accident..." Silas paused.

Swallowing hard, Bridger vaguely recalled the dark room with a roaring fire, a branding iron removed from the flames, and the searing pain. Trembling, he reached for his back.

"It's okay." Silas leaned closer, patting him. "I'm very sorry this happened, but it's in the past now. Try not to dwell on it."

"What?" Bridger stared wide-eyed at Silas "Are you kidding?" He shook his head. "So, there wasn't an accident? And I was... was there a car? I thought there was, but... I remember a dark room, and the cold." He shuddered. "Where was I?"

"You were kidnapped – taken by car, so you might be remembering that. Then they hid you in the old coal cellar where eventually you were found. I know you don't remember too much of it, Bridger, and it's probably best that you don't. All you need to know is that these people–"

"These people!" Bridger yelled. "Who the hell are these people? These Cadre whatever, are they–"

"Hey, what's all the yelling?" Neon asked as he barged into the room. "And what the hell is this place?" He gazed around the room, his wide eyes finally taking notice of Silas. "Whoa! So, I guess *that's* why all the yelling – little family reunion, huh?" He approached Silas with his hand outstretched. "Good to see you, Professor Silas. It's been a while."

"Yes, it has been." Silas stood and shook Neon's hand.

"Yeah, I thought you'd stop turning gray once both of us moved out, but looks like you've still got a few—"

"Could we cut with the niceties?" Bridger interjected. "Uncle Silas was just telling me about the crazy people who put this ugly scar on my back!"

"What?" Neon's mouth hung open as he took a seat.

Silas sat again. "Yes, the Cadre — well, back then, they were a part of a militant faction of the Fourth Tendency."

"You mean communists?" Bridger asked.

"Anti-Stalin communists — a bunch of Trotskyists," Neon specified. "Didn't you ever learn about—"

"So, these Trotskyists..." Bridger pointed toward his scar. "They're the ones who branded me?"

"Branded you!" Neon yelled.

"Oh, and kidnapped me, too," Bridger quipped with a sarcastic smirk.

"What the..." Neon rubbed his scruffy chin. "No, you people are talking crazy-talk here!"

"I'm afraid we're not," Silas replied. "And this is why we've relied on you to watch over Bridger and keep his scar from view — because we knew if these Trots found out—"

"Wait a minute! To watch over me?" Bridger scowled, motioning toward Neon. "You mean you made him my bodyguard? That's his *job?*"

"No, now hold on!" Neon shook his head, looking to Silas. "You and Al said I should watch out for him like any big brother would, because he had this whole fire phobia thing and was all messed up from losing his folks. And the scar... you said he'd probably have more post-trauma if people saw it and asked him about it. I didn't know he'd be in danger if—"

"You were hired to baby-sit me?" Bridger stared at Neon in disbelief.

"No, man! I was hired to be your cameraman, and I grew up with you like a brother! You know that!"

"I don't know what to believe anymore." Bridger turned away, looking back at Silas. "And this number four branded on my back — is it supposed to be some kind of message?"

"The four was meant to represent the Fourth Tendency, a worldwide organization of Trotskyists who've been trying to end capitalism through what they call *Permanent Revolution*. These Trots caused previous Tendencies to dissolve, but they also had their own internal conflicts that led to splinter groups peeling off, each insisting *they* were the true Trotskyists. And there was one particularly violent faction at the University of Michigan that decided they'd prove their supremacy by bombing a bunch of banks in the region, but fortunately their plans were thwarted by an undercover operative the Trots now refer to as Benedict — a man you once knew, Bridger... as Dad."

"My dad? He... he was involved in this?"

"And he's the reason why *you* were dragged into this. This group was devastated by the betrayal of a man they thought was one of their own, and they wanted revenge in the worst way. So, they kidnapped you, and in their desire to distinguish themselves as most worthy of commanding the Fourth Tendency, they used you as leverage against your father."

Bridger shook his head. "For what?"

"They wanted information: the locales of our operation centers and the names of other informants who had penetrated their organizations. That was the deal, and if you're dad didn't deliver, they said they would kill you."

Speechless, Bridger pressed his hands over his mouth.

"Of course, your dad knew these people from his undercover work, and he calculated that the most violent had been arrested from the foiled bombing plot, so he initially thought they wouldn't hurt you. But there were new recruits involved who must've figured that your dad might think them too soft to follow through on their threat, so..."

"So…" Bridger's eyes welled with tears. "So, they branded me."

Silas took a deep breath. "They sent your dad a roll of eight millimeter film of them… doing this to you."

"Good God!" Neon gasped.

Bridger flashed back to memories of his father, barely able to recall any image of the man yet still remembering his reassuring bear-hug and his warm tears dripping onto Bridger's bare shoulder, trickling down his back. "But I *was* rescued, so did he…" Tears rolled down Bridger's cheeks. "Did my dad tell them what they wanted to know?"

"Fortunately, he never had to because another Trot betrayed the group — a woman who witnessed what they did to you and knew these people had gone too far. So she contacted Benedict and told him where you were, and he rescued you and arrested a couple of people involved… but the worst of the bunch managed to escape and regroup, and now they call themselves the Cadre."

Bridger wiped his cheeks. "So, they're still out there."

"Yes, and they had at least achieved a sense of revenge against your father, leaving him so grief-stricken and full of guilt for what had happened to you. He tortured himself by reviewing that film, each time realizing more and more how close he'd come to telling everything. He knew he couldn't let that happen, and he also knew he couldn't bear it if anyone ever hurt you again. So, that's why… he sent you to me."

Bridger cocked his head. "He did what?"

"Your dad made a tremendous sacrifice, Bridger. He loved you more than anything, and that's why he had to let you go."

"You mean he gave me up… for adoption?"

"Well, it was more like witness protection, I suppose. You see, your dad knew that even if he quit his work and walked away, these people would still manage to find him again… and in doing so, he feared they'd find you, too. So, his only choice… was to hide you."

Bridger's heart raced as he continued to recall the tears on his back, his father's embrace, the sound of him sobbing…

"No, that doesn't make sense." Neon shook his head. "You don't hide people by sending them to live with family."

"You're right," Silas nodded, looking down as he twisted his one hand in the other. "So, I guess I also need to tell you that I'm an operative, too." He turned to look toward Bridger. "I worked undercover with your father a long time ago, up until I was assigned to a new job conducting oversight behind the scenes at Mission University; and I also took on my most cherished responsibility... the task of raising and protecting you."

"What? I'm your job?" Bridger stared, his mouth gaping.

"I have *never* looked at it that way." Silas spoke adamantly. "I love your dad – would do anything for him. He's been like a brother to me and–"

"*Like* a brother," Bridger interrupted. "You mean he's *not* your brother."

Silas bit his lip. "No. He's not... but we did this to protect you, Bridger."

"Okay! So, even if I accept that, which I'm not sure I do... then why keep up the lie? I don't understand... Why wouldn't you just tell me after dad died?"

"Bridger, there was no accident, remember?" Silas paused. "We made changes in names, created the illusion of a car wreck so the Cadre would assume Benedict's son was dead. But you're not... and neither is your dad."

"He's... still alive?" Bridge felt the room spinning as he swayed in his chair.

"Whoa!" Neon grabbed his friend's arm. "Are you okay?"

"Okay?" Bridger cried out, rubbing at his damp eyes. "All this time I thought that..." He looked at Silas. "You kept my dad from me, for all these years?"

"It's what he wanted, for your sake." Silas arched his eyebrows. "It kept you safe for all this time, but if the Cadre sees that video of your scar–"

"And you think they will?" Neon asked.

"I have no doubt they will; and when they do, Bridger becomes a marked man."

"I already *am* a marked man!" He snapped, pointing at his back.

"No, you don't understand!" Silas insisted. "This puts you in serious danger, and your dad, too!"

"And I'm supposed to care?" He stood up, the room still spinning as he held the table for balance. "The guy abandoned me, and I don't... What's his name? You call him Benedict? Well, I don't even know who the hell he is, or who you are. Shit! I don't even know who *I* am! So, what's my real name, Silas? Or what should I call you, Agent... whatever." He staggered toward the door.

"Wait! Let me explain what we need to do!" Silas pleaded, chasing after him.

"I think you've explained enough for the moment, secret agent guy." Bridger jerked open the door. "For the first time in my life, I've heard enough secrets, and I don't think I want to hear anymore." With that, he stormed out of the room, slamming the door behind him.

⚜

Chapter 16

Driving through the front gate and along the gravel drive-way, Magdala turned onto the familiar two-track, driving through the high, dry grass that scratched at her truck's underside. Low-hanging limbs filled with leaves of brilliant orange and golden yellow whacked at the windshield, screeching as they were dragged along the length of the truck. Continuing unabated, the cab lurched and shuddered as the fat tires rolled over rocks and through potholes, the ground finally leveling out as Magdala passed the shooting range and barracks. Then, wheeling around the backside of the poll barn, she maneuvered her way through a stand of tall cedars to finally arrive at the old barn where Brother Rami stood, waiting for her in the open doorway.

At the sight of her most beloved friend, Magdala leapt from the cab and dashed to Rami, pouncing into his arms where he embraced her.

"There's my girl," he said to the young woman he'd cared for as if she were his own child. "Glad to see you back safe." Grabbing her shoulders, he held her at arms length, studying her. "I worried about you."

"No reason to. Phalange taught well." She nodded and smiled, speaking with the bits of English Rami had taught her at the Lebanese orphan shelter as well as those she'd picked up since they had arrived in America to bring the battle to the aggressors.

"Yes, your fellow liberation fighters taught you long before I did, but I still worry about—"

"And you..." Magdala added, pushing her finger against Rami's chest. "You taught me."

"Yes... I did." Rami hugged her again. "Come in, come in. Thoreau's here, too; back to his work." Rami waved Magdala into the barn, locking the side door behind them. "From what we've heard, it sounds like everything worked well."

"They explode good! Spread is good!" She walked with her mentor past the empty, run-down horse stalls, a bat flapping in the rafters overhead.

"Well, good... glad to hear Thoreau's crazy idea worked." Rami pointed at his ear, spinning his finger. "Guess it wasn't so crazy after all."

"Not crazy!" Magdala laughed. "It is better – many small bangs, not a..." She stopped in her tracks as she recalled the enormous fireball that had killed her family.

"Yes, it's pretty ingenious." Rami put his arm around her shoulder, walking her forward. "Can't help but wonder if your Phalange comrades could've used such devices in the war. I know it's not a precise weapon, but guess it wouldn't matter if it burned out the Israelis or the Palestinians – they're all invaders."

Magdala nodded. "And imperial... Americans, our true enemy..."

"Yes, the imperialists who meddle in other countries..." Rami clarified as he reached for a door. "You struck a major blow against them today – sparked a lot of fear in the people living around here."

"Good. I want them to fear."

"And you know that shot you took at the casino?" Rami opened the door for her. "You hit a girl! Did you know that?"

"I did?" Magdala smiled, stepping through the doorway. "I did not aim."

"Well, you got her anyway – right in the hand!" Rami followed her into the small workroom. "An excellent shot, especially after pistol-whipping that militia kid, and that worked out well, too. Don't you think so, Thoreau?" he asked the man hunched over a large workbench, his back to them.

"Good job so far, Magdala." Thoreau did not turn to speak, continuing his detailed work under the intense glare of a fluorescent desk lamp. "The fires and now the shooting... they've all elevated tensions with more than just the locals. And now that the media's taking notice and the politicians are getting involved, things will really heat up."

"Especially with tonight's performance, which you've already set up, right?" Rami asked Magdala.

"Yes, done. But tomorrow's... I set those tonight, yes?"

Thoreau set down his tools and slipped off his protective goggles. "Yeah, tomorrow's incendiaries are all attached and ready for delivery. We just need to load the distribution containers." He turned and climbed off his work stool, approaching Magdala. "But something's come up — something I need you to do on Mackinac Island."

Rami tilted his head. "What's this?"

"An extra task," Thoreau replied as he reached into a box on the workbench, withdrawing a Glock 21 with a suppressor.

"How come I didn't know about this?" Rami asked Thoreau. "I think she's been exposed enough already, so if you need something done, then I'll do it."

"No, you won't; you've already got enough to do tonight."

"Well, then you do it!" Rami insisted.

"I would if I could, but I'm recognizable on the island — can't take the risk of someone placing me at the scene. But Magdala's an unknown there. She'll be able to come and go like any other tourist without a thought given to it." Thoreau turned to Magdala and handed her the Glock. "And with all of your experiences fighting with the Phalange in Lebanon, I have no doubt you're the best one to handle this."

Magdala weighed the gun in her hands.

Rami rubbed at his five-o'clock shadow, shifting his weight. "Can't it wait?"

Thoreau grabbed papers from the printer on his workbench. "This order's from the top, marked immediate and high priority." Straightening the papers, he tilted them so Magdala could see the picture printed on the first page. "Do you recognize this?"

"The people I shot at." She pointed at the mob in the picture, apparently taken at the casino incident."

He dropped the first page, revealing another photo. "And this guy?" Thoreau pointed at Bridger kneeling in the picture. "He's got this scar on his back." He dropped the second page, disclosing a close-up photo of the scar on Bridger's back. "It was recognized by our people — apparently this guy is a big find."

Magdala held up four fingers, scowling with confusion over the scar's meaning.

"It's from the Fourth," Rami told her. "It was our symbol at one time, but now we're—"

"Cadre," she interjected.

"Yes, and this guy's Bridger Klein, a reporter. Our people burned that mark on him a long time ago," Thoreau explained. "They were using him to catch a bigger fish."

"Fish?" Magdala repeated.

"His father — a sort of American spy named Benedict who's been a huge problem for us. The Trotskyists tried to nab him a long time ago but it didn't work. After that, they thought the son was dead."

"Son of an American fighter…" Magdala nodded. "I will kill him?"

"No, that's not the plan."

"Then what's she supposed to do?" Rami asked.

"I need her to visit Bridger's supposed uncle, a guy who might know the dad's whereabouts and other helpful information."

"You're going to prep her in time for an interrogation?" Rami's voice was raised. "Her English isn't good enough for that, and she wouldn't know where—"

"I'm not that concerned about it," Thoreau told him. "The more important goal here is to get Benedict's attention — scare him out of the woodwork and throw him off his game. Then maybe he won't cause us any trouble with our current work and, better yet, we might be able to put him out of commission, once and for all."

"I don't know..." Rami shook his head. "She doesn't have time to prepare and she's got to—"

"I can do it." Magdala raised her head with confidence.

"I know you can." Thoreau nodded as he took the Glock from her, tucking it into a worn backpack that he then handed back. "I'll fill you in while we get the truck loaded, so come on — let's get going." He headed toward the door.

"Are you sure about this?" Rami asked Magdala.

"Do not worry." She smiled.

"Easier said than done," Rami replied, then looking to Thoreau. "And what about the son?"

"I'm sure he'll be of help, too..." Thoreau answered. "...all in due time."

⚜

Chapter 17

With the door bolted on the studio's closet-sized sound room, Bridger threw himself into his work, determined to pursue the story he believed held the key to his future. Try as he did, though, his mind kept drifting back to the past, floundering in a sea of unanswered questions.

Taking another peek through the blinds on the room's narrow window, he spotted Silas — or whoever the man was — finally exiting the building. Bridger watched the man climb into his car and drive away from the curbside, heading down the road until his car disappeared beneath a distant stand of colorful maples. He assumed the man was headed back to Mackinac Island, a place Bridger had always thought of as home. But now he couldn't help but wonder what it was — what it had really been for so many years of his life. Admittedly, he longed for answers, but he felt it futile to ask as he assumed the only people who knew the answers were the same people he now felt he could never trust again.

Bridger felt his phone vibrate and pulled it from his pocket, determined not to answer if it was Silas. The incoming call bore no name tag but he recognized the number and answered, welcoming the diversion of a call about the story.

"What've you got now, Dr. Rivard?" Bridger asked without a greeting.

"Knew it was me, huh?" Rivard sounded a bit winded. "Well, I wanted to make sure you got the picture I sent to you — the one of the third copper."

"Yes, I got it. Thanks."

"You bet. And have you had any luck figuring out what it says?" he asked, finally catching his breath.

"No, not yet." We've been swamped here, but we're still working on them."

"Shoot! I figured you'd be the one to solve them, once I heard your uncle is Silas Klein."

Bridger shuddered. "How'd you... where'd you hear that?"

"From a colleague, of course. Your uncle's pretty well known in academic circles. Maybe you didn't know that."

"No, guess I didn't, but I should tell you that I don't have much to do with him anymore."

"Oh... That's too bad because he's a real authority on translations — maybe you could go see him about—"

"Can't right now," he snapped back. "I've got a lot going on here, but I've got an assistant working on the translations and bet she'll come through for us."

"Well, that's good then... Hey, and I've got another picture I'll send to you shortly. It's of copper four — found it at the marina. Maybe this one will help your assistant finally get these things solved."

"Really?" Bridger replied as he wondered how Rivard had managed to take such a picture. "That's weird, because we *have* copper four."

Rivard cleared his throat. "You mean you took the thing even before the cops saw it?"

"Well, yeah. I spotted it and figured we didn't have time for pictures, so we nabbed it and brought it here to the news bureau — thought we'd turn it over to the authorities once we had the syllabics recorded."

"Oh... and still no solutions to *any* of them?"

"No, not any more than you have," Bridger responded, upset by Rivard's insinuation that they should have figured out the code by now. "Plus I'm still trying to figure out how you could've gotten that photo, because we got that copper pretty quickly after the explosion and didn't see you... unless you were right there around the marina when it all happened."

"No, but I wasn't far away. I'd just left the retirement village to head back to my office through Petoskey, and then I heard the explosion and looked back – saw the black cloud go up and wondered right away if there'd be another copper." Rivard paused. "Uh, sorry if that sounds a little insensitive, but guess I think like an anthropologist – always looking for some new relic." He chuckled.

"I see," Bridger answered just as he heard a loud knock on the sound room door.

"Are you *still* in there?" Neon yelled from outside the room.

"Just a minute," Bridger yelled toward the door, then putting his mouth back to the phone. "Well, there's no sense in sending the photo, Dawson, because we've obviously already got that info. But let me know if you find out anything else and I'll do the same. Got to go now–" Hanging up without a further good-bye, he stepped to the door, pressing his ear to it. "What are you doing pounding on the sound room when it's in use? Can't you read the sign?"

"Yeah, I can read," Neon's muffled voice retorted. "It says *in use,* which translates to *too busy sulking.*"

"Sulking? I'm not sulking! I'm trying to get this voice-over recorded, and you're interrupting."

"Open the door, you sulker!" Neon yelled, pounding again.

Bridger twisted the deadbolt and threw open the door, sticking his face into Neon's. "I am *not* sulking. Now, tell me what you need and get out so I can get back to work." Leaving the door open, Bridger turned away and returned to his seat at the recording table.

Neon entered the room, pushing the door nearly closed behind him. "Well, first…" He tossed a piece of paper on the desk in front of Bridger. "K wanted you to have this – said they're translations of coppers three and four."

Bridger picked up the paper, staring at the penciled gibberish.

ᓇᓇᓇ ᐃᓇᒣᑎ ᔭᒥᑕ ᔕᐱᔭᒥ ᔭᓴ ᔭᒥᑕ ᑌᒥᓴᒋᑕᒣ ᔨᐊᓴᑲᒣᑎ
NANANA INAMETI YAMITA SHAPIYAMI YASA YAMITA TEMISACITAME YIASAKAMETI

ᓇᐁ ᔭᒥᑕ ᐃᐱᑌᑕ ᔭᒥᑕ ᓯᓇᔨᒥᔭ ᒋᓂᓇᒣᒣᑕᑎ ᐊᐱᑌᑕ ᒐᑕᐱᐊᒋ
NAE YAMITA IPITETA YAMITA SINAYIMIYA CININAMEMETATI APITETA CATAPIACI

He pointed at the repetitions. "*Yamita, yamita, yamita, yamita...*" He wadded up the paper tossing it aside. "This tells me nothing."

"Hey, don't shoot the messenger," he replied, his hands in the air. "And second, I just wanted to tell you that Silas left... and make sure you were doing okay after that heavy dose of reality he just laid on you."

"Reality?" Bridger turned in his seat, looking up at Neon. "What the hell is real anymore? Man, I don't even know who that guy is, and for that matter, I don't even know who *I* am!"

"Well, that's true — bet you even had a different name before this happened."

"I know!"

"Maybe it was something like... Fabio. Yeah, Fabio Lutz, and now we can just call you Fabu-lous!"

"This isn't funny, Neon."

"I know it's not funny! Fabio? That would suck! I'd stick with BK."

"This isn't something you can just laugh away with one of your jokes!" Bridger snapped as he pointed toward the window. "That guy who just left *isn't* my uncle, and he's telling me my father's out there somewhere, doing whatever it is he decided is more important... than me!"

"Hold on, dude. I was there when this went down, and I heard Silas — or the-agent-dude-previously-known-as-Silas — and he said your dad did this to protect you. So, the guy must've loved you an awful lot to—"

"To fake my death? To give me up and never see me again? Is that what you were going to say? Sounds like he loved his secret operative bullshit a lot more than me, so I doubt he had any problem with giving me up — making me an orphan."

"An orphan?" Neon rolled his eyes. "Look, pal! I'm not going to just stand by while you wallow in this! You're not an orphan, you jerk! You didn't grow up in some freakin' orphanage or on the streets or in some crazy lady's cellar! This Silas guy, whoever he is, gave up a lot to raise you, just like he gave up a lot to take me in when I needed help, too!"

Bridger's eyes widened as he considered the vacant details of Neon's past, feeling ashamed that it had taken his friend's words to remind him that he was not the only one left behind by absent parents. "I'm sorry. You're right," he admitted.

"Of course, I'm right! That guy has given a lot to both of us. He *has* been a father to us, no matter what his name is, and so I think we owe him a bit more than the treatment he just got. Don't you think so?" Neon slapped Bridger on the back.

"I suppose," Bridger admitted. "And I do want to know more about how all of this happened. I just don't know whether I can trust Silas to tell me the truth."

"But it kind of sounds like he's ready to tell it if you just give him a chance," Neon replied. "And since you're the guy who never gives up on a lead, then I can't believe you'd give up so easily on the most important story of your life — the story *of* your life!" He smirked. "From the sounds of it, I think it's going to be a doozy!"

Bridger had to chuckle. "I suppose it will be."

"So, let's get back at it." Neon reached for the door. "We need to check with K-Sue, and I got some new info from Holly that needs follow-up. So, let's get that done and then maybe this evening we can head to the island to talk—"

"Wait a minute." Bridger held up his hand. "Holly called with info… and you took the call?"

"Uh… yeah!" Neon pointed his pinky to his mouth and his thumb toward his ear. "No phone service in the sound room — you've got to come out if you want to play newsman." He swung the door open, motioning for Bridger to follow.

"And what did she tell you?"

"All sorts of stuff, like the fatality count, which was one at Wilderness, five at the retirement village, and two confirmed so far at the marina. And let's see what else," He said as he pulled a folded piece of paper from his pocket.

"The number of injured?" Bridger asked.

Neon looked at the paper. "She didn't give that."

"And you didn't ask?"

"Hey! I'm not the reporter! I just took notes... and you're welcome!" Tipping the paper upright, he read from it. "They set up a shelter for those burned out of their homes over at the Harbor Springs Community Center. Then they're activating CERTs, which are Michigan's Community Emergency Response Teams — I *did* ask what that stood for." He smirked. "They've also dispatched firefighting units from the Mt. Clemens' base downstate, and the tribe has turned the shooting suspect over to the Feds who've stepped in to investigate the overall situation."

"Well, of course they have — that's their job."

"And this is your job." Neon shoved his notes at Bridger.

"Man, I wasn't in that room for more than a half-hour, and you take over my job?" Bridger smirked, studying what Neon had written. "And you did it pretty well, I might add."

"Not looking for a new gig." Bridger stepped from the sound room into the hallway.

"And what's this?" Bridger asked as he discovered a press release printed on the back of the paper.

"Yeah, that's hot off the press from the Governor's office. She's having some joint news conference tomorrow with that Drummond woman."

"What?" Bridger dashed through the doorway, heading for his desk. "We've got to find out what this is about!"

"Ah, the old Bridger..." Neon remarked as he dashed after him. "Not so sure I didn't prefer sulking Fabio."

"There you are!" Kelli Sue greeted him at his desk. "Are you okay? I heard all that yelling from that back room, and then Al took off and Silas left and—"

"I'm fine, I'm fine," Bridger insisted as he shuffled through papers on his desk. "I just need to get a hold of a contact to firm up background on this presser."

Kelli Sue smiled. "Okay then, because Sonny's got a question for you on—"

"K-Sue, I don't have time for the weather girl right now!" Bridger opened his desk drawer, pulling out a cracked mug full of business cards and picking through them. "I've got to prep for this presser tomorrow so we can go and—"

"Hold on a minute, reporter guy!" Neon interrupted

Kelli Sue smirked at Bridger. "Yeah, all work and no patience — vital signs are normal." She cracked her gum as she walked away.

"And he's not listening again," Neon added. "Don't you remember the part about you being in danger with this deal? I mean, I'm glad to help you with the research, but we're not going to that presser tomorrow with all that's happened."

"What? Just because of that stupid video?" Bridger snickered. "And who's going to see that stupid thing anyway?"

"The wrong people, that's who!"

"Maybe…" Bridger paused, looking to Neon. "But you just brought me back to normal — the only normal I've ever known, which is chasing after a story. So, please don't take that away from me now; let me work on this and then we'll go see Silas… or whoever he is… and sort out the facts from the fiction. Once we have that, then we'll decide what's next and what we'll do tomorrow. Fair enough?"

Neon took a deep breath. "Yeah, I guess so."

"Good! Now, let's forget about all this boogey man nonsense and get back to work…" Bridger pulled the business card he'd been looking for from the mug and smiled as he added, "… because there's nothing more important than finding out the truth."

⚜

Chapter 18

The ferry ride back to Mackinac Island flew by quickly for Silas as he rehashed his argument with Bridger, wondering if there might have been some better way of telling him about his past. His questioning led him to further scrutinize everything that had transpired – the separation of Bridger from his father, the remoteness of the boy's upbringing on the island, and ultimately, his placement in a sheltered career at the television studio. All had been done in the hope of keeping Bridger free from detection, but now Silas couldn't stop second-guessing whether he had made the wrong decisions all along.

As the ferry negotiated its way alongside the pier, Silas stepped to the back platform, positioning himself for a quick disembarkment. From there he could see south across Lake Huron to where distant branches of smoke rose up from the autumn-colored mainland, drifting eastward as if blown away by the descending sun. He thought about those he suspected were responsible, troubled enough by the damage they had already done, but even more concerned at the thought of what they might still do. He knew what these people were capable of after witnessing the years of physical as well as emotional damage they had caused through their previous protests, riots, bombings... and in the kidnapping and branding of a little boy. There was no doubt, the Cadre needed to be stopped from causing any further harm, and more importantly, from achieving their ultimate goal.

Grabbing the boat rail, Silas steadied his footing as the ferry bumped against the dock pilings. He waited for the deckhands to secure the lines and drop the heavy metal ramp, then following them as they wheeled bikes and luggage from the back platform. Stepping onto the pier, Silas negotiated baggage carts and mingling tourists until he made his way to the main street where the usual crowds were waning. Paying little attention to the few bicycles and horse-drawn carriages still bustling about the streets, he walked briskly along the sidewalk to the nearby bike rental stand.

"The island's never allowed people to bring cars over here, ma'am," the young bike clerk said to a woman at the counter. "Sorry if that's a problem for you."

"Well, that's ridiculous!" the woman retorted. "There should be room for exceptions."

"Hey, I don't make the rules, lady – I just rent the bikes." He shrugged. "So, do you want one or not?"

"No! I'm not paying to ride some stupid bike when I can just walk," she grumbled as she walked away from the counter.

The clerk rolled his eyes. "Damn Fudgies," he muttered in terminology used by the locals in reference to the thousands of tourists who traditionally purchase tons of fudge from numerous fudge shops on the island.

Silas quickly approached the clerk, flashing his Mission University ID. "I'm running late. Charge it to the university, and I'll drop it off there."

"No problem." The clerk punched the keys on his keyboard and swiped the ID card, then handing it back with a key. "Bike 207 – right over there." He pointed. "Want me to attach a basket?"

"No need." Silas scurried to the bike, popping the key in the lock.

"How about a receipt?" The clerk held up a scrap of paper.

Silas pulled off the chain, keeping it in one hand as he mounted the bike. "No thanks – got to go." Wheeling over the curb, he pulled into the street and peddled hard, hastening toward the communication hub where he could covertly contact field operatives.

Weaving around carriages and pedestrians, Silas rushed past blocks of shops where merchants were retrieving their stands from the sidewalk, preparing to close. Further down the road, he raced passed Fort Mackinac just as they fired the fort's cannon, its thunderous report indicating their five o'clock quitting time. Urged onward by the fort bugler's rendition of *Retreat*, Silas quickly approached the old Indian Dormitory where he had spent the last few weeks assisting an archeological dig. Slowing for an oncoming carriage, he momentarily glanced at the unfinished project. Fluorescent orange netting wrapped like chicken wire around wobbly metal posts still stood as a half-hearted barricade that blocked off the entire backyard perimeter. With mounds of dirt piled high, Silas wondered if the excavation would remain unearthed for the winter. He didn't like the thought of it, but at the moment, it was the least of his concerns.

Once the carriage passed, Silas was about to pick up the pace again when he noticed a young woman sitting on the flight of stairs that ascended to the front porch of the Indian Dormitory. Thinking it odd, he pulled onto the sidewalk and rode up the walkway, approaching her.

"You know this place is closed, don't you?" he said to the woman.

"Oh, it is?" She stood up, holding a long mailing tube in one hand. "Well, that's weird."

"Yeah, the place is still being renovated, so nobody's here." Silas straddled his bike as he pointed at the canister. "Were you dropping off some artwork?"

"Artwork? Well... I don't know."

Silas studied her. "You don't know?"

"Yeah, I don't know what's in this." She held up the tube. "I was just supposed to deliver it here or at Mission U to a Silas Klein. Would that be you?"

Silas climbed off the bike and parked it on its kickstand. "Yes, that's me." He walked up the steps toward her.

"You're kidding?" She laughed uneasily. "But... you don't work here?"

"I've done some work here, but this isn't what I'd consider a mailing address." Reaching the top step, he tucked his hands into his leather jacket pockets. "So, before you hand over that thing, you mind telling me who sent it?"

"Oh, I don't know who she was. She just came in my shipping store over on Market Street and said she'd pay me a hundred bucks if I closed up five minutes early and delivered this." The woman looked over the tube. "Guess there's no info on it, and I didn't ask questions." She held the canister out for Silas to take. "It just seemed like easy money to me, and I could really use it. So, here you go."

"I see," Silas replied without taking the tube. "Well, guess I owe you a tip then." Pulling his key chain from his pocket, he managed to sort out the dormitory's key and turn it in the lock with one hand so he could keep the other in his pocket gripping his Ruger LCP, the 380 pocket pistol he always carried.

"Oh, you don't have to do that, especially since–"

"No, I insist, but I only have plastic on me." Silas pushed open the door and stepped into the foyer. "So, I need to get in my little stash I keep here. Why don't you just step inside here and wait while I get it?"

"Well, I really need to get–"

"But you said you could use the money, didn't you? Look, I'll just be a minute," Silas told her as he hurried away from the foyer, walking into a side room where he stopped and waited, hoping she would take the bait.

"Well, okay," she shouted.

Silas heard the old door creak and footsteps scuttle across the hardwood floor. Once he sensed she had come far enough into the room, he reappeared around the corner with his gun drawn, quickly slamming the front door shut.

Startled by the door slamming, the woman turned, her eyes immediately drawn to the gun. "Oh my God!" she screamed, raising her hands. "What are you doing?"

"Who are you?" Silas demanded to know.

"I – I'm Janet Fas – bender. I–"

"Who do you work for? Are you Cadre?"

"Cadre?" She shook her head. "I — I told you, I work..." She swallowed hard. "I work at the shipping store on Market—"

"Yeah, I heard that one."

"Please, don't hurt me!" the woman pleaded, squinting at the gun.

Silas stepped back from her. "Open the tube."

"What?" she panted. "Okay, I'll..." With trembling hands, she reached for the top of the canister and then froze in place. "Oh my God! You think this is a bomb, don't you?"

"The thought crossed my mind."

"Oh, shit! I don't want to open it! I don't want to blow up! Please don't make me do this!"

"Then why'd you bring it here?" Silas yelled.

"I don't know, I don't know! It was the money!" She held the canister away from herself, nearly convulsing with fear as she dropped to her knees. "Oh my God, please don't make me open it! Just let me throw it away!"

Finally convinced the woman was who she said she was, Silas tucked his gun back in his pocket and held up his hands to her. "Okay, sorry to scare you like that. Just put the thing on the floor and step away from it."

"Okay... okay..." She panted as she carefully lowered the tube to the floor, then crawling backward until she could get to her feet and scamper to the farthest wall. "Dear God, I've got to get out of here!"

"You're going to be okay," Silas tried to assure her.

"No, she is not," Magdala said as she entered the room and fired her silenced Glock, putting a bullet between Janet's eyes.

As the woman crumpled to the floor, Silas reached for his pocket.

"Stop!" Magdala commanded as she pointed the Glock at Silas.

He froze in place, his hand not yet in his pocket. Realizing the armed woman would kill him if he tried anything, he lifted both hands in surrender.

"Better," Magdala said.

Looking down at the body, he shuttered at the gaping wound, brain matter protruding as blood oozed from moistened hair to form an ever-widening crimson pool. "That was an innocent woman!" he said through gritted teeth.

"No, not innocent."

"She didn't do anything... except help you distract me."

Magdala gave the body a split second glance. "Yes, she helped."

"You didn't need to kill her!"

Magdala stepped toward the tube on the floor, her eyes remaining on Silas. "Do you know Frost?"

"Frost? What are you talking about?"

"The poet..." Her eyes never left him as she reached down and picked up the package from the floor. "He writes, 'Poor Silas, so concerned for other folk, And nothing to look backward to with pride, And nothing to look forward to with hope.' — his words." She held up the tube. "And this — you did not open."

"I'd prefer not to blow up."

"Not a bomb." Magdala tossed the package to Silas. "Open."

Realizing he had no choice, Silas ripped at the tape and pulled off the tin lid, relieved when it didn't explode. Then tipping the canister, he withdrew a document from the inside and unrolled it. "And what is this?"

"Read," Magdala insisted.

"Looks to be the 1841 Treaty — the one mentioned at the news conference."

"Yes."

"And it looks authentic... but it's not, is it?"

"I do not know."

"Really?" Silas cocked his head, studying the woman holding the gun. "But you're with the Cadre, aren't you? So, don't you know what your people are trying to do?"

"Yes." Magdala nodded. "Stop imperials."

"You mean imperialists? Is that what you call the freedom-loving people you're trying to conquer with your Marxist-Bolshevik bullshit?

Magdala scowled, stepping closer as she waved her gun at him. "We divide you — stop your wars."

"Oh, and is this how you do it — by killing some innocent girl?" He pointed at the bloodied, lifeless body on the floor.

"Not innocent... American."

"You're not from around here, are you? A new recruit, huh? So, what faction are you working for?"

"I help friend... You do, too." Magdala smirked. "You help Benedict... and Bridger."

Silas' tightened his jaw, alarmed by how quickly the Cadre had made the connection and what it meant for both of the men he had been trying to protect.

"But now..." Magdala nodded as she raised her Glock, pointing it right between Silas' eyes. "...you will help me."

⚜

Chapter 19

Wheeling into the gravel lot adjacent to the Burt Lake Revival Church, Dylan struggled to find a parking place amid the rows of vehicles that extended all the way to the neighboring cornfield. He finally parked askew to the other cars, flattening a patch of dried cornstalks as he nosed into the field with his grandfather's pickup truck. Then leaping from the truck, he dashed toward the front entrance just as the sun dropped below the cornfield behind him, his long shadow disappearing from the flight of steps he ascended to reach the church's open doors.

He entered quietly, taking a seat in the back pew of the packed church where the meeting was already underway. Looking up the aisle, he watched Pastor Creighton gesticulate and move about the crowd as he finished his summary of the day's events with a rationalization for organizing a militia-led response.

"With Governor Thompson and the Feds now involved, this situation could escalate into a military operation at a moment's notice," Creighton insisted.

"You mean, like the National Guard?" asked an audience member.

"Exactly... If these fires continue, then the Governor will likely call up the Guard to help."

Another person spoke from the crowd. "And do you think there'll be more fires, Pastor?"

"I'm not sure, but there's someone here who's pretty certain there will be." Creighton pointed to a clean-cut man in a state park windbreaker who stood and tipped his head to the audience before sitting back down. "Dr. Dawson Rivard is a Ph.D. who specializes in Native American research and does work for the state parks. He's new to us tonight, like so many of you, because he's afraid that these arsons are a part of a larger attempt to scare people off their land. So, he told me before the meeting about some Indian copper shields he found at all four of the fire sites — something he believes attributes the fires to a larger plan on the part of the tribes, indicating that there will be more fires to come."

As chatter erupted, Dylan watched the people in the pews turning to their family and friends with expressions of alarm evident on their faces. He then turned his attention back to Creighton, considering his pastor's words and gestures in a new light as he realized, for the first time, how compelling the man could be.

"Now folks, I don't mean to frighten you, but you must realize there's more to be concerned about here than just the fires," Creighton continued, projecting each word clearly enough to be heard without a microphone. "This is how the governor could justify calling up the Guard — under the pretense of controlling the fires — and then quickly change their marching orders to a new mission: controlling the people."

"Which means taking our guns!" Laski's voice boomed from the crowd.

Dylan heard voices all around him, asking, "Can she do that?"

"The Guard could confiscate weapons under certain circumstances," Creighton responded. "And try as we might to avoid those circumstances, there seem to be other powers at work trying to make them happen anyway… and then we'll have to live with the consequences."

As the crowd murmured, an elderly woman next to Dylan nudged him. "Is that man your Pastor?" she whispered.

"Yes, ma'am."

"I've never heard a pastor like him before." The woman turned to her husband seated in a wheelchair next to the pew, still keeping down her voice as she said, "But he seems to know what he's talking about, Gus. Don't you think so?"

"Maybe," Gus grumbled back. "Phil told me the pastor's some big game hunter who travels all over — calls him the pistol-packing preacher." He chuckled.

"So, folks..." Creighton waved his arms, quieting the crowd. "We're going to pass the plate, but this is one time when I'm not looking for money." He smiled as the crowd laughed. "I just want those cards we passed out earlier as a bit of a survey. So, if you're not in favor of this, then just write *no* and drop it in the basket. But if you're in favor of our plans to prepare – that is, if you're willing to defend yourself... and your neighbor... and your way of life – then I ask you to give us your name, contact info, and a few words on what you're willing to do for the cause."

With a bit of applause and a few whoops from the crowd, three men and a woman came forward to take the offering baskets from Creighton and passed them along the pews.

The elderly woman in the pew leaned toward Dylan. "Are you going to sign up, young man?"

"Oh, I figure I'm already signed up since I'm in the Battalion."

"Really..." the woman whispered with a look of surprise. "Gus, this nice boy's a member of the Battalion – they all seem like good people, don't you think?"

"Now, don't let these cards intimidate you," Creighton continued. "I know some of you have already told me you want to help but you don't want to get caught up in anymore scary situations like the one at the casino today... and I can appreciate that. But remember there are lots of things you could do to help, like working the phones, stocking up supplies, cooking and cleaning, or even just saying you're behind us. Every bit helps, so don't be afraid to join in."

"Maybe I could bake some cookies," Gus' wife whispered.

"I don't think these people are planning a bake sale, Dixie." Gus replied as he wrote on his card. "But if we want them to help protect our home, then I guess we need to sign up." He looked at Dylan. "Is that how this works, son?"

"Well, I suppose so," Dylan replied as a basket came to him.

"Then I guess we're in." Gus took the basket from Dylan, dropping in his card and then handing it to an usher.

"And another thing..." Creighton went on. "I'm sure the national media will show up for that news conference at the

Governor's Mansion on Mackinac Island tomorrow, and so we need to get as many of you as possible to be there with signs carrying our message."

An unfamiliar man in the row ahead of Dylan stood up and asked. "And what exactly is that message, Pastor? Because I've got to tell you, I'm a little surprised to hear a man of the cloth sounding like he's looking for a fight."

Dylan's jaw fell open, astonished to hear anyone questioning the motives of Pastor Creighton — something he'd never heard anyone do before.

"Oh, I'm sorry if you missed it — maybe you were a late arrival." Creighton moved down the center aisle, donning a sympathetic expression as he neared the people in the back of the church. "We're not looking to fight, sir, but if one is brought to us, we need to be ready to defend ourselves and our way of life."

"I understand your argument, but people need to think about how many wars have been waged in the name of self-defense." The man pulled down the high collar on his leather bomber-style jacket, revealing an oblong scar that looked to Dylan like a bullet grazing or knife wound.

"And with good reason," Laski argued from his seat. "Some are willing to make the sacrifice, because we know freedom's not free."

"I hear you both, and let me just say first that we appreciate your service to our country." Creighton bowed slightly in a sign of reverence that brought some audience members to offer a pattering of applause. "But this is not Nam or the Middle East. We're talking about our homeland, and the right to live here as we see fit."

"That's right!" A woman cheered, bringing the crowd to clap louder.

Creighton turned toward the altar, walking up the center aisle as he spoke. "And for those who missed it, let me reiterate our simple message — that no one can take from us our God-given rights."

"Amen!" a man cheered as people in the front pews rose to their feet in applause.

The scarred man remained standing, leaning down toward the woman next to him. "Excuse me," he said in a low voice.

Dylan watched as the people in the next pew turned their legs to let the scarred man squeeze past them. Once the man reached the aisle, he took one last look back at the pastor before exiting out the back doors.

"Yes, our rights are a gift meant for us to keep," Creighton continued. "But today we have unfortunately seen those rights fall under attack. We've heard the threatening rhetoric, and we've seen the fires meant to take our rights to land and property, so it's understandable that we would feel the need to defend ourselves. It's no surprise to hear that this provoked one young man to make a mistake with a gun, and yet the next response we hear of from our government is their plan to take away another one of our rights – the right to defend our land... and ourselves."

"And they can take us!" Dylan added as he jumped to his feet before he'd even realized what he was doing. "They took my friend away today – locked him up when he didn't even shoot anybody! Then they hauled him off to some federal jail before I could even talk to him and..." Dylan paused, suddenly realizing all eyes were upon him. "And his folks didn't see him, either," he added as he sat down, his face flush with both embarrassment and adrenaline.

"That's right!" John Paul bellowed as he stood from his seat. "Those Indians turned my son over to the Feds – the two must be in cahoots on this plan to take everything away from us. It's scary business, and you can trust me on this fact – if they can take away my boy, then they can take away yours, too."

Dylan heard a collective gasp followed by frenzied chatter.

Creighton nodded. "And from what these two men have said, we must now ask ourselves what will be next. Will they take our lands through eminent domain, or worse, by burning us out of our homes? And if we push back, will they take away our means of defense? Just look around this church and ask yourselves this: if they can stop us from keeping our land, bearing arms, or even from gathering and worshiping… if they can do that, then what else can—"

"What the…!" Dylan gasped, ducking with the crowd at the sound of simultaneous pops and bangs exploding above the church ceiling, the rooftop seeming to shudder as people climbed and pushed their way toward the back doors.

"Help us! Help us!" Dixie begged, seizing Dylan's arm. "Get my husband, please!"

Dylan smelled burning wood, glancing up to find smoke accumulating at the peak of the ceiling. Grappling his way into the crowded aisle, he pulled Dixie into the mob and pushed her toward the doors. Then he leaned over Gus, grabbing a hold of the armrests on his wheelchair as he stared into Gus' face.

"What are you doing?" Gus yelled.

"Getting you out of here!" Dylan yelled back as he pushed Gus backwards, using his wheelchair to plow his way through the mob.

"But I need a ramp!" Gus insisted.

"Not today you don't!" Pushing his way through the doorway to the landing, Dylan lifted the man from his chair. "Hold on, Gus!" Dylan shoved the chair off the side of the landing and struggled down the steps with Gus in his arms, continuing into the parking lot past a couple of rows of cars before finally setting Gus down in the gravel-covered ground.

"Don't put me in the dirt, boy!" Gus complained.

"I've got to." Dylan caught his breath. "I'll move you in a minute, once I catch my breath."

"Good Lord!" Dixie exclaimed as she made her way to them. "Thank you, young man! You saved us!"

"He got me all dirty here – that's what he did!" Gus brushed dust from his hands and sides. "And what the hell did you do with my chair?"

Looking back toward the church, Dylan spotted the crumpled wheelchair in the dirt at the base of the stairs, his eyes then quickly drawn upward when flames erupted from the church's rooftop and steeple.

"Oh, my word!" Dixie shrieked. "We... we could've been killed!"

"Is everyone okay? Is everyone out?" Pastor Creighton shouted from the base of the stairs toward the mingling crowd.

"Yes, yes, we're okay!" Dixie spoke up along with a few others.

"You were right, Pastor!" Laski herded the last of the crowd down the steps. "Those Indians are still lighting fires and it's up to us to stop them!"

"Let's get this fire out first and then meet up at, say... the old Pellston Town Hall," Creighton announced to the crowd. "Laski, get on that garden hose 'til the firemen arrive. I'll get the older folks out of — oh, no! It's burning everywhere!" he added, pointing toward the cornfield.

Dylan turned toward the pink hue of dusk on the horizon, looking below it to find the cornfield breaking out in multiple fires.

"The houses, too!" Gus added as he pointed to the homes across the street where smoke and fire broke out from their rooftops.

With screams from the crowd, people dashed for their cars and revved engines, wheeling about in a frantic exodus as Dylan looked down at Gus.

"I need my chair!" Gus insisted.

"No time for that!" Dylan scooped him up from the ground and turned to Dixie. "Show me where your car is!"

"It's this way!" Dixie answered as she headed down the row of cars toward the field.

"Get to it before the fire does!" Dylan yelled to Dixie as he hustled along behind her with Gus in his arms. "We've got to get out of here or none of us is going to live to fight another day!"

⚜

Chapter 20

"We should have waited until morning," Bridger told Neon as their ferry tied off at its Mackinac Island dock. "The next ferry doesn't leave for the mainland until eleven, which means we're going to be stuck over here for almost four hours."

"Three and a half," Neon specified as he exited the ramp and headed for town.

"Whatever," Bridger grumbled, following his friend. "It's still a waste when we could be working our leads and—"

"Don't start again." Neon stopped, holding his hand up to his friend. "We've been over this, and you know Uncle Silas could prove to be our best lead. Besides, you've always wanted to know about what happened with your folks, and so you've got to cut it out with the shying away now that you've got a chance to find out."

"I'm not shying away, but I don't think I have to spend an entire evening with the man just to get a few questions answered."

"Well, since you two have a lot to work through, then maybe you could at least invest a little time in it and see if somehow you can make amends."

"Let's just take this one step at a time." Bridger pushed past him, pulling his jacket up tighter around his neck as he tried to keep warm in the chilly air.

Neon caught up to Bridger and the two walked silently side-by-side past closed shops where brightly-lit displays beckoned bystanders to take a closer look. With the onset of twilight, the antique street lamps lining the street flickered and then glowed, further lighting the sidewalk as the two continued past town toward the university.

"Now what?" Bridger questioned as he pulled his vibrating Blackberry from his pocket and answered. "Hey, K. Give me good news."

"I've got it!" Kelli Sue yelled over the phone. "I found the keyboard!"

"The keyboard? You mean, you solved the syllabics?"

"Yeah, I did! And it's so stupid really — so ridiculously simple once you download the Cree keyboard and make a cipher and then transcribe it backwards."

Bridger slowed his gate at the foot of the fort, his attention focused on Kelli Sue's explanation. "You mean those symbols match up with letters on a keyboard?"

"Yeah, but not in the way they should. Remember when I told you that each syllabic's supposed to represent a consonant-vowel pairing? Well, these don't. Most of them don't even match either the consonant *or* the vowel they're supposed to be paired with. They just match a single letter."

"Well, that's good, isn't it?"

"Yeah, I suppose it is good — really stupid, but good."

Bridger stopped. "So, tell me! What do they say?"

"Well..." She snapped her gum. "I guess that's the next tricky part we've got to figure out."

"What do you mean?" Bridger asked.

"Don't snap at me when I'm helping you!" she retorted. "I'll tell you what I mean — I mean, they don't make any sense! Like the first one... it translates to *I rise up and follow the sacred shell.*"

"...What?" Bridger scowled.

"What is it?" Neon asked, leaning in toward the phone by Bridger's head.

"Yeah, and the next one..." Kelli Sue continued. "It reads *I I a boy born to point the way.* I'm thinking the double-I may be a Roman numeral two, but the rest of it? I'm telling you, it's like they're nursery rhymes... without the rhyme."

"Well, shit." Bridger bit his lip. "Okay, so can you keep working it, K-Sue? I mean, I know it's well past quitting time, but we really need to—"

"Say no more. I'm staying on it."

"Really? Well, that's great."

"Yeah, I don't have anything better to do tonight, and besides, these things are really starting to piss me off. I'll send you what I have so far."

"Okay, then just let me know if—"

"Hey, something else is going on here," Kelli Sue interrupted in a raised voice. "Looks like something else is breaking on this. Got to go."

"Okay, well just…" Bridger pulled the Blackberry from his ear, looking at it. "She hung up."

"Well, what's going on?" Neon asked as they began to walk again.

"She didn't say, but she did figure out the code for those coppers."

"That's what I thought you were talking about."

Bridger shrugged his shoulders, tugging his jacket around his neck once again. "Yeah, but the problem is that we don't understand what they mean. They just say something about a sacred shell and a boy being born which I…" Stopping in his tracks, Bridger glanced across the street. "Do you hear that?"

Neon stopped, too. "Hear what?"

"Those seagulls," he answered, pointing to the screeching flock that was hovering over the backyard of the Indian Dormitory.

"Yeah, like you haven't heard those before?" Neon chuckled. "Damn white crows. Somebody on the excavation crew must've left their French Fries out back."

"At this hour?" Bridger glanced both ways down the street, making sure the road was clear of bikes and horses before he jogged across the road toward the dig site.

Neon followed him. "You think somebody left something else out?"

"I don't know, but people have put a lot of time into excavating that place. Best see what they're after." Bridger continued jogging until he reached the plastic orange fencing wrapped around the perimeter.

"Hey, get lost!" Neon yelled at the birds, waving his arms at them as they continued to hover and caw just out of his reach.

"It's that hole they're after." Bridger nodded toward the farthest ditch from them as he watched two birds dive in for a moment and then exit.

"Or whatever's in it," Neon clarified, chucking a pebble at one of the birds.

"No, you can't do that!"

"What, are you some conservationist now, trying to save the un-endangered white vultures?"

"No, it's the site — you can't disturb anything." Bridger pushed on the plastic fencing, trying to tear it from its connection to the nearest post.

"Oh, but breaking in is okay? I don't think these archeologists want you doing that either."

"Well, I'm going to anyway." He pushed the plastic down far enough so he could swing his leg over, straddling it. "I'll just be careful, and then we can tell Silas — or whoever he is — if there's something besides a dead squirrel in there causing the problem." Pulling his other leg over the fence, he steadied himself before taking his first cautious step toward the ditch.

"They need a light out here — like one of those bright security lamps people have in the country."

"I don't think they want Fudgies climbing around out here in the middle of the night." Bridger waved his arms at the screeching birds, continuing his methodical progress toward the hole.

"Well, they could get one that detects motion to scare off the Fudgies, or the seagulls." Neon pushed on the fencing. "Hey, you want me to come help you?"

"No, we don't need more feet in here."

"Okay, that's fine with me — don't want to get hit with any bird poop anyway."

Two seagulls pecked at each other mid-air over the ditch as Bridger approached the edge and looked downward, swatting the birds out of his way. "Is that…" He paused, unable to focus his eyes as his stomach dropped to his feet. "My God, that can't be!" His heart raced as he made out what looked to be a body facedown in the dirt.

"What is it?" Neon jumped the fence, throwing caution to the wind as he traipsed around and through mounds of dirt, racing toward the hole.

Without hesitation, Bridger leapt into the ditch and rolled the body over, digging away dirt and mud from the person's face as he searched for signs of life. Neon was with him in seconds, checking the neck and wrist for a pulse while Bridger removed blood-soaked mud from the eyes, revealing a bullet hole between them.

"No… no, this can't…" Bridger muttered, barely audible over the still cawing seagulls that hovered overhead as he looked into the lifeless face of Silas.

Chapter 21

"I just want to go home now," Chepi insisted, tugging at the sling around her neck as she sat on the edge of the ER examination table.

"I still can't believe they're releasing you." Takota reached under the backside of her sling, adjusting the ties on the examination shirt she'd been loaned to wear home in place of her blood-stained clothes. "You'd think they'd at least keep you overnight for observation."

"You heard the doctor, Dad. He said my hand's got good function and circulation." She bent the tips of her fingers just a little, grimacing as her palm ached beneath the mound of bandages. "Just be glad it wasn't worse."

"Looks like it's still causing you a lot of pain."

"Yeah, and it's going to for a while, but I'll take some Tylenol and keep it elevated. Look... it's all cleaned up and splinted, and I'm seeing the doctor again in a couple of days, so there's nothing else they can do right now. Let's just get home and I'll sleep it off."

Takota sighed, shaking his head. "You're mother was bull-headed like you."

"And you're not?" She chuckled. "Stop worrying. I'm fine now and we—"

"They won't mind me being back here," Naomi said as she burst into the examination room, a nurse following right behind her.

"If you're not family, you're supposed to wait in the lobby," the nurse told her from the doorway.

"It's okay, ma'am," Takota said to the nurse. "We're just waiting for her release papers and then we're leaving anyway."

"Sorry about that." The nurse scowled at Naomi and then left.

"You'd think the busy-body would have better things to worry about with all these injured people around here," Naomi snapped.

"She's just doing her job," Chepi replied, not in the mood for Naomi's usual criticism of everyone but herself.

"And I'm just trying to do mine," she retorted.

"So, I take it you're okay?" Takota questioned as he pointed at the ace bandage wrapped around Naomi's ankle.

"Just a deep bruise – not enough to stop me. So, that's why I needed to talk to you two, right now."

"Can't it wait, Naomi?" Takota asked. "I'd like to get Chepi home first; then we can talk about the–"

"This can't wait. The governor's office needs info now for their press release. They want the Menonaqua Beach Band represented at the governor's press conference tomorrow, and they're requesting that Chepi make an appearance so they can–"

"Are you kidding?" Takota barked. "She was nearly killed at one news conference today! I'm not going to let her stand up in front of another!"

"That can't happen again at this event – not with all of the security they'll have to protect the governor."

"You know very well that the security will be there to protect Governor Thompson… not my daughter."

"It's all the same."

"No, it's not!" Takota argued. "You said we'd be safe today, but you were the only one with a trooper standing next to you, and my daughter ended up shot. I promised her she'd be okay, and I let her down."

"It wasn't your fault, dad," Chepi insisted, patting her father on the back.

"But I don't know what I would have done if you…" Takota's eyes welled with tears.

"I'm okay now," Chepi reminded him. "And as much as I hate to admit it, I think Naomi's right."

"What?" Takota cocked his head. "But you've been so vocal against this land acquisition. Why would you even want to go there?"

"Because I'm also against all of this fighting, and maybe people need to see what's come of it." Chepi began to lift her arm but then stopped, deciding not to as the throbbing increased. "At this point, it might be the only way to stop it."

Naomi smiled. "Yes, she could promote our desire for a peaceful resolution to these land disputes, and her appearance might swing the public toward agreeing with the governor's call for stricter gun registration laws — something I'm sure you wouldn't argue with now that your daughter's been shot with an unregistered weapon."

Takota took a deep breath. "I'm still against it. She needs her rest, and I don't think it'll be safe even with me there. I can't guarantee her safety, so it's just not worth it."

"Actually... we're thinking it'd be best if you didn't come, Takota," Naomi told him. "Your people need you here at head-quarters coordinating our efforts to tamp this down and to make sure nothing else happens at the casino or with the rest of the band's holdings." She stepped toward Chepi, patting her uninjured arm. "I can take Chepi to the island, and we'll be with the governor's entourage so I'm sure she'll be kept safe."

Takota shook his head. "No, I won't have it. I'll go and—"

"It's my decision, Dad, and I'm going to go," Chepi interrupted. "So, there's no sense in you going, too, when you're needed here."

"I don't want you to do this, Chepi."

"I know you don't for my sake, but there's more than me to be considered here. You've always taught me that — to think of others beyond yourself — and I think this is one of those times when I could really make a difference. I'm going to do this, Dad, and I'm going to be fine."

Takota tightened his jaw, his lower lip quivering. "Only if you have a good night's sleep." He hugged her around the neck, avoiding her arm.

"That's great." Naomi stepped toward the doorway. "So, we'll do the press conference and then go with the governor to a couple of other events she wants to do to show her support for Native Americans."

Takota raised his brow. "Wait a minute... what else do you have planned?"

"Oh, it's simple, really — just a quick tour of the renovation project at the Indian Dormitory, and then back to the mainland where they want the governor to stop by the dinner tent at the Autumn Harvest Powwow." Naomi reached for a pen and prescription pad on the room's desk. "And I almost forgot I need the address. Where are you having the powwow this year?"

"Is that still on?" Chepi questioned, wondering if it would be cancelled due to all that had happened.

"It better be," Naomi remarked. "We need to keep up the PR."

"Sorry about the wait," a nurse said as she dashed into the room. "I'll just go over this with you quick so we can get you out of here before the commotion starts again."

"What's going on?" Chepi asked.

"Another fire, apparently," She answered while jotting notes on her clipboard. "No reports of injuries so far, but we're on alert."

"Takota?" Naomi stood waiting, pen held in her good hand. "The powwow location?"

Takota nodded. "Yes, it's at Granger's Gourd and Pumpkin Patch."

Naomi dropped the pen. "Butane Bill's? You're having the harvest bonfire at the home of a known arsonist?"

"It was a childhood indiscretion, Naomi." Takota shook his head at her. "He's a good man, so you need to stop calling him that."

"Well, so much for PR!" She said as she left without another word.

"Just sign here," the nurse told Chepi, handing her the clipboard.

Chepi sloppily signed her name with her left hand. "Maybe you should consider canceling the powwow, Dad. I mean, it might not look good for us to be celebrating when all of this bad stuff is going on."

"No, we're not going to cancel, Chepi. We're going to show people that we are a peace-loving band, and we're going to do that by putting on the best harvest celebration we have ever had."

Chapter 22

Heat radiated from the wood-burning insert in the fireplace, warming Bridger across the room where he teetered in the familiar rocking chair. He glanced about the beadboard-paneled den, the room teeming with remnants of his childhood. Built-in bookshelves lined one entire wall, each shelf still filled with the books and knick-knacks that all appeared to be in their rightful place, untouched since Bridger had last seen them. Everything looked the same yet it all seemed so different now that he saw it in the new light of all that had transpired.

Bridger stood up from the rocker, heading toward the front door. "Let's go back to the dorm and see what's taking them so long."

"No, the police said to wait here, and that's what we're going to do," Neon insisted as he knelt down by the fireplace, picking through the neatly stacked pile of firewood.

"Al's the one who said to wait here!" Bridger complained as he stopped by the door. "Ever since he raced over here to the island, we've been cut out of the information loop."

"I think he's just trying to protect us."

"I think he's trying to keep us from finding out the truth about this!" Bridger tucked his hands deep in his pockets. "We answered all those questions from the first police on the scene, and we were starting to get some answers in return. Then Al shows up and suggests they give us a break, and the next thing you know, he gets us whisked off to the campus here to wait it out!"

"Look, I don't understand all of his reasons yet, but it seemed like the best thing to do under the circumstances."

"We don't know that! Maybe Al will get them to just cover this up and then we'll never get any answers – never know who killed Silas or who he was and who he was working for or, for God-sake, who *we're* working for!" He began to pace. "I still think we should go back and see what—"

"That's crazy talk, and we're *not* going back there!" Neon lifted a larger log, pulling a smaller one out from underneath it. "It's dangerous, and you're staying here until Al comes to tell us what's going on… so stop pacing!"

Bridger slapped his heels together, glaring at Neon. "But what if Al doesn't tell us the truth? What if he just tells us another story about—"

"You know, we've been working with Al for a long time, and even though he's kept this secret stuff from us, I still trust the man." Neon opened the door to the wood-burner. "He's one of the good guys, BK, so he'll tell us whatever he thinks is safe for us to know." He pushed the small log into the fire.

"Yeah, we'll see," Bridger grumbled, tugging at his collar. "It's hot enough in here, so would you lay off stoking the fire?" he asked, the mere sight of the flames putting him on edge. "There's a furnace in this place, you know, so you don't even have to use that stupid stove."

Neon shut the door on the burner as the fresh log caught fire. "Do you even know why this thing's here? Silas had it put in for you."

"For me?" Bridger stared at the door's glass window as flames licked at the interior, longing to escape. "I hate that thing."

"Of course you do, and he knew it." Neon took a seat in the threadbare wing-backed chair next to the stove. "He had that insert installed in the fireplace so you wouldn't have to deal with an open flame."

"Or he could've not burned anything — now there's a thought!"

"It was controlled desensitization — a way to help you get over your fears."

"Well, I guess it didn't work very well then, did it?" Bridger crossed the room, approaching the bookshelves on the opposite wall. "I never understood him — never really connected. Guess

I should have known all along that he wasn't my uncle, but..."
He paused at the discovery of a stitching hoop crossed with
two Popsicle sticks glued together to form four quadrants, each
wrapped with a different color of yarn. He held it up. "Do you
remember these?"

"Yeah, Sy helped us each make one, but you were so obsessed
that you made a bunch of them. It's a medicine wheel – the white,
yellow, red, and black each represent the different seasons of–"

"I know what it is... I remember." Bridger rolled the wheel
between his palms.

"So, you *were* listening... and you *did* connect." Neon crossed
his arms over his chest. "I think you just butted heads because
you wanted to leave and he wanted you to stay nearby... and I
guess now you know why."

"I suppose..." Bridger admitted, placing the wheel back
where he had always kept it, and where Silas had left it. "I do
miss him, damn it. And my last words with him... I yelled at
him." He lowered his head.

"Don't do that to yourself, BK. I'm sure he understood how
hard it was on you to hear what he was saying."

Bridger shook his head. "All this time I've been avoiding
him, and now I miss him... which seems crazy because I don't
even know who the hell he is!"

"You knew who he *was*." Neon stood up, approaching him.
"He was a father to you, and it's okay for you to grieve him like
you would a dad. I know I am." He patted Bridger on the back.
"Come on and sit down, dude. Al's going to be back here any
minute, and then we'll know more."

Bridger rubbed his eyes, sniffling as he gathered himself.
"Yeah, here we go again – waiting for directives from Al." He
returned to the rocker. "And he's apparently been in on this whole
charade, too, so he should be able to tell me something about my
past. I just don't understand why we have to wait here – why I
can't be there while they–"

"Uh, 'cause we're still worried about your safety, that's why!"
Neon replied as he sat down again in the weathered chair. "If

these Cadre people did this to Silas, then who knows what they'll do to you."

"But I'm not involved with... whatever this is."

"That scar on your back says you are."

"Oh, that was almost thirty years ago! My dad, wherever the hell *he* is, doesn't even know me anymore, so these people aren't going to—" He stopped, startled by loud knocking.

"I got it." Neon rushed to the door, peering through the peephole as he reached under the backside of his shirt.

"Whoa! Have you got a gun?" Bridger shot up, approaching Neon.

"It's us," a deep, muffled voice uttered from the other side of the door.

"It's Al." Neon turned the deadbolt, opening the door.

"Are you carrying a gun?" Bridger repeated.

Neon looked at him with a sullen expression. "Hmm... May-be." He hinted a smirk, like the cat that ate the canary.

"You're packing! Since when?"

"Since I told him to," Al answered as he stepped through the doorway, followed by Pennelope Wirth.

"I think I should know if you're carrying around a gun!" Bridger scolded his friend.

"Okay, so now you know!" Neon arched his eyebrows, his hands held high in a gesture of surrender.

"I am very sorry about all of this," Al said to Bridger as he shook his head. "I was very close to Silas – knew him for a long time."

"Apparently," Bridger muttered, his head held low.

Al sighed. "And I realize you've had your issues with him over the years, but you should know how deeply he cared about you, Bridger. He may not be your real uncle, but he *did* love you like a son."

Bridger took a deep breath. "Thank you."

Al stepped toward Neon. "And he loved you, too." He patted Neon's shoulder.

"Thank you, sir." Neon nodded.

"No, thank *you*," Al replied. "You didn't let us down, Neon, and we hope you'll continue your service."

Bridger cocked his head. "What's that supposed to mean?"

Al looked back at Bridger. "That means he's been the best friend you could ever ask for, son, and that I'm hopeful he'll continue to be just that."

"Because that's what he's paid to do?" Bridger scoffed. "Is that it?"

"No," Pennelope Wirth said as she stepped from Al's side, approaching Bridger. "We pay him to be your cameraman, and that's because your guardian, Dr. Klein, wanted you to be able to pursue your dream of news reporting while keeping you safe." She stepped closer. "Dr. Klein was the one we paid to keep you safe. His job was to protect you, and your father, and this country — and today, he died trying."

Bridger stared back at her, swallowing hard. "I realize that now."

Al stepped forward. "Penne, I don't think you've met these two formally. Bridger and Neon, this is Pennelope Wirth, Director of Strategic Operations for the DIG Foundation."

"Ms. Wirth." Neon nodded as he shook her hand.

"Please, it's Penne," she insisted. "That's what they call me around here." She turned to Bridger, extending her hand to him. "I only wish our introductions weren't under such difficult circumstances."

Bridger shook her hand. "Yes, I... I'm still confused, though. I thought you were VP for Mission Broadcasting. So, is that just—"

"I have many titles, Bridger, but Strategic Operations is my core directive. I oversee investigations and analysis for our organization."

"And that's *not* Mission Broadcasting?" Neon asked.

"I oversee many entities, Neon. The news bureau, this university..." She raised her arms. "This entire complex here at Mission Point is a part of a bigger picture — one that I now must insist on bringing you both into."

Bridger squatted on a footstool, crossing his arms. "Well, that's just fine with me. I want to know what's been going on around here."

"And we'll tell you both as much as we can share. Some secrets will still be kept – information that's need-to-know must be maintained for security purposes. But we know both of your backgrounds well enough to give you a preliminary level of security clearance; that is, as long as you both solemnly swear not to divulge any of what we're about to tell you."

Neon raised his right hand. "I swear."

"Good. Then I need you to go with Al. He has some issues he needs to discuss with you separately."

"What?" Bridger shrugged. "Yeah, I swear, too, but are you telling us info that we can't even talk about with one another?"

"No, we'll share the same Intel with both of you," Al assured him. "But you each have your own unique involvement in this, so we'll use individual approaches in telling you – that's just how we do it here."

"Okay, I suppose, but what about..." He swallowed hard. "Where'd you take Silas? What did you find out?"

"He's one of our own, Bridger." Al sounded choked-up. "We will care for him properly, with the dignity and honor his sacrifice merits." He patted Bridger on the shoulder.

"The FBI's taken over, so we'll coordinate with them," Penne added. "They found a woman dead inside the building – shot just like Silas. They also found that Treaty of 1841 document that will be analyzed, and they found a note... in Silas' hand."

"What?" Bridger exclaimed, his eyes wide. "Something he wrote?"

"No, it was put there by the killer. It's being analyzed, too."

"Well, what was it? What'd it say?"

"A simple message, meant to be a warning... It reads: *The son of Benedict lives.*"

❧

Chapter 23

"The campus is secure," Penne told Bridger as she ended her cell call. "Now we need to take a walk." She opened the front door of the Klein home, motioning Bridger to exit.

"After you," he replied, allowing her to go first and then following. "So, you make a call and, just like that, some security detail locks down the premises?"

"Not quite, but something like that." She strode briskly along the well-lit pathway, her heals clicking against the brick pavers. "We need to head over to the old boardinghouse."

"Silas' office?" he asked as he walked at her side.

"No, mine," she replied. "And we have rooms there reserved for overnight guests. We'll have you and Neon stay there for the night."

"No, that's not necessary. We missed the late ferry but I can still arrange a puddle-jumper to fly us back tonight."

"You need to stay here," Penne insisted, never breaking her stride. "We need to sort this out before you go anywhere – decide if you want to change your identity again or if we need to set up more security for–"

"I'm not changing my name or running away from this. My life may be mundane, but it's still my life and I'm staying here and getting it back."

"Don't make any hasty decisions, Bridger. First let me explain everything so you can think on it for the night. Will you at least do that?"

"I'll hear you out, but don't be expecting me to change my mind."

Penne glanced at him. "You *are* bull-headed, you know – Silas always said you were."

"Yeah, he told me that, too," Bridger admitted. "We bucked heads even when I was young. Back when I lived here, I always wanted to check things out for myself, but he kept trying to rein me in and I'd get so pissed about it."

Following the walkway along the backside of a townhouse complex, Bridger kept pace with Penne. Rounding a corner, they approached the university's central and most architecturally distinctive edifice — a sixteen-sided structure crowned with unusually steep trusses, creating the semblance of a tepee towering nearly forty feet into the air.

"I was always exploring all the nooks and crannies around here, but he didn't want me snooping around — told me to stop hanging out in the teepee," Bridger recalled. "But I couldn't help myself, especially on those days when we were waist-deep in snow and there was nothing else to do." His memory drifted back to happier times. "That place was an awesome spot for cowboys and Indians or hide-and-seek, and I could never understand why he didn't want me goofing around in there... but now I guess I know why."

"Yes, there are secured areas in that building," Penne confirmed as they turned to pass by the teepee, following another path that crossed an open field.

"Yeah, but to a kid, it was a tempting playground, and even more so after I found out it was built to look like a teepee." Bridger laughed. "Silas told me it was supposed to fulfill some Indian prophecy that said a great tepee would be erected on the east side of the island, and that all nations would gather at it to learn about peace... or something like that."

"That's what they say," Penne smiled. "Sounds like Silas taught you a lot about the island; so, did he tell you about the organization that built all of this?

"You mean that kooky Moral Re-Armament group?" Bridger pulled up his jacket, tightening it around his neck as the night breeze swept in from Lake Huron. "Yeah, the MRA was some cult for rich people who gave up their worldly possessions in their search for a morally-centered life."

"A philosophy that has saved millions of alcoholics since AA was created from the tenets of the MRA."

"Guess I *didn't* know that," Bridger admitted. "So, are they the ones behind this DIG thing?"

"Indirectly, I suppose, since they established this base of operation."

"Yeah, and they had the money to do that. I saw it with my own eyes one time when Neon and I stumbled into a storage room full of MRA loot. The place was packed with furniture and jewelry, shelves full of beautiful crystal, loads of silver and gold… We thought we'd found buried treasure!"

"Yes, a lot of wealth was stored here… and a lot of secrets, too. The people here wanted to change the world for the better but never seemed sure how to do it. Then right about the time they decided to give up on this facility and go overseas, that's when DIG came in." Penne pointed toward the boardinghouse on their right. "We need to go in there."

"Silas said most of the boardinghouse was off limits, too," Bridger recalled as he followed her toward the entrance. "All the signs still say *staff only* – not real conducive to professor office hours, if you ask me."

"This building was here long before the MRA – built in the early 1800's by the missionaries who came here to convert the Native Americans; thus the name, Mission House." Stepping onto the porch, she turned a key in the door's lock. "We did a lot of remodeling and excavating to make this place work for our purposes." She turned the knob and pushed open the door, stepping into a small, steel reinforced entryway. "This building best suits our purposes for this facility," she added as she worked a keyboard and then lowered her face, centering her chin in a metal cup for an eye scan. "It's aged exterior projects an image of insignificance, which helps us maintain our anonymity. But trust me…" With the clicks and whirs of an intricate time piece, a steel door slid open, revealing a stairwell. "…this place has been modified to withstand penetration." Penne headed down the steps, motioning for him to follow.

"Are you kidding?" Descending two steps, Bridger heard the door abruptly slide and lock behind him. "Holy crap!"

Penne glanced back at him. "It's okay. It's supposed to do that." She continued down the stairs.

Bridger steadied himself, following behind her. "And you said DIG – this Domestic Intelligence Group – is a privately funded, nonprofit? Man, I can't believe even the MRA's money was enough to fund something like this."

"You'd be surprised how many deep pockets are willing to contribute to a cause like ours, Bridger… especially when it means their safety and security."

"You mean, like capitalists who don't want a bunch of communists taking over?"

She stopped, turning to look up the stairs at him. "More like *Americans* who don't want to lose their Constitutional freedoms." She turned back, taking a couple more steps before heading into a corridor dead ahead, leading her out of Bridger's range of sight.

Bridger took the last few steps, catching up to her in the fluorescent-lit tunnel. "But doesn't our government protect us? Why the private funding?"

"It allows us to do work that governmental entities can't legally engage in."

"Oh, I see. So, you're private spies… and my dad's one, too?"

Arriving at another steel door at the end of the corridor, Penne tapped at the keypad. "We have senior investigators in the field, and yes, your father is one of them." The door slid open and Penne stepped to the other side, lights blinking on to reveal the space ahead. "As you can see, we also have researchers and analysts; people who evaluate and disseminate information deemed pertinent to past and current intimidation activities."

Bridger followed her into the large, open space, gazing across the room at the enormous wall of glass that provided a panoramic view of DIG's operations nerve center. "You people… built all of this?"

"Actually, the MRA constructed most of these underground facilities, and they're well fortified since they were built during the Cold War — meant to withstand nuclear fallout if need be." Penne motioned back toward the door that had closed behind them. "We added a few new access points, and we upgraded the technology to state-of-the-art standards, of course."

Bridger stared through the window at banks of computer stations manned by about a dozen or so people, all of them wearing headsets as they typed on keyboards, occasionally glancing up at the maps and images on large screens above them. "This looks like a mini NORAD, or something the CIA would use." He scratched at his head, grimacing as he bumped the tender spot he'd long since forgotten. "Yeah, that's it... you're like the CIA, except you spy on citizens, which the CIA can't do. So, how do you get away with that?"

"It's not illegal to observe people's actions," Penne replied as she stepped close to the window, nodding at a man who nodded back at her.

"Really? Is that how you look at it?" Bridger smirked. "So much for the Constitutional right to privacy."

"The Constitution does not specify any right to privacy." Penne turned on him. "I have every right to look at you, watch you, study your every move... and I can communicate whatever I may think about your actions, because the First Amendment of the Constitution *does* specify my right to speak freely."

"Okay..." Bridger conceded. "So, you're a bunch of paranoid people-watchers put out there to stop the next 9/11 or Oklahoma City bombing. Is that it?"

"Yes, we look for terrorists, if that's what you mean. But we've been looking since long before those events — for decades now, as a matter of fact." She walked to the lone desk in the middle of the open room, taking a seat in the leather executive chair and wheeling herself up to an open laptop. "In 1975, the Church Senate Committee discovered that CIA operatives had been conducting unauthorized domestic surveillance and interventions. Of course, these clandestine programs were immediately terminated, leaving us with a major void in our intelligence capabilities." She tapped a key, bringing the computer to life. "This action worried people in the intelligence community, especially those who'd been monitoring home-grown radicals hell-bent on inciting violence and overthrowing the government." She tapped more keys and rolled the mouse. "They knew that domestic insurgents wouldn't just disappear when they shut down operations; they would be left unchecked as they continued their seditious efforts — out there radicalizing new recruits and provoking the kind of mayhem meant to undermine our Constitutional way of life."

"So, these intelligence people... They created DIG?"

Penne's eyes remained on her computer. "Yes, starting with only two facilities: one in DC and the other here, appropriately named Mission Point. Since then, we've expanded to other locales, but we're all working toward one common goal: to eradicate all domestic endeavors meant to collapse our union."

"Like what al-Qaeda's been trying to do? I know those hijackers weren't home-grown, but they definitely operated domestically." Bridger tipped his head toward the glass. "Guess your team missed that one."

Penne looked up from her screen. "Yes, like other intelligence communities, we didn't discover that plot, but we have enjoyed some successes." She turned her computer so Bridger could watch a series of mug shots roll across the screen. "Our efforts have thwarted threats for decades; and now with newly established, government-run, fusion centers cropping up across the country, we've established a multi-leveled liaison with law enforcement and the intelligence community, further increasing our success rate." She closed the laptop. "Unfortunately though, this business can be very dangerous — a point proven today when Silas was killed, and one I don't want made any clearer with the loss of anyone else." Leaving her seat, she walked back to the glass, nodding again at the man on the operation's floor. "In addition, I now have to pull my lead investigator off this arson case because he has knowledge of our most critical intelligence and I can't risk the possibility of him being coerced into revealing that information."

"You're talking about my dad, aren't you? You're worried he'll talk if these people get a hold of me again."

"I *know* he'll talk if it comes down to saving you; that's why we're trying to track him down now." Penne gazed through the glass as the man on the other side shook his head and shrugged. "But apparently we're not having any luck." She reached downward, pressing a button on a lower panel. "Keep trying."

"We will," the man's voice projected back through a speaker.

Penne reclined against a ledge below the glass, looking to Bridger. "Our Intel suggests that elements within the Cadre provoked all of these incidents today. We just haven't yet been able to track down the person or persons behind this." She motioned toward the enlarged satellite image in the operation center. "But we do know that the fires, the protests, the treaty, the shootings… they're all meant to incite fear. That's how the Cadre goads the masses into committing subversive acts — make them think the wolf is after them and they'll follow one another like sheep off the side of a cliff." She shook her head.

"Well, then somebody's got to convince them that the wolf's a fake." Bridger smirked. "Yeah, and I could help with that. Tomorrow when we head back, Neon and I will do a story on—"

"Wait a minute." Penne held up both hands. "I don't need you getting any further into this. Besides, you were supposed to think on it tonight — decide if you were even going to stay around here."

"But if you're pulling my dad, then I'm no longer you're problem."

"No, it's not that simple. They could still try to—"

"Look, it's my decision!"

"And it's my station! You work for me, remember?"

Bridger took a deep breath. "Then I'll quit, and I'll do my own story." Tucking his hands in his pockets, he moved slowly toward the door. "Yeah, I can do that, because freedom of the press is also specified in the First Amendment."

"Good God, you are just like your dad!" Penne tapped her foot, scowling at him. "Okay, by morning I'll come up with *some* safe way to get you back to work." She rolled her eyes. "Damn it, I went through this with you thirty years ago, and I refuse to go through it again!"

"You mean my kidnapping?" Bridger asked. "Were you around then?"

"You still don't remember much, do you?" Penne shook her head. "I was there, Bridger; I was the next operative to infiltrate the Trots after your dad took some of them down. It was me that led your dad to the basement where they kept you."

"What?" Bridger scanned his memories, unable to recall seeing her.

Penne shook her head. "I did try to stop them, but they held me back." She cleared her throat. "I am so sorry I couldn't help you, Bridger, but I was there when you were branded."

⚜

Chapter 24

Gazing at the fishing bobber floating on the calm surface of Mullett Lake, Magdala could see more clearly now that dawn was breaking on the horizon. She found it easy to keep her distance from other boats as anglers preferred to fish in their own space, revving their motors and moving themselves if Magdala's Boston Whaler dared to float anywhere near them. Now all she had to do was keep propped up far enough in her seat to appear to be fishing despite knowing full well that no fish would ever bite at her baitless line.

Magdala yawned as she reached for her thermos, hoping another cup of coffee would rouse her from her stupor. She hadn't slept well beneath the boat's forward shelter canvas, the night's brisk air biting at her nose and cheeks while she bundled up in a down-filled sleeping bag. The chill kept her alert enough to recall the man she killed earlier, his final words suggesting that the Cadre would prove itself a greater war-monger than the United States ever was. Refusing to believe it, she fulfilled her orders to interrogate and terminate. Yet the man's words lingered in the recesses of her mind, resurfacing every time she drifted between sleep and consciousness. Her misgivings about the Cadre had caused her a restless night, and now they haunted her as she struggled to face the new day. She poured coffee into the thermos lid and guzzled down the lukewarm brew, hoping the caffeine would bring her back to her senses.

"Is that...?" she muttered as she thought she saw something small and dark wriggle beneath the shelter canvas. "Get out!" Dropping her thermos and pole, she swatted at the creature. "What is wrong?"

Flopping out from under the canopy, a lethargic bat took flight, seeming to wobble in the air as it attempted a flight for the nearby western shore.

She swatted at the air. "Go on!" Turning back to pick up the thermos and pole, she placed both in the compartment below a bench seat. Then closing down the hatch on Thoreau's release mechanism, all was prepared for her departure.

"I'm first!" someone cheered from the shoreline, followed by more shouts that echoed across the lake.

Looking to the west, Magdala spotted the source of the commotion; the Mullett Creek Kids' Camp that she had visited much earlier, long before dawn. She watched a cluster of children scramble from a sizable, log-style bunkhouse toward a nearby lean-to, each grabbing what must have been a cane pole before running out on one of the camp's three docks to fish.

Turning the key in the ignition, Magdala kept the idled outboard in neutral as she searched the shoreline, gathering her bearings so she could find the boat launch where she was to leave the boat. Brother Rami promised she would find his Ford Ranger pickup parked on the gravel road by the launch, its bed carrying another release container loaded with incendiaries, ready for distribution. She would drive the truck to the abandoned Topinabee Par-T-Mart near Mullett Creek and wait there until the set time for completing her current mission, then drive to her next destination to deliver her payload.

"I got one! I got one!" a child shouted from the dock.

Magdala watched a boy yank a small fish from the water, holding it up for the other children to see. She could make out their voices over the putter of the outboard, their squeals of delight melding with the scent of the damp shoreline, triggering Magdala's recollection of her young brothers when they netted fish in Jounieh bay just north of Beirut. She could still recall their unbridled enthusiasm, brimming with wide grins as they basked in the glory of their catch. Smiling at the thought, she then snapped back, reluctantly returning to the reality of the present.

"Look at it!" another child yelled. "It's too little! Throw it back, throw it back!"

Fighting her emotions, Magdala clenched her fists, wiping her eyes on her jacket sleeves before the tears could fall. "I turned to speak to God about the world's despair," she muttered, recalling Frost. "But to make bad matters worse, I found God wasn't there."

Tapping the throttle, she drove the boat slowly forward while continuing to watch the children, pondering what was yet to come. They would shriek again when their emotions inverted, as hers once did, from abundant joy to overwhelming panic. Then the parents of theses children would know of a terror much greater than any they'd ever experienced – the overwhelming fear of losing their most precious loved ones in one random flash of fire. It was a painful lesson Magdala knew too well, and one she was prepared to share with others until everyone had learned their lesson.

Cranking the steering wheel, Magdala headed for shore where she would take up her position and wait until she completed her greatest assault yet. Then all would be in motion and there would be no turning back once people were incited by the most formidable of terrors... a threat to the lives of their children.

⚜

Chapter 25

Gazing out the window from the guest quarters' kitchen, Bridger watched the whitecaps break as they rolled in from Lake Huron, the waves glistening in the dawn sunlight. Sipping his third cup of coffee, he scrolled through the news on his Blackberry, searching for more details on the Burt Lake Revival Church fire that had happened last night. Then he glanced back at the translations Kelli Sue had sent, noticing that the first syllabics of each created a Roman numeral.

ᐊ ᐊᐊᒉᐟ ᑲᓴ ᐱᐟᐳ ᐃᔑᔑᓭᐢ ᐳᒉ ᒉᐱᐊᐊᒐᐟ ᒉᒉᔑᔑ
I RISE UP AND FOLLOW THE SACRED SHELL

ᐊᐊ ᐱ ᐊᔑᐢ ᐊᔑᐊᐟ ᐳᔑ ᐍᔕᐊᐣᔑ ᐳᒉ ᐤᐊᐢ
II A BOY BORN TO POINT THE WAY

ᐊᐊᐊ ᐃᐊᐟᐣ ᐳᒉ ᐍᐱᔑᒉ ᐳᔑ ᐳᒉ ᐅᒉᔑᐟᒉᐟ ᔑᐊᔑᑲᐟᐣ
III FIND THE PATH TO THE CHOSEN GROUND

ᐊᐁ ᐳᒉ ᐃᐱᐊᐟᒐ ᐳᒉ ᐟᐊᔑᐢᔑ ᒉᐢᐊᐟᐟᒐᐣ ᐊᐱᐊᐟᒐ ᐤᒐᐱᐊᒉ
IV THE FACE THE LIGHT SKINNED RACE WEARS

"And *yamita*... is *the*? That's it?" he muttered. "It still doesn't make sense."

"It sure doesn't!" Neon concurred as he entered the room. "I still can't believe this whole DIG thing." He poured himself a cup of coffee from the pot. "So, how long have you been up?"

"Since maybe around four — I'm not sure." Bridger's eyes remained glued to the Blackberry.

"Yeah, I couldn't sleep much either." Neon added sugar to his mug, stirring. "I kept thinking about this place — how we never knew this was here." He took a sip. "Never knew about Silas... and I just keep thinking about him."

Bridger took a deep breath. "Yeah, I'm sick about it." He sighed. "I was awful to the guy, and even though he kept secrets from me, I'm coming around to realizing how much he did for me – how much he must've sacrificed." Picking up his mug, he pressed it between his hands. "And now he's dead because of me."

"He's dead because these Cadre people killed him, BK." Neon took a seat at the table. "Don't go blaming yourself for their evil deeds. Man, you didn't even know all of this was going on."

"Yeah, but he tried to warn me." He took a drink. "And now I do know about this, so I need to follow up – it's the least I can do for him."

"You mean, investigating this deal? Yeah, Al told me you were determined to keep chasing this story, so he told me to stick with you."

"To be my bodyguard again, I suppose?" Bridger cocked his head, studying his friend. "I don't think I'd ever seen you with a gun before, so when'd you get comfortable with carrying?"

"You know, I did a lot more than just drive people around when I worked at the Indian Embassy," Neon reminded him. "Silas helped me get that DC job; in hindsight, maybe that's why he trusted me to look out for you."

Bridger tipped back in his seat. "And so, that's it? You're sure there's not something more to this I should know about?"

"Dude, I'm telling you, that's it!" Neon insisted. "I've told you before, there's stuff about my embassy work that I'm not supposed to talk about – most of it I'd *rather* not talk about – and you've always respected that. But trust me; it's got nothing to do with all of this insanity... except maybe my skill set." Neon patted his chest. "You know, my body *is* a lethal weapon."

Bridger had to laugh. "Yeah, I've been told that... by you." He looked into his coffee. "It's just that I feel kind of betrayed, I guess. With all of this secret stuff whirling around me, I'm just not sure what to believe anymore." He set down his mug. "But I am going to get to the bottom of this. I want to know what's going on with all of these fires — give people the straight story." Looking at Neon, he pointed to his Blackberry. "Did you hear there's been another fire?"

"Yeah, Al told me before he left in the night."

"He already left? Then why are we still here?"

"Because you still want to be a reporter," Penne answered as she entered the kitchen, taking a seat at the table. "If you're going to cover this, then he's still got a TV station to run."

"Well, then let's get going!" Bridger jumped up from his seat. "I need to talk with some people, starting with my dad."

"Hold on." Penne held up her hand. "First, we need to clear up a few things about how we're going to handle this."

Bridger eased back into his seat. "Like..."

"Your position... I'd prefer you to work from the bureau office for the time being — at least until we've pieced this together and figured out your new security."

"But I thought once my dad came in, then I'd be able to—"

"You're father refused to come in." Penne crossed her arms. "What?"

"You heard me." Withdrawing a pen from her jacket's interior pocket, she pushed one end against the table and drew her fingers along it, flipping it to do so again. "He sent word that he's on the verge of a breakthrough and can't come in just yet, so he requested that I keep you safe until he wraps this up... Like I said before, he's bullheaded like you."

Bridger ran his fingers through his hair. "Okay... well, I still want to go back, and I'm not going to sit there in that office when I want to—"

"I know you won't..." Penne's eyes remained on the pen as she continued to flip it. "Guess I thought it might be worth asking, but I figured you'd say no." She looked up at him. "We won't take the ferry. I scheduled a flight back that leaves at nine, so we can take that; that is, unless you want to stay here for the governor's press conference." Her eyes returned to the pen. "Chepi Weatherwax will be there, in case you're interested."

"Really?" Bridger leaned forward. "I'm surprised she's up to that already."

"Oh, yeah." Neon laughed, slapping Bridger's arm. "He's interested."

"Oh, give it up, Kashkari!" Bridger mandated. "Yeah, I'd like to cover that, but I think it's more important to follow-up at the latest fire site – maybe talk to some witnesses. Then I also need to check with K-Sue on those translations."

"Al's bringing her into the loop this morning," Penne informed them. "We hired her for the news bureau in hopes she'd eventually work out to be a DIG analyst. Guess we're making that transition sooner than expected, but it's best to have her up to speed with us if she's going to be a resource."

Neon leaned back in his seat, clasping his hands behind his head. "Oh, man, she's going to flip out when Al tells her about this."

Penne handed her pen to Neon. "And like her, you gentlemen will need to sign some agreements I have for you before we leave. Then I'll be going with you to the Revival Church."

"You're going with us?" Bridger questioned. "But that's not necessary."

"Oh, yes it is," she insisted. "If you're going to do this reporting for my station, then you just got yourself a new producer."

"Dude! I've always wanted a producer!" Neon smiled.

"Well, I haven't!" Bridger disagreed. "So, does this mean you're going to control my work? Because you know that's not going to happen."

"I wouldn't dream of trying to control you, Bridger, but I do think you could use me as a guide since this is definitely new territory you're entering into." She curled her lip. "It is my station, and those are my conditions; so if you wish to work for me, then that's how it's going to be. Otherwise, you and your compadre here are going to have to come up with a new program, which will involve more time and money – things you don't have to spare right now. So, what do you say?" She extended her hand toward Bridger.

Neon reached across his friend, shaking Penne's hand first. "I'm in! Welcome to the team." He smiled, releasing his grip.

Bridger took a deep breath. "Okay, whatever." Standing up, he reached to her and shook on it. "So, let's clean up here and line up a pony cab so we can get to the airport on time."

"It's all arranged." Penne stood, too. "One other thing, though. As your boss, I want to be very clear about your mission here."

"Mission?" Neon smirked. "Does that make us spies now, too?"

Penne ignored him. "Our work with the news bureau has been more than just protecting you, Bridger. The network has provided us with a way to strike a balance between facts and fallacies."

"Network? You mean WHAM?"

"No, I mean ONUS – Operation: Neutralize Undermining Subversives."

"You mean…" Bridger paused, stunned by the revelation. "DIG operates the entire national network?"

"Think about it, Klein." She leaned toward him. "Insurgents are more than just some limited, momentary threat. Their subversive efforts aren't isolated to some rural sliver of Northern Michigan; it's a national challenge in need of a national solution." Her eyes narrowed. "We launched ONUS in response to the escalating manipulation of the media, hoping we could be the voice of reason by cautiously determining what to present and how to present it… because news should inform and educate, not disrupt or motivate."

Bridger scowled at her. "What are you saying?"

"I'm saying there are many reporters, just like you, who are dying for a big break; and for that reason, they're willing to engage in all kinds of sensational reporting that plays right into the hands of extremists bent on inciting the public. So, when radical sects stage incidents meant to frighten people into acting irrationally, then it's up to us to offset that."

"So, you choose what facts to report and which one's to hide? You know, that's manipulating the news, too!"

Penne shook her head. "I knew you'd see it that way, but it's not like that at all. The idea is to practice responsible journalism — to avoid being tricked into disseminating some conspirator's propaganda."

"Like the Twin Towers," Neon interjected. "On 9/11, the networks kept playing the video of the planes hitting and the towers falling. They played it over and over again until somebody said enough; give the dead some dignity and stop scaring the crap out of people, because that's exactly what these terrorists want us to do."

"Yes, exactly," Penne nodded. "At least one of you gets it."

"Okay, yeah, that was the right thing to do in that case," Bridger admitted. "But I still think it's wrong for a news network to have an agenda in reporting the news."

"Are you kidding?" Penne laughed. "*Every* network has an agenda, Klein! So, get that straight in that hard head of yours; we're going to report this the right way or we're not going to report it at all!" She headed for the door. "Now let's get going, gentlemen, because we've got a plane to catch."

⚜

Chapter 26

A smoky haze still rose from the smoldering remnants of the fire as the sun climbed over the treetops to shed light on the escalating crisis. Bridger kept a watchful eye on the gray patches ascending from behind the colorful treetops as he stared dead-ahead through the windshield of the Chevy Malibu they had rented at Pellston Regional Airport.

"That was Al," Penne said from the backseat as she set aside her cell phone. "He'll have some cameraman named Kodak pick up your car in Mackinaw City after he finishes covering the governor's news conference with that Dais girl."

Bridger sighed, rolling his eyes. "Sonny..."

"Hey, dude, you said you weren't going," Neon reminded him from the driver's seat. "Al has to send somebody else if you're not going to be there."

"Yeah, I know." Bridger turned sideways in the passenger seat. "With all the money you're sinking into saving the country, Penne, don't you think you could hire another reporter and get the weathergirl off the air?"

"Oh yeah... that's definitely a matter of national security," Neon added, glancing at Penne in the rearview mirror.

"I'll take it under advisement." Penne adjusted her jacket. "Meantime, let's focus on investigating this latest fire. My sources gathered Intel through the night; they're telling me the fire broke out while the Michigan Battalion was holding an organizational meeting in the church."

"That's militia... like the shooter at the casino," Bridger recalled.

"Yes, and they invited guests," Penne continued. "They're pretty riled up over the governor's involvement – starting to think the government's colluding with the Native Americans in an effort to take their land."

"Well, they kind of are, aren't they?" Neon smirked

"I don't know if I'd call it that, but that's the militia's perception," Penne replied. "And that press conference today won't help matters. After that happens, then the Battalion will have more ammunition for recruiting people to their cause."

"Recruiting?" Bridger scratched at the scruff growing thicker on his cheek. "So, the people who've lost their homes in these fires are getting involved?"

"They're enlisting people who've lost property or who think they might lose their property... anyone who's afraid of what might happen next is on the militia's radar." Penne pointed ahead. "Turn right there."

Neon turned at the next crossroad. "And they're arming these people?"

"Most of them, I'm sure," Penne answered him. "There should be a church lot you can park in at the end of this road."

"Look at this!" Bridger's mouth gaped open at the site of the smoldering wreckage. "They must have burned maybe a dozen houses!" he approximated as he looked at what remained of the neighborhood through a swath of scorched tree trunks and limbs.

"Our count is ten," Penne told him.

"Ten homes..." Bridger muttered to himself as he watched three firemen with a fire hose douse a windowless brick two-story in a deluge of water. "Most of these burned to the ground, and those still standing look like a total loss."

Neon turned into the parking lot. "And it looks like the party's still going."

Bridger glanced the other way, spotting a crowd mingling about the charred remnants of the church. "Well, we won't have any trouble finding people to interview."

"But we *will* have trouble finding anyone with any helpful info," Penne leaned forward between the seats. "That group's going to be packed with ambulance chasers, all eager to cry on command if it gets them on TV."

"Yeah, well we know how to weed out the actors," Bridger insisted. "You know, Neon and I *have* been doing this for a while and we have a pretty well established routine for handling a scene, so it'd probably be best for you to just follow our lead."

"No, Bridger. It's not going to work that way."

"Uh, oh," Neon responded as he parked the car and popped the trunk. "I put a camera in the back when we stopped by the bureau, so I'm just going to get that out now." He opened his door. "I'll take some footage while you two fight this one out..." He glanced back at Penne. "...that is, if it's all right with our new producer."

"Go ahead." She waved him off.

"Good deal," he said as he climbed out of his seat. "And may the best man win," he added, slamming the door shut.

"As your producer, I'm going to ask some initial questions, and then we'll decide who to interview on camera or where to go from there. Agreed?"

"Do I have any choice?" Bridger climbed out of the car, not waiting for an answer.

Penne exited the backseat. "And you're to stay *right* with me."

"I wouldn't dream of doing anything else," he retorted, never looking back at her as he approached the crowd.

"Hey, Bridger!" Dr. Dawson Rivard yelled as he stepped from a group of bystanders. "Did you see it yet?"

"A copper, I assume?" Bridger replied.

"Yeah, I can show it to you if the police haven't moved it yet."

"I'm sorry. We haven't met." Penne extended her hand toward him. "Pennelope Wirth of Mission Broadcasting."

"Oh, I'm Dr. Rivard — call me Dawson," he replied with a handshake. "So, you must be Bridger's boss."

"Oh yeah." Bridger nodded, his eyes rolling upward as his annoyance grew. "She's just tagging along today, making sure I'm doing my job right."

"Actually, I'm his producer; I just came along to help since this is such an enormous story." Penne smiled. "Bridger told me you're helping with these coppers, which must be a major find for an anthropologist like yourself!"

"Yes, they're an incredible discovery," he answered her and then turned to Bridger. "So, did your researcher figure out what they mean yet?"

"As a matter of fact, she did manage to translate them, but they're meaning still isn't clear. She's going to call me shortly with an—"

"Oh, that's right! You're a historian with the state parks, aren't you?" Penne interrupted. "So, what's bringing you so far south of your stomping grounds? I mean, the park commission probably prefers you working on their lands, so it's somewhat surprising that they'd let you chase these fires looking for coppers when I suppose the police could do that work."

Rivard scowled, shaking his head. "I'm not going to let the police track these down and throw them in some evidence locker where they'll never see the light of day again!"

"So, where's the new one?" Bridger blurted. "I want to see it."

"It's over here, just beyond the yellow tape." Rivard walked toward the edge of the scorched cornfield where a cluster of people huddled together by a State Trooper's Jeep Grand Cherokee, the truck's red dome light still spinning on top.

"Yes, please show us." Penne glared at Bridger as she walked side-by-side with him, following Rivard's lead.

"I didn't expect to see you here, Bridger," a familiar female voice said as the group parted, revealing Holly Ward dressed in uniform.

"Detective Ward," Bridger replied with a smile and a nod.

Holly stepped from the crowd, approaching him. "I heard about your uncle." She patted his arm. "I'm so sorry for your loss."

"Thank you." He motioned toward Penne. "This is my new producer, Pennelope Wirth. She's helping me work this story."

"Afraid I can't give you much right now," Holly said as she shook Penne's hand.

Penne released her grip. "What about the coppers? Have you lifted any prints?"

"They're pretty clean, except those from a certain news man we both know." Holly scowled. "We also cleared Dr. Rivard's prints since he handled most of them. The perp must've used gloves." She pointed toward Rivard. "The good doctor here just told me your gal Friday at the station broke the code. Would you mind passing the info on to me and the Post Commander?"

"Pass it to me, too, along with this one!" Rivard motioned toward the copper planted at the outer edge of the burned field.

"I'll get on it," Bridger replied as he poked the keys on his Blackberry. "I'm afraid they won't be too helpful at the moment, but K-Sue's still trying to track down their meaning."

"Well, it's a start," Holly replied. "Our people can work it, too."

"So, quid pro quo, Detective?" Penne inquired. "What's the preliminary word on how these fires were ignited?"

"Sorry, but it doesn't work that way, Ms. Wirth. Bridger and I don't conduct tit for tat business. We give each other everything we can, and nothing more... and trust me, he's always gotten the better end of that deal." She smirked at Bridger.

"Oh, I don't know about that." He laughed, sending his text. "But you'll have the translations shortly, just the same." Leaning across the yellow tape cordoning off the field, he took a photo of the copper with his Blackberry. "I'll send this, too, so K-Sue can get us the translation ASAP."

Neon approached the group, carrying his camera. "I got some footage, so what's up next?" He looked first at Bridger and then at Penne. "Oops. I asked the wrong person."

"That should be enough," Penne told him.

"Wait a minute, team." Bridger grabbed both of them by the shoulder. "I'm thinking we should get some people on camera talking about what they've seen." Arching one eyebrow with a smirk, he tilted his head toward Penne, hoping she'd take his

suggestion. "We can always dump it later if it doesn't help our...
story," he added.

Penne studied him with narrowed eyes before turning to
Neon. "Go ahead; we'll edit later."

Neon hiked the camera up on his shoulder, turning the lens
on Bridger. "Ready for whatever you want to do."

"Are you Bridger Klein?" Pastor Creighton asked as he
emerged from the mingling bystanders.

"Yes, he is," Penne answered as she interjected herself with
an extended hand. "I'm his producer, Pennelope Wirth, and you
must be Pastor Creighton."

"Why, yes I am." He smiled as he shook her hand. "The
collar must give me away."

Bridger cocked his head, surprised that Penne knew who
this man was when he did not. "Have we met before?" he asked
as he, too, shook hands with Creighton.

"No, but I've seen your work on TV," Creighton answered.
"Then I also saw that horrible video of you at the shooting;
looked like you got pretty banged up there on your back. Are
you okay now?"

"Oh, I'm fine. It's actually just an old—"

"Yeah, Bridger's pretty resilient," Penne interrupted. "Of
course, *you* must be, too, now that you're here dealing with the
loss of your church. What a tragedy; how are you and your
parishioners coping?"

"We're in shock, Pennelope... absolute shock. The people
gathered here cannot believe what these land-grabbing arsonists have done!" He turned to Bridger. "Please do right by them
in your coverage, son." Turning slightly toward the crowd, he
waved his arms toward them. "They've come here to see the remnants of what these violent, hateful people have brought down
on us — destroying our house of worship along with the homes
of our families... Why, they even put some of our members in
the hospital!" He looked down, shaking his head. "It's unbear-
able, and it needs to be stopped before more lives are destroyed.
But as you can see, the police haven't been able to stop it."

"We're doing everything we can, Pastor Creighton," Holly insisted from where she stood nearby, her hands tucked in the pockets of her jacket. "But it's not helping for all of these people to be mingling around here when we're still gathering evidence, so it might be best if you encouraged them to head home."

"Home!" he snapped. "Detective Ward, some of these people don't *have* a home anymore!"

"Yes, of course," she nodded. "But we have set up a shelter at the—"

"Our members have that covered, Detective. We care for our fellow man when something like this happens." Creighton looked back at Bridger. "So, we want to encourage people interested in volunteering to come and help us over at the old Pellston Town Hall where we've temporarily rented space for organizing our relief efforts."

"Well, that's nice of you people to do that," Holly told him. "I'll have our people get in contact so maybe we can coordinate our..." She paused as her radio crackled with the faint sound of a dispatcher, the woman's voice barely audible as the volume was low. "Pardon me." Holly turned from the group, pulling the radio from its holster and holding it near her ear.

"I wonder what that's about," Bridger muttered, stepping after her.

"Bridger, you and your cameraman should come by the hall this afternoon," Creighton continued, glancing toward Neon and then taking a step backwards until he was in view of the camera once again. "There's a meeting at two o'clock for those interested. It'd be a chance for you to see what volunteers are doing to help these people who are under attack and getting little assistance from a government that's more interested in assisting the perpetrators than the victims."

"Are you suggesting that because of the governor's news conference today?" Bridger questioned.

"It's not a suggestion, son; it's a blatant fact," he insisted in a louder voice, catching the attention of some of the bystanders who stepped up behind him.

"Seems more of an assumption," Penne countered, pointing at her watch. "And we really need to get going, Bridger."

"Really, Pennelope?" Creighton cocked his head, scowling. "So, why's the governor chosen to have only Native American representation at her side today? And why is she speaking from Mackinac Island instead of any of the fire locations? I haven't seen her around here showing any support for these people who are the real victims of this tragedy."

"Yeah!" a man cheered from the crowd, followed by other supportive shouts and claps.

"Wrap it up, Kashkari," Penne said to Neon, dragging her finger across her throat to cut filming. "We *really* need to head back now."

"Oh, so is this news you don't want to hear, Ms. Wirth?" Creighton retorted. "Is the media now choosing sides, too?" He turned back toward the gathering people. "Do you see how this works, people? We can't seem to get these so-called reporters to report on the real victims!"

"You're in charge here now," Holly yelled at a fellow trooper who nodded back as Holly stepped toward the driver's side of her Grand Cherokee.

Bridger followed her. "Wait! Where are you hurrying off to?"

"Hey, Klein!" Penne yelled, following after him.

"You don't need to chase this," Holly told Bridger as she pulled open her car door. "I'll call you with the info if it's related."

"It's another fire, isn't it?" He grabbed her door, holding it open.

"Another one?" Rivard questioned, jogging to the police truck. "Where is it?"

"Cut it out, Klein!" Holly grabbed her door handle. "I've got to go!"

"Aw, come on... just tell me where," he pleaded.

"It's only one house — it's off to the east, near Afton," she answered. "It may have nothing to do with this, so just give it a rest, Bridger." She yanked at her door, unable to shut it. "Now let me go or I'll have to cuff you and take you along!"

"There's a thought!" Neon joked as he approached with his camera off, pointing it downward.

"Thank you, Holly." Bridger smiled, shutting her door for her and stepping back as she drove away, gravel flying out from beneath her tires.

"Come on, you two!" Bridger shouted at his partners as he turned for their car. "You said it was time to go."

Rivard walked briskly after him. "A house fire... but that doesn't sound like the other incidents. Are you sure this—"

"Can't hurt to find out," he answered.

"Yes, it can," Penne argued as she hustled over to his side. "This incident here is a perfect example of why it'd be better for us to cover this from the bureau."

"I'm not going back until I at least check out this fire." Bridger grabbed the door handle, pulling up on it to find it locked. "So, are we staying here with our new-found friends, or going off to make new ones?"

Penne popped the doors. "You're incorrigible."

"Hey, Klein," Creighton yelled as he approached their car "Don't forget about us – about what the real story is, despite your producer."

"I'll do my best," he answered, climbing into the passenger's side.

Neon climbed in, lobbing his camera into the backseat. "What's up with the crazy preacher man?" He turned the key in the ignition.

"He's a Battalion Commander," Penne explained as she settled in beside the camera.

"Oh, I see." Neon shifted, backing out of his parking place. "So that must be why he's more zealous about the government than Jesus!"

"And that's why we shouldn't put his propaganda on the air for him," Penne added.

"So, you think he's Cadre?" Bridger wondered as he pulled his vibrating Blackberry from his pocket.

"Maybe, or else being manipulated by them – can't be sure yet, but it's worth looking into." She pulled out her phone, too, poking at the keys to text.

"Hey, it's a text from Kelli Sue; says she figured out what those coppers mean!" Bridger smiled, looking over at Neon. "I'll call her while you get us to Afton, dude. Looks like we're finally getting somewhere!"

Chapter 27

Protestors gathered behind a white picket fence, kept at bay from where Chepi stood with other guests to form an arc around the backside of the governor's podium. Despite her distance from the chanting mob, Chepi's heart raced as she questioned how well the crowd was contained. Wiping sweat from her brow with her uninjured hand, she shuddered as the breeze off Lake Huron swept across her clammy skin, the light winds bringing leaves from the maple overhead tumbling down around them.

"The national media finally showed up," Naomi whispered from her spot next to Chepi. "It's about time."

Chepi glanced at the cameras positioned to one side, some with spotlights pointed toward the podium despite the bright sunlight of late morning now trickling down on them through the half-barren tree branches. The image caused her to flash back to yesterday, recalling her reluctant appearance at that press conference, the beginning of Naomi's speech, the screams and the searing pain. Shaking her head, Chepi gasped.

"What's wrong?" Naomi asked in a quiet voice.

"Nothing," she whispered, gathering herself back to the moment.

"Good. We need to give a positive image here so we can muster public support." Naomi turned her head, scanning the camera crews. "I don't see that Klein reporter. Don't you know him?"

"We just met," she answered, scanning the crews herself. "Apparently his station sent someone else," she noted as her eyes fell on the WHAM logo emblazoned across Kodak's camera. "I see their weather girl over there," she added, noticing Sonny Dais standing off to the side.

"Weather girl?" Naomi scoffed while maintaining her phony smile. "Not a cloud in the sky — seems a no-brainer to me."

"Ladies and gentlemen," a man announced into the podium's multiple microphones. "Please join me in welcoming the Governor of the great state of Michigan, Ella Thompson." He clapped along with those surrounding the podium while an audible mix of cheers and boos ascended from beyond the fence.

"I don't know about this," Chepi muttered as she glanced at the police and security personnel interspersed with the bystanders. "Are you sure they've got this covered?" she asked, taking notice of a tattoo-laden woman in short sleeves and chains as well as a weather-beaten man in a bomber's jacket and combat boots — both looking riled.

Naomi leaned toward her, still clapping. "It's just fine, Chepi. Take it easy," she replied out of the corner of her mouth. "Just keep smiling."

"When there's nothing to smile about?" she replied, unnerved by the sight of two barrel-chested men standing with arms crossed firmly, dressed in camo-pants and hats. "I don't think so…"

Governor Thompson's expression looked sullen as she stepped to the microphones, placing her speech on the podium. "Thank you," she said as she brushed back tufts of her blonde and light brown highlights that meandered in the gentle wind. "I appreciate your coming here today to what we consider to be the gem of Michigan — this breathtaking island set between the two beautiful peninsulas that we call home." She adjusted her half-moon reading glasses near the end of her nose. "I chose to speak to you from this tranquil location today because it ably represents who we are and what we choose to be — a peaceful place that welcomes people from all walks of life with open arms."

Chepi nodded with agreement, unable to clap as others did around her.

"Unfortunately, we here in Michigan, just like people in all of the other forty-nine states, must contend with individuals who, from time to time, attempt to disrupt our otherwise amiable balance; and to do this, these agitators often employ some disconcerting methods that, all too often, become violent. That is just the sort of situation we've faced for the last day and a half as arsonists have attempted to dissuade us from pursuing a fair and equitable means of rectifying the past wrongs committed against the indigenous people of our state. There is no doubt that these malicious acts are meant to provoke an insurmountable conflict, much like what we see happen in foreign land disputes where negotiations are thwarted by the violent acts of militant factions determined to undermine the peace. They are meant to incite violent reactions such as what we witnessed yesterday with the shooting at the Menonaqua Beach Casino which injured Chepi Weatherwax, the daughter of the band's chairman... and we are so pleased that she has recovered well enough to be with us here today."

Chepi nodded again to the sound of polite applause, all of it this time directed at her. Still photographers turned on her, flashes popping as their cameras raced through multiple clicks, searching for the best shot.

"Best face," Naomi insisted as she looked admiringly toward her.

"Chepi is one of us," Governor Thompson continued, smiling at Chepi and then gazing back at the cameras. "She is a reasonable, rational representation of what citizens in this state wish to be — everyday people living everyday lives in a state that provides equal rights and equal protection. That is what every citizen wants, what every citizen deserves, and what I intend to deliver."

"We want the fires stopped! That's what we want!" the protestors yelled, their signs bobbing on the other side of the fence while the arc of guests proffered polite applause for the governor.

"We do need to stop these fires," Governor Thompson responded before her eyes returned to her prepared speech. "And with the incredible work of the many dedicated firefighters of Northern Michigan, we have managed to contain all of these fires, with most now extinguished." She pointed past Chepi to

an easel holding a large map of Northern Michigan with circles
indicating the locations of the fires so far.

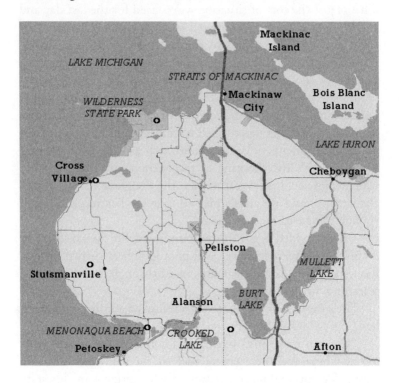

   Chepi looked at the map, taking notice of a discernible arc
created by the fire locations.
   "However, this is not enough," Governor Thompson continued. "We must stop these criminals dead in their tracks, for they
are not only arsonists, but they are killers and agitators, as well.
For this reason, I will be accepting the National Guard's offer
of limited assistance in dealing with this current rash of arsons."
   Chepi saw two signs pop up from the crowd, both reading:
Military State? Just Say No!
   "The Guard's assistance will be limited to firefighting and
technical support, such as aiding with research and other investigative work behind the scenes. Their roll will not involve any

policing at this time; however, that possibility has been discussed with advisors and even the President, given that he now has the authority to supercede me in calling out the Guard for a state emergency — an authority granted to the President by the US Congress when they tweaked the 200-year-old Insurrection Act in the aftermath of Hurricane Katrina. So, the public can rest assured that we do have the manpower to work the situation 24/7, and if additional assistance be deemed necessary, then the Guard is ready and aptly prepared to further assist us."

Chepi noticed a flutter among the reporters, some scribbling on notepads while others nodded at one another, all seeming to take the utmost interest in what the governor had just said.

Governor Thompson clasped the sides of the podium, leaning in toward the microphones. "So, with the fires contained and the resources in place, we will now redouble our efforts in law enforcement. I have invited our Attorney General Mitchell Pletcher here today." She nodded toward a lean man in a pinstriped suit standing at the opposite side of the arc from Chepi. "He will continue his current directive to vigorously prosecute violent offenders, but will adjoin my newest edict for the AG's office to relentlessly pursue all malicious agitators who attempt to incite violence, as well."

"That's me!" someone yelled from the crowd.

"Uh oh," Chepi muttered, her heart racing once more.

"It's okay." Naomi patted Chepi's back. "Keep it together — almost done."

"We must not allow violence to beget violence, and so these fires will no longer be considered an excuse for vigilante mentalities to be tolerated. People cannot be allowed to take matters into their own hands, for we are a government of laws — laws that will be enforced. And now I'd be happy to take a couple of questions."

The press jumped to life, reporters shouting as they vied for position.

The governor pointed to one. "Karen…"

"Thank you, Governor. Karen Marcus, NBC... Some of the victims of these arsons are complaining that you aren't spending enough time with them addressing their concerns. They take issue with your appearance here with the United Tribal Consortium, suggesting that your attempt to resolve this land dispute in the face of these fires indicates your willingness to compromise with terrorists."

"These people are not terrorists." Governor Thompson shook her head as she motioned toward Chepi and Naomi. "They're Michiganders, just like you and me, and to suggest that they and their people are responsible for the vicious, cowardly acts of these arsonists is ludicrous. I'm concerned about our indigenous population along with all of the citizens of this state, and I will be meeting with some of the victims this afternoon. But I kept this previously planned meeting with UTC so we could continue to correct such misguided, divisive thinking." She pointed to another reporter. "George?"

"George Tatum, AP... Will you and your guests still be visiting the Indian Dormitory despite the shootings that occurred there last night, and do you have reason to believe the incident is related to the fires and/or shooting yesterday?"

Chepi gasped audibly at the thought of more shootings, her eyes wide as she gazed at Naomi's reproachful expression.

The governor took a deep breath. "Tragically, two island residents were killed last night, and it is still too early to determine if the incident is connected to events on the mainland. So, no, we will not visit the dormitory built here as a part of the assimilationist vision within the Treaty of 1836 - constructed at the direction of then Indian Agent Henry Schoolcraft, who's known for his discovery of the Mighty Mississippi's water source as well as for being Longfellow's inspiration for *Song of Hiawatha*," she added. "However, the restoration of the building will continue, converting the dormitory into a museum for exhibits reflecting the art and culture of all people native to the Straits of Mackinac region." She paused.

"And the shooting?" George from AP brought her back to his main point. "Do you know who the victims are? Did they have ties to the other incidents?"

The governor shifted her weight. "The female victim's name has not been released, pending family notification, and the other victim was a professor here at Mission University. I know of no ties, and his name was..." Flipping a page, she glanced at her notes. "Silas Klein."

"Oh, my God," Chepi said under her breath yet loud enough for some heads to turn, including Naomi's.

"In the red blouse," Governor Thompson said, pointing to Sonny Dais.

"A follow-up," George of AP interjected before Sonny could speak. "Is it true that the original 1841 Treaty was found with one of the bodies?"

"I won't be commenting further on the shooting investigation," she replied. "An official from law enforcement will speak shortly after we finish here, so you can direct those questions to him. Now, back to the lady in red..."

"Yes, Governor! Sonny Dais of WHAM-TV, affiliated with ONUS News... and might I add, such a pleasure to meet you!" She smiled.

"And you," she replied with a smile and nod. "Your question?"

"Yes..." Sonny glanced at her notepad. "Is it true that your office received a request from the Michigan Battalion to meet with them regarding your pursuit of a land deal for the tribe, your use of the Guard in dealing with this situation, and, um..." She glanced back at her notes "...your position on gun control?"

"Ban the guns!" a protestor yelled as she held up a sign reading *Guns Kill*. "Let's ban you!" another yelled as the distant crowd shifted in a commotion, police moving in to address the disturbance.

"I will not be meeting with any militia members, but now I *will* be meeting with the representatives here today, and so thank you for coming." She stepped from the podium, turning to her guests. "Now, let's head inside." She walked with her security detail past Chepi and the map, the group of guests following her toward a nearby conference room.

Chepi used her good hand to open her cell phone and press the buttons, taking a few steps and then lingering by the map with her phone pressed to her ear.

"What are you doing?" Naomi asked as she strode past her.

"I'm calling Bridger to see if he's all right."

"All right? Oh, he's fine, so come on!" She stopped, pointing at the rest of the group as they walked away with the governor. "We have to keep up with them."

Chepi held up her finger as she spoke into the phone. "Hey, Bridger, it's me, Chepi. Listen, I'm at the governor's press conference and just heard about a shooting here that… well, maybe involved someone you know. So, I just wanted to find out what happened and…" She paused, staring at the map. "…and…I need to meet with you right away, because I think I just figured something out. So, call me when you get this; I'll be on my way back to the mainland." She shut the phone and tucked it in her pocket while looking to Naomi. "I've got to go."

"What?" She glowered. "No, you're coming with me!"

"No, need to catch the next ferry and explain this to Bridger." Chepi turned, scurrying off in the opposite direction. "Maybe he can help with this before the tribe gets blamed for another fire."

⚜

Chapter 28

"**Y**ou solved it!" Bridger said into his Blackberry as he stared out the car window at tall pines hurdling past the speeding Malibu.

"That's all you've got to say?" Kelli replied in a shrill voice. "Didn't Al tell you we're working for spies now? What am I saying? We've been working for them all along!"

"I know, I know, K-Sue. It's a big shock for all of us but—"

"And your uncle, Bridger! I'm so, so sorry about Silas. It's just awful!"

"I know, thanks." He sighed, the image of his dead uncle persisting in his mind. "And I want to figure out who did this, so I need your help. You're still in this with us, aren't you?"

"Of course, but good God, Bridger; Al told me about those Cadre nut-jobs! Did those crazies really brand you?"

"Apparently, yeah, but I need you to get past all the revelation stuff and help me out here. Now, what've you got on those coppers?"

"Put her on speaker phone," Penne insisted from the backseat. "I want to hear what she has to say."

Bridger pushed a button on his cell. "You're on speaker, K."

"So, no foul language, young lady!" Neon quipped.

"Whatever," she responded. "I sent an e-mail explaining the translations, so open it on Neon's phone while we talk."

"Just a minute," Neon said as he dug in his pocket while driving, pulling his cell from his pocket and tossing it to Bridger.

"Okay, we're looking for it," Bridger said, catching the phone.

"I included the translations of all five coppers you've found so far, and then there should be two more coppers yet to come," she answered.

"And what makes you think that?" Penne asked.

"Because the messages are from the Seven Fires Prophecy. Didn't you open that email yet?"

"I'm working on it," Bridger told her as he scrolled through the emails. "So, what's this Seven Fires Prophecy?"

"The email explains it in detail, but basically it's an Anishinaabe Prophecy that was passed down from their Midew, which is what they call their medicine men. Anyway, the prophecy outlined what they expected to be the eras of their life on what they called Turtle Island."

"You mean Mackinac Island?" Bridger questioned as he brought up the email on Neon's cell.

"I know people refer to Mackinac as the Great Turtle, but my research says this prophecy refers to the entire continent of North America."

"Yeah, I see that here," he said, scanning Kelli Sue's explanation as he scrolled through the email. "And so, why do they call it the Seven Fires Prophecy?"

"It's the prophecy of seven different eras on the continent with each period referred to as a fire. It tells what will happen during each fire; like with the first fire, it says the Anishinaabe will rise up and follow the sacred shell to the chosen ground — a turtle shaped island that is linked to the purification of the earth. It also says that such an island will begin and end the journey with seven stopping places along the way."

"Wow! Well, that's helpful!" Neon mocked. "So, what the hell is all of that supposed to mean?"

"Hey, I didn't make this up!" Kelli Sue cracked her gum.

"I know, and you're doing great, K," Neon said as he swerved the car around the remains of roadkill in his lane.

"Well, this means more fires, for one thing," Penne pointed out. "It also places culpability back on Native Americans, provoking just the kind of blame game the Cadre thrives on."

Bridger studied the details of the email. "So, the first is supposedly about the Anishinaabe coming to this region, and the second fire is a period where they camp by a large body of water."

"Which the research suggests is Lake Superior, but maybe it's Lake Michigan," Kelli Sue added.

"Okay." Bridger nodded. "And the second has a boy who points the way back to their traditional ways…"

"Maybe that's you, BK," Neon suggested, slapping at Bridger's shoulder.

"That's what I'm afraid of," Penne said under her breath.

"Oh, for crying out loud — it's not me!" Bridger scoffed. "They didn't even know about me until after this all started, so don't get off track with that nonsense!"

"And the third fire…" Kelli Sue continued. "It's where they move their families again along a path to some chosen ground — someplace in the west where food grows on the water, which doesn't make any sense to me. I was thinking rice maybe, but I'm still looking into that one. Hold on…" She paused. "Tossed out my stale gum."

Bridger had to laugh when he noticed Penne rolling her eyes.

"Okay, and the fourth fire — the one about the face that the light skinned race wears?" Kelli Sue said. "That one's different because there are actually two prophecies: one if the light face comes with weapons and one if he comes without."

"Sounds a bit ominous," Bridger responded.

"Well, get this," Kelli Sue replied. "Historians say that the light skinned race came in the form of French fur traders, or what the Anishinaabe called the wooden-boat people. That means they came with knowledge and a hand-shake instead of weapons, which is a good thing according to what the prophecy said to look for. However, the tribes didn't initially realize that the French also came with the intent of colonizing, followed by the British who wanted the same thing, and that's what brought about the fifth fire."

"Which is…?" Bridger looked at the fifth translation on the screen of Neon's cell phone.

▽ ᐱᐊᑕᐱ ᒥᐳᐊᑊᑏᑊᑕ ᒪᑊᑏ ᐱᐊᓇ ᐱᑏ ᑐᐱᑉᐊ∇ᑕ ᔑᑕᐧᑐᑊᑕ
V GREAT STRUGGLE WILL GRIP ALL NATIVE PEOPLE

"The great struggle is the conflict that the French and the Brits brought to the continent," Kelli Sue explained. "The fifth fire talks of this era as a time of war. It suggests that if the Anishinaabe abandon their old teachings and accept the promises of living a new way under new governance, then the struggle of this fire will continue for many generations."

"Leading up to right now," Neon suggested.

Bridger read from the email. "It also says the promises made by the light skinned race will prove to be false, causing the near destruction of the Anishinaabe – a prophecy that turned out to be all too true."

"Yeah, and the sixth and seventh fires address the consequences of the false promise," Kelli Sue told them. "The sixth speaks of imbalance and sickness as children turn against their people's teachings, causing their elders to lose their reason and purpose for living. Then the seventh fire says the people will struggle as they turn back to their elders, finding that many of them can't help since they've been ignored and neglected for so long. And here's the interesting part." She paused. "The prophecy tells the Anishinaabe that, if they remain strong, then there'll be a rebirth of their nation with the – and get this – rekindling of old flames as the sacred fire is again lit. How about that?"

"This is great info, K," Bridger told her. "But did you happen to see anything that suggests *where* the next fires will be started?"

"Uh… so I'm now supposed to be a miracle worker?" she snapped back. "No, not yet, Bridger, but I'll keep trying to figure that out."

"And that's all I ask," he replied.

"Yeah, but there is one more thing," she continued. "Did you see my note at the bottom of the email, just below the fifth copper's translation?"

"No, I don't think so," Bridger scrolled to the bottom.

"Yeah, Al suggested I look into how all of this ties in with this Cadre's ideology, and I found something I think might connect with them."

"Let me see that," Penne insisted, taking Neon's phone from Bridger.

"Grabby!" Bridger mocked her. "Tell me what it is, K."

"Well, the seventh fire prophecy also mentions a choice the light skinned race must make, and that the right choice would lead to the lighting of an eighth and final fire – one of peace, it says," she added.

"So, what's the wrong choice look like behind door number two?" Neon asked.

"That choice brings suffering and death to all the earth's people."

"Oh, that's all," Neon quipped.

"Yeah, so I researched the eighth fire," Kelli Sue continued. "There's not much out there, and the few sources I found were sketchy. But I did find general agreement that the eighth addresses all people of every color and creed, telling them that they must make a choice that will determine their final destiny."

"A choice between materialism and spirituality," Penne read from the phone.

"Basically, yeah, that's right," Kelli Sue confirmed. "The eighth says we must change our ways and follow the wise path of mutual respect for one another as well as the planet – a way that leads to a kind of spiritual illumination."

"And if we don't change our ways?" Bridger asked.

"If we continue to follow our materialistic path, then it'll be the end of us," Kelli Sue answered. "Sounds a bit like a Marxist mantra to me."

"You've got that right, Kelli Sue," Penne replied. "Great background – let us know if you get more."

"Okay, but before you hang up, Al wants to know when you're going to be back here. He's pretty anxious, you know; and I kind of am, too, guys."

"Tell him we're hitting one more fire site and then we'll be back," Penne instructed her. "I'll keep him posted."

"Okay, Ms. Penne Wirth, ma'am," Kelli Sue said, a hint of edginess in her voice. "Just get those boys back here soon, will you?"

"We'll be back in no time, K. See ya," Bridger said, ending the call.

"Penne Wirth," Neon repeated. "I get it; like Alfred of Batman fame... but I bet that's not your real name, is it?" He raised an eyebrow, smirking.

"It's a legally adopted name, Mr. Kashkari," Penne told him. "And that's all the more you need to know about that. Now, how close are we to the fire?"

"Coming up on it," Neon answered. "Not much smoke, but I can see enough to find it."

Bridger glanced out the window. "Yeah, I see the plume, too, and I've got to admit it doesn't look like much." His phone vibrated. "But we should still check it out while we're trying to solve this prophecy stuff." Punching his Blackberry's buttons, he dialed his voicemail.

Penne leaned forward between the front seats. "I think we may be asking the wrong questions here, Bridger."

"Oh, yeah? And how's that?" He held his phone to one ear, still listening to her with the other.

"We keep trying to figure out what these clues mean when maybe the real question is this: *Why are there clues to begin with?*"

"Hey, this message is from Chepi's number!" Bridger punched another key and listened.

"Did you hear me, Klein?" Penne asked.

"Of course, he didn't," Neon said as he slowed to take a turn. "He's now in Chepi-land!"

Bridger punched him, still listening as he glanced at his watch. "Well past eleven — presser must be over, but..." He paused, intently listening as her voice suggested that they meet. "She says she thinks she figured out something." He pushed more buttons, dialing her back.

"And as I was just saying, I think these clues are just the Cadre's way of playing us," Penne said. "Did you hear me?"

"I heard you," Neon replied. "And I think you make a good point."

"Thank you." She nodded at him.

Completing his turn, Neon kept one hand at the top of the steering wheel as he shifted his weight, turning slightly toward Penne and Bridger. "Yeah, those clues don't seem to lead to anything except the tribes, so maybe they're just meant to make the local bands look bad."

Penne patted his shoulder. "There's hope for you yet, Kashkari." She leaned back in her seat.

"Yeah, Chepi, it's Bridger returning your call," he began after the beep. "Guess we're playing phone tag here, but I do want to meet. Tell you what — I'm heading to a house fire near Afton but shouldn't be long, so why don't you call me back with your idea for the best place for us to meet afterward."

"The WHAM bureau," Penne spoke over him. "That's where we're going next."

"Just give me a time and I'll be there. See you then," he finished, hanging up.

"You'll meet her at the bureau," Penne insisted.

"First, let's see what she's got to say," Bridger replied "Now what was it you were saying before?"

"She was saying that she didn't want to be played by these Cadre people," Neon responded. "But it looks like she needs to worry more about being played — by you."

⚜

Chapter 29

Flames leapt from the dormers of the one-and-a-half story Cape Cod as Bridger walked up the driveway, closely followed by Neon and Penne. Together they approached the backside of the fire truck, staying clear of the hoses as firefighters in fluorescent gear pulled them from large reels and dragged them across the lawn to douse the fire.

"You should back up, boys," one firefighter said to the three school-aged boys huddled together by the truck.

A woman closer to the house turned on them. "I told you to stay back!"

"I'm sorry, Mom!" The tallest of the three boys pleaded through teary eyes. "It got on the curtain, and I tried to put it out, but..." He buried his face in his hands, sobbing with his brothers.

"Thank God you didn't get hurt," the mother said, stepping to them and embracing all three. "It's going to be okay."

Neon held his camera at his side as he leaned toward Bridger. "I'm not filming the family – I won't do that."

"No one's asking you to," Bridger agreed. "Let's find out the deal here."

"It's all contained to this one spot," Penne said, pointing at the house. "No other structures are on fire; not even the detached garage."

"Nothing in the trees or in the field next door," Neon added. "No pops or bangs – just one starting point, and sounds like it was the kid."

Bridger looked at the family, scratching his head. "Wonder why they're home on a school day?"

"They're home-schoolers," Holly answered as she walked up behind them. "The mom teaches them – said she'd had the TV on because she was worried about the fires getting closer and she wanted to make sure there wasn't something going on she needed to know. Then next thing she knows, junior's left the kitchen table to run a little science experiment of his own."

"Ah, the old playing-with-matches experiment..." Neon shook his head. "Yeah, that one never ended well for me, either."

Holly shook her head. "The kid said he heard on the news that an eyewitness heard a bunch of bangs like a roll of caps going off. So, he lit some on a paper plate in his room — wanted to hear what that sounded like — and the match lit the plate which lit the curtains which then... well, you can see what happens when some news story gives a kid an idea."

"What?" Bridger scoffed. "Hey, it's not like this is *my* fault!"

Holly's hands went to her hips as she rolled her eyes upward in a huff. "Yeah, well, maybe you could do a piece on telling your kids not to play with fire; given the current circumstances, it might be the one helpful thing you could do." She shook her head. "So, that's all I've got here, and now I've got to go." She turned and headed for her Cherokee parked at the end of the driveway.

"Wait up." Bridger followed her. "Where are you off to now?"

She kept walking while tucking loose strands of her gray hair back into her cap. "Really, Klein... I can't keep babysitting you. Can you help me out, Neon?"

"Can't seem to keep this dog on his leash today," Neon replied from behind them.

"We were just leaving ourselves," Penne told her as she strode along behind them. "But I must admit, I'm also wondering where you go from here."

"We continue to investigate," Holly answered. "I'll follow-up at some of the scenes, but first I need to coordinate with the Guard since they're now deploying their own search operation."

"Which is?" Bridger asked.

"Which I don't know yet; that's why we're meeting," Holly snapped, stopping in her tracks. "Look, the other thing you can do is to tell people not to be alarmed if they see members of the Guard patrolling in their area. A few have been dispatched to watch over the previous fire sites, but most of them will be patrolling areas deemed as suspicious. So, assure the public that these people are there to keep them safe."

"Can we get it on camera?" Neon asked, lifting his camera to his shoulder.

"No, I don't have time." She turned, taking the last steps to her SUV.

"And what are the areas of suspicion?" Bridger continued to question her.

Holly opened her car door. "They're focusing on this area and to the east along M-68 and south along I-75."

"But why?" Bridger asked.

"It's just a theory," she answered as she reached into her car and pulled out a printed map of Northern Michigan.

Bridger took the paper from her, studying the marks on the map.

Penne looked at the map over Bridger's shoulder. "The X's mark the shootings, the O's mark the fires..."

"And they put a star here for this fire," Holly added, pointing at the map. "I guess they marked it just in case, even though they know the fire doesn't fit the MO. But anyway, they're working theory is that the arsonist – or arsonists – will follow the roads, moving away from where he can be easily trapped and into more populated areas with plenty of room for redirection and escape."

"Interesting..." Bridger nodded. "Can I keep this?"

"No, you can't." She took the paper from him and climbed into the car.

"Really?" Bridger replied. "And just when I was going to give you something."

Holly started the car, rolling down her window as she closed the door. "I did get the translations, thank you. So, did you figure out what they mean?"

"Yep," he answered. "They're a part of a Native American prophecy that I'll send to you. Just thought you'd want to know that there are either seven or maybe eight parts to it, and each one is referred to as a fire."

"Meaning more fires – great." She leaned out of her window. "And it ties this to the tribes again, which could definitely cause more problems than even the fires." She looked at Bridger. "Thanks. I'll pass it on once you send it." She began to pull out of the driveway. "Now, go get something helpful on the air, will you?" With those last words, she drove away.

"Yes, that's exactly what we're going to do now," Penne said as she headed for their car. "Come on, you two."

Bridger followed with his Blackberry in hand. "But wait – we've got to meet Chepi!"

"I told you, we'll meet her at WHAM."

Bridger checked his texts. "But she already sent me a message to meet at noon at the old Topinabee Part-T-Mart, and she says it's important." He scrolled. "Says she thinks the next fire will be near there!"

Neon jogged passed Bridger and Penne. "Well, I wonder what makes her think that." Popping the car doors with the toggle, Neon jumped in and started the engine.

"Call her and find out," Penne insisted as she returned to her backseat, taking Neon's camera from him and placing it beside her. "I want more info."

"You can't call her there – it's a dead spot," Bridger said as he hopped into the passenger seat, waving his phone in the air. "There's nothing around there – no service."

Penne rolled her eyes, tapping her foot. "You do have an excuse for everything, don't you, Klein?"

"I take that to mean we're going to meet her?" Neon questioned as he made a U-turn from one shoulder of the road to the other.

"I suppose so, Mr. Kashkari," Penne replied. "We'll meet just long enough to see if she's really onto something and then have her follow us back to the office while I have my people handle it." She punched the keys of her cell phone. "I'll get them in position now."

"Fine," Bridger agreed. "But let's step on it, Neon. It sounds like she's onto something, and I want to get there before we miss out on whatever's about to happen."

Chapter 30

Passing by boarded up cottages along the shoreline of Mullett Lake, Bridger took notice of the kids' camp complex up ahead, spotting smoke drifting up from the bunkhouse chimneys. The facility was the first place to show any signs of life since they'd passed the half-dozen cars parked out front of the Café Noka, a restaurant in Topinabee where the locals preferred to have lunch.

"We should've gotten sandwiches at the Noka," Neon said, scratching his head. "I know we're in a hurry, but we could've gotten them to go."

"Maybe on the way back," Bridger told him.

"Lost my signal," Penne complained, tossing her phone aside.

"I told you it's a dead zone," Bridger reminded her. "And what's this?" he pointed up ahead at a group of preteen girls trying to cross the highway by the creek. "Camping on a school day? Doesn't anybody send their kids to school anymore?"

"Don't you remember?" Neon crossed the center line, driving at a safe distance around the pack of giddy girls. "Cheboygan and Indian River send their middle school kids here for camp. We did a story on it a couple of years back."

"Yeah, I remember — I was just kidding." Bridger looked out his window at the noon sun reflecting off the lake. "I came here years ago with my Cub Scout troop."

"Cub Scouts?" Neon snickered. "Man, you shouldn't admit to stuff like that!"

"Silas made me do it," he recalled. "He volunteered for pack leader and then forced me to join even though I didn't want to." Thinking back, Bridger remembered his misgivings. "Everything

revolved around camping skills and wilderness training, like
how to start a fire."

Neon turned the steering wheel without slowing, barreling
through a curve in the highway. "Silas sure did push the whole
desensitization thing, didn't he?"

"At the direct request of Bridger's father," Penne noncha-
lantly contributed.

"Really…" Bridger looked back at her. "So they both
thought more torture might somehow help the situation?"

"Therapy can be brutal, Klein, but it's not torture," she
argued. "Your dad didn't want to see you living with the scars of
the whole horrible ordeal, so he made sure you had skin graphs
to help with your physical wounds and desensitization therapy
for your emotional ones." She turned her gaze from him, looking out the side window. "Apparently, neither one worked very
well."

"I'll say…" Bridger turned back, looking straight ahead.
"Hey, you missed the lot, Neon!"

"What?" Neon glanced in his rearview mirror. "Ah, shit."
He slowed and pulled onto the shoulder, waiting for an oncoming car before turning around.

"It's not much past the kids' camp – I can't believe you
missed it."

"He was distracted," Penne said. "We all were, and we can't
afford to be."

"Well… okay," Bridger conceded. "So, back to my dad…
Was he really still that involved in deciding what happened with
me after he left?"

"He never really left you, Bridger," Penne answered. "He's
always been around, taking in little snippets of your life while
you were growing up."

"Really…" Bridger bit his lip. "Must've been nice – an
indulgence I was never allowed."

"Actually, it was pretty miserable for him," Penne argued.
"To be that close and yet so far away – to watch from a distance

as your child grows up without ever being a part of your life...
that's a pretty selfless sacrifice to make, if you ask me."

Bridger took a deep breath, empathizing for the first time
with what his father must have gone through. "I suppose it was."

"That's why I missed it," Neon said as he slowed to turn into
the gravel lot at the abandoned Topinabee Par-T-Mart. "That
tree limb broke; it's covering the sign on the other side." He
pointed at the wooden sign on posts, the weathered paint dis-
colored and faded, chipping off at the outer edges of the frame.

"There are *three* cars waiting," Penne snapped. "What's the
deal?"

"People carpool from here," Bridger replied. "Take it easy."

"I don't like it." She leaned forward. "Are you checking this,
Kashkari?"

"Yeah," he replied, slowly turning in the driveway. "Which
car is hers?"

"I don't know what she drives," Bridger answered.

"Great!" Penne reached under her pant leg. "Try those two
first," she told Neon, pointing at the Toyota Highlander and
Ford Ranger parked to one side, two car lengths apart from one
another.

"It's no big deal, Penne!" Bridger insisted. "People meet up
here for trips downstate – leave there cars here so they won't get
towed away." He looked back to see her withdrawing a Smith &
Wesson Chief's Special 38 from a holster strapped to her ankle.
"What the hell are you doing?"

"Being cautious," she answered, fisting the pistol.

Neon edged his side up toward the two vehicles, approaching in a way that blocked Bridger from their view. "Neither lady
looks like Chepi."

"That's because neither one is her!" Bridger told him, pointing at the Pontiac Vibe behind them just as Chepi popped the
door, climbing out. "She's back there!"

"Got it," Neon said as he backed away from the two cars and
headed across the lot toward the Pontiac.

"You need to learn some things about meeting places, Klein," Penne said as she tucked her gun back in her ankle holster.

"Yeah? Well, you could learn a few things about manners; like that it's not nice to point guns at people who're trying to help you," he came back at her. "Pop the backdoor and hand me the camera so she can get in… or do you want to frisk her first?"

"Funny, Klein…" Penne handed up the camera and then unlocked the door opposite her.

Stepping up to the side of the Malibu, Chepi tucked some papers into her sling, freeing her hand to open the car door and climb in. "Thanks for meeting me."

"Thank you for meeting us." Bridger smiled at her. "I can't believe you're already up and around. How're you feeling?"

"A little achy, but I'm fine, thanks."

"Chepi, I'm Pennelope Wirth, Bridger's producer." Reaching across the seat with her right hand, Penne took a hold of Chepi's left and shook it. "What is it you think you've figured out?"

Bridger frowned at his boss. "Pardon Penne – she likes to cut to the chase."

"That's fine," Chepi responded. "Well, it's the fire locations. I spotted them on a map they had at the governor's news conference, and I noticed that they looked perfectly aligned in an arc."

"Yeah, the trooper's detective told us the authorities are looking at that," Bridger replied. "I guess they think it has to do with the layout of the roads that the arsonist is probably taking."

"No, I don't think so." She reached in her sling and withdrew her papers, awkwardly flipping them in her left hand. "I've got a map in here I picked up at the ferry dock before I left the island."

"Let me help you." Penne took the disheveled papers and thumbed through them until she located the map, spreading it out on the seat between them.

"Yeah, that's it, thanks." Chepi pointed at the four fire locations she had already penciled onto the map. "See how they form a half-circle? And I think these arson people will try to complete it."

"You mean a circle?" Bridger questioned. "Well, I suppose that's possible, but what makes you think that?"

"Because it would connect the fires to Native Americans," she answered. "Now, don't get me wrong; I'm not blaming my people for this. But I do think someone's trying to make it look like we're responsible."

"I'll give you that." Bridger nodded.

"But how does the circle tie it to your people?" Penne asked.

"The circle is probably the most significant symbol in our culture. It's a part of nature, found in the shape of the earth and the sky, the sun and the moon. We use it in our daily lives and our ceremonies because it signifies the seasons of our own personal life journey, represented in what we call a medicine wheel."

"The medicine wheel," Bridger repeated as he remembered making them in his childhood, and finding one on Silas' bookshelf last night. "It's divided into four quadrants, isn't it?"

Chepi nodded. "Yes, typically they're white, yellow, red, and black, going clockwise, but the colors can vary... as can their meanings. But I don't think that matters here. What's important is that someone's trying to make this pattern appear to be a medicine wheel." She looked at Bridger. "Do you have a pen?"

"I've got it." Neon pulled a pencil stub from his pocket, handing it back to her while he kept the car idling in park.

"Thanks. Now look here."

Bridger looked back at the map as Chepi drew lines across it.

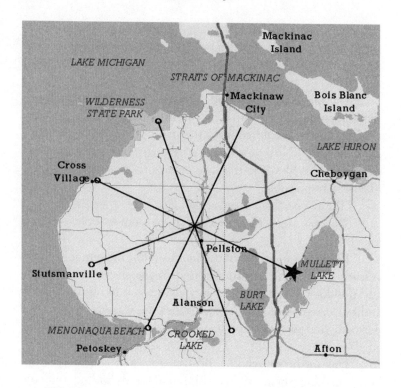

"If you connect the first and the most recent fires, then cross that line dead center from the third fire at the retirement village… then you get four quadrants. Now, if you cross that center point again from fires two and four, then you see the circle."

"Plus you get more specific points of potential fires," Penne added as she reached for her cell phone.

Bridger nodded. "Yeah, and you get eight points, which ties in with the Eight Fires."

Chepi's eyes went wide. "What did you say?"

"Oh, yeah, I haven't told you; we figured out the coppers. Each one tells a part of the Seven Fires Prophecy, and then Kelli Sue at our office said there could be an Eighth Fire Prophecy, as well."

"That's right," Chepi nodded. "Then this all makes sense."

"Damn it!" Penne lowered her phone into her lap. "There's still no signal. Neon, we need to head back to the office so I can get some bars and call for help. Chepi, why don't you follow us there?"

"We can't just leave, Penne!" Bridger argued.

"Oh, yes we can, Klein! I've had enough of this risk-taking business." She pointed at the two vehicles still waiting across the lot. "For all we know, they could be involved in this, so we need to let the professionals handle this."

"What? You're going to be scared off by a couple of mothers car-pooling for some downstate shopping extravaganza? I don't think so!" He argued as he punched at his Blackberry, relieved that at least the GPS application was working.

"And for all we know, the next fire could blow any second," Neon added. "It could kill somebody, Penne, and we can't just ignore that."

Penne gritted her teeth. "Yes, but we had an agreement..."

"Well, and there's a reason why I had you meet me here." Chepi pointed at the spot on the map directly across from the second fire. "Look, the sixth fire's supposed to be in this area, which is right where we're parked."

Penne looked at the map. "Damn..."

"Pretty darn close," Neon agreed. "What's the GPS say, BK?"

"I can't tell for sure without mapping this all out on a really accurate grid, but I'll tell you one thing." He pointed out the car window toward the Mullett Creek Kids' Camp. "That's the only place around here that makes sense."

"Okay, I buy it, boys, but we had an *agreement*," she reminded them. "We don't want to risk anyone getting hurt... like Chepi back here," she added.

"Thanks for your concern, Ms. Wirth, but I agree with them," Chepi replied. "If all those kids are maybe in danger, I think we should at least stop by and give them the heads up. Don't you?"

Penne sighed. "Okay, okay... but then we need to do some *editing*, right boys?"

"Absolutely." Bridger nodded. "Are you sticking with us, Chep?"

"For now, yeah. Let's go."

Dropping the car into drive, Neon wheeled out of the lot. "So, we're *all* in?" he asked Bridger as he pointed low, out of Penne's sight, toward the camera on the passenger-side floor.

"Oh, definitely!" Bridger nodded.

"Don't get any wild ideas, boys," Penne stipulated. "We need to be in and out of there quickly and without causing a panic; so as your boss, I'm going to take charge and do the talking. Is that understood?"

"Oh, yeah," Bridger answered, a Cheshire grin spreading across his face. "I have no doubt who'll take charge."

⚜

Chapter 31

Poking at the touch screen of her cell phone, Magdala redialed Brother Rami's number and listened for the ring tone that never came, the call failing due to no signal. She hung up, realizing she'd lost her opportunity once the Malibu left the Par-T-Mart lot, taking with it the one she recognized from a photo to be the branded one named Bridger Klein.

Looking out the side window of Rami's Ford Ranger, she glanced at the nearby Toyota Highlander just as the woman inside of it looked back, meeting eyes with Magdala. Feigning a smile, Magdala returned her gaze to the cell phone in the seat next to her, uneasy that the woman had looked her over and yet averse to taking any lethal action given that her current task was not yet complete. Instead, she maintained position, continuing to pose as a person who was merely waiting for a ride.

Poking again at the touch screen, Magdala typed an urgent text to Brother Rami — the only person she had learned to trust since the deaths of her parents and brothers. Prior to meeting Rami, self-reliance had been Magdala's only option on the war-ravaged streets of Lebanon. Even under the tutelage of the militant Kataeb Party's Maronite Christians within the Phalange, she remained detached from her mentors, heeding their advice to trust no one amid the incessant, erratic shifts in alliances within the civil war. This was the directive she lived by until Brother Rami took her into the orphanage, resurrecting her from her solitary purposelessness with his plan to right the wrongs brought upon Lebanon by the war's guarantor — the United States of America.

She sent the text with the hope it might go through with any momentary reception of a signal, but it did not, the screen flashing that the transmission had failed. "Damn this all!" she cursed at the phone just as a Ford Windstar slowed on the highway and turned into the lot, pulling up to where the woman exited her Toyota. She watched intently as the woman locked her car with an electronic fob and then, with a friendly wave to Magdala, climbed into the van carrying two other women. "Lucky for you," she muttered with a smile and wave back at the woman, concluding it best to let this loose end go as the minivan exited and drove off.

Watching the van head down the highway, Magdala saw in the distance where the Malibu had pulled into the Mullett Creek Kids' Camp, a move that triggered a new sense of urgency within her. Starting her own vehicle, she pulled out of the parking lot and headed away from the camp while holding up her phone, desperate to find a signal. In a matter of two miles, a couple of bars appeared, so she pulled onto the gravel shoulder just shy of the biking and snowmobile trail that wound along side of Mullett Lake.

Then dialing Rami again, she heard an electronic voice announce that the caller she had tried to reach was unavailable, dumping her into his voicemail. "It is Magdala," she said. "Call me now." Then she hung up, clicking her tongue in frustration. She wished she had time to wait for Rami's instructions, knowing his would be the best advice since the two of them were so like-minded in their beliefs and motivations. But time was a luxury she no longer had, and so she dialed a different number, resorting to contacting Thoreau.

After three rings, Thoreau answered, "What's wrong?"

"The Bridger man – I saw him."

"Where are you?"

"Just past store – I had to move."

"And Bridger… is he alone?"

"No – has cameraman and light lady – I do not know her. They met Indian I shot."

"Hmm…" Thoreau paused. "Sound like strange bed-fellows."

Magdala shook her head, not understanding the bed reference. "No, they are in car."

"They're probably protection for him, but why would they be there?"

"They are not here," she told him. "They drove away – stop at camp."

"*Our* camp?" he asked. "Our next target?"

"Yes."

"Interesting," Thoreau paused again. "So, maybe they're finally on the trail."

"Yes," she repeated. "Do I wait? It is not time?"

"Yeah, but we can't wait very long or they might find the devices." He paused. "Has anyone made you, Magdala? Are you still in play?"

"Made me?" She recalled the woman waiting in the car. "They do not know me, if this is what you mean."

"Good. Then let's give it until 12:30."

"That will work," she told him. "What about Bridger? Should I follow him?"

"No, I know you'll have some extra time now, but that's still a bit risky, especially now that he has an entourage."

"Okay," she replied, wondering if Rami would have chosen to do the same or to shift with the changing circumstances – something that the two of them had always been quite adept at doing. "I will wait – for now."

"Yeah, if Klein's on the trail, then our chance at him should be coming soon, just as we planned," Thoreau told her. "He may have protection, but if he keeps chasing this, he'll eventually be vulnerable – and you'll be ready."

"Yes, I will be," Magdala assured him. "I will not miss chance."

⚜

Chapter 32

"**N**o one's at the front desk," Bridger told Neon when he exited the office building with Chepi and Penne in tow. "Did you find anything?"

"Yeah, a bunch of giggling girls and squirrelly boys — every one of them hormonal." Neon pointed toward the beach at a picnic pavilion, the sound of childish laughter emanating from the shaded space beneath it. "They're heading over there from the lunch line, fighting over who they're going to sit by."

"I can't believe there's no sign of adult supervision around here," Chepi noted, looking back toward the office.

"Well, there's got to be someone in charge around here somewhere." Bridger took a few steps downhill toward the pavilion. "Let's spread out. Keep your eyes open for a copper."

"No, you're not wandering off, Klein," Penne insisted as she hurried to catch up with him. "We stick together."

"You know, we could accomplish more if you'd just loosen the leash."

"Okay," she replied, striding at Bridger's side as she looked Neon's way. "Hey, Kashkari, go check the bunkhouses for the grown-ups and let me know what you find."

"Got it, boss." He turned, jogging away with his camera tucked beneath his arm.

"That should help." Penne smirked at Bridger.

"Well, I don't like this at all," Chepi said from behind them.

"Oh, I'm sorry, Chepi!" Bridger stopped for her, now taking notice that she was struggling to walk downhill with her arm in a sling. "Let me help you." He took her by the left arm, helping her to hike the rest of the way down the hill.

Penne glanced at her cell phone. "There's GPS but no bars still." Still walking, she looked to Chepi. "I'm sure that office has a landline behind that locked door, but I'm not sure it's safe for you to wait here for help. Do you think you can make it?"

"I'm fine," she told them as she leaned on Bridger. "I'm just kind of scared about this. Something doesn't seem right."

"We shouldn't have brought you along," Bridger acknowledged.

"Well, we're too late for regrets," Penne noted as they stepped into the shade of the pavilion, nodding toward two adult women standing at the opposite side. "But at least we found the big people," she added, heading in the direction of the ladies. "So, let's pass along a word of caution and then get the heck out of here."

Bridger lingered behind Penne, helping Chepi negotiate between the picnic tables. "I'm really sorry I dragged you into this," he told her.

"You didn't drag me – I came. Remember?"

"Yeah, I do." He smirked.

"And I'm sure we'll be fine if we just stick together." Chepi grinned at him. "You're friends really look out for you."

He scoffed. "They're overprotective – I can't stand it."

"Don't be upset; be glad."

Two wrestling boys bumped into them. One muttered, "Sorry."

Bridger scowled at them, then looking back at Chepi. "They're coddling me like a baby. Why would I be glad about that?"

"Because it shows that they care about you," she answered. "It means you're loved, and that's nothing to take for granted."

"Can we help you?" the tall woman asked Penne.

"Yes, we're looking for the owners of this establishment."

"That would be me," the short one said, smiling as she stepped closer.

"Well, I wanted to inquire about your facility." Penne pointed back at Bridger and Chepi. "My colleagues and I wondered when you might have an opening for a retreat we were considering for our children's organization."

"Sure!" the short one nodded. "What group is it?"

Penne motioned up the hill. "Well, we can discuss that on the way to your office, if we could leave these young people in your friend's care," she suggested, nodding at the tall woman.

"Of course," the short one said as she left the tall one with an anxious look on her face. "Let's go see what we've got."

"E-yew! E-yew!" a group of girls screamed, pointing at the roof over their corner table.

"What is it?" the short one asked, darting around the picnic tables as she made her way toward the girls.

"They're bats!" the nearby boys cheered with excitement as everyone looked to the ceiling.

"They're all bunched together!" one boy observed. "Look at 'um!"

A man stood up from the end of one table where a group of adults were eating. "Just move away from them," the man suggested. "Take your food and move to the next table."

"No! Cooties!" the boys at the next table complained, bunching up as the girls approached them.

"E-yew! Yuck!" the children screamed from another table.

"There over here, too," another adult said as he stood up, pointing at another corner of the roof. "Come on kids. Let's go back in the cafeteria."

"Aw, come on!" they complained as they picked up their trays, moping away from their tables.

"Uh, maybe they should take their meals to the beach instead," Bridger suggested to the short woman. "I think they'd be better off there... at least until we talk."

The short woman cocked her head. "What do you mean?"

"I found the copper!" Neon told them as he jogged up to the group. "It's over in the cattails by the creek."

"Are you with the media?" the short woman asked, pointing at the camera under Neon's arm.

Penne looked at the woman. "Ma'am, I don't want to alarm you, but we're investigating the area fires and we think it'd be best if you sent the children to the beach until we get the authorities here to check things over — just as a precaution."

"What?" Her eyes went wide. "You think the—"

"Don't panic..." Penne insisted. "...for the sake of the children."

"Mrs. Kinney," the short yelled to the tall. "Don't go in the cafeteria — take the children to the beach to eat."

"What?" Mrs. Kinney questioned. "But I thought—"

"There may be bats in there, too," Neon added, contorting his face into an awful grimace.

"Oh, dear!" Looking alarmed, Mrs. Kinney whistled for the children's attention. "Eat on the beach, kids."

"Yeah!" They cheered, heading toward the shoreline as the adults followed.

"We need to use your phone," Penne told the short woman as they all hiked up the hill together.

"And a couple of questions," Bridger added, still supporting Chepi as he walked behind the woman and Penne. "Did you happen to notice any unfamiliar people around before we—"

The sudden multitude of explosions sent them all diving for the ground, Bridger sheltering Chepi as Penne and Neon scrambled to do the same for him. The short woman screamed at the terrifying sound of countless, simultaneous bursts erupting all around them, her shouts quickly dissipating as the distant shrieks of the children intensified.

"We've got to help those kids!" Bridger rose to his feet, remaining low to the ground as he scurried downhill.

"I've got him!" Neon left his camera behind, dashing after his friend. "Wait up, Dude! I'll help!"

"Kids, run in the water!" Bridger shouted as he approached them. With a quick turn back toward Penne, he yelled, "Call for help!" Then barreling onward with Neon, they herded the mob until they all stood thigh-deep in the cold waves of Mullett Lake. Turning back, all Bridger could do for the moment was stand there, helplessly watching what he feared most — a rising fire.

⚜

Chapter 33

Abank of news cameras lined the far wall of the Pellston Town Hall as reporters milled about the area Pastor Creighton had roped off for their use. In the middle of the room, Creighton mingled with volunteers who worked the donation tables, sorting piles of food, clothing, and other assorted contributions into boxes so they could be shipped to shelters in the area.

"This wall's nearly full of boxes, ladies!" Creighton commented to a group of women who were organizing the stockpile of canned goods. "I can't believe the response!"

"We take care of our own," one elderly woman commented as she stacked cans of soup.

"Yes, we certainly do," Creighton agreed, giving the woman a one-armed hug around her shoulders.

"Excuse me ladies," a reporter said with a smile as she walked through the group of women. "Pastor Creighton, it's now a few minutes past two, so the media pool's wondering if you're still planning on saying a few words. Otherwise, we've got to get back to the Mullett Creek fire to get more—"

"Sorry if I was holding you up," Creighton said with a nod as he scanned the camera crews, spotting the WHAM weatherwoman standing with her cameraman. "I was just waiting a few minutes to make sure all the local affiliates had time to get here, but I guess we can get started," he told her, now feeling certain Bridger Klein had not accepted his invitation. "Tell everyone I'll be right over,"

Glancing across the room, Creighton waved for all three members of the Tamarack family as well as J Paul's attorney to join him at the podium. "Keep up the great work, ladies," he said as he walked away, approaching the cluster of microphones situated in front of the cameras.

Stepping into the bright lights, Creighton placed his notes on the podium and cleared his throat. "I'm grateful to the media for coming to see our operation here where we're trying to help those who've been burned out of their homes by the arsonists ravaging our land here in Northern Michigan." He shuffled his papers as John Paul and Millie Tamarack escorted their son J Paul up behind him. "We invited Governor Thompson to come see our efforts here, but she refused our offer. Apparently she's occupied with meeting tribal union representatives as they collaborate on seizing privately owned lands in the area." He smirked. "Such are the efforts of a state government that continues to attack our rights, one by one. However, I'm pleased to announce that the concept of *innocent until proven guilty* is still standing, at least at the federal level, now that a judge has allowed bail to be posted for the beloved son of Mr. and Mrs. John Paul Tamarack, the young J Paul Tamarack who is with us here now." Creighton reached out to J Paul, shaking his hand as still photographers snapped a series of flash photos.

One reporter was quick to shout, "Just a question, J Paul; did you fire the gun that shot the girl?"

"No!" he insisted. "I didn't do it!"

"My client's not here to answer questions," the attorney interjected, pulling J Paul back to his parents, his mother embracing him.

"A number of members of my organization, the Michigan Battalion, have contributed to a fund being used to cover J Paul's defense expenses. So, we stand behind him, believing that a rush to judgment led to his premature arrest and allowed the real shooter to escape — maybe striking again on Mackinac Island."

"So, you believe the shooter is still at large," another reporter speculated.

"I have no doubt the shooter is still at large," Creighton replied. "State officials and the feds are eager to blame these shootings on the militias, using both incidents as an excuse to further restrict people's Second Amendment right to protect themselves. Meanwhile, they're after people's Fifth Amendment right to keep their property, using this phony 1841 Treaty as an excuse to rob landowners of due process." Creighton glanced down, shaking his head. "So, to sidestep the Fifth and take people's land, they're sidestepping the Second and taking people's weapons so they *can* take their land — and they're organizing to do all of this using our own military against us, sidestepping both the Insurrection Act and the Posse Comitatus Act in the process!"

"Wow! That's quite an accusation!" Sonny Dais commented as fellow reporters looked at her with wide eyes. "Uh... so Pastor Creighton, you think the Guard is here to do more than fight fires and assist the police?"

"I believe Governor Thompson has a misguided belief that the Northern Michigan citizens who cling to their property and their guns and religion are the problem, and she thinks sending in the Guard is the solution," Creighton answered, flipping a page in his notes. "She fails to realize that the problem isn't us — the problem is the arsonists; and it's the handful of tribal union leaders looking to steal prime real estate; and it's the Guard turning our region into a military state; and most of all, the problem is the governor herself."

"Yeah!" a volunteer cheered as the room broke into applause.

"Thank you," Creighton muttered as the applause trailed off. "So, I don't want to keep you media folks here because I know you need to head back toward Topinabee to cover the latest fire." Creighton looked to the ceiling, shaking his head. "Good Lord, I don't know how these... these ruthless demagogues can live with themselves, trying to kill innocent children!" He covered his mouth for a few seconds and then lowered his hand. "*That's* who the governor needs to be protecting, and that's who *we'll* protect if she won't." Scanning the cameras, he stopped at the one in Kodak's arms, gazing at the WHAM audience. "We'll have a meeting here at 6PM for individuals and families who want to help…" He paused, picking up his notes. "…and that's all I have for now." Then he turned around to the Tamaracks.

"We'll be here then, Pastor," J Paul told him. "Me and my mom will help."

"That's great, J Paul." Creighton patted both mother and son on a shoulder. "It's good to have you back with us."

"Thank you, Pastor Rod," Millie nodded with tears filling her eyes.

Creighton smiled at her, nodding as he turned to face her husband. "I could use a hand, John, if you've got a moment."

"Always," John Paul answered.

"I'll be in touch, Rod," the attorney said. "And I'd like a few minutes with mother and son before I go," he said to J Paul and Millie, guiding them away from the microphones.

Creighton walked John Paul in the opposite direction, heading toward a stand of boxes. "I need you to head to the compound for a quick check-in with Laski and the group leaders up there, just to make sure plans are still on track."

"Glad to." John Paul nodded.

"Can you do that and still be back to your place for our meet-up at three?"

"Not a problem." John Paul tucked his hands in his pockets. "I'll be back early enough to let you know how things are progressing before we even walk out to the burial site."

"That's great." Creighton extended his hand. "I knew you were the right guy to go to when we put this together."

Withdrawing his right hand from his pocket, John Paul shook with his pastor. "Well, we always figured this day would come, so it's a good thing we prepared."

⚜

Chapter 34

"The public deserves to know where these fires might strike next!" Bridger insisted as he stood on the lakeshore some distance from where the buildings and trees still smoldered. "I say we put this map on the air." He waved Chepi's map in the breeze.

"I can give you a dozen reasons not to," Penne countered. "It'll let the Cadre know we're onto them, and they might change locations because of that. It'll also play into the Native American implications, which is exactly what they want us to do. And it'll scare people who—"

"It's already scaring people! Look at this!" He waved his arms toward the girls' bunkhouse, now roofless and gutted; the only building still partially standing amid the torched trees and structures burned to the ground. "Did you see those parents who showed up here? They were frantic! And the kids were scared out of their minds!"

"I did get video of the parents, but not the kids," Neon said as he approached the two of them with his camera in tow. "I won't do that, even if the other networks will."

"Where's Chepi?" Penne asked.

"She said she was going with some parent she knows to get her car and that she'd be right back to follow-up on that map of hers."

"Good." Penne stared at Neon, her hands going to her hips. "And as for that video you took, I don't want even those frightened parents on the air."

Bridger snickered. "Didn't you hear what he said? They're going to be on TV whether you like it or not, because the networks *will* play it all!"

"But we won't be a party to it on either our national or local broadcasts."

"Fine – stick your head in the sand!" he replied, then turning to Neon. "What about the copper? Did you get the photos?"

"Done... but can't send them without a signal."

"Well, get them to K-Sue and that Rivard guy as soon as you can."

"Uh, oh," Neon muttered as he glanced toward the trees. "Here comes more trouble."

Following Neon's gaze, Bridger saw Al emerge from a clearing in the trees.

"And why in hell are you still here?" Al demanded to know as he made his way through the reed grass lining the beach, untouched by the fire. "You were all supposed to be back hours ago, and then when I couldn't reach you–"

"No signal." Bridger held up his phone.

"Yeah, I figured that," Al snapped. "Then word broke on this latest fire, and I waited, and worried, and then finally said screw it – I'm going to go see if the great manipulator still has Penne tied up at that fire... and surprise!" He held up his arms. "Here you are."

"Sorry, Alphonse, and you're right about this one." Penne extended her thumb, indicating Bridger. "He's been multi-tasking, playing rescuer and reporter all wrapped into one."

"And what did you want me to do?" Bridger threw his hands in the air.

"Leave with me!" she retorted, looking back to Al. "But he wouldn't do that; not even long enough for me to get word to DIG. So, I left him with Kashkari just long enough to drive down the road for a signal. Sorry I didn't call you then, but I needed to get word out about the map we're looking into."

"What map?" Al asked

"Chepi Weatherwax came up with it," Bridger said, handing the map to Al and then looking to Penne. "So, did you send field investigators out to canvass those areas where they might strike next?"

"Our people are on it."

"Our people... including my dad, I suppose."

"Yes, he's still involved with operations, Bridger; and believe me, I'm going to pull him in as soon as possible... which is what I'd like to do with you, too, but you can see how well that's been going!"

"You know, I'd go back if I had something you'd let me show on the air, but you've got me so bottle-necked with all of your political correctness that there's nothing I can do but keep chasing this thing until I find something worth reporting that you'll let me use!"

"Well, look at this," Holly said as she walked toward them from the clearing, Chepi following at a slower pace behind her. "The gangs all here... and Ms. Weatherwax says you've got a map I might be interested in."

"Absolutely," Bridger replied, tugging the map from Al's hands and turning it over to Holly. "Maybe you could get some resources to the next two potential locations, here and here." He indicated the spots on the map. "Bet if your people scan these areas, then you might be able to stop the next one before it blows — or better yet, catch them in the act."

"That'd be worth a try," Holly nodded. "Thanks for the lead, Chepi."

Chepi smiled. "I just hope it helps."

Holly smiled back. "Yeah, now we just need the manpower to do something with this." She glanced over the map. "It's kind of a broad area and we're stretched pretty thin right now."

"Really?" Bridger questioned. "I mean, they don't seem that broad to me. And even if your police and fire resources are spread thin, you've still got the Guard now, so you should have plenty of people to patrol these spots."

"We'll have to see about that," Holly answered. "The Guard may be assisting, but we don't have authority over them. They make their own decisions — have their own leads, their own bosses—"

"...there own agenda," Neon added.

"Hmm..." Bridger scratched the scruff on his chin. "This sounds a bit conspiratorial, Detective."

"More territorial, if you ask me," Holly replied. "Turf wars can get ugly when new powers are in play."

Bridger studied her. "Or is there more to it? Could it be that people do have a reason to be concerned... that the Guard's prepping to up the ante?"

Al crossed his burly arms across his chest. "If you want to report this, then you need to just present the facts and keep the speculations to yourself." He stepped back from the group. "Now, I'm going back to the office to see what Sonny and Kodak have for me, and I'd appreciate it if you'd come back, too, Bridger. I need you to get something useful on the air, like maybe letting people know that none of the kids here got severely injured or worse."

"But the kitchen help's headed to the hospital," Bridger pointed out. "One was hurt pretty badly by falling debris."

Al tapped his foot in the sand. "Guess I'll just have to get Sonny to do it."

Bridger tightened his jaw. "Yeah, have her do your *happy story* — we've got more important stuff to deal with, like where the next fire's going to strike."

"He's all yours, Penne." Al started to hike away but turned back to add, "But you might want to get back at some point so you can talk to the funeral director. You do have a funeral to plan, you know." With that, he walked away.

Bridger swallowed hard, kicking at the sand. "God... I almost forgot."

"I'm sorry..." Chepi patted his shoulder. "Can I help in any way?"

"Maybe it *would* be a good time to head back to WHAM," Neon suggested. "Chepi and I can help with the arrangements, and we'll also keep working the story — buy a map and get this accurately plotted out so we can—"

"We'll handle tracking down the fires," Holly insisted. "You need to—"

"I'm not going back yet," Bridger told them.

"Klein!" Penne shouted. "Enough with this!"

"No!" Bridger glared at her. "We need to get a map and find a place near the next location where we can sit down and plot this out."

Neon grimaced. "Does this involve food?"

Bridger looked over Holly's shoulder, studying the map in her hands. "Docksiders Restaurant on the Cheboygan River — we'll go there."

"Yes!" Neon headed inland.

"No!" Penne scowled.

"I'll leave you media types to figure this out," Holly said, backing away. "But Bridger, you keep me in the loop and let us handle this," she added, turning away to head down the lakeshore toward the fire site.

Bridger leaned in toward Penne. "Look, I know you're really tired of this tug-of-war, and I am, too. But the heart of our agreement was that I get to keep on being a reporter as long as I've got protection at my side. And look... I've got you and Neon with me." He lowered his voice, nearly whispering in her ear. "If someone's determined to find me, they can look at WHAM, too. It's not necessarily any safer there."

Penne bit her lip. "We'll go get lunch and decide what's next from there."

"Thank you."

"What is *that?*" Chepi sounded alarmed as she pointed toward a couple of dark objects rocking to and fro in the waves as they lapped at the shore. "They look like dead rats!"

Bridger approached them. "They're not rats — they're bats, like the ones we saw on the pavilion's ceiling." He picked up a nearby branch and dragged one from the water into the damp sand. "And what's that on it?"

Penne stepped to his side. "It looks like..." She paused, kneeling down for a closer look. "Oh my God! Get back!" She pulled at Bridger, yanking him toward the woods as Chepi followed.

"What is it?" Bridger shouted as they scrambled up the beach toward the woods.

"What'd you find?" Holly yelled as she ran toward them.

"Stay back!" Penne shouted back. "We found one of the bombs, and it looks like it hasn't gone off!"

Chapter 35

Militia members who could take time from their workday gathered again at Tamarack's Tree Farm, continuing what began last night. They huddled together around the patch of older trees banned from harvest, fenced off from where the locals traipsed in search of their family Christmas trees. This was the one area deemed off limits to all but a handful of militia members who were in the know, the only ones aware of what was buried in the soil beneath the towering pines.

"Keep digging men — there're plenty more," Creighton encouraged his entourage as he, too, plunged his spade into the rock-solid clay soil, withdrawing another shovelful and tossing it aside.

"Man, how many did you bury, Mr. Tamarack?" Dylan asked as he tossed more dirt into the growing mound of dirt by the stand of towering Blue Spruce.

Ted Laski stopped digging, looking at Dylan. "He didn't do it by himself, son. Trust me — he had plenty of help. Right boys?"

"Oo-rah!" one man bellowed, followed by chants of agreement from the rest of the men.

Removing his cap, John Paul wiped sweat from his brow on his shirt sleeve. "Yeah, by my count, I figure we're just a little short of two hundred by now."

"Holy crap!" Dylan drove his shovel in again, striking something. "Hey, got another one!"

"I'll help you," J Paul offered, stepping to his friend's side as the two of them jammed their spades beneath the long piece of PVC tubing, lifting it from its grave. "There you go!"

Creighton approached them, picking up the capped tube. "So, let's see what you got this time, boys." Removing the cap, Creighton tipped the canister until a rifle slid from inside, dropping into his hand. "Another Ruger Mini-14." Holding it with the barrel pointing upward, he passed it to Dylan. "Add it to the rest of them."

"Sure." Taking the rifle from his pastor, Dylan walked around the excavated plot toward the large crates on the opposite side, adding the semi-automatic to the box that stood nearly full of similar rifles. "Are these going to the Michilimackinac Compound?"

"Most are," Creighton answered. "But we need a few to stay here."

John Paul shoved his spade into the soil, leaning against it. "Yeah, now with that fire at Mullett Creek, we've got to prepare for when those Indians strike next." He spit. "They went after kids! Can you believe it? Frankie and Tom aren't here digging 'cause they're with their kids — got the shit scared out of them at that fire. It's awful, I tell you. What kind of people go after kids like that?"

"The same kind that locked your son up," Creighton replied, patting young J Paul on the side of his head. "Glad you're back with us, son, but you best stay out of what's likely to come next — don't want you in trouble over the conditions of your bail."

"What do you think happens next?" J Paul inquired.

"Well, I already showed this to your dad and the other men here, but guess there's no reason not to show it to you boys." Creighton pulled a map from his pocket, opening it to reveal where he had drawn an incomplete circle in the area known as the Tip of the Mitt.

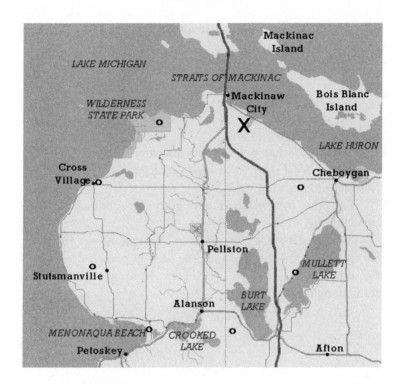

"The fire locations..." Dylan pointed to them. "They're forming a circle."

"It's an Indian symbol," Laski scowled. "Makes it look like they're the ones trying to trap us with these fires, but they're just pawns in a much larger assault."

"What do you mean?" Dylan asked.

"It's the governor... and her Guard. Don't you see it, son?" Laski grabbed the map from Creighton and pointed to out each fire location on the map. "The Guards been dispatched to each one of these fire sites, *supposedly* to fight the fires. But what are they *really* doing? Ask yourself *that!*"

Creighton took the map back. "What's more important to ask at this point is where will they strike next?" He held the map out for both young men to see.

"And he means both the arsonists and the Guard," Laski added as he began to dig again.

Dylan looked to Creighton. "The next spot... it's right here!"

"Exactly... and X marks the spot that completes the circle."

"That's the compound!" J Paul jabbed his finger at the map. "What are we going to do?"

"We'll do what we've always prepared to do," Creighton answered. "We'll meet them head on; defend our land and our freedom — that's what we'll do."

The other men whooped with guttural sounds as they continued to dig.

"So, let's get these guns up, men," Creighton said, thrusting his spade into the dirt and jumping on it to press it deeper into the soil. "Looks like we're headed for a showdown, so we best be ready to fight back."

⚜

Chapter 36

With the Michigan map purchased at the BP station draped over the sides of the restaurant booth tabletop, Bridger smoothed out the northern portion of the Lower Peninsula, then penciling in the exact location of each fire. "Move your glass," he demanded, staring at Neon seated across from him.

"Oops! Sorry." Neon slid his Mountain Dew onto the wood top at the outer edge of the table, then wiping away the damp ring left behind on the map. "I didn't think it was in your way."

"Here are your smelt," the young waitress said as she slid three paper-lined plastic baskets heaping with fried fish onto the table's edge. "And I'll be right back with the burger, sir."

"Could you also bring me something with a straight edge that's longer than a ruler; like a yardstick if you've got one?" Bridger asked her.

"I'll see what we've got," she answered before scurrying off to wait on the next table.

"This Docksiders place is known for their smelt." Neon passed a basket to Penne who was seated next to him. "Save some for Chepi to eat when she gets back from calling her dad."

"Do you really think I'd eat all of this?" Penne took the basket and set it to her other side against the wall. "Oh no," she grumbled, looking across the room at the flat screen mounted on the wall. "Do you see this?"

Bridger turned to find the TV tuned to their cable news competitor's channel, the network now broadcasting footage from earlier when sobbing children were led from the lake, around the fire, and into the arms of panic-stricken parents. The news package continued with a montage of incensed adults condemning law enforcement for failing to keep their children safe, all of it followed up with a clip of Pastor Creighton at the Pellston Town Hall rebuking the governor for neglecting her responsibility to protect the people and then announcing a six o'clock meeting for those interested in taking matters into their own hands."

"He's meeting at six? But that's our broadcast time," Bridger complained.

"Is *that* all you're worried about?" Penne shook her head.

"Yeah, and you should be worried about it, too," he snapped. "That's our time to get out *our* story, but it won't help if people are at that meeting with their minds already made up, never even seeing what we put on the air."

"Good point, I suppose." Penne took a sip from her iced tea.

"And I want to do a story on those crazy bat bombs," Bridger noted as he took a drink from his bottle of Bud Light, then leaning over the map to study it. "I think people ought to know how these fires are started so they can be on the look out for unusual sightings of bats."

"Yeah, that is one wild way to firebomb a place!" Neon muttered through a mouthful of fried fish. "Wonder who came up with that bizarre idea."

"Kelli-Sue's compiling background on the concept, so we should know soon," Penne said, resting her elbow on the table to cradle her chin in her hand.

Neon pushed more fish into his mouth. "And I wish we could've stuck around for the bomb squad. That would've been some sweet footage!"

"Well, at least you got film of the dead bats floating in the water before they made us leave the area. I know we were far off, but you were able to zoom in for a clear close-up, weren't you."

Still chewing, Neon gave the thumbs up with one hand while lifting his glass of Mountain Dew with the other, sucking it all down with a straw until the last drops gurgled in the bottom of the glass.

"Make sure Al or I check that video first," Penne insisted. "I don't want to give away any critical info that could help the arsonists; and you should check with Holly on that, as well."

"What? Do we work for the police now, too?" Totally flustered, he got up from the table and stepped to the window just behind them, staring across the river at the salmon fishermen having no luck on the opposite bank. "I know your pain, guys," he muttered to the glass. "I'm not catching any breaks, either."

"The waitress said to give you this," Chepi said as she walked up to Bridger, handing him a yardstick.

"Thanks," he said with a smile. "How're you doing?"

"Just took my pills, so I'm flying high!" She laughed. "But I really should eat something."

"Yeah we got some smelt and that Diet Coke you ordered." He walked her back to the booth. "So, you must've reached your dad. Was he upset to hear you were with us at the fire?"

Chepi slid along the bench seat to the wall. "Yes, but he'll get over it, especially now that he knows I'm safe." She dipped a smelt in tarter sauce. "I told him I was having a quick lunch with you and then I'd meet him to help set up for this powwow we're having later," she added, biting into the fish.

Bridger sat down next to her. "You've got a lot left to do, and you must be worn out."

"I'm okay."

"Yeah, but I bet your dad's concerned, and I'd hate to see him worry."

"You should talk!" Neon said with a laugh.

Bridger ignored him, taking another drink from his bottle and then slapping the yardstick onto the table. "Okay, so now we're going to get somewhere." He slid the stick across the map, positioning it between juxtaposed fires. Drawing a line to connect fire one with five and another to connect two with six, he next measured the distance of each, comparing the two. "They're close, but not quite the same."

"Use the median between the two," Chepi suggested.

"Ah, we have a math whiz," he joked. Then following her suggestion, he dragged the pencil from the third fire location at the retirement village toward an area of farmland to the west of where they were currently sitting in Cheboygan. "Well, there's not much at that spot." He drew the next line from the marina fire, the pencil landing at a spot just short of the Mackinac's Historic Park at Mill Creek. "Not quite there, but the park could be the target." He screwed up his face, taking a bite of a smelt. "Guess I expected something a bit more... definitive."

"Well, the first two lines prove that the arsonists weren't perfectly accurate when they put this together," Penne suggested. "They probably generalized an area, which is going to make it that much harder to pinpoint the next strike."

"Then why don't we go drive around this general vicinity?" Bridger pointed to the patch of farmland to the west. "At least we could be trying to find them instead of just sitting here doing nothing."

"Speak for yourself," Neon said with his mouth full of smelt, bits of chewed fish spewing out onto the map. "Sorry," he added, using his napkin to wipe the map clean.

Penne took another drink from her tea. "I told you, Klein, we're not going to drive aimlessly around when there are police and possibly military personnel out there searching for these people. Let's just leave it to the professionals for now and wait to hear something."

"And eat while we're waiting," Neon added. "Wonder why my burger's taking so long."

Feeling his cell phone vibrate, Bridger removed it from his pocket to see a message coming through. "It's from Kelli Sue," he announced, opening it to find the translation for the sixth copper.

∇ᗡ ᐃᗡᐊᒥᑊ ᐃᗡᐊᐸᑕ ᑌᐱᖴᑕ ᗡᎢ ᐱ ᐃᐱᒋᑕᑕ ᑲᎪᒪ
VI FIRST FIRE CAME IN A FALSE WAY

"So, what is that supposed to mean?" Bridger asked, tipping his phone so Chepi could read the message.

Chepi lipped the words as she read them. "It references the false promises made by the white man — how they will be our ruin if we fail to turn away from them and rekindle our own ways," she explained. "But with these actual fires burning at each site, who knows how we're supposed to interpret them."

"Either way, it's a message meant to divide people," Bridger suggested as his phone vibrated again, this time with an incoming call that he accepted, pressing the phone to his ear. "Thanks for the translation, K-Sue. So, what else have you got?"

"I've got worries, Bridger Klein!" she answered. "You and Neon could've been blown to kingdom come with just that one little bomb. Do you know that?"

"No, but I do now. What's the deal with them?"

"Speaker phone," Penne insisted.

"I've got Chepi, Neon, and Penne here, so I'm going to put you on speaker. Is that okay?"

"Yeah, I get it." Kelli Sue lowered her voice. "I'll be careful about what I say — keep DIG stuff on the QT."

"Good idea," he replied, pushing the speaker button. "I've got you on now, so tell us about these bat bombs."

"Okay... So, as crazy as all of this initially sounded, you need to know that this whole idea of firebombing with bats stems back to a Marine Corps operation named Project X-Ray developed during World War II."

"What?" Bridger leaned toward his phone. "You're saying this idea was once a military operation... in the United States?"

"Yep... After the bombing of Pearl Harbor, a lot of Americans were sending the government some pretty insane ideas for payback, one of which came from Dr. Lytle Adams, a dental surgeon and inventor who lived in Irwin, Pennsylvania. He'd recently seen the world's largest bat colony found in New Mexico's Carlsbad Caverns, and his recollections of millions of bats flying around at night gave him the idea to harness them with incendiaries and drop them in mass from a plane, sending them off to spread a massive fire across Japan."

Penne brushed back her bangs. "And the military took this seriously?"

"At the order of President Roosevelt himself," she answered. "He forwarded the idea to one of his colonels with a handwritten note…" she paused, the sound of shuffling papers carrying over the phone. "*This man is not a nut. It sounds like a perfectly wild idea but is worth looking into* — that's what Roosevelt wrote."

"So, they actually planned to attach bombs to bats like what we saw today?" Bridger washed down another smelt with the last of his beer.

"They didn't plan it — they did it! People went to caverns in Texas and New Mexico and netted thousands of Mexican Free-tailed bats, then brought them back and stored them in refrigerators designed to induce hibernation so they wouldn't need feeding. Then some engineers designed this bomb-shaped container with a delayed parachute that, when it opened on descent, would also peel back the outer shell of the container to lower the twenty-six trays inside, each one holding forty bats in individual compartments. So, if you do the math, it comes out to just over one thousand bats in each bomb-shaped container."

The waitress handed Neon his burger basket. "Sorry about the wait."

"Just in time," he told her, handing her his empty smelt basket.

Taking the basket, the waitress looked at the phone on the table. "Did she just say bats in a bomb?"

"She's kind of crazy," Neon whispered back, spinning his finger by his head.

"Oh." The waitress smiled, backing away.

Neon kept spinning his finger. "Yeah, so K-Sue… What about the part that makes this whole bomb go boom?" He laughed, taking a huge bite out of his burger.

"You can thank the chemist Louis Fieser, the guy who created military-grade napalm, for that one," Kelli Sue answered.

"They put his thickened kerosene concoction in these oblong-shaped celluloid case-thingies with a time-delayed ignition that would trigger when a chemical corrosion process ate away at a metal barrier, tripping a firing pin – complicated, I know, but all pretty ingenious, you've got to admit," she added. "Then they used surgical clips and string to attach bombs to the loose skin on a bat's chest, so when bats were let lose, they'd fly off to hide in a barn or a belfry – some building somewhere – and a lot of times they'd gnaw through the string and leave the bomb before it even detonated. That's the good part – where at least the bats live."

"Unlike the people," Bridger added.

"Actually that's not true, Bridger. Bat bombs aren't nearly as deadly as you'd think because they're meant to detonate in places like eaves and attics that are hard to reach, well away from people. That means the sticky, flammable, napalm-like substance is supposed to stick to the structure long enough to get a fire burning but it's not meant to get on people in the way you probably think of napalms used in the Vietnam War. That must be why the bat bomb inventor Dr. Adams was so bummed when his project was cancelled."

Penne cocked her head. "But I thought you said the military did this, and now you say they cancelled the project even though it worked? So, which is it, Kelli?"

"–Sue," Neon interjected, swallowing down another bite of burger. "You shouldn't leave off the Sue-part."

Penne shook her head. "Did the bat bombs work or didn't they?"

"Uh, they worked, but at the wrong place," she answered.

"And what's that supposed to mean?" Bridger asked.

"They ran a test on the base with just a half-dozen bats, and apparently the bats came out of hibernation too early and flew away… and then they burned the whole base to the ground."

Neon laughed. "Nice job!"

"Well, it did prove they were very effective," Kelli Sue chuckled back. "But they obviously had some fine tuning to do.

So, they kept working on it, setting a target date of mid-1945. But by then, the military was anticipating the completion of the much more formidable atomic bomb and they didn't want to keep sinking money into both projects. So, they cancelled X-ray, which seems like such a tragic decision in hindsight if you read this quote from Adams where he imagined… *thousands of fires breaking out simultaneously over a circle of forty miles in diameter for every bomb dropped. Japan could have been devastated, yet with small loss of life…* end of quote. Makes you wonder what would've happened if they hadn't wiped out over two-hundred thousand people with Little Boy and Fat Man and had gone with the bat bombs instead."

"Well, we'll have time later to mull over that moral dilemma, K," Bridger replied. "But in the meantime, we've got to figure out how these old techniques tie in with the new."

"Yes, and we need to pass along word of this finding to the authorities," Penne added, picking up her cell phone and punching keys. "They need to be looking for someplace where they're storing these bats."

"If they're inducing hibernation, then they could store them in a very small space," Kelli Sue told her. "Al's checking on some…" She paused, starting again. "Al has some connections he's pursuing here, trying to see if he can trace the shipment of the bats. We're passing our info on, too… to Holly, of course," she quickly added.

Bridger laughed. "Of course… Thanks, K."

"Yeah, and I'm sure the fire marshal's already onto the whole napalm substance thing," Kelli Sue continued. "But we should probably be looking into that, too. Don't you think so, Penne?"

"Yes, good job, Kelli… Sue," she quickly added, still punching keys. "I'm on it."

"And thanks again for the sixth prophecy," Bridger added. "Will you shoot that off to Dawson Rivard, too? Guess I kind of owe him that."

"Yeah, I've still got his number, so will do. But here's a question… Do you even want me to keep bothering with those things? I mean, they don't seem to lead us anywhere, except to pointing back at the Native Americans who don't really seem to be to blame here."

"Amen, sister!" Chepi cheered.

Bridger smiled at Chepi. "Yeah, those happy pills are working, aren't they?"

Chepi covered her mouth, her cheeks turning flushed.

Bridger leaned back toward his phone. "We'll decide when we find the next copper, K, but for now I'm thinking we keep checking them."

"Okay, whatever." she replied, snapping her gum as she hung up.

Chepi looked at her watch. "Oh, my gosh! I'm late — I've got to go!"

Bridger jumped from his seat. "Sorry if we distracted you."

"No, it's my fault." She slid out of the booth, jerking upright and then swaying, leaning against the table.

"Hey, are you okay?" Bridger caught her by her good arm. "Maybe you shouldn't go, or I should drive you."

"No!" Penne told him, never looking up from her phone.

"I'm fine, really. I've just got to drive to Grangers' farm out on Levering Road, just past the airport," she told him, pointing at the location on the map still draped on the table.

Bridger glanced down her slender arm to where her finger rested on the spot juxtaposed to fire three, then looking back up to her. "That's it!"

"What's it?" she asked.

"The next strike — it must be the gourd farm."

Penne looked up at him. "You don't know that. There must be other farms around there, too."

"Not where they're having a powwow with a whole lot of people attending," Bridger argued.

"But they're Native Americans," Chepi pointed out. "If whoever's doing this is trying to make it look like my people are responsible, then why go after my people?"

"She's got a point there," Neon said, chewing the last of his burger.

Bridger looked at Neon. "It's still too much of a coincidence." Sliding the yardstick into the seat, he grabbed the map and folded it. "Leave the fries and let's get going."

"But the fries are the best part."

"Then grab a fistful, and let's go!" Bridger drew his wallet from his pocket and threw three twenties on the table. "You, too, Penne."

"We should wait, Klein," Penne answered.

Bridger glared at her. "Look, I don't care if I go in the rental or with Chepi, but I *am* going — just thought you'd want to come along since that was our deal."

Penne curled her lip, sliding out of the seat and walking away from the table. "Hope this isn't another cell dead zone," she grumbled.

"Won't know 'til we get there," Bridger answered, holding the door for the two ladies as they walked out. "And Neon, will you hurry up?" he added, then leaving himself.

"Hey, don't you want your change from this?" the waitress asked, picking up the three twenties.

"Yeah, but there's no time," Neon told her, grabbing a fistful of fries. "Guess I hear the bat bombs calling." He laughed, biting into the fries as he rushed out the door.

⚜

Chapter 37

Looking at his watch fashioned to resemble a medicine wheel, Takota thought of Chepi who had given it to him, wondering why she hadn't arrived at 4:30 as she had promised. Even though she was only fifteen minutes late, it worried him given her condition, especially considering everything she had encountered during the course of the day. Distracted by her absence, Takota found it difficult to focus on all that still needed to be set up in the patch before people began to arrive in a little over an hour.

"Your men did a great job with the tent setup," Naomi said to Takota as she wobbled through the dry dirt in heels, her one leg still wrapped from the incident yesterday. "Things are going to be decorated a bit nicer, though, aren't they?"

"Once Chepi gets here, she'll see to it." Takota glanced again at his watch.

"Are you going to have enough time to get this together? I mean, we want it to look good for the cameras once the governor gets here."

"We want it to look good when everyone gets here." He nodded. "I've got at least two dozen tribe members here setting up the tables, running the electrical cords and stringing up lights. And those men over there are stacking the bonfire." He pointed to a group huddled together about a hundred feet away from them.

"Well, you better make sure they get that right," Naomi said, her hands on her hips. "We sure don't need them starting the patch on fire given everything that's happened."

"I'm well aware of that, Naomi."

"You sure you want to do this, Chief?" Butane Bill asked as he hobbled on his walking stick from his yard toward them.

"We haven't had rain in a while, and with all these fires, I'm surprised they haven't banned us from doing this."

"We have special permission from the governor," Naomi told him. "That's why we're going to make sure it's done safely. Right, Takota?"

Takota didn't answer her, looking back to Bill. "We appreciate you letting us use your land again this year."

"You know I'm always willing." He leaned with both hands on his stick. "I just don't want there to be trouble because of it."

"I'm hoping this will bring about the opposite," Takota replied, brushing windblown strands of gray hair from his face. "When the cameras show up to film the governor, then we'll have a chance to show people the peaceful nature of our traditions. Maybe that will calm things down a little bit."

"Plus the governor will be making some very supportive remarks," Naomi added. "She might be able to sway a few minds."

"Not counting on that," Bill muttered. "But I sure hope you're right about this, Chief, and I'm sure the members will do everything they can to help." He turned toward his house. "Got a couple more things to do inside before I'll be back out to help."

"Take your time," Takota told him.

"But there's lots still to do, Takota," Naomi complained. "You seem a bit lackadaisical about all this. When's your daughter getting here, anyway?"

"I'm not sure." He glanced at his watch once more. "I'd expect she'd be here any—" He stopped and dropped to the ground, startled by the sudden bursts and bangs coming from seemingly everywhere. "Get down!" he yelled to Naomi and all the surrounding people and sparks flew in the distant trees and smoke began to rise.

"It's a — another fire… is-isn't it?" Naomi stuttered, crawling in the dirt.

"Head for the road!" Takota directed her, then turning to yell at Bill. "Stay away from your house!"

"No!" Bill yelled back, hobbling toward his home. "I've got stuff inside I've got to get out."

"I'll help you!" he shouted, moving toward the house where he saw smoke beginning to fume from the eaves. "We don't have much time!"

"Get back!" voices yelled from behind him.

Takota turned back just in time to see the tent burst into flames, tables tipping as those underneath scrambled to get out.

"Don't go in the house!" Takota yelled back at Bill and then turned away from the house, hurrying toward the collapsing tent of fire. "Get them out of there!" he shouted to people outside the tent's perimeter.

"We can't!" a man screamed as another wailed, running as flames leapt from his jacket.

"Roll in the dirt!" Takota yelled with others as they watched the man drop to the ground, flailing about yet unable to smother the fire.

Takota yanked off his jacket, beating the man with it. "Somebody call 911!"

"We did!" a man yelled as he threw his coat over the screaming man and thrashed against him with his bare arms. "This — won't — go — out!"

"The dispatcher said they're backed up!" another man shouted. "I don't know when they're coming!"

"You've got to drive this guy to the hospital," Takota told the man across from him as they finally extinguished the flames, the man now gurgling over his guttural moaning. "A couple of you help carry him — anyone else hurt?" he asked those nearby.

"Not sure, but we'll check," one man volunteered himself and another.

Takota looked from the injured man and the burning tent toward the edge of the patch where fire leapt at random between the trees. "There's got to be an irrigation system around here somewhere. Go search along this side of the trees for the water source – Quick! See what you can find!" he shouted, sending them running toward the escalating fire as he turned back for the house, still yelling. "I'll be right there – soon as I save a friend…"

✤

Chapter 38

"See the smoke rising over there?" Creighton asked his fellow militia members, pointing over the trees. "That's got to be where the explosions went off."

"That's my place — my grandpa's farm!" Dylan shuddered. "I've got to go help him!" He dashed for the gate.

"We'll be right behind you, son," Creighton assured him.

"Thanks," he yelled, never looking back as he exited the place they were excavating and took off running through the trees.

"I've got to help him, too!" J Paul headed for the gate.

"Hold up, son," his father told him. "That's not a good idea given your bail situation."

"We're helping put out a fire!" he protested.

"Your dad's right," Creighton told him. "We might meet up with the people behind these fires, and I don't want you involved if things get ugly."

"So... helping out the Indian neighbors, are we now?" Laski asked, leaning on his shovel.

"Helping ourselves," Creighton answered. "That fire's not far from here, so we can't stand by while it creeps up on John Paul's farm."

"That's for sure!" John Paul nodded.

"Plus we've got a bone to pick with whoever's behind these fires, so I say we go survey the situation — see how we can be of help."

Laski grinned. "Well... guess that's the kind of assistance I'd be happy to offer." He stepped over to the crates filled with semi-automatics. "Now which one should I take with me?"

"We'll use these," Creighton instructed them, pointing into another crate. "These were dug up earlier — they're cleaned and tested, ready for use." He looked to J Paul. "You want to be of help, son? Then you get the rest of that ammo together up at the house, ready for when we get this shipment out."

"Okay, Pastor," J Paul answered, passing through the gate and heading toward his house.

"The rest of us need to split up here," Creighton told the remaining men as he lowered his arm down between them. "Laski, you take these men on your side, and the rest of you are with me." He pointed toward a smaller crate off to the side. "There's plenty of ammo in there for our current purposes, so get what you need, gentlemen - just in case we run into the enemy."

"The enemy…" Laski repeated, approaching the smaller crate. "So, would that be the Indians setting the fires or the Guard backing them up?"

"That would be the arsonists *and* those defending them, oo-rah!"

"Oo-rah!" the group bellowed back.

"People have chosen sides; the authorities have, too," Creighton said as he slid an ammo box from the crate. "Now *we* have to choose — either you're with us or you're with the enemy." He opened the box, withdrawing a handful of bullets. "We're the last line of protection, men. Do not let our enemy escape."

⚜

Chapter 39

"We're already too late!" Bridger complained as he looked through the Malibu's windshield at the back of Chepi's Vibe, both cars racing toward the smoke now billowing into the sky. "You should pass her!" he told Neon.

"No, you shouldn't!" Penne said from the back, poking at her cell phone as usual. "Let's not get crazy again, boys; keep our heads in the game."

"Don't you get carsick doing that?" Neon asked, glancing at Penne in the rearview mirror.

"Yes, I do." She kept texting. "But I'm trained to tolerate pain."

"That's not pain," he argued. "That's just... being sick! You don't ever hurl, do you?"

She glanced up at him. "No... I don't *hurl*."

"Keep focused, will you?" Bridger scolded Neon, pointing at Chepi's car. "Look, she's pulling off there — on the shoulder!"

"I can see that!" Neon pulled over behind her.

Chepi climbed from her car and walked quickly toward them, grimacing as she hugged her injured arm with the other.

"Roll down your window!" Bridger demanded.

"Slow down, dude!" Neon yelled as he rolled it down.

Chepi leaned in. "I see my dad's car next to those others up ahead, but I don't see him or the others anywhere." She grimaced, biting her lip.

Bridger leaned toward Neon's open window. "You're in pain, aren't you?"

"No time for that!" She took a deep breath. "That's Bill Granger's house catching fire, and I'm worried Dad might be in there."

"Get in!" he told her, leaning into the backseat to pop the door open for her.

"What are you up to, Klein?" Penne demanded to know as Chepi climbed in beside her, closing the door.

Bridger ignored Penne. "Neon, pull in that turnaround driveway and park just past those cars."

"Got it," he said, driving ahead.

Penne leaned forward between the seats. "You should park where we can get away when this fire gets out of control, Kashkari. We've got people to keep safe here, remember."

"I can drive right out the other side," he said as he parked on the driveway's shoulder, pointing ahead to where the pavement continued in a half-circle until it returned back to the road.

"There's dad!" Chepi yelled, opening her door and climbing out.

Bridger popped his door and jumped out, spotting Takota with a young man, the two of them dragging the garden hose from the side of the smoking house toward its front door. "Don't fool around with that, Takota!" he yelled, bypassing Chepi as he ran to him. "You need to get away from here!"

"I think Bill went in there!" he answered in tears. "Dylan and I've got to help him."

"He's my grandpa!" Dylan added. "We've got to get him out of there!"

"I'll do that!" Neon said, grabbing the spray nozzle and squeezing its handle to release the water as he dashed up the front steps, the hose trailing behind him.

"You need to get back from here," Bridger told them all. "Chepi, get your dad back, and Dylan, you need to go help those men save your granddad's farm," he added, waving toward the men in the field.

Dylan held up his hands. "But I've got to—"

"We'll get your granddad, so go put out the fire!" Bridger insisted. "Now, go on!"

"Uh, okay!" Dylan agreed, running off.

Penne headed for the farmhouse's front door. "Kashkari, hurry up – this place is about to blow!" she shouted.

Bridger approached the door, his hands trembling as he noticed smoke creeping from the eaves. "Neon, you got him?" he yelled as he watched the hose continue to slither, then noticing where it dragged along side of a copper shield jammed into the ground at the foot of the steps.

"Come on, Neon!" Penne demanded. "Is he even in there?"

Bridger tapped his foot, glancing at the smoke and fire that he thought he feared most; then staring at the open front doorway at the top of the stairs, he realized what he feared even more. "I got your back, dude!" he yelled to his friend as he ran up the stairs, bursting through the doorway and into the smoke-filled house.

"No! Get back out of there, you two!" Penne yelled from the steps.

The fire crackled as the white paint along the roofline began to singe and glow, but from inside, no one answered.

Chapter 40

The concealed space between the back of the farmhouse and the detached garage provided good cover for Magdala to remain unnoticed while she observed events unfolding — so far, all going as planned. Since triggering the multiple incendiaries, she had watched the tribe members disperse in multiple directions, most of them dashing toward the outer edges of the patch where flames leapt without restraint through the dry trees and shrubs. Assuming the men were searching for the irrigation system, Magdala was pleased to know they would find it no longer functioning since she had sabotaged the pump and ruptured the main pipeline. She found satisfaction in witnessing the men's futile efforts to stop the inevitable — exactly what she had felt so long ago when she had lost everything to fire.

Then she spotted her signal — the Battalion members creeping toward the fire zone, searching for their prey. Little did the militiamen realize that *she* was the one they should be looking for; but she knew they would be much more content to stalk the tribe members, blaming them for what she had done and making them pay with their lives. All they needed now was a little push.

With the silencer still attached to her Glock 21, Magdala took aim for the militiaman closest to her yet a good distance away from the others. Pulling the trigger, she took him down, leaving her victim crumpled in a patch of ripe pumpkins where he would be found soon enough by his fellow men. Turning slightly, she next pointed the Glock at two tribe members still nearby in the patch, one helping the other limp away from the burning tent. Squeezing the trigger, she struck one, sending them both tumbling to the ground. Lowering the gun, she smirked, pleased that she had managed to strike both targets.

From the corner of her eye, Magdala suddenly noticed some-one moving inside the smoke-filled house. Concerned that who-ever it was might have seen her, she raised the Glock and fired, taking a quick shot through the window that dropped the per-son to the floor.

"Bull's eye," she muttered.

"What was that?" a distant voice yelled from inside.

Unable to see who had yelled, Magdala crouched at the sound of the voice, creeping away from the broken glass to make her way around the side of the house. Flames were now breaking out from the roofline, forcing her away from the protective cover the farmhouse had provided. Ducking behind a landscaped row of cedar shrubs that had not yet caught fire, she peeked through the branches, trying to catch a glimpse of whoever was still in the house.

"Get out of there!" a woman's voice carried from the front yard.

Following the sound, Magdala crept quickly along the row of shrubs until she spotted the tall blonde whom she had seen earlier in the car with the Klein man. She raised her Glock, tak-ing aim just as the woman scurried up the front steps and into the house.

"Damn," Magdala cursed, lowering the Glock.

"Somebody get me out of here!" another woman screamed from where she stood by the parked cars in the driveway.

Magdala turned to see the woman she recognized as the Drummond lady — the one she had taken aim at when she had pulled the trigger at the casino.

"I need a key, damn it!" the Drummond woman cursed as she kicked at a rusted-out Ford Bronco in the driveway. "Is any-body coming?"

"I am here!" Magdala shouted as she ran toward her, keep-ing her gun hidden at her side.

"Oh, thank God!" Naomi shouted back. "They all ran off and left me! Crazy fools!"

"Yes, crazy!" she answered, jogging to where she could take cover behind the cars, coming closer to Naomi.

"So, which one's yours?" Naomi demanded to know as she motioned toward the vehicles, ducking at the sound of limbs snapping from tree trunks and dropping along the roadside, further dispersing the flames. "Hurry up! We don't have much longer!"

"No, we do not," Magdala replied as she raised the Glock and fired, striking Naomi in the chest.

"No—" Naomi screamed, the sound cut short as she tumbled backward, emitting a guttural yelp when she struck the ground.

Magdala kept herself hidden behind the parked vehicles as she crept to Naomi's side, looking down at her wide eyes that looked so familiar — the kind of pained eyes she had seen so many times before. The gurgling sound was familiar, too, drawing Magdala to study the blood oozing from Naomi's nose and pooling between her lips as she attempted to move them, unable to form words. Looking downward, she took notice of the blood stain widening across Naomi's blouse as her arms remained limp at her sides, powerless to reach up to where blood seeped out of the hole in her chest.

"No… not much longer," Magdala whispered, leaning closer to watch as Naomi's wild gaze faded to a blank stare.

⚜

Chapter 41

"I think I see him!" Bridger yelled, crawling below the dark smoke as he made his way across the dining room's carpeted floor toward the faint figure of a man lying on his back.

"Leave him, Klein, and get out!" Penne shouted from somewhere behind him. "We'll get him!"

"He's right over here!" Bridger yelled back as he grabbed at Bill's shirt, finding it soaking wet.

"Oww..." Bill moaned at Bridger's touch.

"Bill... Bill?" Bridger hovered close to him, squinting with burning eyes at Bill's stomach as he tried to make out the dark patch of moisture contrasting against the lighter hue of his shirt. "Is that... blood?"

"I heard glass break!" Neon barked at Bridger as he reached Bill's side. "Maybe it's—" He coughed and spit, choking on the smoke. "Shit! He's shot!"

Bridger gagged, struggling to breath. "What?" Sweat dripped from his face as he sweltered in the heat radiating from the ceiling, his heart racing at the mere thought of the fire ever-intensifying overhead.

"We've got to get out!" Penne coughed as she crawled to them. "Shirt over mouth!" she told Bridger, tugging at his shirt while pulling her own over her mouth.

Bridger pulled the collar of his shirt over his nose. "Back door!" he yelled through the sweat-soaked fabric as he motioned toward the nearby spot where he'd seen hints of a sunbeam. "You push," he added, grabbing Bill by the shoulders and dragging him backward.

"I got him," Neon insisted, pushing Bridger out of the way to scoop up Bill and dash blindly into the smoke.

"Neon! Don't stand!" Bridger yelled, fearing for him.

"Follow him!" Penne insisted, giving him a push.

With snaps and bangs increasing all around them, Bridger crouched as he scurried for what he hoped was a door.

"The roof's going to go!" Penne pushed from behind, yelling, "Hurry!"

The cracks and pops continued as they tumbled out the back door and down the steps, landing nearly in a pile where Bill was sprawled on the grass, grunting as he writhed in pain.

Bridger sat up, hissing as he grabbed at the painful welt on the back of his head. "Must've split that spot open again," he said, looking at his hand to find it moistened with blood.

Neon looked at Bill. "They got him in the stomach," he told them, wiping beads of sweat from his face as he glanced around at the fire spreading around them. "And we've got to get out of here!"

Penne scanned the grounds as she stepped to Bill, kneeling down and pulling back his shirt to reveal blood oozing from a gaping hole. "In here," she assessed, rolling him.

"And it came out there," Neon observed on his backside. "But no sirens yet, and he's already lost a lot of blood."

More bangs sounded, but now Bridger realized they were not coming from the burning house. "Is that gunfire?"

"Get down, Klein!" Penne yelled, swatting at him.

"Where's Chepi?" Bridger's eyes darted about until he spotted her hurrying through the patch with her father toward the distant blazing trees where tribe members brandished shovels and heavy branches, beating them against the irrigation pipes. "Don't go out there!" he yelled after her.

Penne reached for her ankle, drawing her Chief. "We're getting out of here," she insisted, cringing as more shots rang out.

"We can't leave Chepi and her dad!"

"Oh, yes we can! They can fend for themselves."

"I'll get Bill," Neon said, kneeling at his side.

"And I've got Klein," Penne replied, grabbing Bridger by the shirtsleeve.

"No, you don't!" He pulled away from her, dashing toward the field.

"Wait!" Neon sprang to his feet, chasing after him.

"You're going to get killed!" Penne ran after both of them, her gun in hand.

"We'll switch, Bridge!" Neon shouted, gaining on him. "You take Bill – someone's got to help him!"

Bridger slowed as he noticed up ahead that Chepi and Takota had turned back, fleeing the gunfight. "I don't want you shot at," Bridger yelled back to Neon, tumbling into the patch vines at the sound of more shots.

"Ditto!" Neon answered as he crept up to him, drawing out his nine-millimeter Colt Defender from under the back of his shirt. "But I've got this!"

"That's your gun?"

"Yeah!" Neon snapped. "What's wrong with it?"

"It's fine – just cover those two, will you?" Bridger pointed at Chepi and Takota hurrying toward them.

Penne caught up to them. "That's a deal, Klein, *if* you come back with me," she told him. "Right, Neon?"

"Right, so go!" he answered, dashing off to meet up with the two.

"Come on!" Penne demanded, pulling at Bridger while scanning the area around them.

Bridger stayed low as they dashed around the vines in the patch, hurrying back toward Bill. Shots echoed through the field again, Bridger glancing back to see Takota tumble to the ground. "No!" he yelled.

"Trust your friend, and keep going!" Penne insisted. "You've got to help Bill."

Bridger's jaw tightened as he ran onward, sliding into the grass at Bill's side. "I know it'll hurt for me to lift you, but we're going to get you some help," he told Bill as he shoved his arms under him, lifting his bloodied body and hurrying around the house toward the Malibu.

Penne continued to search the tree lines as she walked nearly backwards at Bridger's side. "Oh, no — Kashkari still has the keys, doesn't he?" she guessed, her eyes darting about the area.

"We left the car... in a hurry." Bridger panted and grunted under the weight of Bill in his arms. "Bet he left them in the car."

Penne popped the backdoor. "Slide him in," she told Bridger as she glanced in the driver's side window. "Yeah, keys are in there. You drive so I can ride shotgun," she insisted, heading around the car.

Bridger lowered Bill into the backseat, feeling for a pulse as he yelled to Penne. "But I can't drive!"

"You can now!" she yelled back.

"No, I never learned!" he replied, finding Bill's pulse weak but still there. "Hang in there," he said to the unconscious man, tucking his legs into a contorted position as he rushed to shut the door. "I just can't—" he stopped abruptly as he righted himself, finding a gun pointed in his face.

"You drive — now," Magdala said to him, opening the door and motioning for him to get in.

"But I..." he stammered. "Where's... Penne?"

"She is gone," Magdala answered. "Get — in!"

"What?" Shaking uncontrollably, Bridger climbed into the front seat, still stammering through his words. "But I... I told you, I don't... know how..." He swallowed hard. "I don't drive."

Keeping the gun leveled at Bridger, Magdala made her way around the front of the Malibu and climbed into the passenger seat. "Yes, you do," she said, closing the door and then jabbing the gun into his side.

"Okay, okay!" Bridger turned the key in the ignition, holding it there as the engine revved.

"Let it go," she told him.

Bridger released the key, the car now idling. "I told you, I don't know how!"

"Learn!" she yelled at him.

"I don't know..." He trembled uncontrollably, his heart throbbing in his throat.

Magdala pointed the gun into the backseat at Bill, pulling the trigger.

"Jesus…" He shuttered, squeezing shut his tearful eyes. "You killed him!"

"Your friends are next!" she yelled, jabbing the hot silencer into his side. "Drive!"

Pulling down on the gearshift, Bridger trembled through the motions, recalling the process as best as he could from watching Neon drive. With the car parked for an easy exit, he tapped his shaking foot against the accelerator and moved the car slowly forward, keeping both hands on the wheel as he followed the circular driveway. As he neared the road, he heard the distant sound of sirens approaching, wondering if he could hold off long enough for help to arrive.

"Help is coming," Magdala said to him, smirking.

"Yes," he replied, his voice shaking. "Can I pull Bill from the car – leave him here so he might have a chance?"

She shook her head. "He has no chance."

"And my friends?" Bridger asked, bringing the car to a stop at the end of the driveway. "Do they have a chance?" He glanced in the mirror at the yard behind him, gasping when he spotted Penne slumped in the grass.

"Maybe – if you drive," she answered, waving the gun in his face. "Take right to expressways – now!"

Fearing for his friends as well as himself, Bridger turned the wheel and tapped the accelerator again, making his way onto the road. He trembled at the sight of the fire nearing the road, burning trees and tall grass swaying with the flames as they continued to spread. Glancing at the farmhouse, Bridger's stomach dropped when he saw where the roof had finally given way, flames now raging out of broken windows as the home went up in fire. Breaking out in a cold sweat, he found his only respite when he spotted Chepi and Neon walking with Takota's arms over their shoulders, helping him from the patch.

"For you friends…" Magdala said, pointing at the three walking together. "Maybe they make it." Then she pointed ahead at a police car barreling toward them, its red dome flashing on top as it passed them by. "Help is coming," she repeated, still pointing ahead as a military transport truck followed the police car, speeding past them. "Or is it help?" she asked.

"Is that... what you want?" Bridger asked, confused.

Magdala studied him, not answering.

"And my friends..." Swallowing the lump in his throat, he struggled to keep the car steady between the lines as he squeezed the steering wheel, his heart racing. "Will my friends be okay?"

"Help is coming." She shrugged. "So maybe..."

"And Penne?" he added. "What did you do to her?"

Magdala scowled, shaking her head without answering.

Bridger blinked, fighting against the terror raging within him. "And what about... me?"

Magdala's scowl faded, her lips curling into a sinister smile. "Help is coming," she answered. "I am sure."

⚜

Chapter 42

More shots rang out from the trees as Creighton held his position hunkered down behind the dying limbs of a fallen pine with his forty-five caliber Benelli R1 at his side. From there he could see his men working their way to where the fires burned, stalking those who had taken down one of their own.

Laski scuttled from tree to tree with Bushmaster Carbon 15 gripped in both hands, making his way back toward Creighton's position. "They got Miller — he's dead!"

"Good Lord." Creighton crossed himself.

"Great man — damn shame!" Laski pressed his back against a wide tree for protection. "But the men picked off a couple Indians and took down a Guard."

"Guard?" Creighton questioned. "So, the military's already moving in?"

"Just as you predicted," Laski shouted over more distant gunfire. "But you've got to go, Rod. They'll expect you at the compound for that meeting, and you've got to be there if we want things to progress as planned."

Creighton shook his head. "No, I can't just leave the men here."

"You have to, and they'll understand why." Laski shouldered his rifle. "The mission's too important."

Pushing aside a dead limb, Creighton surveyed the field until he spotted one of his men aiming his rifle and firing, taking down another tribesman. "I think we've accomplished enough here," he told Laski. "If I leave you in charge, can I count on you to pull the men back before reinforcements arrive?"

"You *know* you can."

"Yes, I suppose I do." Creighton nodded. "Don't bring the men to the compound, though. When you leave here, I want all of you to head right for the final rendezvous point – get the men started sealing off the perimeter so we're ahead of the game."

"I'll do that… and then I'll take off for my final mission."

More gunfire echoed across the field as Creighton laid eyes on his loyal comrade. "It'll be rough, but if anyone can pull it off, I know it's you."

"Well, guess we won't know that until I try," Laski replied with a smirk before dashing from the tree to advance on his men.

"Good luck, my friend!" Creighton ran the opposite way heading back toward the tree farm where he'd left his car, yelling back an added, "Godspeed!"

Chapter 43

Sirens screamed from all around Penne, rousing her to consciousness. With one cheek pressed against the cool grass, she reached to the other side of her head, groaning in agony as she touched where her hair was matted with clotting, warm blood. Sensing the scorching heat against her backside, she carefully rolled to her back, the cool earth relieving the burning sensation as the intense heat from the raging house fire now radiated against her throbbing head and along her side.

A woman's voice shouted over the sirens. "Penne? Penne..."

Blinking her eyes open, Penne squinted at what sunlight cut through the smoke from where the sun hovered just above the burning trees. "What is..." she muttered through parched lips, stopping as pain seared through the right side of her head.

"Are you shot?" the woman asked as she pressed at the side of Penne's head.

"Aahhh!" Penne screeched, writhing in agony.

"Sorry — just need to see what happened," the woman said. "Maybe a graze, or did somebody hit you?"

Penne squinted at the woman, blinking her eyes until the figure in uniform came into focus. "You're... Holly..." she muttered.

"Yeah, and I think you're going to be all right," Holly replied, turning to yell at someone next to her. "Get that body moved before the media sees it."

"Media?" Penne murmured, unsure if that meant her or someone else. "But I'm not..." Her words trailed off.

"Just hang in there," Holly encouraged her. "I just need to get you away from here, but the gurneys and stretchers all went to the field."

"Where's... Bridger?" Penne asked, straining to recall what had happened.

"I don't know – figured you would."

"No... I was..." She squeezed her eyes shut. "Help me... up."

"I'm not sure that's a good idea," Holly advised her.

Penne pushed against the grass with her elbows, forcing herself upward. "I need to see..." She hissed, reaching for her head.

"Okay, just let me help you," Holly offered, lifting her from the shoulders until she sat upright.

Penne looked over to where a fire truck was dousing the farmhouse in water, taking note of the military transport truck parked right behind it. "The Guard... they're here?"

"Yeah, a few were already scouting the area based on that map Chepi gave us; then it looks like the militia came in here and shot at some unarmed tribe members. They killed at least a couple we know of, and who knows how many more are dead or injured." Holly shook her head. "This put the governor right over the top – she signed an order moving the Guard into a police presence."

"But she can't..." Penne leaned sideways, overcome with a wave of nausea.

"Well, she just did!"

Penne spit out bile flecked with smelt. "Oh, God..." she muttered, wiping her mouth. "That's a mistake! She's playing into... their hands."

"I don't know about that, but I do need to go help with the other injured around here just as soon as we get you moved out of the way."

"Where's my..." Penne muttered, glancing about for her missing gun.

"If you lost something, we'll need to look later." Holly stood up. "Right now I need to move you back a little. Maybe I can get a firefighter to help–"

"My grandpa!" a young man yelled, dashing toward them. "They got him out, didn't they, lady? Where is he?"

Penne studied him. "He was... shot."

"Shot!" He pulled at his hair. "What? Where is he?"

"He was..." Penne pressed against her forehead, unable to suppress the pain.

"Hold on, son," Holly said, grabbing the young man by his shoulders. "What's your name?"

"I'm Dylan, and my—"

"Okay, Dylan," Holly continued. "You help me move this lady, and then we'll go find your grandpa." She reached down under Penne's arm. "Get her other arm, Dylan."

Dylan picked up Penne from the other side, both of them lifting as she staggered to her feet.

"You've only got to walk a few yards," Holly told her.

Still feeling woozy, Penne draped her arms over their shoulders, walking forward as she poured her all into repressing the pain. "Bridger moved him," she recollected. "He put Bill in... the car?" Still gimping forward, Penne tried to look back. "Where's the car?"

"Let's put you here," Holly said as she and Dylan guided Penne back to the ground. "Now, what car?"

"A rental..." Penne struggled to remember. "It was blue and, um... a Malibu, I think."

Holly stood up. "Well, I don't see it, so Bridger must've taken Dylan's grandpa to the hospital, don't you think?"

"No. He said... he doesn't drive," Penne insisted.

"Then where are they?" Dylan demanded to know.

Penne pointed back to where Holly had found her. "The car was there when I—"

"Finally!" Neon interrupted Penne's thought, running over to her. "We've been looking all over for you guys!"

Chepi followed. "My God, Penne, are you okay?"

She rubbed at her eyes. "Yeah... something hit me, I guess."

"Is she shot?" Neon asked Holly as he knelt at Penne's side.

"No, but I'm not sure what happened," Holly answered. "Looks like another pistol-whipping like the one that kid got at the shooting."

Penne looked at Neon. "Bridger... he carried Bill and..."

"And you hurled, didn't you?" Neon smirked, tugging his shirtsleeve over his hand and using it the wipe the side of Penne's mouth. "So, we got Takota — twisted his ankle, but he's fine — and you guys got Bill, so he's... where?"

"I'm not sure," Penne stammered, the image of his lifeless body flashing in her mind. "He was in the car and..."

"...and what?" Neon asked, looking back to where the Malibu had been. "Where's BK?"

"I... I don't know!" She raised her hand to her mouth. "I'm telling you, I don't know where he is!"

"What?" Neon brought his face close to hers, gazing at her with wild eyes. "Where is he, Penne?"

"I... I told him to drive, and he said he couldn't"

"He doesn't drive!" Neon snapped.

"Where'd he go?" Dylan yelled at them all. "Where is my grandpa?"

Penne closed her eyes, forcing herself back to that moment. "He was on the driver's side, and I ran around to the other side and I saw... Naomi Drummond, shot dead."

Chepi gasped. "No!"

Holly nodded. "My men already moved the body."

"Then I saw a shadow, and I turned..." Penne recalled her gun in hand but now realized she hadn't turned quickly enough. "Somebody hit me and... they must've taken Bridger."

Neon shot up, turning to Chepi. "I need your car!"

"Then I'm going with you," she insisted, drawing her keys from her pocket and tossing them to Neon.

Holly threw up her hands. "What makes you think somebody took Bridger?"

"Long story," Neon answered, backing away.

Penne rolled onto her knees, pushing herself through the pain. "I'm going with you."

"No you're not!" Neon turned, heading for the road.

"*Please*, take me with you!" Penne pleaded, struggling to lift one foot. "This is my fault... and you know how that feels."

Neon stopped, glaring back at her.

"I'll help you." Chepi took hold of Penne's arm, helping her to her feet.

"Is anyone going to help me?" Dylan questioned, his eyes filled with tears.

"I've got you, Dylan." Holly wrapped her arm around his shoulder. "We'll make some calls and figure out where they've taken your grandpa."

"And I'll let you know what we find out," Neon told Holly and Dylan.

"You do that, Neon," Holly insisted as she turned and walked Dylan toward her police car.

Neon moved to Penne's other side, supporting her free arm. "We're going to have to hurry, you two."

Penne grit her teeth. "I am."

"You're doing great," Chepi encouraged her as they neared the car.

"And all that pain tolerance training you said you had," Neon reminded her as he opened the Vibe's backdoor for her. "You'll need to use it now."

"Got... it!" Penne grimaced as she crawled into the back.

"No hurling in the car," he told her, slamming the door shut.

Chepi climbed into the front seat, looking back at Penne. "I know you've been trying to keep your reporters safe, but now *you're* hurt, so are you sure you're all right to go?"

Penne leaned back, hissing in pain when her head made contact with the head rest. "Doesn't matter – I'm going."

Neon jumped in and revved the car. "You're right, Penne. I know how it feels to blame yourself – it's easy to do." Shifting to drive, he hit the accelerator, sending gravel flying from the road's shoulder. "The hard part is recognizing when you shouldn't blame yourself; it's admitting that sometimes, no matter how hard you try, you can't control everything."

Penne pondered his words as she looked out the side window at the chaotic scene. Despite the best efforts of rescuers, the fires continued to burn and some people lost their lives. Not all were saved, but some were… and some still could be.

"You tried your best to protect him, Penne," Neon added as he drove past the farm, heading for the expressway. "God knows, we both tried." He sniffled, pinching tears from the bridge of his nose.

"So, where are we heading?" Chepi asked.

"We follow the circle," Penne answered from the backseat. "We find Bridger, and we get him back… because I am not done trying."

Chapter 44

With his hands now tied behind his back, Bridger sat on the stool in the horse stable looking around the interior of the vacant barn. He couldn't see much in the only light shed from a single light bulb dangling almost directly over his head, but he had caught a glimpse of a nearby workbench on his way into the barn, noticing it piled with capsules that resembled the one he had seen attached to the dead bat at the Mullett Creek fire.

"Please..." he pleaded. "Just tell me – did you kill Penne?"

Magdala scowled at him with wild eyes. "No! I could not." She knelt by his legs, wrapping a rope around them. "I almost did," she admitted, tying a knot. "But I need her."

"Need her for what?"

Magdala glanced up at him. "To tell..." Tugging at the rope, she tied his legs to the stool. "...we have you."

"So that word gets to my dad; is that it? You think he'll try to save me."

"They say he will."

"They," Bridger wondered aloud. "You mean your Cadre people."

"I am *not* Cadre." Magdala raised her chin, studying him. "I am Phalange."

"Phalange? And what is that?"

"It is Greek – means Battalion," she answered.

Bridger shook his head. "Like the Michigan Battalion?"

"No! Kataeb Party... of Lebanon."

"What?"

"Lebanese Social Democrat?" she said, her head cocked. "We fight invaders – the Jews, the Palestinian Refugees..."

"You're some kind of Lebanese freedom fighter?" Bridger shook his head. "You've got to be kidding! What's that got to do with me?"

"Everything!" Magdala yelled. "Imperials... Americans... You came to fight!" Looking up toward the rafters, she shook her head. "Your money, your weapons... *You* kill my people... my family!" She raised her Glock, leveling it at his eyes.

"Okay, okay!" Bridger shuddered, cringing at the gun. "So, you want payback for American involvement – I get it!"

"We stop it!" she insisted, lowering her gun.

Bridger caught his breath. "Guess I thought American involvement in Lebanon ended a long time ago, but maybe I was wrong."

"Your involvements – it does not end." Magdala tugged at the ropes around his legs. "America fights everywhere." She tied another knot. "You bring war to us... Now, we bring to you."

"Okay..." Bridger tried to gather his nerves. "So, you're with this Phalange group, but why are you working with these Cadre people?"

"We want the same."

"Same, as in what?"

"To stop Imperials."

"You mean, like, destroy us?"

"Maybe!" She smirked. "Weaken, at least... Divide you and conquer!" she suggested, shaking her fists triumphantly.

"So, is that why you started these fires with these bat bomb things? What, are you trying to burn people off their land so you could take over?"

"Burn people off?" she questioned.

"Yeah, with the bat bombs – we know about them."

"Of course, you do... But burn you away?" Crossing her arms, Magdala rubbed her chin. "If only so simple..."

"So, then why the fires?"

"To make you blame," she answered. "Americans do this – blame others, and then fight them."

"And the coppers — we translated them into the Seven Fires Prophecy. Why did you make those?"

"To blame your Indians," she told him. "That was Rami's idea."

"Rami? Who is he?"

"What you call missionary? He missioned for orphans — saved me. We saw war together — saw the killing." Magdala lowered her head. "Rami had to leave, and he brings me. So we are safe... but others? Americans still bring war," she said, looking back at Bridger. "We must stop them."

"So, you and this Rami — you are waging your own war against America?"

"No need." She chuckled. "You will fight yourselves."

"And the fires and coppers were all just supposed to make us blame the Native Americans?"

"And your leaders," she added. "You blame them too."

"Especially the Michigan Battalion — militias don't trust their government."

"My Phalange hated government... They are not loyal... change sides in one minute."

"Sounds just like our government," Bridger replied with a nod, hoping he was building a rapport with his captor. "Yeah, you can count on them to shift like the wind."

Magdala nodded, agreeing.

"Okay, so you're saying the whole idea here is to weaken the United States by turning our people against one another, creating our own kind of civil war."

"That would be good." She smirked.

"Then, uh... why am I here? I mean, what do I... well, and my dad... what do we have to do with this?"

Magdala paused, seeming almost unsure. "Information, I guess."

"But you don't know?"

"I do as told." She nodded.

"Yeah, but you don't strike me as a do-as-your-told kind of girl."

She smiled at him. "Yes... but we scratch backs."

"So, the enemy of your enemy is your friend?"

"Ah... Mark eight-fifteen," she nodded. "Jesus said *Watch out! Beware of yeast from Pharisees and Herod.*

"You quote Jesus, huh? Yeah, I suppose it's never good when your enemies break bread with one another. Are you Christian?"

"Of course... Maronite Catholic, as you say." She drew back. "What do you think?"

"Well, I didn't know," he answered. "I mean, I'm Christian, too, and so... well, I guess I have a hard time imagining a Christian person wanting to hurt people like this – wanting to wage a war like–"

"American Christians!" she yelled. "You are full of killers! You think you are righteous! But you Christians kill us!" She knelt down, pulling her knees to her chest and rocking on her feet, her eyes wide with hate and pain. "You kill... my family!"

"I'm sorry," he said to her. "I know how it feels to lose your family."

"You do not know!" she insisted. "Your father lives!"

"But I didn't know that until yesterday!" Bridger argued. "I lost my parents when I was five! My mom died, and then I thought I was in an accident that killed my dad... but it was the Cadre that took him from me and ruined my life, so they're no better than the people who killed your family!"

"You are wrong!" Stepping behind him, Magdala tied a line to one of his wrists. "He left you." She moved to his right, threading the other end of the line through a large eye bolt screwed into the stall's support beam.

"He had to, because those Cadre people tortured me! He was trying to protect me!" he yelled as he accepted the truth in his own words for the first time.

"Your father had a choice," Magdala insisted as she tied a separate line to his other wrist. "My father, my family... they get no choice!" She moved to the support beam on Bridger's left side, pushing the end of the line through the eye bolt directly juxtaposed to the other.

"What're you doing?" Bridger asked as beads of sweat dripped from his forehead.

"I am preparing." With the end of the line in hand, she stepped back behind Bridger and picked up the end of the other line from the floor.

"For what?" He trembled as he felt her press down on his bindings, jerking them back and forth.

"For your father," she answered

"But he hasn't done anything to you – I haven't done anything to you, so please, just let me go!"

"You have done enough," she said in his ear as she cut away the rope that had bound his hands together.

Despite the lines still tied to each of his wrists, his hands dropped to his sides. "Oh, my God, thank you!" he said as he brought his hands up in front of him, reaching to loosen the line.

"Imperial! Do not thank me!" she yelled as she yanked on the two lines.

Bridger's hands snapped from one another, jerked in opposite directions for as far as his arms could reach. "Ouch!" he yelled at the pain in his yanked shoulders and the burn of the line digging into the skin on his wrists. "What're you doing to me?"

"I told you," she answered, tying off the lines.

"But this... Why the arms like this?"

"Enough talk..."

"No, not enough." He shook in fear of what was about to happen. "I want to know more about what happened in your country, in your past. You know, I'm a reporter and I could do a story about what happened, because people need to know! I didn't know all of this, and I think people should know what happened – how we were involved in whatever terrible things happened to you and your people when–"

"Hold still," Magdala commanded as she grabbed Bridger's shirt by the collar.

"What're you doing?" he yelled, stiffening as he felt her ripping at his shirt, tearing open the backside from top to bottom.

"Now, let me see," she said from behind him as she folded open the shirt.

"What're you looking at? My scar — is that it?" His words flowed quickly. "You see what they did to me? That's why my father left me — that's how they ruined my life! And I don't imagine him coming for me now because he doesn't even know me! So, you might as well let me go, because the only ones coming would be my friends." He thought of Neon and Penne — his only hope. "Yeah, they know about the circle — the medicine wheel thing — so they'll be coming. They'll be looking here for the last fire, and then they'll find me and—"

"Last fire?" she questioned. "No, there is more."

"More? What are you talking about? It's the Seven Fire Prophecy with seven coppers — which the last one would be here."

"No, there are eight."

"Yeah, we know about the eighth, but this would be the eighth fire, completing the circle," he insisted as his stomach churned, the ropes the only thing keeping him from falling off the stool. "This is it, and my friends know it, so they'll be here."

"This is *not* it!" she shouted from behind him. "*We dance round in a ring and suppose, But the Secret sits in the middle and knows.*"

"What? A riddle?" he asked of the familiar stanza. "No, I know that. It's Frost, isn't it?"

"Yes," she answered, pulling his shirt further back to reveal his scar.

"And so, if we've been dancing around the ring when the secret sits in the middle, then that must mean the last fire will be where the lines cross — in the center of the circle."

"Yes."

"Which must be right around Pellston somewhere — I'll have to look at a map to guess better. So, will I... get to do that?" He swallowed hard.

"Maybe," she answered, running her finger across his scar.

He cringed at her touch. "Yeah, uh, I'm a little sensitive about that ugly mark back there — pretty awful what they did to me, don't you think? And I was only five when they did it, so I've kind of suppressed it. Can't remember my folks too well either—"

"I remember," she muttered. "I was twelve... I saw them die."

"Oh, my God... I am so sorry." Suddenly he felt something else against his skin — colder, sharper. "What... what are you doing?"

"I must finish this."

"Finish what?"

"What the fourth began," she answered in a monotone voice.

"What... what do you mean?"

"I must change four." She pressed harder with the cold blade. "For anarchy; it must be made *A*."

Feeling the knife slicing into his skin, Bridger shrieked at the pain searing through his shoulder blade... just as it had so many years ago.

❖

Chapter 45

"Looks like the men are locked and loaded, ready to move," Creighton said with a smile as he climbed down from the passenger's side of J Paul's jacked-up Ford Ranger, striding to the front of the truck. "Thanks for the ride, son — couldn't have gotten here without you."

"Well, thanks for letting me come!" J Paul replied as he came forward from the driver's side. "I wanted to help, and your truck being gone made a good excuse for making Mom let me leave."

"Well, your mother was none too happy about it, but we do need the help of everyone now that we're fully engaged in this battle," Creighton told him as they walked together to the covered entrance on the side of the compound's house-sized poll barn. "She'll be a big asset over at the temporary shelter, and I know I'm going to need your help here." He pulled open the door, holding it for J Paul. "I can always use a good man I can count on."

"Well, that's me, Pastor Rod!" he replied as he stepped through the door onto the cement flooring into the enormous open-space.

Creighton came in behind him, looking with pride at the orderly movement of men in camouflage as they went about their delegated tasks, preparing for the operation that was already in motion. Three bulky men in military-like garb approached him together, extending their hands to Creighton.

The short one with a beer gut spoke first. "Got to hand it to you, Rodney — you saw this coming before the rest of us." He shook Creighton's hand. "Your quick reaction made it possible to get this thing off the ground."

"Only worked with a quick deployment of your people," Creighton responded, releasing the short one's grip to then shake with pallid freckle-faced young man. "And yours, as well."

"Yeah, you probably didn't notice on your way in how well my top team has secured the perimeter of the compound," the freckled man pointed out as they shook hands. "But trust me, even though you can't see them, they do have this place surrounded – they're just very good at what they do." He smirked, nodding. "No arsonists will be getting in here."

"That's good to know." Creighton nodded, moving on to shake with the eldest of the three, a Hispanic man with deep wrinkles and red eyes. "And your men have already moved out, I assume."

"Of course," the eldest answered with a firm shake. "They've been in position for some time now, just waiting for us to give the order." Releasing his grip, he crossed his arms across his barrel chest. "I'm assuming that will come shortly."

"Yes, all is happening even faster than expected, so we'll have them move in shortly. I take it you've all been updated on what happened at that farm over by the Cheboygan Airport."

"Yeah, and we informed our people of the Guards involvement," Freckles replied. "Seems hard to believe those Indians would set fire to land owned by one of their own, but guess they were desperate to get the blame off their backs."

"And then the Guard engaged?" The eldest shook his head "Those men will have nightmares when they think about how they attacked their own citizenry – poor guys are at the mercy of this crazy government gone totalitarian!"

"Hey, those weekend warriors chose their side," Shorty argued. "They didn't have to shoot at our people, and now there are men dead on both sides!"

J Paul looked at Creighton, his expression twisted. "My dad... you said he was okay, right?"

"Of course, yes, he was fine," he answered, turning back to the others. "We pulled back before government reinforcements arrived, so I sent my men on to the final rendezvous so they can assist in taking control of that situation before the authorities can react. But it won't take the governor long to go after our people, especially our families. So, are we in motion with their relocation?"

"As we speak," Shorty replied. "Buses are in position and ready to move out with our families and any other willing participants on board. They're gathering up people from that 6PM town hall meeting, and the trucks there are being loaded up with all the supplies. So, as soon as we take possession of the final site, we'll immediately move those people and supplies in before anyone has a chance to react."

"Good, good," Creighton nodded.

"And will my mom be with them?" J Paul asked.

"Of course!" Creighton patted him on the back. "Why do you think I sent her to the shelter? I'm sure she's already on the bus, and you'll see her and your dad soon enough." He looked back to the men. "And those cards we collected from the people at the church — did you use those to call in more volunteers?"

"My wife ran that operation," Eldest said, his chin high. "She could sell a poor man waterfront in Kansas, so believe me, she saw to it that we brought in as many people as possible."

Creighton chuckled. "I do believe you, thanks."

"Pastor Creighton?" two young men dressed in a mishmash of olive drab and khaki clomped over to Creighton in their hunting boots, each with a shotgun slung over a shoulder. "This man says he knows you — needs to talk to you," one of the men said, pointing to someone behind him.

Creighton saw that it was Dawson Rivard. "The historian, from the church meeting," he said. "Yes, I know him — He's okay, guys."

"All right, then," the other of the two men replied, both of them turning and heading back to their posts.

"Boy, you've got quite the set up here, gentlemen," Rivard said to the group, his eyes wide. "I need to show you something," he insisted as he held up a copper.

"What is it?" Freckles asked.

"It's one of those shields," Creighton recalled. "There was one at our church when they burned it down. It has some significance to Native Americans."

"And to the fires," Rivard added. "There's been one at every fire site so far, including one I took a picture of at the fire over at that Granger fire." He held up his phone, displaying the photo of the copper to the men. "I've been tracking these with this reporter guy from WHAM News named Bridger Klein."

"Yeah, I know that guy from the TV," Freckles said. "I'm not so sure he'd be sympathetic to our cause."

"Well, he's been really helpful to me so far," Rivard replied. "He's sent me information on all of the coppers up through six, and then he helped me get them translated into the Seven Fires Prophecy."

"And what's that?" Shorty asked.

"Really, it's a kind of prediction from the area's indigenous people," Rivard explained. "It outlines a number of periods they will go through until their people return to their origins, living on their land according to their own culture once again."

"That's what they've wanted all along," Eldest insisted. "And our own government's against us, trying to give everything back."

"What do the latest coppers say?" Creighton asked.

"Well, I just worked it out according to a cipher Bridger Klein gave me," he answered, bringing up the translation on his cell phone.

ᐁᐊᐊ ᐀ᑕᒧ ᗞᑕᐦᐃᒃᐸᕐ ᒪᐊᕐ ᑕᐟᑕᐊᐸᑕ ᐊᑕᓇᐊᐟᐊᕐᐊ᐀ᐸ ᕐᕐᐁ ᐃᕐᐱᐊᑫᑕᕐ
VII NEW PEOPLE WILL EMERGE REKINDLING OLD FLAMES

ᐁᐊᐊᐊ ᐂᕐᑕ ᕐᐊᑌᐊᑕᐁ ᐃᐊᐊᑕᑕ ᒪᐊᕐ ᐃᐱᐊᐊᐟ ᐊᑕ ᕐᐊᕐ
VIII THE SACRED FIRE WILL AGAIN BE LIT

"Did you say it's the *Seven* Fires Prophecy?" Freckles asked, pointing at the shield in Rivard's arms. "Because according to your numbers there, that one's number eight, which would mean another fire's in the works."

"Yes," Creighton agreed. "So, if you're holding the eighth copper, then where did you find it?"

"Well, that's the most important point," Rivard told them. "I used a map I received from Bridger Klein to track the next spot... to right here."

"You found that copper thing here?" Shorty questioned.

"Yes... right outside your front gate."

Freckles laughed. "I'm telling you guys, that's not going to happen – not with my men in position."

"Hey, you better check this out," Eldest said, pointing at the three flat-screen televisions on a nearby table, each broadcasting a different cable news network from their satellite feed. "Looks like SNN is first to send out footage of the Granger fire."

"And that's the fire that will make the public most sympathetic to the Native Americans, of course," Creighton complained as he approached the monitors, the rest of the men following.

"Look, there's no fire video on the ONUS network," J Paul pointed out. "How can a channel claim to be all about the US and *not* be covering these fires?"

"ONUS is docile and worthless," Freckles argued.

Shorty picked up the controller to the TV carrying the Satellite News Network, turning up the volume. "Hey, quiet everybody! The Queen of Michigan is about to speak."

The room quieted to a minimal shuffle of paper and feet as more men and a couple of women gathered around the monitor just as the governor's face appeared on all three monitors.

"Good evening, or so I wish it was," Governor Thompson began, rattling her paper in hand. "As all of you across the state and across the entire country must be aware of by now, the citizens living in the northern region of Michigan's lower peninsula have found themselves under assault from a terrorist faction determined to wreak havoc on our peaceful way of life. What began as horrible acts of arson that have so far destroyed hundreds of acres of land and property, has now spiraled into violent uprising involving lethal weapons that have injured and even killed a number of individuals, including the head negotiator for the UTC Ms. Naomi Drummond."

J Paul gasped. "That's the lady they thought I shot at!"

"Now, these deliberate, destructive, and deadly acts of violence must be brought to an immediate halt," the governor continued. "It is for this reason that I have requested more members of the National Guard to be disbursed to assist police forces in various hot zones across the region. In addition, I am calling for all divisions of the Michigan Volunteer Defense Forces to converge in this area to further assist efforts as we pursue the apprehension of any and all individuals involved in these heinous acts."

"The MI-VDF is a fairly new entity, a post-9/11 creation," Creighton pointed out. "They're Troopers wearing Guard uniforms."

"Isn't that like wolves dressed in sheep's clothing?" Shorty laughed.

"In light of these fires and further devastation, I am requesting that Emmet and Cheboygan Counties be declared disaster areas so that federal funds can be made available in assisting our communities. Furthermore, I have spoken directly with President Siudara regarding this matter, and I can assure you that he supports our need to dispatch whatever security forces are deemed necessary in order to protect this region. For those of you who may not be aware of recent changes in the Insurrection Act of 1807, you should know that it provides the President with the ability to deploy troops within the United States as a police force to disperse insurgents obstructing enforcement of the law."

"Another 9/11 reaction?" Shorty asked.

"No, that one's post-Katrina from when local authorities couldn't get their shit together," Freckles answered.

"This would include those individuals who not only think they are above the law, but have somehow come to the deluded conclusion that they *are* the law. I am referring, of course, to those people who have taken up arms with plans to execute their own perception of justice. We are a country of laws, and so these types of vigilante activities will not be tolerated and they will be shut down."

"Yeah, from my cold, dead hands, lady!" Eldest sneered at her.

"We have identified a need for further air support beyond the firefighting jets already in use, and so the MI-VDF will provide three aircraft for transport, plus we will also have the use of two C-21A's out of Battle Creek. This will allow us to move reinforcements into the area and then transport the injured out of the overwhelmed hospitals in the region to where they can receive medical treatment downstate. So, in order to coordinate this effort, we will be closing the Pellston Regional Airport to the public as of eight o'clock this evening, allowing our personnel to convert this into a base of operation from which we plan to reclaim our state and return to the peaceful way of life we have previously enjoyed."

"Reclaim, my ass! Take over is more like it!" Eldest blurted, muting the sound on the television. "I've heard enough."

"Yeah, you were exactly right on the air base!" Freckles said to Creighton.

"Just wish I hadn't been." Creighton sighed. "But apparently the time's arrived, folks. This is when the powers that be try to takeover, and when we push back," he barked to those gathered, the group cheering in reply. "I know you've prepped all day, so this should go smoothly, but stay on top of this as all must be coordinated in order for it to work. So, let's send out the command for those on the perimeter of the Pellston Airport to move in and takeover. In the meantime, let's get those buses rolling with our volunteers and supplies on board so they're at the gate ready to come in as soon as our people have control."

"We've got it covered," Freckles replied, spinning his hand in the air with a loud whistle. "Let's move it out, men!" he yelled to the group, all jumping into motion at his command.

"Wow!" Rivard responded to all that had just transpired. "So, you really think the government's jumping into some sort of police state mode?"

"Of course, they are!" J Paul answered. "Didn't you hear what they're doing — taking over the airport and bringing in more troops. That change in the whole Insurrection Act was the beginning of this, and here comes the next part."

"Which we need to keep you out of, J Paul," Creighton said to him. "You've been in enough trouble today already, and I promised your mom to keep you on the sidelines."

"But I want to help!" he complained.

"Tell you what," Creighton said, turning to Rivard. "Maybe you could go with Rivard here and the two of you could do something really important."

Rivard held to his copper. "I don't think I want to get involved at that airport — sounds kind of crazy."

"Not the airport," Creighton told him. "I need you to go talk with this Bridger Klein that's been helping you. I tried to get him to cover our perspective on this, but I haven't been able to get through to him — maybe you could."

"What do you want me to do?" Rivard asked.

"Just tell him what you've witnessed here — how we see this and what we're trying to accomplish." Creighton pointed at the news monitors. "This is a battle for hearts and minds as much as anything else, and we can only win it if the people begin to see what's going on here."

"I think we can do that," J Paul said. "Are you in, mister?"

It's doctor," Rivard replied. "Dr. Rivard, but if we're working together, I suppose you can call me Dawson." He smirked, reaching out a hand.

J Paul took it, shaking. "Okay, then, let's go!"

"Hey, and if you don't mind, I'd like to send a couple of other guys with you as couriers," Creighton said.

"As long as it's not Mutt and Jeff from the front gate," Rivard replied with a chuckle.

"No, I've got to keep those two on fire duty to keep the arsonists out now that you alerted us to that one, thanks. I'll just get these guys," he said, stepping a few feet from J Paul and Rivard to two men seated at computer screens and leaning between the two of them. "I need you to go with them to the WHAM station to help them get our story on air."

"Yes, sir," they both answered, closing their laptops.

"You better take those National Guard uniforms with you to use later." Creighton told them as he leaned closer, his voice lowered to near a whisper as he handed the men a video CD. "Use force if necessary, but get this story out."

The men nodded, standing up from their seats and heading toward the door.

"I'll drive – I know the way," Rivard insisted, following the men.

"Okay, well, I'll leave you my truck then," J Paul said to Creighton, tossing him the keys.

"I appreciate it, son," he replied, following to see the boy off on his mission with the others as the sun dipped low in the sky. "I appreciate it, more than you could know."

⚜

Chapter 46

Desperate to reach for his open wound, Bridger tugged in vain at the lines that held his arms outstretched. He could still feel the tracks where warm blood had trickled downward, now coagulating in thick globs as the chilly air crept across his vulnerable back.

"Where... where are you?" he asked, answered only by the beating of wings in the rafters overhead. "Is this it? Is this all you wanted to do... was to torture me?" Pausing for an answer, he again only heard fluttering, wondering now if it was the wings of birds or bats.

Outside of the barn, he could hear the sounds of multiple vehicles — doors slamming, engines revving, brakes screeching — all amid distant voices shouting to one another. His yells for help had gone unanswered, probably not heard by anyone over the noise. But he assumed his captor had heard him and chosen to ignore him, just as she had when she had sliced into his back, seemingly indifferent to his pain.

"What's that I smell?" he questioned as he noticed an intensifying scent of gas or kerosene. "Is that the cars leaving... or the bat bombs?" He paused, but she did not answer. "I know there's supposed to be a fire here, so is that next? Are just going to leave me to die in here?"

Hearing no answer, he dropped his head, his mind racing with thoughts of how he had come to be in this situation. It had all happened so fast — the fires and the casino shooting, and then hearing everything about his past... and seeing Silas, shot dead.

"You're the one who killed my uncle, aren't you?" he screamed at her. "You shot him in cold blood, you evil bitch!" He yanked at the lines around his wrists. "I don't care what happened to you! Do you hear me? I don't care about your family if this is what you'll do to mine!" He panted; then biting his lip, his eyes welled with tears.

The past few hours churned in his mind as he remembered the fires where children ran for their lives, men shot and killed one another in the fields, and now this barn – this torture. Events flashed liked snapshots in his mind, the remnants of all that had happened both recently and well into the past now coming to light. His head throbbed with the dizzying recollection of petrified expressions worn by those who had witnessed the horror – of frantic people staring in disbelief at the flames. Suddenly, they were the faces of people he'd known long ago – friends of his parents standing around him, staring at him from behind an old movie camera. And there was Penne, younger and even thinner than now, yelling at the top of her lungs as someone held her back from him. Then a voice whispered so closely to his ear that he could feel the words: *Be brave.*

Bridger screamed away the nightmare, returning to another one in the present as he hung from his bindings. "My father... he let this happen to me before, you know." He looked to the rafters. "He wasn't there the first time they marked me, so he's not going to come now when he doesn't even know me anymore. You see, you killed the one that cared about me – you killed Silas, and that was stupid, because *he* would have come for me." He lowered his head, barely able to say, "He always came for me." With these words, he sobbed, his body heaving as he tried to catch his breath.

Then Bridger thought he heard the slightest movement nearby. "Are you there?" he asked, first thinking it was his captor, but then wondering if it was someone else. "Who is it?" He paused, hearing nothing but the distant sounds of the cars and commotion outside. "Hey, whoever you are; if you're here to help me, I think this is a trap. There's a crazy woman with a gun and a knife in here, so watch out for her!"

Turning his head, Bridger heard the rustling sound again, stirring the winged creatures overhead to flutter about once more. The bright light over his head made it difficult for him to see into the deep recesses of the barn, but for a moment he thought he saw the dark outline of someone moving in the shadows. Straining his eyes to see, he made out what looked to be an older man, gray-haired, wearing a dark jacket. Keeping his eyes on the figure, he saw the man slowly raise a hand, pointing his index finger upward as he raised it to his lips.

Bridger only lipped the words, "Dad?"

Bursting like firecrackers, a dozen or so capsules erupted in the rafters, sparks flying as the smell of smoke began to fill the room.

"Oh, shit!" Bridger blurted. "I smelled fumes in here before!"

More bursts could be heard outside, and then a single bang erupted over everything, blowing the man in the shadows backward to the floor.

"What the..." Bridger seized up as he watched the man convulse in the burgeoning flickers of firelight. "What did you do?"

Crawling from a hidden spot behind the workbench, Magdala emerged in the escalating glow of the room, an over and under shotgun carried in her hands.

"No!" Bridger's chest heaved. "Is that my dad? Did you... oh, my God! He *did* come, and look what you did!"

"Yes." Magdala nodded, stepping over to Bridger as small fires began to burn. "Thank you for help."

⚜

Chapter 47

"**M**y GPS shows some kind of unmarked campground behind the Mill Creek Park complex," Penne said from the backseat, gripping her cell phone in one hand while holding her aching head in the other. "Do you know how to drive back in there?"

"Yeah, I'm pretty sure I know how to access it." Neon kept both hands on the steering wheel of Chepi's car as he raced off the exit ramp. "We use to party back in there as kids until a half-dozen hunters in camo face paint scared us out of there. Seems like a prime spot for some of these militia types to be hanging, so I think you're onto something there."

"So, are you sure we should just drive back in there if it's some kind of private hunting grounds?" Chepi asked. "They sound like they can be overly protective, and they've probably got guns back there."

"Oh, we've got that covered," Neon assured her.

Penne glanced up from her GPS app, alarmed by what he had just said.

"What do you mean?" Chepi asked. "Do you have a gun?"

"The station required him to get a gun... well, a concealed weapon permit, and that was a few years back," Penne told her, trying to regain her wits. "For news reporters, there can be safety concerns."

"Well, I see that now." Chepi nodded. "And how about you, Penne? Do you carry a weapon, too?"

"Uh... well, I did, but I don't now?" she answered.

"Aw, crap!" Neon looked at her in the mirror. "Did you lose your gun back there?"

She glared back at him, gathering her senses enough to be angry at him for blowing her cover. "Yes, I suppose whoever whacked me took it."

"Wow!" Chepi turned to her with a look of surprise. "So, is that typical for news people to carry guns? I mean, did Bridger have one, too?"

"Unfortunately not," Penne answered, leaning back in her seat.

"Come on, Penne," Neon said to her. "You know, if Chepi's going in there with us to look for Bridger, then she really should know what's going on."

Penne tightened her jaw, the tension painfully searing through the side of her head. "Kashkari, I don't think that's such a good—"

"No, I'll handle it," he insisted, turning to Chepi. "You see, Penne is actually a guard with a security firm that the station hired to protect Bridger and me while we work on this story. Isn't that right, Penne?"

She smirked at him. "Yes, if you say so."

"And that's why we figure they've kidnapped Bridger — because he's a reporter and they want to use him to get their story out."

"Kind of like the movies when a bank robber or some criminal gets a reporter to cover the story the way they want it told," Chepi suggested. "Never thought about how dangerous the news business can be."

"Hey, you're not kidding," Neon replied, glancing back at Penne. "So, since you're the security professional, I defer to you on how to approach this. Got any plans in mind."

"Still making this up as we go," she admitted, punching at her cell phone. "I am bringing in some resources from my company, of course."

"Oh, good!" Chepi said. "I was kind of nervous about this, you know, since I don't have any kind of background in security or guns or, well, whatever it is you do. And with my arm still in this sling—"

"I think you best stay in the car while Penne and I check things out," Neon insisted, glancing back at Penne. "And we need to get you another weapon."

"Yeah, I won't be much help without one. Damn it all! I just can't believe I let that jerk get the best of me," she bemoaned, pressing her hand to her head. "I had my gun drawn, but that Drummond woman's body on the ground... it threw me."

"Dear God! That would throw me, too!" Chepi admitted. "I can't believe she's dead."

"Well, she pissed off a lot of people, but she sure didn't deserve that," Neon replied.

"Yeah, and now she's dead, and Silas is dead, and then I lost Bridger..." Penne's voice trailed off

"Hey, he's going to be okay," Neon insisted. "We're going to get him back, and we're going to figure out who's behind all of this so we can put a stop to it."

"I sure hope so, or else all hell's going to break loose."

"Look at that!" Chepi raised her hand, pointing at the dimming sky. "Is that what I think it is?"

"Smoke!" Neon jammed the accelerator. "This has got to be it!"

"Yes, it does," Penne replied. "I just hope we're in time."

⚜

Chapter 48

Fire flashed and crackled from the rafters overhead as Bridger stared at the man, his body going still. "You killed him!" he yelled.

"Only stun gun," Magdala told him as she held up the odd yellow-barreled shotgun for him to see. "I cannot kill him… yet," she added, leveling the shotgun at the man once more.

"Good God, don't shoot him again!"

Magdala ignored him, firing another oversized bullet into the man's chest. "I subdue him."

"Haven't you done enough?" he yelled, watching the man's body writhe about the barn floor.

"No, I must take him," she said lowering the shotgun. "We need him, but you… not so much." She set down the gun and stepped to the side of the stall, retrieving some more rope.

"What?" Bridger's eyes shot around the barn as the fire spread. "You're just going to leave me here!"

"I can carry only one," she replied, approaching the man with the rope.

"Are you kidding?" he yelled. "Just cut me loose and let me go!"

"I cannot," Magdala told him as she knelt at the side of the man's listless body, grabbing his wrists.

Bridger jerked back as he saw the man suddenly shoot up and grab Magdala by the arms, rolling over her and beating her to the ground. They wrestled, Magdala kneeing the man in the groin and tossing him back, her shirtsleeve sparking with fire as she slapped it out. The man lunged at her, slamming her back against the stall railing. She freed an arm, punching him in the face to send him staggering backward. Catching his footing, the man went for Magdala again as she dove for her Glock sitting on another stool in Bridger's stall.

"She's got a gun!" Bridger screamed.

He watched the man reach to his backside and draw a weapon, leveling it at Magdala as she reached hers and turned. With earsplitting bangs from both weapons, the man tumbled backward while Magdala struck the stall's support beam, a dark stain of blood emerging dead center in the fabric of her shirt.

Magdala stared at Bridger with wide eyes, blinking as she slid down the beam to sit at its base. Her lips parted, blood coming from them and dripping from her nose as she said, "Blood has been... harder..." She gasped, licking at the blood. "...to dam back..." she quoted from Frost. Her lips were still moving but no more sound came from them until they went still, all life draining from her body as her eyes transformed to a vacant stare.

"Shit!" Bridger's eyes darted from her to the surrounding fire. "Help!" he screamed. "Get me out of here!"

"I've got you," a voice said to him.

Bridger turned to find the man who had been shot three times now squatting at his side, cutting the ropes from his ankles. "But how did you...?"

"No time for that," he said, standing up and cutting the ropes from his wrists. "We've got to get out of here while we still can."

Freed from his bindings, Bridger negotiated the fiery patches burning throughout the barn, fleeing the building with the man following right behind him. Once outside, they found other buildings and the surrounding trees in flames, and so they jogged down the road away from the fire to an open field lit only by the setting sun.

Catching his breath, Bridger finally laid eyes on the man well enough to study his face, finding it to be all too familiar. "You're... Benedict?"

"Yes," He nodded, unzipping his leather jacket as he stepped to Bridger's backside where his shirt flapped open, lifting one

side to reveal the new cuts. "Dear God... I'm *so* sorry about..."
His quavering voice trailed off.

"That crazy girl said she'd make it an *A*, for anarchy."

"Yeah, now they like to think themselves anarchists, I suppose," Benedict told him while slipping off his coat. "I... I don't
want to hurt you, but I think it'd be best to cover that cut until
we can get it looked at." He held up his jacket toward Bridger.
"How about you put this on?" Lowering it, Benedict guided it
over Bridger's arms.

"Thanks." Bridger hissed at the pain as he slid into the
jacket. "I just... I don't know how you're still alive!" He studied
Benedict, noticing a deep scar across his neck. "Are you hurt,
too?"

Benedict scratched at his neck. "No, this is just an old
wound, like yours." He grimaced. "God, I'm so sorry I..."

"But she shot you!" Bridger recalled.

"Yeah," he said, unbuttoning the collar of his chamois shirt
to reveal a bullet-proof vest. "I wear one of these in my line of
work."

"So, the bullet hit you there... and the stun gun?"

"Same thing..." Benedict reached for the front of the leather
jacket Bridger was now wearing, plucking off a pronged capsule
that was shaped slightly smaller than a wine cork. "The XI2
Taser gives a wireless shock, but it hit my vest... so I faked it."
He tossed the bullet aside.

"So, you're okay then?" he asked, meaning it more broadly.
"And you're... alive."

Benedict sniffled, rubbing his nose. "Yeah, I'm right here,
Bridger. I always have been... and I'm sure you hate me for it."

"No... no, I don't." Bridger's voice wavered. "I'm glad you're
all right." Raising his arms, he refused to give in to the pain as
he reached for his father's shoulders.

Benedict returned a gentle embrace to his injured son. "I've
tried to keep you out of this, but now you've been dragged right
into the middle and..." He placed his palm against the leather
where it covered his wound. "They've done this to you again!"

His voice raised as his chest heaved, unable to suppress his tears. "I swore they wouldn't hurt you again, and then this!" Pushing back, he grasped Bridger's arms. "But I'm going to take care of you now, and I'm going to stop these zealots if it's the last thing I do."

"I want to help... Dad." Bridger nodded.

Benedict smiled, wiping his tears. "First, we need to—"

Bridger cringed at the sound of nearby gunfire.

Benedict sheltered him, grabbing his son's arm and pulling him toward a stand of trees that had not caught fire. "First, we need to get you out of here — this battle's far from over."

"Who's shooting now?" Bridger asked.

"Must be the militia thinks they've found whoever started the fires — little do they know that their real arsonist's gone."

Bridger glanced at the barn where they had nearly died, the building now fully engulfed in flames that would take with it the body of the woman who had started it all. "But the fires aren't done," Bridger said, recalling Magdala's words. "She said the secret sits in the middle — meaning the last fire, I think."

"What?" Benedict questioned his son. "She told you there'd be another attack?"

"Yeah, come on!" Undeterred by more cracks of guns firing and braving his way past the fires, Bridger started to jog, motioning for his father to follow. "And if I got the map right, I'm pretty sure I know where it's all going to go down."

⚜

Chapter 49

"**T**hese crazies are shooting again!" Neon shouted as he parked Chepi's Vibe close to a couple of oversized pine trees near the front entrance to the compound. "Look at those guys!" he pointed, barely making out a couple of men in olive drab ducked down with their rifles in the distant shrubs. "How're we even going to get in there?"

"I see my people," Penne answered, popping the back door.

Neon reached back at her. "Don't go out there! You haven't got a gun!"

"Yeah, but I need to get one!" She grimaced, grabbing at her head as she slid out the door.

"I'm going with her," Neon told Chepi. "You just hunker down in here and you'll be fine."

"Hurry back," she said, sliding down in her seat.

Neon jumped from the car and slammed the door shut, drawing his Colt Defender from his backside as he followed Penne into the trees. "Wait up," he insisted in a muffled tone just as one of the olive drabs pinched off another shot. "Shit! What are they shooting at?"

"Anything that moves near them," a woman said from the shrubs. "Just glad it's not us."

"Seems we didn't get here in time to preclude events," Penne said to the woman as well as the man standing next to her, both dressed in dark wool jackets and caps. "Are we getting on top of this, though?" she asked.

The man nodded. "We've got people moving into position, and a couple of them were already inside, as you well know."

"Then they've got troubles now!" Neon kept his voice low as he gazed at the mounting fire behind the fence. "And so does Bridger if they've got him in there, so we need to move."

"What's your Intel on Klein?" Penne asked the man, holding out her hand.

"Our operative inside is checking to find out," he replied, handing over a Walther P99 to Penne. "You know there was no stopping him."

"Yeah, I figured." Ejecting the clip, she checked the rounds in the P99, then slamming it back in. "So, I need you two to distract our olive drabs long enough for us to get through the gate. Are you game?"

"We'll make a go of it," the woman said as she turned to head deeper into the trees.

"And get the word around that nobody gets out of there with Benedict," Penne added. "We can't let him fall into their hands."

"You've got it," the man answered, sneaking off to follow his female colleague.

"Okay, let's do this," Penne said, tilting her head and stretching her neck.

"You sure you're up to this?" Neon asked, studying her eyes to find her pupils looking dilated in the dwindling daylight. "I think you've got a concussion."

"I'm fine," she quietly insisted, walking through the trees toward the gate. "Best leave Chepi in the car so we don't involve her – better to sneak in on foot."

Neon agreed but remained silent, moving more rapidly and sure-footed through the wooded area as he bypassed Penne, hurrying toward the gate. As more shots were fired, he glanced toward the olive drab defenders, finding they had turned their guns toward the diversion offered by Penne's colleagues. Taking cover behind a stand of cedars, Neon watched a couple of four-wheel-drive vehicles race from the compound, leaving the gate ajar on what continued to burn inside.

Penne made it to his side. "I'll cover you while you go."

"Thanks." He smirked and then made a run for it, trying to keep low as he scurried passed the fenced perimeter and headed down the roadway. With the sound of more shots fired behind him, Neon glanced back only a moment to see he was still in the clear, continuing to jog into the sweltering heat radiating from the ever-increasing fire.

"Hey," a voice yelled from up ahead.

Neon dove to the gravel drive, rolling sideways to the grass where he leveled his Defender at the silhouettes moving toward him.

"Don't shoot us, you idiot!" the familiar voice yelled.

Rising up from the grass, Neon dashed forward toward the two men as they emerged from the blaze that now encroached upon the entire complex. Picking up speed, he could now see the pained look on his best friend's face. Opening his arms wide, he ran to hug him.

"Not too hard – he's hurt!" Benedict yelled at him.

Coming to an abrupt stop, Neon looked upon Bridger, barely able to ask. "What did they do?"

"I'm all right now," Bridger insisted.

Neon struggled to hold back the tears, grabbing Bridger by the arms of the leather jacket. "A new look for you," he chuckled. "Is it Armani?"

"Funny." Bridger patted Neon's cheek. "I'm all right, dude," he repeated, pointing toward Benedict. "I've found my dad, and now I'm going to be fine."

Neon turned to set eyes on the man next to him, finding him to be a wrinkled, gray-haired image of his friend with a face that looked more than familiar. "Have we met?"

More shots fired, sending all three men diving to the grass.

"No time for the niceties," Benedict answered. "We've still got to get out of here."

"Yeah, I'll say!" Neon brushed himself off as he stood back up next to Benedict. "But for what it's worth, big guy, welcome to the family!"

⚜

Chapter 50

Not far down the driveway to the Michilimackinac Compound, Holly encountered a sergeant and private with the Guard who had barricaded the road. Driving her police SUV off the shoulder, she added a quick blare of her siren to the red light already spinning of her rooftop, expecting the men to let her pass. But to her surprise, the private positioned himself squarely between the front headlights of her Cherokee while the sergeant stepped to the driver's side, motioning for her to roll down her window.

Doing so, she leaned out, staring into the flashlight the sergeant pointed in her face. "You need to let me pass, gentlemen."

"Can't do that, ma'am," sergeant told her. "I'm under strict orders — no one in but Guard responders at this time."

"Are you kidding me?" she scoffed, grabbing her badge on her jacket and lifting it for him to see. "This is your strict order to let me in right now or I'll place you and your buddy there both under arrest!"

"No ma'am, I'm sorry, but your orders must be the same as mine, handed down from the governor herself."

"Really..." Holly grabbed her radio mike from its cradle and depressed the side button. "This is Detective Ward calling for you to inform the Lieutenant that the Guard's denying me access to the Michilimackinac fire zone under some misguided supposition that those are the orders of the governor, over." She released the button, looking forward through the windshield at two women in Guard uniforms guiding two handcuffed men in olive drab toward a military transport truck. "And what are you doing with those people?" she asked.

"They're detainees headed to the detention facility we're establishing at the airport," the sergeant answered.

The car's radio crackled. "Detective Ward, your message will be passed to the Lieutenant when he's available shortly, but our orders in hand are to allow the Guard to handle the situation at the militia compound and to redirect our efforts to investigating the previous fires, over."

"Ten four, over," she answered into the mike, returning it to its cradle.

"Sorry ma'am, but just following orders," the sergeant said. "The governor's directed us to contain the situation before it burns out of control."

"Seems like we're well past that." Holly stared through her windshield at the flames raging just beyond the trees, watching the military fire trucks still setting up to battle the fire. "I'm going to have a SWAT unit here shortly, but I suppose there's no chance of them getting past you, is there?"

"There's no need, ma'am. All militia exited the interior as the fire started, so the only one's left were on the perimeter... and we've already rounded them up."

"Well, then, who are they?" She asked, pointing at the high-beams glaring in their eyes as a car came from the exterior of the gate and slowed at the barricade.

The private turned and brought up his rifle, directing it toward the oncoming car. "Hey, who's that?"

"You stay put," the sergeant told his comrade as he raised his rifle, too. "I'll check it out."

The car dimmed its brights and turned sideways, revealing the open driver's side window from which Neon shouted. "Hey, we're good guys! Put down the guns!"

"Get out of the car!" the sergeant yelled at them as other Guardsmen approached the car with guns lowered.

"Don't shoot us!" Chepi yelled as they all began to climb out the doors.

"Hey, guy! They're okay!" Holly yelled at the sergeant as she leapt from her vehicle. "I know them — they're media! I can vouch for them."

"Are you sure?" the sergeant shouted back to her, his gun still pointed as the five exited the vehicle. "That's a lot of people and I don't see a camera."

"I've got a camera if you want to see it," Neon offered, reaching back toward the car.

Holly heard the clicking of the rifles. "Hold up, hold up, guys!"

Neon threw his hands in the air. "Or maybe you don't want to..."

"Put your weapons down before somebody gets hurt!" Holly shouted, approaching the five as they piled out of the car. "I told you, I know these people, except..." She paused, noticing Benedict.

"He's my dad," Bridger told her, his hands held up from the waist as he then addressed the Guardsmen. "We're with WHAM, if you want to see a press pass."

"There's no need," Holly insisted, waving off the Guardsmen as they finally began to lower their rifles and return to their duties. "Kashkari, drive the car through — that is, if it's okay with you," she said to sergeant.

"Fine, let him through," he told the private who stepped from the front of Penne's police vehicle long enough to move the barricade.

"Man, I would've been a goner, Holly!" Neon shouted to her as he climbed back into the Vibe and drove it through the opening, then parking by the Cherokee.

A military transport truck followed, driving past where Neon had parked to reveal its open backside where armed Guardsmen held vigil over their handcuffed prisoners.

"And where are they going with those people?" Penne asked as she walked a bit unsteadily toward Holly.

"Word is they're setting up a detention center at the airport for dealing with these militia members. Guess they qualify as home-grown enemy combatants, and the governor wants to deal with them as such. So, no police presence — we're banned from the compound."

"You're kidding! So, they *are* moving the military into policing?" Bridger's jaw dropped. "I cannot believe this is happening!"

"It's good to see you're all right, Klein," Holly said to him. "But sad to see all of this. Geez, I don't even know *what* the governor's thinking, but somebody's going to call her on the carpet for this one."

"Yeah, but it'll be too late if the damage is already done, so we need to get to the airport," Benedict replied, heading for where Neon had parked the car.

"So, Dad's another ambulance chaser?" Holly chuckled at Bridger. "It must run in the family."

"No, it's not like that. He's, uh… well, we think the airport's another target."

"What do you mean?"

"No time to explain it all," Penne said, heading for the car with Chepi. "But you'd be wise to tell the powers that be that, uh…" She scowled, tilting her head.

"You better get your head checked," Holly suggested, recalling the hit she'd taken at the farm fire.

"I'm fine," Penne insisted, continuing toward the car. "But you should expect a grand finale to all of this, probably at that airport — the arsonist said as much."

"The arsonist?" Holly questioned, following them. "Who is he?"

"She," Bridger corrected her as they, too, headed toward their cars. "It's complicated, but I'd describe her as a foreign militant looking to overthrow the government."

"As in starting a revolution… with fires?" Holly shook her head. "And now she's going to start another one?"

Bridger opened the Vibe's backdoor. "She's not going to start anything — she's dead."

"What? You killed her, Klein?" Holly grabbed his car door, holding it open. "You better stay with me so we can talk about whatever happened."

"That's not going to happen," Benedict bristled.

"Leave that problem to the Guard," Penne said as she slid into the opposite side of the backseat, moving Chepi to the middle. "Her body's in there," she added, pointing at where the fire continued to burn up ahead. "Makes it Guard jurisdiction... not much else you can do."

"I'll tell you everything later," Bridger promised as he rolled down his window and closed the car door.

"Or you could tell me now while I drive you wherever you need to go," she replied, persisting.

Benedict leaned back from the front passenger seat, glaring at her. "My son's injured and is heading to the doctor's right now, so he'll have to speak with you later."

Bridger smirked at Holly. "Yeah, but you should still go to the airport and make sure there's no trouble."

"I'm supposed to go follow-up on the other fires," Holly said as she glanced at the nearby flames and smoke, noticing the Guard still struggling with their hoses. "But I'll head to the airport first... and I imagine I'll somehow end up running into all of you there."

"No, not all of us," Benedict insisted.

"Yeah, it's well past my bedtime!" Neon turned over the engine.

Holly noticed Chepi cradling her arm and Penne holding her head. "Looks like the whole backseat could use some help, so make sure they get it, Neon."

"Will do, Detective," he answered, dropping the car into drive and heading back for the highway, gravel flying as they sped off.

Climbing into her own vehicle, Holly paused for one last look at the men and women of the military who now worked in her stead. She believed them to be good people, each and every one of them, but their mission was misguided and she feared what consequences would come of it all. With this in mind, Holly started her engine and turned away from the calamity, shaking her head in disbelief as she muttered to herself, "God help us all."

⚜

Chapter 51

With traffic heavy on the southbound side of Highway 131, Bridger stared impatiently at the taillights of the Ford Windstar ahead of them, watching the red brake lights flash on and off with the constant pauses in the procession. "It's like the guys got his flashers on!" he complained. "Can't you get around him?"

"And then what?" Neon snapped back, weaving across the center line for a glance ahead of the van. "This convoy goes on for a mile!"

"It's best to just stay in the lane and not end up like them," Chepi said as she pointed at two dented cars on the shoulder, their drivers yelling at one another as they passed by them.

"You're sure you can't get around?" Benedict asked as he pressed his face against his side window. "I think there might be a break up ahead."

Neon laughed. "Yeah, I'm sure I can't get around... and you remind me of somebody, big guy."

Bridger leaned forward. "Man, I've never seen traffic like this! Are these people just getting out of Dodge?"

"I'd say so," Penne answered. "Look at that van... piled to the hilt."

Bridger looked in the back window of the Windstar, noticing the bags and clothes pressed against the glass. "Yeah, and it looks like they're taking everything with them."

"I don't blame them," Chepi said. "According to our prophecy, the eighth fire has deadly potential."

"You know, we never saw the eighth copper at the compound, so I don't even know what it says."

"It's considered a prophecy of transformation, and the change it brings is dependent on the path chosen by the light-skinned people," Chepi explained. "If the path of mutual respect and spirituality is chosen, then catastrophe can be avoided and an era of enlightenment will abound. But if the path of materialism is followed, then the selfish will reap what they sow... and the people of the earth will experience much suffering and death."

"Well, that's interesting," Benedict said. "Sounds like a socialist, Marxist, anti-capitalist slogan if I ever heard one — wouldn't you agree, Penne?"

"It's something they'd appreciate," she answered.

"My people aren't socialists or Marxists," Chepi protested. "They just love the earth and don't want it ruined — which is what's happening with all of these fires."

"I'm sorry," Benedict responded. "I didn't mean to offend you or your people. I was just saying that I know some people who might like to hijack that mantra and make it their own."

"People do like to steal good quotes like that," Neon chipped in. "They'll plagiarize your words and twist them for their own use, like what happened to me when my so-called friend stole my line, *There once was a kid from down under.*"

"I didn't steal that — it was *my* line," Bridger complained. "But that reminds me about that crazy lady." He shuddered at the thought but continued. "She quoted from Frost. That's where she got that line, *We dance round in a ring and suppose, But the Secret sits in the middle and knows*; which led her to telling me they planned to strike at the middle of the ring. Then she also quoted the Bible, saying to beware of Herod and the Pharisees break-ing bread — a passage that's the foundation of the idea that the enemy of my enemy is my friend. She said that was why she and Brother Rami paired up with the Cadre — to fight their common enemy: America."

"And who's Brother Rami?" Penne asked.

"She said he's the guy that got her off the streets of Lebanon where she'd been fighting with this Phalange group. He took care of her during the civil war which it sounded like got to the both of them. She was pretty battle scarred..." Bridger paused, unnerved by the memory of her ruthlessness. "…Maybe this Rami guy is, too."

"Okay, so we'll need to be on the lookout for this bad character, as well, Penne," Benedict said to her. "But are you sure you're up to going in with me?"

"Well, you're not going in alone," she answered with a grimace, poking the keys on her cell phone and pressing it to her ear.

"I can go in with you," Neon offered as he braked for the van, cursing under his breath. "Damn traffic's getting slower!"

"Thanks, Neon, but I need you to be Bridger's wingman." Benedict told him.

"Is that what you call it?" Bridger scoffed. "Yeah, I know how this works. Just wish you'd let me go in with you guys."

"That can't happen," Benedict told him. "I need to be able to focus on the situation without worrying about these people coming after you again. And besides, I need you and your pal here to get back to the station and put this story together so people know what's really going on. Can you do that?"

"Of course, we can!" Neon answered. "And we'll put Chepi to work for us, if she's game."

"Yeah, as long as I can maybe get a little shut-eye, too." She adjusted her sling, yawning.

"I still can't get through to Al." Penne lowered her phone from her ear. "All the lines are busy — either the circuits overloaded or it's been taken out by fire."

"Yeah, I couldn't reach Kelli Sue earlier — same thing," Bridger said.

"So, we don't have a doctor lined up for Bridger yet, either?" Benedict asked.

"Afraid not," Penne answered. "And that could be tough to line up anyway with all the demands on the hospitals right now."

"I'm okay for now," Bridger said. "I'll just pound the Motrin and have Kelli Sue clean it up — she's pretty good with first aid and the whole TLC thing."

"Yes, but your... scar," Penne said. "I just... don't want it worse."

Bridger looked across Chepi to Penne, noticing the stress in her expression. "Are you all right?" he asked.

"I'm fine," she insisted. "It's just... I shouldn't have... let this happen, again."

"It's not your fault," Bridger told her. "And I wanted to tell you that, when I was tied up..." He swallowed hard, remembering. "It all came back to me, and I remembered you."

Penne's jaw trembled. "I am... so sorry."

"No, you shouldn't be," he said, speaking somewhat ambiguously in Chepi's presence. "What I remembered was that you tried to help me, and I was glad you were there."

"Thank you," she said, biting her lip.

"And there were others, too, that I knew," he added.

"Yes, there were," Benedict said. "And we'll have to talk about that later, but for right now we need to keep focused on the present and get this situation under control."

As the car slowed, Bridger could see the flash of emergency lights up ahead, the traffic coming to a near standstill. "What's the deal?" he asked.

"I don't think we're going to get much closer," Neon said. "Look, they're detouring traffic around the area."

Benedict looked back at Penne. "He's right, so are you ready to bail?"

"Ready as ever," Penne answered, releasing her seatbelt.

Benedict pointed off to the right. "You're going to drop us on the shoulder up ahead, just before the detour turn, okay?"

"Got it," Neon said, pulling off the road.

"This doesn't look promising, Pen," Benedict said, popping off his belt. "I hope we're not too late."

"So, you're just going to get out here?" Bridger asked. "But you won't have a car or a way to get back to the bureau."

"Lot's full of rentals, Bridger." Benedict told him as he unlocked the car door. "And I know where the office is — passed by there from time to time over the years."

"I have seen you around, haven't I?" Bridger strained to remember.

"You just saw me yesterday at the casino." Turning backward, he grinned at Bridger. "Plowed into me at the foot of the handicapped ramp, in a hurry as usual."

"That's right!" Bridger laughed. "How many times have I. . ."

"Lot's more," Benedict said to him. "And I'll tell you all about it once this crisis is over. Got some catching up to do, I suppose, so I'll be right back." He winked, jumping out of the car.

"I'm right with you," Penne said as she exited a bit slower.

"I hope she's going to be okay," Chepi said to Bridger as she slid over into the vacant seat.

"Yeah, I do, too," Bridger replied, tapping his father's shoulder. "Sure you don't want another set of hands?"

"Nope, we're good," he answered as he opened the door and climbed out. "Let me go do what I do best while you go do what you do best. Just promise me you'll get this story told right."

Bridger nodded.

"Then off with you." Benedict slammed the door and never looked back, heading off toward the airport in the distance.

As Neon pulled away from the shoulder and headed for the detour, Bridger looked out the back window at the two walking away, saying aloud his promise, "I will, Dad."

⚜

Chapter 52

The five old school buses owned and operated by the militia drove along the interior perimeter of the airport, following the fence line past where Creighton stood beside John Paul, both observing the arrival of the many volunteer protestors and the handful of media personnel seated on board. Battalion members guided the buses to park side by side right in front of the airport's hangar; the building standing with its doors wide open to reveal a number of planes and jets parked off to both sides of the interior, leaving a large, vacant area in the middle.

Creighton leaned toward John Paul. "So, we've vacated the compound but lost our perimeter team there in the transitions, poor guys. And I've got to say you did a great job here getting everyone in position — made the operation go smoothly."

"All because of your planning," John Paul replied. "We got those buses and the last of our people in here just soon enough to avoid a police confrontation, and the Guard... well, they're still trying to get their shit together."

"We figured as much." Creighton nodded as he looked west across the open airfield, well above the pink horizon to where a couple of jets soared through the deepening blue sky. "They look like meteors when they're lit up like that," he said, pointing out their exhaust trails so brightly illuminated by the sun that had already set from their view. "I'm sure TSA will clear this airspace once they realize we've taken control." He looked to John Paul. "So, those Homeland Security and Delta Airlines personnel that our men subdued when they came in here... did we unload any of that unwanted baggage?"

"There weren't that many of them — only four total when we got here because a couple were sent home in advance of the planned military takeover," John Paul informed him. "It was a simple take down of a very unsuspecting facility, and so we released all but one gal from the airline — kept her in case we needed any information since she seemed the least likely to give us any trouble."

"Good, because I don't want to worry about anybody on the inside getting some idea about stopping us now that everything's in motion." Creighton smirked.

"Yeah, we won't let that happen."

"No, we won't," Creighton agreed as he looked toward the buses, watching the people unload. "So, now we need to get the media pool separated from the rest of those folks over there. How about you come help me with that?" Creighton started toward the buses.

John Paul followed. "Not a problem."

"Yeah, it's all culminating as intended, and our final stand here is going to show the public the true colors of our government officials," Creighton said as he walked briskly to the back of the buses and weaved his way with John Paul through the meandering crowd. "They're finally going to see the lengths to which our elected representatives will go to hold onto their power — how they're willing to push our fine men and women in uniform to confront the people they're supposed to be here to defend." Emerging from the front of the buses, Creighton stepped into the hangar, looking to John Paul as he pointed toward a nearby Lear jet. "I need you and the men to congregate the protestors over there while I speak to the media."

"Got it." John Paul walked toward the jet, giving a loud whistle and waving his arms at the milling mob. "Hey, folks, I need all the volunteers to step over this way so we can talk to you about the protest we have planned. Media, you need to go over there," he added, pointing toward Creighton.

Sonny Dais emerged from the crowd, scuttling in her high heels toward Creighton. "I'm with the pool," she announced, racing up to him. "What did you need to tell us?"

"Just that you're in for the scoop of a lifetime, ma'am," Creighton answered.

"Really?" she questioned.

"What's up?" Kodak asked as he made his way to her side, his camera gripped firmly in both hands.

"No matter what happens, and no matter what others tell you, you're going to want to keep your cameras on those protestors once they take there positions," Creighton advised him. "I will guarantee you a prize from your peers and the public for your coverage of this event... if you just do what I say."

Kodak smirked, nodding. "So, you know what's going to happen next?"

"Yes, I know what's going to happen next! A lot of really brave people are going to stand against tyranny, and you'll be the one to capture that historical moment," he replied as a couple other media members straggled over to him. "First, I need to speak to the protestors gathered here to fill them in on what's happened and to give them further directions. Then once I'm finished with that, you'll be able to go with them to their staging ground. However, I do want to remind you of what you agreed to when you stepped on that bus – that'll you'll stay away from the perimeter fencing and only leave with the assistance of at least two of our members should you need to. Are we still clear on that?"

"Yeah," Sonny nodded as she twirled her finger in her hair.

The reporter from SNN scowled. "Did your people commandeer this airport from officials?"

"With guns?" a competitor chimed in.

"We did what we had to in an effort to protect the public from this military coup d'état. If you are not comfortable with that, then you do have the right to leave with an escort as I told you before; but remember you won't be allowed to return."

"We're out of here!" The SNN reporter motioned toward her cameraman. "We can't stand by while you do this – we could be considered accomplices."

"Guys, can you come over here?" Creighton flagged over a couple of nearby militiamen. "I need you to escort these reporters back to the main terminal and see them to our men in charge there. They'll make sure they're safely escorted from the premises."

Sonny looked at Creighton with wide eyes. "Are we going to get arrested?"

"Of course not." He shook his head. "You're the press and you're just doing your job, covering a story — you're not responsible for it."

"And you're guaranteeing people's safety? I don't think so!" the SNN reporter retorted as she and her camera walked away with their militia escort.

"You *will* be safe," Creighton tried to assure them. "We have every reason to protect you because we want this story told — so, are the rest of you in?"

Glancing at one another, the remaining media members nodded timidly.

"Good... Now, I need to talk to these folks over here," he told them, turning from the media group and heading over to where John Paul and other militiamen had congregated the volunteer men, women, and children into a semi-circle.

"Here's the bullhorn, Reverend," a woman in camo garb said as she handed him a megaphone.

"Thanks." Depressing the side button, he brought the bullhorn to his mouth. "I want to thank you all for your willingness to come here this evening to protest the military's attempt to takeover our regional airport and regional police force; in essence, an effort to topple our sovereign rights in the name of safety and yet an act that will not make us safe. Quite the contrary, such an occupation will rob us of our security, taking away from us the personal rights we were granted by our creator and guaranteed by our constitution."

"Here, here!" a man cheered, the crowd following with whistles and applause.

"But right at this very moment, these plans are already in motion. More military vehicles are heading here, military planes are being flown in, and more troops are being dispatched to take charge of Northern Michigan." Creighton waved his hand over the crowd. "I can tell you of the people I know who are missing from this gathering – men and women I left to guard private property we own up toward Mackinaw City, and who were taken into custody for doing so. These are everyday citizens like you and me who were taken away in handcuffs for trying to protect their land, and nothing more. They've been taken prisoner because of their affiliation with this group… and not by the police, but by our very own military. They haven't been Mirandized, they haven't been given legal council, and their rights of habeas corpus have been suspended because they are being detained as insurgents… Insurgents!" he yelled into the megaphone. "Can you believe that?"

The crowd rumbled with shouts of outrage and disbelief.

"They've stripped these Americans' of their rights and their freedom, loaded them into military transport vehicles, and sent them off to be held indefinitely in a detention center… or so they thought." He chuckled, nodding. "But they ran into a bit of a kink along the way, because their detention center… is right here," he told the crowd, pointing at the cement beneath his feet. "This hangar is where they planned to keep our fellow citizens, but we didn't allow that to happen… and we won't let it happen – not on our watch!"

"Yeah!" the crowd cheered in agreement.

"When in the course of human events it becomes necessary…" he quoted the Declaration of Independence. "…we *will* stand against tyranny using nonviolent acts of resistance as taught to us by Thoreau and Gandhi and King. We will stop the military from using these grounds for their operations or detentions by simply blocking their entrance to them. Our friends of freedom from all around the state have already helped us with securing the entire perimeter, holding back the Guard from entering by either foot or vehicle. But there still remains one method of entrance that must be impeded, and that is the one overhead."

People in the crowd went quiet, parents looking down at their families as children looked toward the darkening sky.

"Now that may sound daunting to many of you, but it will be much easier than you think," he told them. "It's Civil Disobedience 101, a sit-down strike — the easiest, most effective trick in the book. All you have to do is go out on the tarmac, line up along the lines, bundle up in some warm blankets we'll provide for you, and just sit with your family and friends, enjoying the stars on a clear night."

"On the tarmac?" one person said from the crowd. "You mean sit on the runway?"

"Yes," Creighton nodded. "Thus the phrase, *sit-down strike* — so simple, and so effective."

"Cool!" a teenager said, a younger sibling then punching him.

"But that sounds pretty risky if these planes are on their way here," a woman said above the growing unrest in the crowd. "What will they do if we're in the way?"

"They'll hit us!" another woman said, cuddling her young child.

"Are you kidding?" Creighton replied. "They're not going to hit you! They're human beings, loyal to country, sent on a mission they will refuse to complete if you're in their way. I mean, honestly! Is there anyone here who believes there's a single pilot in the National Guard who's going to attempt to land an airplane if it means crashing into a hundred plus people on the runway?"

The people looked around at one another, no one saying a word.

"You see? That's the beauty of this. They will not land, I tell you! I have seen this done before in foreign countries during times of war, back when I was a missionary during the Lebanese Civil War. You will be safe, and I will sit with you, right in the center of where the two runways cross. So, who's with me?"

"I'm in, dude!" the teenager said, his family also raising their hands.

Surrounding militiamen and women raised their hands, as well, and then more hands went up in the crowd.

"We'll do it," Gus Levering said as he sat in his wheelchair to the side of the crowd, his wife Dixie looking less sure as she stood behind him.

"That seems like enough of you, and hopefully others will join in once they see us in action," Creighton said with a smile. "So, anyone not ready to participate yet needs to head over to the lower level of the terminal over their and wait in the chairs where people normally wait for their flights. The rest of you need to form two lines, one behind John Paul over there and the other with Charlie holding his hand up on the other side," Creighton told the crowd, pointing to the two men as they waved in reply. "Those two men will walk you out on the runways and I need you to sit on the center line or as close to it as you can, if you would please. So, go ahead and I'll be out with you shortly."

As the crowd shifted with people lining up and a handful leaving for the terminal, Creighton withdrew his cell phone from his pocket, punching in Laski's phone number. Pushing the phone to his ear, he listened to it ring, finally dumping him into voicemail when his friend failed to answer.

"I've got plenty of volunteers here, so we're all set on my end," Creighton said into the phone. "Hope everything's coming together for you. I'll expect a call if there's problems – otherwise, good luck," he added, hanging up.

Then looking back at two long rows of people, Creighton grinned as he saw his efforts finally coming to fruition. All the years invested in positioning himself within the militia and the church, and all the additional time spent with Magdala preparing the sites, stocking the supplies, researching the history, plotting the maps, making the coppers... today it would all finally pay off as they dealt the Americans a terrible blow, weakening and dividing a country that had become way too powerful and needed to be brought back in line.

"We're all set here, Reverend Rod," John Paul yelled from the front of his line, nearly a hundred people in his row and the same in Charlie's.

"Then take them out and enjoy the show," he replied as the runway lights suddenly blinked to life, the crowd oohing and aahing at the red lights atop the nearby barricades, blue lights lined the taxi areas, and white lights running along both sides of the runways.

Creighton rang up another number on his cell, pressing the phone to his ear. "Thoreau, it's Rami," he said to the voicemail. "I'm all set here – just waiting for you and Magdala to show." He hung up, looking back at the beautiful site of the lights and the people and the entire plan coming together. He took a deep breath of the cool air, smiling at the thought of sharing this moment with his dear Magdala. She would be so pleased to see this grand moment – the fight they'd brought back to the United States about to be delivered tonight.

Chapter 53

"I let you down again... and I'm so sorry," Penne said to Benedict as they walked across an open field toward the airport parking lot, a light breeze rustling her tufts of blonde hair.

"It's not your fault, Pen," he insisted. "It's them — they won't let it go."

"I know, but I still let Bridger get to me — let him come along on this wild goose chase." She rubbed at her neck, still walking toward the lot where emergency vehicles filled the lot, their lights flashing. "I should have... reined him in."

"But I know how hard that's been with him — that apple didn't fall far from the tree, you know." He laughed, striding along at her side with his hands tucked in his pants pockets. "You've watched over him and kept him safe for a long time — you and... Silas," he added, shaking his head. "I've counted on you two for thirty years — always trusted you to look out for him... and I still do."

Penne kept her eyes down, watching her every step through the thick, matted grass. "Yeah, you counted on me, then and now — and both times, I let you down."

Benedict stopped, staring at her. "No — you are *not* the one who let me down — you didn't betray me, and you didn't betray him, Ms. Pennyworth." He took her chin in his hand, lifting her face to make her look into his eyes. "You've been an ever vigilant guardian. Why else would I call you that?" He smiled.

She grinned back. "Okay, then I get to give you a better name — Benedict has never suited you."

"Yeah, I suppose I shouldn't have let my enemies name me," he replied, starting to hike toward the airport again. "Guess I'll have to let you pick my new alias after this is over — when I have to disappear."

"What?" she stopped. "You're going away... again."

He looked back at her. "Well, I'll have to, I guess — or else Bridger will need a new identity, but he sounded reluctant. So, I'll have to go deep again if I want to keep him safe — and me and my secrets, as well."

Penne continued to walk once more, feeling a sickness in the pit of her stomach that was from much more than a concussion. "I think there's got to be a better way of dealing with this."

"Well, we'll have to see," Benedict said as he raised his arm, pointing at a nearby satellite truck for SNN. "Meantime, we've got to deal with them."

"Oh, no," Penne responded. "They'll be looking for blood. I wonder if we could cut their live feed — that'd hold them back at least a little while."

"Maybe we will, but let's see what else we need to deal with first," he said as they reached the parking lot, walking up to the nearest state trooper. "Yeah, officer, we had a flight out tonight but I heard the military's moving so I wondered if the airport's totally closed off to the public or what?"

"Uh, no, you're not going to be able to go near there now. The military didn't even get in — we've got a hostage situation now."

"What?" Penne gasped, playing it up. "But what happened?"

"Can't say much, Miss," he replied.

"Oh, it must be those awful militia people. So, are they just in the terminal or did they take over the whole field?"

"These people are out there with weapons around the entire perimeter, Miss, so we need you to stay away from the entire area until we get more help here to lock it down from the outside." He tipped his hat. "Sorry about your flight, folks, but I've got to go."

"Thank you, officer," Penne said as she turned away with Benedict, drawing her cell phone from her pocket. "DIG's got to get through to the governor and convince her to back off." She frantically poked at the keys, mixing them up as she tried to type her message. "It's kind of... blurry."

"Let me," Benedict said, taking it from her and quickly typing out a message. "It's going to be hard to get this out since the system's overloaded."

"Well, at least we can try," she replied as she studied the perimeter of the airport. "In the meantime, we've got to try to get in there, but that's not going to be easy."

"Yeah, we won't get in this way," Benedict said, placing his hand on Penne's back and guiding her away from the lot. "Let's go back where we came from and get a closer look at the perimeter before the authorities move in."

"Okay," she agreed, walking back into the field. "I think I saw a possibility back at the—whoa!" Stumbling on a clump of packed down grass, Penne tripped and nearly fell to the ground."

"Hey, let me help you!" Benedict insisted, taking her by the arm. "You shouldn't have come out here." Turning Penne toward him, he brushed the blond tufts from her eyes, gazing at her oversized pupils in the fading light. "What happened to you?" He looked closer, turning her head to see where dry blood flaked from her hair. "Did that bitch whack you?"

"I think so," she answered, grabbing at her head and blinking her eyes."

"God, I didn't know! We need to get you to a doctor."

"No, I'm fine. I'm staying with you. I. . ." She took a deep breath. "I can't lose you!" she cried out, throwing her arms around him.

He embraced her, gently stroking her head. "I can't lose you either, Pennyworth. That's why I want to get you to a doctor."

Catching her breath, she held him back away from her, taking hold of his hands. "No, I'm fine for now, and I've got you to keep an eye on me like I'm going to keep one on you," she said, pointing to her eye. "So, we're going to stay together, and we're going to get in there and take care of this, once and for all."

"That's my girl." He winked at her, brushing at her cheek. "Then let's go find that one weak link and get this party started," he said, taking her by the hand and heading off into the shadows.

⚜

Chapter 54

"For the longest time, this is all I've wanted," Bridger told both Neon and Chepi. "I wanted a big story like this so badly, but now..." He shook his head. "All of this is just a nightmare."

"And it's not over," Chepi added. "From the looks of things, it's just going to get worse."

"Which is why we've got to get this on the air, pronto," Neon said, glancing at the two of them in the rearview mirror. "We've got to get people to just settle down and let calmer heads prevail."

"Yeah, I just hope we're not too late," Bridger commented as he glanced forward to the front passenger window, noticing his father's handprint emerging as the glass fogged up. "And I hope Dad and Penne are careful, too. It'll be good when this is finally over and I'll have time to talk to them — to sort out all of this because... Man! So much has happened."

"Well, you'll get time soon enough." Neon flipped on the defroster, then reaching up to wipe away the fog with his hand. "Your dad and Penne — they know how to take care of—oh crap!" he yelled, swerving as a doe and fawn ran from the trees into the road.

"Hold on!" Bridger yelled as he tumbled toward Chepi, the wheels screeching and the car sliding sideways until it came to a stop in the dirt just short of the ditch.

"They always do that shit at dusk!" Neon accelerated, the wheels chucking gravel as he sped back onto the road.

"Well, keep your eyes peeled, dude!" Bridger sat back up. "We didn't make it through all of this to be wiped out by a couple of deer!" He glanced at Chepi. "Are you okay?"

"I'm fine," she answered, her eyes drooping. "But I'll be better once we get there."

"If you take more happy pills, you'll be out like a light!" He chuckled, then grimacing at the pain radiating from his back. "And maybe you could spot me a couple."

"Can't — I'm all out of them," she told him. "Tried to text my father to bring me more now that it turns out his ankles fine, but he said he's going to the airport — thinks he needs to be available in case anything more is blamed on our people."

"Did you actually talk with him?" Bridger wondered as he glanced down at his Blackberry. "Because I can't get a phone line — wonder how you did."

"No, it was only text — signal must be too weak to make a call."

"Thought so..." Bridger scrolled to a new message. "I just got one from Holly, but it's worthless — says she's too busy and there'll be a presser later, but no time given, so that doesn't help at all. Guess we'll just have to work with the video we've already got of her."

"Yeah, that'll be fine if you just do a voice over," Neon agreed.

"Man, I can't believe K-Sue hasn't texted me — they must be overwhelmed there." Bridger scrolled through his other messages. "I sent a text to Rivard to see if he had anything more, and he texted back asking me who I was. What the hell?" he scoffed. "It's Bridger," he keyed in, sending it. "You know, the guy you've been bugging for the last two days," he added sarcastically. "You'd think he'd have that one down by now."

"What a doofus!" Neon laughed. "Well, I doubt he'd be much help, either, and I think you've got plenty to work with. I'm just not sure what footage you'll want to use of what I took today." Neon reached back between the seats, holding his hand open to Bridger. "Hand me up my camera, would you BK? I'll maybe take a look."

"No, not while you're driving," he answered as he glanced around the back. "And I don't see it back here anyway."

"What?" He glanced back, scowling. "It's got to be back there."

"Eyes forward please," Chepi insisted.

"It's not back here, dude," Bridger told him, leaning forward to look in the front. "You sure it's not on the floor up there?"

"No, I moved it to... oh, crap." He smacked his own head. "It's in the Malibu!"

"Which is back at the compound," Bridger added, slumping back in his seat. "Even if the rental's still there, we'd never get at it now, and we haven't got time to go back there anyway."

"I can't believe it!" Neon beat his palm against the steering wheel.

"Hey, just keep us on the road and don't worry about it," Bridger told him. "We've still got earlier footage to work with and most of what we got today wouldn't work for this anyway. It'll be fine."

"It'll be fine?" Neon stared at him in the rearview mirror. "Now that doesn't sound like you, Captain Intensity! We definitely better have the Doc examine your head," he joked as he turned into the WHAM parking lot.

"Hey, we just need the facts at this point," Bridger said as his phone vibrated and he glanced at it. "More text from doofus," he announced. "He says sorry – he thought maybe someone else was using my phone and wonders where I am. What difference does that make?" he questioned as he texted back that he was minutes from the station. "And just when I thought I could use this guy on the story, he turns out to be clueless."

"Well, Kelli Sue's really the one you should use," Neon replied, parking the car close to the building. "I mean, she's the one who researched the coppers and translated the Cree, so who's the real authority?" Popping his door, he climbed out of the car.

"Good point." Bridger nodded as the phone vibrated. "Now what does he want?" First getting out of the car, he looked at the text. "He just heard I was kidnapped – wants to know if I'm all right... Yeah, obviously!" he said, texting back that he was fine and the arsonist was dead. "Man, I need to ditch this guy."

"Which way do we go?" Chepi asked as she slid out of the car.

"Need a hand?" Neon offered, helping her out and shutting her door. "We use the emergency exit back here," he told her, walking her to the door. "Al doesn't like it, but we do it anyway."

"You got the key?" Bridger asked, following behind them.

Neon pulled it from his pocket, unlocking the door. "At least I didn't lose this." He smiled at Chepi, holding the door for her.

"Thanks," she said, heading in first.

Bridger followed behind her. "I wonder if Kodak's around, too, so he can help us."

"If not, we could call him in," Neon said as he closed the door, locking it behind them. "That is, if he's not out there working it with Sonny."

"Don't remind me," Bridger told him, continuing behind Chepi as they entered the quiet newsroom. "Hey... where is everybody?"

"Honey, I'm home!" Neon shouted, but no one answered. "Uh... this doesn't feel right," he muttered, reaching for the underside of his jacket.

Bridger heard a click and turned around to see what Neon was doing, only to find him frozen in place with a Glock 21 pressed to his head by Rivard. "What are you doing?" Bridger yelled at him, noticing him garbed in a National Guard uniform.

"Ah-ah-ah," Rivard uttered, turning the gun toward him and Chepi.

"No!" Chepi screeched, crouching behind Bridger.

More guns clicked around them, Bridger glancing about as two other men dressed in National Guard uniforms emerged, pointing pistols at the three of them.

"Aren't you Guard?" Neon demanded to know as he held up his hands. "What the hell is going on?"

"Shut up!" a man bearing the stitched name Finland on his uniform yelled at Neon, stepping closer to him. "We're not

Guard… and I'll take that," he added, reaching under the back of Neon's jacket to withdraw his Defender.

"What are you doing? Where'd you put K-Sue and Al?" Bridger demanded to know.

"They're in the studio," Rivard answered, glowering at Bridger. "But the more important question is what are *you* doing here? You're supposed to be with Magdala."

"Magdala? You mean the crazy girl?"

"You might call her that," Rivard nodded. "Did you really kill her?"

"My dad killed her… and I take it you were working with her?"

"She was working for me," he answered. "And she was supposed to take care of you and Benedict, but apparently things didn't work out as planned." Rivard moved closer to Bridger, shoving the Glock in the small of his back. "So, I guess that means we'll need to come up with a new strategy."

⚜

Chapter 55

"**A**re you two all right?" Bridger asked as knelt beside Kelli Sue and Al who were gagged and tied back-to-back on the studio floor.

"Get these off," Neon said as he ripped electrical tape from Kelli Sue's mouth.

"Cut it out!" yelled another man in a Guard uniform, giving Neon a hard kick.

"Oh-my-God-oh-my-God!" Kelli Sue licked at her lips, trembling. "What are they doing? Are you okay, Neon?"

Neon got back up, glaring at the man as he took notice of the name Gomez stitched on his uniform. "Yeah, I'm fine – can't get hurt too bad by a white guy named Gomez."

Bridger ripped the tape off Al's mouth. "Sorry," he told him, yanking at the ropes that held him to Kelli Sue.

"*I'm* the sorry one, son!" Al shook his head. "I couldn't stop the–"

"Shut up!" Gomez yelled, kicking Al in the stomach and shoving Bridger aside.

"God, do you have to keep doing that?" The youngest militiaman dressed in a Guard uniform cringed at the sight of Al spitting up on himself.

"You need to get with the program, son!" Finland barked at the youngest, giving him a rough elbow in the side.

"Okay, enough with this," Rivard told them all. "Those two stay tied up and the girl – tie her up with them."

Bridger tried to shelter Chepi. "You can't tie her up – she's hurt."

"Just watch me." Finland grinned, approaching her.

Bridger kept between her and Finland. "Just sit with your back to them." He told Chepi as he helped her back up to the others. "It's best for the moment."

"Okay." Chepi slid back, her eyes wide.

Finland smirked as he took a rope to Chepi. "Yeah, listen to your boyfriend, girly." He laughed.

"Tie Klein up separate," Rivard said.

Gomez stepped to Bridger with rope in hand. "I got it."

"What do you want? What are they doing, Bridger?" Kelli Sue persisted.

"You'll know soon enough, Blondie," Finland answered, tying Chepi to Kelli Sue.

Then you…" Rivard pointed his Glock at Neon. "I need you to come over here." With a few flicks of his pistol, he motioned for Neon to move toward the station's broadcasting equipment. "Bet you know best how all this stuff works."

Neon stood up, walking toward Rivard. "That stuff? No, man, I haven't got a clue."

"Then figure it out!" Rivard shouted at him, holding up a CD. "I need you to broadcast this."

"Are you kidding?" Neon laughed. "I've got no idea how to do that."

Rivard pointed his pistol at Neon's face. "I told you — figure it out!"

"Just do it, man!" Bridger insisted, hissing and grimacing at the intense pain in his cut up shoulder blade as Gomez yanked his arms back to tie his wrists.

Neon took the disc from Rivard. "Yeah, but I can't just override the network like that. They've already got shows on at this hour and—"

"Where there's a will, there's a way," Rivard said, turning the Glock toward Bridger.

"Okay-okay!" Neon pushed a couple of buttons. "Just turn the gun from him — you're making me too nervous to work."

"You'd rather I point it at you?" Rivard turned the gun back to Neon.

"As a matter of fact, yeah." He pushed a few more buttons.

"Use the emergency broadcast system override," Bridger told him.

"Yeah, that's what I'm trying to do, but I could use an extra pair of hands."

"I bet you could." Rivard smirked.

"I don't mind helping," J Paul said, approaching Neon.

"J Paul, you stay back and let him do it," Rivard told him.

Chepi gasped. "J Paul! He's the one who shot me!"

"What?" Bridger stepped toward him. "You're the guy?"

"No! I swear I didn't do it! Somebody pistol-whipped me and they took the shot!"

"Are you kidding?" Finland laughed. "Shit, if somebody blamed me for shooting that Indian, I'd say hell yeah I did it, even if I didn't!"

Bridger glowered at Finland. "Yeah, and that says a lot about *you* if you'd be so proud for shooting a girl, you stupid army boy!"

"Yeah, and I'd be proud to shoot you, too, asshole!" Finland raised his gun to him.

"Shut up, Klein!" Al yelled.

"Enough men! Back off!" Rivard demanded, then turning back to Neon. "You must've gotten that on by now."

"Yeah, almost there," he answered, sliding the disk into a slot and pushing a couple more buttons. "We'll see how that works."

Rivard glanced up at the silent monitor overhead. "Where's the sound?"

"Right here," Neon said, grabbing a remote and turning up the volume.

The sitcom on the screen disappeared, replaced with an image of Reverend Rod Creighton reading from a script.

"The preacher guy?" Bridger questioned. "He's doing all of this?"

"He's our Battalion's leader," Finland said. "He's a great man."

"If you like ministers that shoot people," Neon muttered.

"Under the guise of emergency management and martial law," Creighton began. "Governor Thompson is moving hundreds of National Guard Troops into our homeland, taking away our civil rights that we are guaranteed under the United States Constitution. And so, as a pre-emptive measure, concerned citizens of the area have taken refuge at the Pellston Regional Airport, initiating a sit-down strike intended to block the military from turning it into a point of operation for coordinating this takeover and for detaining the multiple citizens they've already taken prisoner. For this reason, we're sending you this advisory with suggestions for what you should do during this current state of emergency. If you wish to remain at home, we recommend that you gather with family and friends, stockpile supplies if time permits, lock all doors and windows, and do not allow anyone unknown into your home — especially anyone wearing a uniform. As for those who wish to help and join in the protest, we encourage you to come to the Pellston Airport and approach the fence around the perimeter."

"He's trying to get people there for the final blow," Bridger muttered.

"As brave citizens, do not be deterred by those in uniform pretending to act in your best interest by barring you from the area. You have every right to see what is happening inside, to bear witness to the events that are unfolding — for if you don't, then no one will know of the ways in which the government has betrayed us. Please... come if you can come, be safe if you can be safe, and pray for God to bless the United States of America. Thank you."

"So, you finally figured out the prophecy," Rivard said to Bridger. "It took you long enough."

"That's because it wasn't even in real Cree," Kelli Sue told him.

"It did what it needed to do," Rivard replied.

"Your crazy woman told me about the center of the ring," Bridger said to Rivard. "She quoted a Frost poem."

"She liked to do that," Rivard nodded. "Apparently Rami taught her a lot of Frost poetry at the orphanage."

"You mean..." Bridger cocked his head. "You're not Brother Rami?"

"Me? No, that's Creighton," he answered. "He was a missionary to Lebanon and rescued Magdala from the war there." Rivard shook his head. "And he is *not* going to be happy that your dad killed his protégée."

"She tried to kill us!" Bridger protested.

"Yeah, she does that... and seems to take great pleasure in the process." He smirked. "Like killing your uncle — she almost seemed happy when I asked her to do that."

Bridger's stomach turned as anger raged through him. "You bastard!" he shouted, lunging at him despite his bindings.

"Save it, Klein," Rivard told him as he raised his gun, warding him off. "You'll have plenty of opportunity for further outrage before the evening's over, so let's get going."

"Where're you taking us?" Neon asked.

"I'm not taking you anywhere," he told him. "I'm just taking Klein."

"No your not!" Al shouted, wriggling in his place.

"Will you shut up, fatty?" Gomez punched him, knocking him out.

"Al!" Kelli Sue cried out. "What's wrong with you?" she screamed at Gomez.

Neon lunged at Rivard but never made it, knocked to the floor by Finland. "Can I shoot him now?" he asked Rivard.

"No!" J Paul protested, all eyes turning to him. "We might still need him for another message, right?"

"Then you deal with him," Finland said, giving Neon a swift kick and a shove.

"Tie him up, J Paul," Rivard told him. "Guess you and Sam can hold down the place while we head to the airport."

"Shit, really?" Gomez said.

"Yes, really Sam," Rivard answered. "Now, come on, Klein. Guess we've got to make another date with Dad before things get anymore crazy."

Neon crawled up, struggling to go after Bridger as J Paul tried to tie him up.

"Don't Neon," Bridger told him as he headed for the door. "You've got to stay here – protect the others."

"Listen to your friend or you'll all get killed," J Paul told him as he tied his arms.

Bridger glanced back at all of them, their expressions of terror seared into his mind. "I'll try to be back for news at eleven," he told them with a stiff upper lip.

"I wouldn't be making plans," Rivard said as he pushed his Glock into Bridger, forcing him through the door. "Once I catch up to your dad again, I'll have other plans for you."

Chapter 56

Accompanying the more than two hundred protestors out onto the runways, Sonny Dais took up position just to the side of where the two runways intersected in the center of the open field. Surveying the situation, she found herself amazed and a bit shaken by the blind trust these people placed in those who had directed them to their positions. Most protestors accepted the gift of donated blankets from the militiamen, bundling up and waiting patiently in two long, staggered rows that ran along the runway centerlines to where they crossed perpendicular to one another at the spot where Sonny now stood.

"Can you get a good shot of this from this position?" Sonny asked Kodak who was still setting up his camera.

"I might do better to move back, but then the lightings going to be a big problem," he answered.

"Yeah, I see what you mean," she replied as she looked back at the people and beyond them to where multiple white lights gleamed in the twilight, the airfield resembling the view of city lights twinkling in the foothills. "Well, we'll just have to adjust as we go along," she told Kodak.

"Okay, if I can have your attention over here," a man said at the intersection a short distance from Sonny.

"Get this," she told Kodak.

He started filming. "I do know how to do my job, Sonja," he answered using her real name.

"For those of you I haven't met yet, my name's John Paul," the man said into the bullhorn. "I guess I'm going to be directing you until Pastor Rod gets back out here shortly, so now that we've got you in position, I just want to make sure you all know the plan." He pointed toward the nearby windsock surrounded by brightly lit barricades. "By the way that windsocks flopping, we can tell that the wind's barely blowing, but it's the direction that matters — it determines which way a plane will land and which runway they'll use. Unfortunately, with the way the winds blowing right now, these pilots coming in could attempt to use either runway, so that's why we've got you spread out on both." He motioned with his arms down the rows. "However, if a plane should even think about coming down near the ground, trying to intimidate us, then that's when we'll make our move."

"Out of the way..." one protestor assumed aloud.

"No, *into* their way," John Paul corrected her. "If you're on the runway that the plane is *not* approaching, then we want you to hustle over to the other one where it's acting like it's going to land." John Paul laughed. "Man, people! Can you imagine that pilot — what he's going to be thinking when he sees all you getting in his way? He's going to crap him pants — excuse me ladies," he added. "And then that guy is going to high tail it out of here!"

"Are you... sure?" another protestor asked.

"Am I sure he's just going to go back up and head on out of here?" John Paul replied. "No, if he's some hotshot who's trying to be some hero, then he might buzz you, folks, and you need to pre- pare your younger ones for that reality. Moms, if you think that might be too much for your kids, then we still got room inside for the little ones. But I'd think you'd want them out here sharing in the moment. I know my wife is," he said, pointing down the runway to where Millie stood, waving her arm at him. "And our son's supposed to be here shortly — wouldn't want him to miss this moment for the world! I'd expect that if your kid's like mine, then he'll probably get a big kick out of some big jet buzzing low to the ground — that doesn't happen to often, now does it?"

Some of the children in the crowd laughed and jumped up and down at the thought, their parents nodding at their amusement.

"So, I guess that's about it for now until Pastor gets out here. If you've got more questions, we Battalion members will be out amongst you to answer them. So, thanks for your attention," he ended, handing off the bullhorn to another militiaman.

Kodak turned off the camera. "I've got to tell you, Sonja, this gig's the freakiest one yet today!" he told her, tucking his long hair behind his ear. "I cannot believe these crazies are willing to sit out here on those painted lines, making their kids be human shields. This is going to be pretty amazing stuff!"

"It's not just a story, Cody!" Sonny retorted, her eyes darting about the scene. "Look at this! Some people are acting like this is some afternoon picnic with their kids!" She blinked hard and often, forcing back the tears.

"Hey, are you okay?" Kodak stepped to her side.

"No, I'm not!" she admitted, rubbing at her eyes with her woolen gloves.

"Hey-hey-hey! It's okay!" He put an arm over her shoulder, giving her a hug. "It's been a really long and emotional day, so it's understandable that you'd have a moment here, but you've got to try to keep it together just a little bit longer."

"Yeah, I know, I know." She sniffled, her hands trembling as she tried to straighten her jacket. "I just... needed to catch my breath."

"You know, it's okay for you to be upset by this. You're not just a reporter — you're also a human being. And I think it'd be good for you to tap into some of that emotion while you're talking to people."

"You really think so?" she asked as she headed toward the protestors.

"Absolutely!" He followed her with his camera in hand. "I think it'd play well — just be yourself and it'll be great."

"Okay, I'll try that," she said as she approached a middle-aged woman in a parka who was holding a toddler in her arms. "Hi, ma'am. I'm Sonny Dais from WHAM News — just wondered if I could ask you a couple questions on camera."

"Sure, I guess," the woman answered.

Sonny nodded to Kodak to begin taping, then turning back to the woman. "Could you tell us why you came here tonight and who you brought with you?"

"I came with my daughter and son-in-law and their two kids. This one's their daughter Tracy who's two," she said, hugging the little girl. "My daughter's up ahead of me with her boy Michael who's five," she added, pointing to her daughter and grandson just a few feet past her on the center line. "And my son-in-law's around here somewhere. He's militia, so he's got to move around the crowd to check and make sure we're warm enough and have water or anything else we need."

"So, your son-in-law — is he the reason you came out here?"

"He's the reason I knew about this, but I came because I wanted to." She smiled, bouncing her bundled granddaughter on her hip. "I've got property the governments been after and then one of the fires came real close to our backyard. So, I'm here to take a stand because we're just not going to take this anymore."

"And you brought the kids and grandkids?"

"Of course — it's their country, too, that's at stake here."

"And are you... afraid?"

"Afraid?" The woman nodded. "Yeah, I'm a little afraid, I suppose — you feel kind of vulnerable standing out here. But I've got to tell you, I feel more afraid about not doing anything — about standing by while the government and the military just take over." She glanced at her granddaughter. "I'm afraid for her and her brother, and what'll happen if we don't take a stand."

"I see. Well, thank you," she said as she walked from the woman and headed further along the line.

Kodak followed her. "They're a pretty determined bunch!"

"I'll say," she responded as she walked up to an elderly couple, the man in a wheelchair with his wife seated next to him in a folding chair provided by the militia. "I'm Sonny Dais with WHAM-News — would you mind answering a couple of questions on camera?"

"Oh, my goodness," The woman held her hand to her mouth. "Well, this would be our second interview in as many days, and with the same TV station, to boot! Can you believe that, Gus?"

"I *can* believe it, with all of this craziness going on," Gus replied.

"I'm sorry, have we met?" Sonny extended a hand to the woman.

"Oh, no, I'm Dixie," she said, shaking hands. "My husband and I spoke with Bridger Klein yesterday at that awful scene at the casino — nearly got shot ourselves, I'm telling you!"

"Really?" Sonny replied as she shook hands with Gus, motioning for Kodak to film. "Well, I'm glad you're all right, but I'm surprised you'd dig right into this again, showing up here for this protest after all you've been through."

"That ain't the half of it!" Gus replied. "We've been neck deep in this mess, young lady!"

"Yes, we were also at the Burt Lake Revival Church when it caught on fire!" Dixie added. "Probably would have died there if it hadn't been for a lovely young man that helped us get out."

"Wow! That's amazing! Who saved you?"

"Oh, this nice boy named Dylan who's around here helping out — he's a militiaman, you know," Dixie added as she glanced around for him.

"I'll have to keep an eye out for him so we can talk to the hero," Sonny replied. "But with everything you've been through, you still volunteered for this protest?"

"Well, it wasn't our original plan," Dixie told her. "We just wanted to help people that'd been burned out of their homes, so we showed up at the town hall to help with the donations for the people at the shelter."

Gus nodded. "Yeah, and the next thing you know, they show up with these buses and start loading them with supplies, and then they tell us we should get on board them if we want to be of help."

"Didn't they tell you what you were going to do?" Sonny asked.

"Told us we were going to stop the military from taking over our airport," Gus answered. "They said to dress warm because we'd be outside having a sit-down strike, and the next think you know, here we are. Just wish I'd listened closer to the dress warm part." Rubbing his hands together, he tugged at his blanket, tightening it around his shoulders.

"And so you sit here waiting for the planes, prepared to act as human shields against these military aircraft," Sonny noted. "So, are you afraid?"

"No ma'am!" Gus insisted. "I'm not going to be scared off by these Indians or the government or even the military trying to take my land. I'm staying right here, daring them to hit me!"

"Which they won't," Dixie added, shaking her head. "The government's trying to make the good men and women of the military do something they never signed up to do. They're decent people who enlisted to defend us, not harm us; so they're not going to turn around now and land those planes on top of us, especially with all the innocent women and children out here. No, they just won't do that."

"That's good," Kodak said, shutting off the camera. "Now we better go get your sign off filmed before it gets too dark."

"Okay, let's—Wait!" She gasped as all of the lights on the tarmac suddenly went out. "What happened?"

"It's all right, folks," the militiamen announced over the restless crowd. "It's normal – the lights go out to conserve power and then planes turn them back on when they want to land, so don't worry about them."

"Yeah, don't be scared people," Kodak muttered to Sonny. "You only need to worry if they come back on."

"Which they will," Sonny said, nodding.

"You really think those planes are going to come in here and kill all those people, don't you?"

"Yeah, I do! And you don't?"

"No, I don't!" Kodak insisted. "They're going to get called off long before that happens, Sonny, because that *would* cause an uprising like you have never seen before."

"Yes, it would," Sonny said as she searched the sky for any signs of flight. "That's why I hope I'm wrong... and you're right."

Chapter 57

The camouflage Hummer H3 pulled into the airport parking lot with Bridger bouncing around in the backseat, Finland bringing it to a stop right by two police cars blocking the front entrance. Straightening himself in his seat, Bridger grimaced in pain as he watched an officer approach the vehicle, figuring this might be his one chance to get out of his situation.

"I think I know this guy," Bridger lied about the approaching officer.

"You better pray you don't," Rivard told him as a pleasant grin spread across his face.

"Evening officer," Finland greeted him. "We've got our bad guy in the back that we're supposed to deliver."

"Well, that's not going to happen, sir," the officer told him. "Don't you know the situation here?"

"Yes, we do." Rivard leaned from the passenger side toward the driver's window, lowering himself enough to make his confiscated Guard officer's hat and jacket visible. "We know this militia riff-raff nabbed our airport before we got in there, and we know they're holding one of ours, so we've been sent in to make a switch with this worthless piece of shit." He pointed toward the back seat with his thumb.

"What are you talking about?" The officer scowled.

Finland opened his door and climbed out. "We're just here to follow our orders." He opened the back door and pulled Bridger out by the arm.

"Ouch!" Bridger screeched in pain. "Don't yank me like that!"

"Yeah, now the guy wants coddling," Finland scoffed.

"I don't know anything about this, do you, Carl?" the officer said to his colleague.

Rivard exited his side, coming around to put another hand on Bridger. "Sorry, gentlemen, but you don't know anything about this because this is now the governor's show," he told them as he flashed the Captain's bars on his uniform. "She's calling the shots – including this one."

Carl stepped up to them. "Yeah, she's taking over, I know, but we still didn't hear anything about some prisoner swap, sir."

"That's because there isn't one!" Bridger yelled. "These guys are the bad guys and they kidnapped me!"

Finland laughed. "Shit, now that's a good one!"

"Oh, my God, yeah!" Rivard chimed in. "Guess this guys none to happy about going back in with his buddies now that they know he betrayed them." He slapped Bridger on the back, right where Magdala had cut him. "Time to go, buddy!"

Bridger doubled over in pain, the two men pulling him back up and dragging him toward the door.

"Sir, you can't go in there!" Carl insisted as the three continued past him.

"Sorry Carl, but orders are orders," Rivard told him as they kept going.

"They're not who they say they are!" Bridger dragged his feet, pain searing through his whole body as he hung from his arms, the two men dragging him toward the front doors. "Help... me!" he cried out as he thought he heard the click of weapons behind him.

"You need to stop, sir!" the first officer shouted.

Finland paused. "Really?"

Rivard stopped, too, turning back. "Yeah, really guys? You're going to shoot two Guardsmen." He shook his head. "Look, we're going to be right back with our guy in a minute, and then we'll be out of your way." He turned back, continuing to drag Bridger with Finland's help on the other side.

"No!" Bridger yelled. "Don't let them take me! Don't... let... them!"

"Hey, you need to stop!" the officer shouted, firing a volley into the air.

"Hold your fire! Hold your fire!" Carl yelled. "That's all we need is a shoot-out!"

"Gets me every time," Rivard chuckled, unflinching as he and Finland dragged Bridger the rest of the way through the automatic doors that slid open for them, then closing behind them.

"What are you doing? Good God, you've got to let me go!" Bridger yelled inside the building, heads turning to glare at the scene he was making.

"Too late, so give it up, cry baby," Finland barked at him as he released his arm, slapping him on the back and sending him tumbling toward the base of the enormous fresh water aquarium standing in the center of the room.

"Okay, show's over," Rivard said to the bystanders, then looking to Finland. "Get me some rope to tie him up with and find the Ready Team — get the video equipment they brought with them and bring it to me upstairs in the observation room."

"Got it," Finland said as he dashed off past the black bear and other stuffed wildlife about the pine paneled interior.

"I'd like to..." Bridger muttered defiantly under his breath as he crawled up on his knees.

"Yes, I'm sure you would." Rivard nodded. "Now get up on your feet or I'll drag you onto them... and I'm sure you wouldn't like that."

Bridger stood up, glaring at Rivard. "What do you want from me?"

"I want you to go right up those stairs," he said, pointing at the staircase constructed of knotty pine.

Bridger marched over and climbed the stairs, glancing around the familiar airport fashioned from natural timbers harvested within the region. Turning at the top of the stairs, he made his way past the stuffed mountain lion and wolverine, heading down the hallway past doors marked with large home-land security emblems.

"Keep going," Rivard told him, giving him a shove in the back.

"Hey, help me!" he yelled again, hoping he might here a voice from the other side of the doors, but no one answered.

"They've all gone home for the night," Rivard said from behind him. "Now, go through that door." He gave him an extra push toward the right.

Stepping into a dimly lit room that overlooked the airfield, Bridger took immediate notice of the darkness outside. "Where are the lights?"

"Off for now, so have a seat." Rivard pushed him toward an armed chair with wheels.

Bridger sat down, still looking out the floor-to-ceiling windows. "I can see people out there — a lot of them. What are they doing?"

"They're blocking the runways so the planes can't land."

"What do you mean?" Bridger caught a glimpse of the crowd as the searchlight rotated past them, flipping from white to an aqua blue. "They're just going to sit there to stop them from landing?"

"Looks like it," Rivard answered as he took a seat and wheeled up next to him.

"I heard you made it," Creighton said as he hurried into the room, taking notice of Bridger. "You… what are you doing here? You're supposed to be…"

"Gone? Dead?" Bridger wondered what word he was searching for. "No, things didn't go as planned."

"What's that supposed to mean?" Creighton glared at him, then turning his eyes to Rivard. "How'd he get away… and get here?"

"I caught up to him and brought him here," Rivard answered. "It would seem that Magdala wasn't able to take care of our problem with Benedict."

"That was *your* problem, not mine." Creighton looked back at Bridger. "And she's not one for showing any mercy, so how did you get away?"

"My dad rescued me." Bridger held his chin high. "And he took care of your crazy friend."

Creighton's jaw tightened in a grimace, his eyes wide with rage. "You... killed her?" He lunged at Bridger, grabbing him by the neck and chocking him.

"Cut it out, Rami!" Rivard shouted at him, gripping Creighton's hands and prying them from Bridger's neck. "We still need him!"

Creighton released him, panting. "*You* need him — I don't!"

"No, you need him, too," Rivard argued. "You need him if you want to catch the one who killed her."

Still panting, Creighton slapped his hands against his fore-head. "Dear God! How could you kill her?"

"How could I kill her? Are you kidding?" Bridger snorted in outrage. "She's a freakin' sadist!"

Creighton lunged for him again, but Rivard held him off.

"You're all a bunch of sadists!" Bridger shouted at them.

Creighton's chest heaved. "It's so easy for you, isn't it, Klein? You can't even begin to imagine the life she lived — the horrific nightmare she lived!"

"That doesn't excuse you bringing that nightmare to every-one else!"

"It does if it changes minds! It's about time we make all the war-mongers in America think twice before they go off wag-ing wars in other people's backyards!" Creighton lowered his head, falling back into a chair and rocking. "After all we've been through... God, I can't believe she's gone."

"I'm sorry," Rivard told him. "But don't let her death be in vain, Rami. We've got to press on."

Creighton looked at him with moist eyes. "This is how you Cadre people operate, isn't it? You don't care about anybody — it's just about the cause."

"The cause is all about caring for people," Rivard argued, shaking his head. "We do this for the sake of people — to stop the capitalists from their wars and their greed."

"People don't want this!" Bridger shook his head. "They don't want this chaos you're bringing down on them!

Rivard ignored Bridger, his eyes focused on Creighton. "You didn't do all of this to quit now, Rami. You need to see this through — it's what Magdala would want you to do."

Creighton wiped his eyes. "She would..." His lip trembled.

"They'll be time to grieve later, and I promise you revenge," Rivard added, glaring at Bridger. "But for now, we've got to stay on track, so I need you to go down to that field and keep those people in line. Can you do that?"

Creighton nodded as he stood up, leaning toward Bridger. "I'll deal with you — and your father — later!" Wiping his nose, he turned and stormed out.

Finland passed Creighton as he entered with the video equipment in hand. "Found what you need, and here's your rope, too." He handed a spool of clothes line to Rivard.

"Good job," he replied, pulling some line from the spool. "Pull out the tripod and get that thing set up, will you? We've got to have that ready when the time comes — that film's going to be a great propaganda tool for us."

"It's going to be nothing," Bridger countered as Rivard went about tying him to his chair. "Those pilots won't try to land without lights if you think that's how you're going to do it."

"No, that's not how we're going to try to do it," Rivard said back as he tugged the ropes tightly around him. "We have a better plan — one that will finally turn the people against the capitalist ruling this country."

"Really?" Bridger scoffed. "Well, you're in for a big disappointment because those National Guard pilots are never going to crash into those people."

"But that's the point. I don't have to count on the Guard pilots when we have our own pilot in play — one on his own mission to shake things up, and who's willing to risk his life to do so."

Bridger felt his throat tighten. "Who are you talking about?"

"You'll know soon enough, Klein," Rivard answered. "But for now, let's just say I know of someone who has the will and wherewithal to do what it takes to finally show this country what it's come to."

Chapter 58

Tugging at the rope tied around his wrists, Neon found enough wiggle room to finally slide one of his wrists from the bindings. He had realized they were loose from the moment J Paul tied them, finding himself wondering if the young man had done so intentionally since he sounded so alarmed by all that was happening. But at the moment, Neon was less concerned about why he could untie his wrist and more worried about what he was going to do now that his hands were free.

"Don't know why I was so pumped about staying here with these chumps," Gomez said from where he sat reclining in a computer chair, his hand still wrapped around the Glock that rested in his lap. "Now I wish I'd gone to the airport — been there when the big battle finally goes down, oo-rah!"

"Well, you can still go," J Paul told him as he leaned against the wall. "Take their car and head over there."

"Nah, I said I'd stay here, so I'm staying." Grabbing the remote control, Gomez surfed the channels. "It'd be hard to get in without the Hummer, anyway, so might as well get comfortable and watch it all unfold on the boob-tube."

"Al..." Neon whispered out the side of his mouth. "My hands are loose. Can you distract the morons?"

"Happy to," he muttered back.

"Hey, look at this!" Gomez pointed toward the screen with the remote. "SNN's got a live feed from the fence! At least that network's got its shit together."

"Oh-oh!" Al moaned in pain.

"What's wrong?" Kelli Sue yelled at him.

"What is it?" J Paul added, stepping toward Al.

"My... heart," he stammered. "Feels... like... an elephant..." he choked. "Can't... breath!"

"Oh-my-God, you've got to help him!" Kelli Sue demanded. "Call an ambulance – get him help!"

"Call 911!" Chepi chimed in.

"Yeah, like that's going to happen," Gomez scoffed.

"Al! Al!" Neon knelt by him, keeping his hands behind him. "Hey! Hang in there!"

"Oh, what the hell!" Gomez set down his Glock and tossed the remote aside, swaggering toward Al. "You sure it's not indigestion, fatty?"

"We've got to help him!" J Paul insisted, reaching for Al's bindings.

Gomez booted J Paul away from him. "No we don't – he'll be fine."

"Are you kidding?" Kelli Sue shouted, kicking at Gomez with her foot.

"Hey, cut it out, girly!" he kicked back.

Al gurgled. "Can't... get... air..."

"Oh, for shit sake, take a breath!" Gomez leaned over Al, punching him in the gut.

Neon pounced, knocking Gomez off his feet and shoving him to the floor. Gomez swung and missed, Neon landing a return punch on the side of his jaw. Rolling to his side, Gomez tried to get up, crawling toward his gun; but Neon came at him again, grabbing him by the waist and pile-driving him into the side of equipment console.

"What... the..." Gomez muttered as he tried to sit up.

"Just take a breath," Neon said to him as he leveled one last punch into his face, knocking Gomez unconscious. "That should help."

"Help Al!" Kelli Sue yelled to Neon.

Quickly crossing to Al's side, Neon untied his hands as Al coughed and gasped from the gut-punch.

"Is he going to be okay?" J Paul asked with his Glock still pointed at the group.

"I hope so," Neon answered as he untied Kelli Sue, looking to her. "Help him out there, K."

She reached for Al. "Lie down and we'll get you an ambulance!"

"Can I help?" Chepi asked as Neon untied her, as well.

Al caught enough breath to say, "Just... faked it... I'm fine."

"You scared me!" Kelli Sue yelled at him with a light slap to his shoulder. "Is your stomach okay?"

"It... will be." He nodded back, swallowing hard as he rolled onto his side.

"So, he's okay." J Paul took a deep breath.

"No thanks to your friend there," Neon answered as he got to his feet.

"He's not my friend! I'd never met the guy before today."

"So then, what's it going to be, J Paul?" Neon asked, pointing at the gun.

"Oh," J Paul looked at the Glock in his hand as if he'd forgotten he had it. "Yeah, this is so out of control — it should've never come to this." Lowering the gun, he handed it to Neon. "So, what're you going to do... with us?"

"With you?" Neon took the gun, shaking his head. "Nothing."

"What?" Chepi shuddered with outrage. "He shot me, and he would've shot us!"

"I never would've done that, lady!" J Paul insisted. "I just... I only joined the Battalion because my dad wanted me to. Guess I was just trying to make him... proud of me."

"Proud!" Chepi yelled at him as Neon helped her up. "You make him proud by aiming guns at people? That's sick!" She stepped toward him.

Neon held up his hands, blocking her. "Hey, you don't know him or his life, Chepi, and I believe he didn't shoot you — probably that Magdala girl did, and that's why the courts let him out."

"I swear I didn't do it!" J Paul repeated. "And I sure didn't want all of this to happen, so for now, I'd rather help you than them," he added, motioning toward Gomez on the floor.

"Okay, you're on," Neon replied. "Take the rest of that rope and tie-up your ex-compadre here."

"I'm on it," J Paul told him.

"I can't believe you trust him!" Chepi snapped at Neon.

"Hey, I'll take the help of anybody right now if it means getting Bridger back before they hurt him again... or worse." Neon looked to Al. "Are you really going to be all right if I leave you here with K-Sue?"

"Yes," Al answered, holding his stomach. "I should come... with you."

"No, you'll slow me down, big guy." Neon patted his shoulder then looking to Kelli Sue. "Can you handle this until we can get him a doctor?"

"I'll take care of him and keep trying the phones — maybe get in contact with Penne's friends, too."

"Good idea, K," he winked.

"So, where you headed?" she asked.

"To the airport — I've got to get Bridger back."

"You won't be able to get in there now," J Paul said as he finished tying up the unconscious Gomez. "The militia took the place over, so I bet the cops and Guard won't let you near that place."

"Well, that sucks," Neon scoffed. "So, guess I'll need your help with that, too, J Paul. Maybe you and that uniform can help us out somehow."

"I'll try," he answered. "So, you want this guy left here?"

"I don't want to have to deal with him if he comes to," Kelli Sue told them.

Neon walked over to Gomez, grabbing his limp body under one of his tied-up arms. "Help me out here."

J Paul dropped the rope and grabbed under the other arm, the two lifting and dragging Gomez across the room to a closet. Neon opened the door and the two lowered him into it, Neon giving the legs of Gomez a few extra kicks to shove him the rest of the way in before slamming the door. Then grabbing a folding chair from a sidewall, Neon jammed it under the doorknob so it couldn't be opened.

"That should do it," Neon said as he brushed off his hands. "Now, we've got to go."

"I'm going, too," Chepi insisted as she walked toward the doorway, hugging her injured arm to her chest.

"No, I know you don't want to hang with bad-guy J Paul here, and besides, you should stay here where it's safe," Neon to her.

"I want to help Bridger, too, and besides, my father's supposed to be at that airport. So, if the militia's taken over, I want to make sure he's okay."

Neon shook his head. "I don't have time to argue, so come on." Moving past her, he headed out the studio door. "You can do whatever, but you can't slow me down because I've got a friend in need of saving."

⚜

Chapter 59

"Hey, the runway lights... they're coming back on again," Bridger noticed as he glanced out the bank of windows from where he sat tied to his chair. "Did you do that?"

"No, but it's a little early," Rivard answered as he looked at his watch and then to the sky. "That can't be Laski yet."

"Laski – your pilot," Bridger assumed. "So, he can turn on the runway lights from his plane?"

"That's the beauty of a non-tower airport – the lights are turned on from the cockpit, so the pilot's in total control of his arrival."

"Do you think somebody else is trying to come in?" Finland asked.

"Yeah, I do, but it shouldn't be a problem," Rivard replied. "It's probably a media bird, and they'll keep it back."

"Wishful thinking," Bridger retorted. "Bet it's a military chopper trying to come in here to shut this down."

"They may have deployed choppers by now, but they'll still be too late," Rivard answered him.

"So, if something awful goes down here, then the militia's going to take the rap for your little Cadre Tendency conspiracy." Bridger looked to Finland. "You know, this Rivard guy isn't who he says he is. He's a part of some Marxist fringe group trying to overthrow the United States, so you shouldn't trust him."

"And who ever said I'm militia?" Finland snickered as he pointed his thumb at Bridger, turning to Rivard. "This guy's kind of got us pegged, doesn't he?"

"He's been listening to Benedict's girlfriend, Pennyworth," Rivard replied. "I'm sure she's been filling his head with all sorts of nonsense about us."

The term girlfriend surprised Bridger, but he said nothing of it as he glared at Rivard. "Nonsense, huh? Then clear it up for me — just who in the hell are you anyway?"

"We're liberators, Bridger, just trying to free the Bolshevists from their capitalist captors."

"Bolshevists?" Bridger scoffed. "You mean Communists."

"He means the majority," Finland corrected him. "That's what the term means in Russian."

"Fine, but I meant you specifically," Bridger said to Rivard. "You're not some historian, and I'm sure your name's not Dawson Rivard..."

Rivard smirked. "We're all set here," he told Finland. "I need you to go out on the tarmac and make sure Creighton holds it together. Can you do that?"

"No problem," he answered as he looked to Bridger. "Then you and I... we'll catch up later," he added with a grin, grabbing the spool of rope and leaving.

Bridger glared at Rivard. "So... who are you?"

He glowered back. "They call your father Benedict for a reason — because he had no sense of loyalty and he betrayed the people who trusted him. It's a name he should be ashamed of, and yet he wears it like some badge of courage." Rivard turned his eyes, gazing through the Plexiglas at the people organized on the runways. "They call me Thoreau after the great dissident who refused to give in to the demands of an unjust government, and because I choose to live deliberately — to make a difference."

"You are nothing like Thoreau," Bridger scoffed.

Rivard chuckled. "Thoreau believed in civil disobedience, a method of revolt that gave me the idea for this little demonstration you're about to see."

"His acts of civil disobedience didn't lead to people dying!"

"True, but if they had, do you think they might have changed things?" Rivard stepped to his video camera. "It's not the disobedience that makes the change — it's the violent acts committed against the peaceful demonstrators that make people stand up and take notice." He looked into the camera lens. "These people just standing or sitting out on that tarmac wouldn't alter a damn thing, but wipe them out with a US military jet in a fiery explosion and you'll turn all the hearts and minds you need for a revolution."

"But they'll know it's not a military jet," Bridger insisted. "So there's no sense in killing those people!"

Rivard looked at him. "You're mistaken — it *is* a military jet."

"But that... can't be!"

"Yes, it can, because our man Laski trains pilots at the Air National Guard Base over in Alpena, just a short jet flight from here. So, nobody's going to question his access to the Combat Readiness Training Center where they all know him, and they all trust him."

"But he can't just stroll in there and take a jet without their knowing it."

"Oh, I think he was already set for a training mission tonight — long before this situation arose." Rivard glanced at his watch, then moving the tripod and adjusting the camera's position. "Of course, I'm sure they're on heightened alert, but we have help on the inside. Trust me, our power is far reaching."

Bridger stared at the people amid the glow of the runway lights, shuddering at the thought of what he could now envision happening. "So, once the jet comes low enough, those people aren't going to just stand there and take it."

"By the time they try to get out of the way — especially the elderly and the people with kids — it's going to be too late."

"No, it won't! Once people see his wheels hit the ground, they'll run for it!"

"Ah, but you see, that's not going to happen," Rivard told him as he looked into the camera lens again, letting out a sigh. "Damn. I'm just not high enough to get a good angle on this — have to take this up to the tower bar."

"What's not going to happen?" Bridger asked.

"Like I said before, we have help on the inside — someone who had access to Laski's jet before he let him take it." Rivard grabbed the legs on the tripod, folding them into one another.

"Yes, that Laski's a patriot. He knew the risks and was willing to do the job anyway. We just had to make sure that after all this work we still got the images we needed to sell this to the public."

"You sabotaged his plane, didn't you?" Bridger's mouth gaped open as he shook his head.

Rivard leaned the camera and tripod against the wall, walking over to Bridger. "Laski's landing gear won't deploy properly, but he's a good man and he'll still do what needs to be done... unlike your father who was never loyal to his people or his cause." Grabbing the back of Bridger's chair, he wheeled him up against one of the floor to ceiling windows, pressing his knees against the Plexiglas. "And here's a front row seat just for you — wouldn't want you to miss this."

"Sooner or later the FAA and the Alpena Guard Base are going to know he's headed in here."

"And then what?" Rivard laughed. "They're going to try to move those people with bullhorns and scary stories about how they're going to get killed, but we already prepared them to ignore their voices." Rivard leaned to Bridger's ear. "They're not going to listen to the bad guys," he whispered, then backing away.

Bridger cranked his head, grimacing at the pain in his back as he looked back at Rivard. "Those Guardsmen won't stand by while you do this!"

"Do you really think that our military has had the time or forethought to prepare any kind of contingency plan for shooting down one of its own aircraft?" He picked up the camera and tripod, tucking it under his arm. "By the time they realize they have a problem, it'll be too late — and that plane is going to come skidding in here, blowing up everyone in its path."

"People will run — you'll kill some, but not many."

"Yeah, we thought about that, too," Rivard said as he headed for the door. "So, I made sure our man inside packed the leftovers from our bat bombs in the underside of that jet.

As you should know by now, there's nothing like napalm to get a fire going." Turning off the lights in the room, he left Bridger to stare out the windows, helpless to stop what was soon to come.

Chapter 60

"**W**on't be long before they notice… they're down two guys," Penne rubbed at her neck as she looked down at the couple of men Benedict had knocked unconscious, leaving them sprawled out on the cement floor of the hangar. "If they come to… they'll call the cavalry."

"Then we'll need to shut them up," Benedict told her as he pulled one up and flung him over his shoulder. "What I'd give to send in *our* cavalry to deal with this, but the Cadre will instigate a shootout if those Guardsmen come near the runway." He walked to the open door of a storage room, unloading the unconscious man inside before going back for the other. "We've just got to come up with some way to scare those people back to their buses without it looking like it's the military doing it."

"Don't know how — a bulldozer maybe — that might move them," she joked.

"Hey, that's not a bad idea, Penn!" He told her as he lugged the other man into the closet and shut the door, then jamming a small shovel under the doorknob to lock the two inside. "I saw a snowplow when we broke in here, back behind the two Learjets. Check it out — see if the keys are in it."

"That's your plan?" She asked as she eased her way between the two jets. "If you take that plow… They'll shoot it up."

"Hey, that's what the Kevlar's for," he replied, beating at the chest of his bulletproof vest. "I can take it."

"Your head can't," she said as she staggered to the snowplow, nearly falling over when she yanked the door open. "No keys," she told him, straining to focus her vision enough to recognize the ignition.

"Shoot! Maybe something else will work." Jogging over to a service truck, he tried the door handle. "Locked up…" He pressed his cheek to the window, sheltering his eyes with his hand. "And no keys," he added, elbowing the door. "What about a plane?"

"How's that work?" Penne asked, doubling over and dropping to her knees.

"Penn!" He ran to her, kneeling at her side.

She vomited, wiping her mouth on her sleeve. "Oh, that's attractive."

"You need a doctor — I've got to find somebody to help you."

"We need to stop... these people!" Tilting to her side, she sat down on the cement, catching her breath. "Picked a bad time... for a concussion."

"Okay, so just sit here while I check for keys," Benedict told her, leaving her side to dash about the hangar, checking plane by plane for one that was unlocked with the keys in the ignition.

"Did you find any?" she asked, pressing her hand to her forehead.

"I think so!"

Penne gazed at the blurred image of him opening the door on what appeared to be a single-prop Cessna. "We're taking that?"

"It'll do," he insisted, leaving the plane and jogging to her side. "I'm taking it — you're staying here." He lifted her up in his arms.

"No, you need me," she argued.

"You'll be in the way," Benedict said as he carried her over to a nook in the wall and set her down where she wouldn't be easily seen. "I'll be too worried about protecting you to do what I need to do."

"You're leaving me... again." She wanted to fight him on this but she didn't have the strength. "Please be careful."

"Just worry about yourself while I finish this," Benedict told her as he reached beneath her pant leg and withdrew the Walther P99, placing it between her hands and propping them up on her knees with the barrel pointed outward. "Stay alert until I get someone to help you." He gently kissed her forehead. "I'll be right back."

Her vision still skewed, she squinted to watch the image of him boarding the plane, her head spinning with confusion as she wondered, like always, if she would ever see him again.

Chapter 61

Driving the car up close to the airport fence, Neon left it double-parked as he jumped from the driver's seat and dashed toward the nearest state trooper.

"You can't park there," the trooper told him.

"I'll move it in a minute," Neon answered. "First I need to talk to Detective Ward."

"I don't know where she is and we're too busy here to be tracking her down."

"Well, you need to now – it's urgent."

"Did you find her?" Chepi asked as she walked up with J Paul.

"What is it you want with her?" the trooper asked with a tilt of his head. "Maybe I can help you."

"It's about a friend of hers who's been taken hostage by these people," Neon answered. "Trust me – she's going to want to know about this."

"Did I overhear you say a hostage?" a Guardsman asked. "I'm Captain Nickerson – tell me the situation."

"My friend's been taken hostage by some fringe element of a group involved in this situation," Neon told him, then turning back to the trooper. "Please, make the call to Detective Ward."

"Hold on." Captain Nickerson held his hand up to Neon. "We've got probably well over two-hundred people in there who could all be potential hostages of this Michigan Battalion."

"But it's not the Battalion doing this, sir," J Paul offered. "It's some other group that's infiltrated the Battalion."

"Now that sounds like a lot of horse hooey to me, Bucholz," the Captain said to J Paul, addressing him by the name stitched to the National Guard uniform he was wearing. "Where'd you get an idea like that stuck in your head?"

"I stuck it there, Captain," Neon said, covering for J Paul. "We told Bucholz here about it at the entrance to the airport, so he escorted us to the fence to talk to someone senior."

"I'll get that car out of the way, sir," Bucholz said, dashing back to where the Vibe sat running and driving it off to the back of the lot."

"You need to get us Holly Ward," Chepi insisted to the trooper. "My dad might be stuck in there, too."

"A whole bunch of friends and family members are stuck in there, ma'am, and we're doing everything we can to get them out unharmed," the captain replied. "So, you need to let us get back to that."

"What's that?" Neon asked as all heads turned toward the chopping sound of a helicopter's rotors beating against the air.

"That's not one of ours," the captain said to the trooper. "Is it yours?"

"No, sir!" he answered as his two-way radio crackled with voices asking the same question.

Neon searched for the chopper's lights amid the myriad of blinking stars that filled the midnight blue sky. Looking to where the crescent waxing moon hovered just above the treetops, he finally spotted the helicopter, its familiar SNN logo visible even in the darkness.

"It's a media chopper, for Pete's sake!" Captain Nickerson roared. "What're they doing up there in restricted air space?"

"Don't know sir, but we'll call them down," a nearby sergeant assured him as he depressed the button on his two-way radio, barking orders into it as he strode away.

"Bet they think the first amendment let's them be up there, but I've got news for the news media!" the captain barked. "We're not going to have that kind of a public relations fiasco on my watch, so get those people down from there!"

"Captain, are you dealing with that SNN chopper?" Holly Ward asked as she approached the fence.

"Holly!" Neon moved toward her. "It's Bridger! He's been—"

"Hold up, Kashkari," she told him, still looking to the captain for an answer.

"Yes, it's under control, Detective. Now let us get back to it," he added, turning away from her with his entourage.

"Could've fooled me," she muttered, frowning as she looked to where the helicopter still hovered in the sky. "What is it, Neon?"

"Long story short — we were ambushed at the radio station by some Marxist radicals trying to start a civil war between the military and the militia."

Holly's hands went to her hips. "And they're doing a fine job of it."

"These guys had guns, Holly, and they had Guard uniforms."

"What?"

"They beat the crap out of Al, and then they took Bridger at gunpoint!"

"And you think they brought him here." She nodded. "That's no good."

"So, I need to get in there, Holly! I've got to get to him out of there!"

"Yeah, him and another two hundred plus out on that field!" she said back. "I want to bring SWAT in here and get this over with, but now the governor's shown up to call the shots from her suite at the Holiday Inn across the street!"

"What?" Chepi scowled.

"Shouldn't have said that," Holly said to herself, shaking her head. "Your father's there, too, Chepi — hopefully getting a chance to talk some sense into her."

"He is?" She sighed with a grin. "Thank God he's all right."

"Yeah, at least he is," Holly replied. "But all I can tell you is that this is all wrapped up in politics right now, so I can't be of much help. My hands are tied."

Neon bit his lip, giving her a nod. "I get it."

Holly looked to the sky where the news chopper was finally turning away. "It's all we can do right now to keep the governor from sending the military in there and confronting those citizens, because if that happens and the country sees it, then we'll have civil unrest the likes of which we haven't seen in a long time."

"No doubt," Neon agreed as he took notice of J Paul waving at him from where he'd parked further down the fence line. "If you can't protect people, then they'll try to protect themselves." He started toward J Paul.

"Hey, where're you going?" Chepi asked, following him.

"What're you up to, Neon?" Holly shouted after him.

"I'll let you know if I find him," he yelled back to her.

With her injured hand swinging from her neck, Chepi hustled up to Neon, keeping pace with his stride. "Now what?"

"Like Holly said, she can't protect him," Neon told her. "So, I guess we'll have to protect him ourselves."

❦

Chapter 62

Blocking everything else from his mind, Bridger focused solely on escape as it seemed the only chance for saving himself as well as everyone else. Steeling his mind against the pain across his back, he jerked and tugged against his bindings, searching for some weak point that just wasn't there. His eyes darted about the room in hopes of finding some sharp object, but he found nothing.

"Damn it all!" He panted, kicking at the Plexiglas that reverberated in reply. His eyes darted downward, noticing a sliver of imperfection in the pane where his foot had struck. Straining to focus in the darkness, he leaned closer to find the lights from the runway refracting through a hairline fracture in the window.

"Yes!" Striking out with both feet, he pummeled the window until he broke through, chips the size of ice cubes exploding from the football-shaped hole. Most of the Plexiglas remained in place, now crackled with a multitude of fractures that made it impossible to see through. Still in need of a larger piece, Bridger reached through the hole with his shoe, curling his toes toward him and tapping at the outside of the Plexiglas to push it inward.

"Ouch!" he yelped, the Plexiglas slicing through his sock into the top of his foot. Refusing to give in, he tried again, finally managing to break away a larger chunk of the glass that fell to the floor.

"Now the hard part," he muttered to himself, rocking his chair until it finally tipped over, throwing him onto the scattered pebbles of broken Plexiglas. Despite the biting cuts that ripped through his pants at his skin, he wriggled about until he finally managed to position himself over the shard. Enduring the added agony of his throbbing head and shoulder blade, he twisted and contorted his position in the chair, struggling to pull his tied hands out from between his back and the chair. Finally freeing them to one side, he reached with all his might for the large fragment, oddly gratified to feel it cutting against his fingertips as he realized the shard was now within his reach. Stretching just a bit farther, he tilted the chunk up between his middle and index finger, maneuvering it to where he could grasp it in his other palm.

"Okay..." He took a deep breath, sawing quickly but cautiously as he knew one deep gash could cut a ligament and end his chances. Hacking at the rope, he felt warm blood ooze and smear about his fingers and palms. Sweat trickled from his hairline and dripped down his face, a clammy chill enveloping him as he shuddered in the night air blowing in through the hole in the window. "Come on, come on..." he muttered, egging himself on as he kept whittling away at the line, feeling it give way. "Almost... there..." he gasped, cutting and tugging until the rope finally broke loose.

Sliding his hands free of their bindings, he quickly managed to untangle the rest of the rope holding him to the chair. Then he climbed to his feet, knocking away shards of Plexiglas from his father's leather jacket as he crept in the darkness to the door. Quietly taking hold of the doorknob, he turned it slowly until it clicked, pulling it open just enough to peek out to the hallway.

"He's still up in the tower bar but I'll give him the message," a not too distant voice said.

"And you three keep a lookout for this Benedict guy until he comes back down here," another voice replied.

Bridger carefully shut the door, figuring he would never make it past the three or more men who were likely positioned at the end of the hall. He needed to find a different way out but had to protect himself in the meantime. Glancing at the chairs, he found them all to be on wheels, making them impractical for jamming against the door. He continued to search until he spotted a wedge normally used to prop open a door, taking it and jamming it under the door with a few taps of his heal. Figuring that would slow down Rivard when he returned, he still knew it wouldn't stop him for long.

Keeping the lights off, Bridger staggered back to the windows and looked downward past the first floor and walkout basement to the pavement two-stories below. It was a jump he'd make if he had to but he hoped there still might be another way. Then glancing out to the runway, he made out someone climbing a step ladder near the center where the runways crossed. With the window broken, he could hear the person he thought to be Creighton bellowing into a megaphone, "They're going to try to scare you into leaving, but we're not going anywhere."

Bridger realized that, for the moment, he wasn't going anywhere, either; but he knew he had to find a way to get to those people soon or else they weren't going to survive.

⚜

Chapter 63

"This could get dicey again, Chepi," Neon said as he headed toward where J Paul stood near the airport hangar. "You're dad's safe so you should go to him and stay out of this mess."

"Bridger tried to save me yesterday, so now I want to try to help him," she answered, cradling her injured hand as she strode to keep up with Neon.

"Okay, well, let's see what J Paul can do for us," he replied as he jogged up to the man still dressed in Bucholz's Guard uniform.

"I spotted my friend Dylan and flagged him over," J Paul said. "He's so pissed at these people — says one of them killed his grandpa in his home this afternoon and he wants payback, so he'll help us get in."

"The kid from the Granger farm," Neon assumed.

"He must be Bill Granger's grandson," Chepi added.

"Yeah, he is." J Paul nodded. "So, you know him?"

"We met at the scene, unfortunately," Neon explained. "Kid could be a powder keg, but I'm game if he can get us in. So, where do we go?"

"Come on!" J Paul motioned for them to follow him as he moved along the fence. "He's letting us in through the hangar."

"That could be a challenge with all the Guard around," Neon said as he and Chepi followed him.

"Hey, I'm one of the guys now!" J Paul said, tugging on the shoulder of his uniform. "Just be cool," he quietly added as they neared two National Guards, both of them women who stood facing the fence, staring at the man speaking into a bullhorn on the other side.

"Captain says we're just going to hold for now," one woman said to the other, both of them nodding to J Paul as he passed them by.

He nodded in reply, waving his hand in a circle for us to follow. "Come on, you two."

Neon put his hand to the small of Chepi's back, seeing her past the two at the fence. "Evening," he said, both nodding in reply to him and Chepi, as well.

J Paul made his way to an attached shelter on the side of the hangar, entering it on the front side and stepping to the door. "It's right here." He wrapped three times, paused, and then knocked three times again.

"What've we got here, Private?" a Guardsman asked as he approached.

"Oh, yes... evening there!" J Paul stammered, looking like a deer in headlights.

Neon quickly approached. "Sorry, but the little woman and I were being a bit of a pain to Private Bucholz here," he chuckled, approaching the Guardsman with his hand extended. "Afraid we've had a bit of a family emergency, so we've got to get to our plane in there."

"Sorry, but you can't take your plane up, sir. Everything's grounded."

"Oh, I know, I know!" Neon replied. "We weren't going to fly it, of course! No, we just needed to get some papers out of the—"

Suddenly the door swung open, Dylan sticking his head out to find us all standing there.

The Guardsman's eyes went wide. "What the—"

Neon didn't let him finish, taking a quick swing that caught the man right in the jaw and sent him tumbling to the ground. "Get inside!" Neon told all of them as he dragged the unconscious Guardsman up by the door, propping him upright in the corner of the shelter. "Sorry, dude," he whispered to the man. "I really did have to get in there," he added as he turned around and followed the others through the doorway, locking it from the other side.

"Keep it down!" Dylan whispered, waving his palms downward. "I think someone's in here... Hey!" He pointed at Neon and then Chepi. "You were there... at my grandpa's!"

"Yeah, sorry again, kid." Neon frowned, nodding. "So, where's the person?"

"Over there," he pointed toward a plane across the hangar. "I heard him clicking at stuff in the cockpit, so I stayed over on this side." Dylan looked to J Paul. "They killed Grandpa... I can't believe it!"

J Paul opened his arms and embraced his friend. "God, I can't either." He slapped Dylan's shoulder. "This has all gone so wrong!"

"Okay, keep it together, guys, or things are going to go worse," Neon told them, keeping his voice down. "Now we need to—" He stopped at the sound of a plane's engine revving.

"Is that the militia?" Chepi said just loud enough to be heard over the engine.

"Not sure who's at play here, but we best move on," Neon answered. "That sound's going to get the attention of someone on one side or the other, and we better not be standing here when it does. Where's the best way out?" he asked Dylan.

"Better go this way," he said, crouching behind other planes and jets as he moved toward the opposite side wall.

"You think that pilot's the only one in here," Neon asked as he brought up the rear, keeping watch behind them until the group abruptly stopped. "What the—"

"I'm in here," a familiar woman's voice muttered.

Neon turned and stepped up to Dylan. "Penne!" he quietly exclaimed, rushing to where she sat up against the wall with a gun pointed at them.

She lowered the gun, tilting her head. "Neon?" she squinted, looking bewildered. "But I thought... you were... where's Bridger?"

"Long story, as always," he answered. "You look out of it!"

"I guess I am." She held her head. "Don't have... a hard head like... Bridger, where is he?" she asked again.

"Penne... the Cadre nabbed him again, and I'm betting he's here."

Penne gasped. "You can't tell... him." She pointed toward the Cessna.

"You mean his dad, right?" Neon asked. "Is that who's in the plane?"

"Yes," she answered. "He's going to... move those people."

"He's going to fly at them?" Chepi wondered.

"No, he doesn't have to," Neon said, realizing what he was up to. "He's just going to drive at them — good thinking, big guy!"

Penne rolled to her side, beginning to get up. "And we've got to... get Bridger."

"Oh, no-no! *I'm* going to get him — *you're* staying here so Chepi can keep an eye on you."

"But we can't stay in here, Neon; you said so yourself," Chepi told him. "Someone's going to come poking around in here any minute, so we've got to move... and we'd probably be best off leaving in the custody of these two," she added, pointing at J Paul and Dylan.

Dylan nodded. "Yeah, we're still on the good side with the guys here, so we could walk you out without a whole lot of questions."

"But we better go before that Guard dude you knocked out decides to wake up," J Paul added.

Penne got to her knees. "We'll go to that... terminal over there."

Neon helped her up. "Okay, good plan." He glanced to Dylan and J Paul. "If anyone asks about us, you tell them we were snooping around our plane in the hangar and you're taking us to the terminal for safe keeping."

"Got it!" Dylan replied, leading the way out.

As the Cessna began to taxi toward the large open doorway, Neon ducked down behind a jet to keep out of view. "Don't let Benedict see you, Chepi, or he might know something's up."

She ducked, too, making her way behind a couple of planes as she followed Dylan toward the door.

Neon exited the hangar just as the plane rolled out the large doorway, turning away from where the five now stood and following the row of blue lights along the taxiway. Turning to head the opposite way, Neon lead the group toward the main terminal, the sound of the Cessna diminishing with distance so that they could now here the megaphone blaring from the center of the field.

"This is how they'll test our resolve," Creighton said into the bullhorn, his voice carrying across the field. "They'll try to clear us out of the way, but we're not going to budge — whether they come at us on land or from the air!"

Glancing up toward the sky, Neon glanced about for any sign of an incoming plane. Spotting a blinking star that could be something more, he pointed it out to the others. "It's not Antares. Maybe a satellite… or something closer to home?" he asked.

"I think that's a jet!" J Paul replied. "But even if it's not, you know that sooner or later, they're going to try to fly in here."

"Yeah, that's what I'm afraid of," Neon said as he turned and moved more quickly toward the terminal. "Because once they've done that, then who knows what'll happen to Bridger."

⚜

Chapter 64

"I don't know where that guy thinks he's going!" Creighton chuckled into the megaphone as he stood on the second step of his step ladder, pointing toward the distant Cessna on the taxiway. "Guess he didn't get the memo from the government that they're taking over the airport... and everything else!"

"No, they're not, Pastor!" a man yelled from the crowd, others cheering and clapping in response.

"That's right, they're not!" he replied over the loud speaker, waving his free arm in the glare of the media floodlights pointed toward him. "That whole bunch of big-headed politicians we voted into office forgot who they're working for! We don't answer to them — they answer to us!"

"People on the runway, we need your attention now," a voice blared from a bullhorn in the parking lot just beyond the fence. "There is a rogue aircraft approaching, so you need to clear the runway immediately."

"What?" Creighton scowled, acting surprised as he switched on his megaphone and lifted it back to his mouth. "Can you believe that one? Now they're going to pretend like they have no radio contact with their own jets? Are you kidding me?" he scoffed, bending a bit with a chuckle. "Now *that's* desperation, people! Can you *believe* the lengths to which your own government will go to try to scare you out of their way? Well, I've got news for you, buddy! We're not buying it!" he bellowed toward the fence, the crowd whistling and clapping at his rant.

"Seriously!" the bullhorn voice from the parking lot replied. "We have no contact with that incoming military jet, so you must move immediately!"

"It's a military jet, and they have no contact with it!" Creighton barked back. "Now I've heard everything, folks!"

He looked to the sky, spotting the first clear glimpse of what appeared to be a plane on approach. "That's one of their own jets coming in here, and I have no doubt they've been instructed to give us a show, so sit back on your blankets if you like and enjoy your own little private air show!" he coached them, waving his arms toward the sky. "Hey, buddy! We're over here!"

Creighton looked beyond the glare of the camera lights, spotting the children laughing and giggling as people pointed toward the blinking red light in the sky. For a moment his mind drifted back to the children he'd once known, recalling the brief, frivolous moments when the orphans played without a care in their war torn world. Then in the blink of an eye, another explosion would snap them back to reality, bringing them more orphans... until that one day, when he and Magdala were away, when the bomb struck the orphanage...

"We'll show them, Pastor!" a teenaged boy yelled from the crowd, abruptly returning Creighton to the present.

"Yes, we will... yes, we will," he nodded as he thought of his dear Magdala and all the lost children, his range of view now broadening from the perspective of just the one young man before him to the entire mass of people on the runway. "The needs of the many..." he quoted to himself from Dickenson. "They outweigh the needs of these few..."

The parking lot megaphone blared its adamant message again. "You need to clear the runway immediately, people!"

"Could they be right?" Sonny Dais asked from behind Kodak's camera. "Maybe these people need to move."

"They're bluffing, Ms. Dais," Creighton replied off-megaphone. "And you should remember you're here to report the story, not participate in it."

"Fine," she replied with her hand on her hip, then turning to point at the taxing plane. "Hey, that Cessna — I think he's headed this way, Kodak. You should get some of that."

"Already on it," Kodak answered, turning his camera toward the plane as others did the same.

Alarmed by the media's change in focus, Creighton kept his bullhorn at his side as he barked to his nearby militia personnel. "You need to deal with that guy! We can't let him ruin everything!"

Heads and cameras turned back toward Creighton, people gazing at him with anxious expressions. "Pastor?" one woman spoke up. "Whoever it is in that plane, maybe they just don't know what's going on here."

"Of course, I'm sure that's the case." He smiled, nodding as he hoped he'd recovered quickly enough to keep the people in his camp. "Why don't we all wave to the guy so he knows we're friendly," he added, waving his arm as many followed his lead.

"Hey, how's it going?" one young girl yelled toward the Cessna, others following her lead as they waved and shouted kind greetings.

"The plane approaching is *not* responding to our call," the bullhorn voice insisted again. "You must get out of the way!"

Creighton raised the megaphone back to his mouth. "It's time to do what we've come to do, people! We must do as all great civil rights protestors have done before us – sit peacefully as human shields, blocking any plane. Whether they are on the ground or in the air, and whether they are friend or foe, we must *not* allow anyone to pass here or our mission will have failed. Are you with me?"

"Yeah!" the cheer went up, the people holding they're positions in the line.

Spotting Finland at his side, Creighton waved him over, leaning down from his stepladder to speak so only Finland could hear. "I need you to take a group out to meet that plane and get it out of the way."

"Permission to engage?" he asked.

"No, if you shoot, you'll scare off this crowd," he replied. "But I need them subdued one way or another before they ruin all we've accomplished."

"Understood," Finland replied.

Creighton maintained a grin as he glanced about the crowd. "I know I can count on you, so no gunfire, but do whatever else it takes!"

⚜

Chapter 65

At first it looked to be a twinkling star, like Antares or Arcturus or any one of the many he had gazed at through the telescope with Neon and Silas. But as the flickering light bore down on the airport, it became clear that it was an aircraft approaching, and Bridger felt quite certain it had to be Laski's jet.

Panic returned to him as he scuttled about the room, momentarily oblivious to his multiple injuries as he searched for some way to reach the people on the field. In desperation, he knelt by the broken window, wondering if any of them might here his voice over the dueling megaphones if he shouted his own warning.

"That jet could try to land, so you must get out of the way!" a distant, magnified voice echoed across the field.

"We know they answer to you and the governor!" the familiar voice of Creighton reverberated back from where he stood center stage, a semi-circle of camera enveloping him so that he was clearly visible even at a distance.

"Don't listen to him, people!" the frantic voice returned. "Dear God, for the sake of your children, get out of there!"

"You're lying to us just as you have all along," Creighton barked back. "The people here know your tactics, and we know what lengths you'll go to force your way in here! But we won't give in, will we? We won't give in, we won't give in, we won't give in..." he chanted over the speaker, the crowd chiming in with him.

"No!" Bridger shouted, unable to contain himself. "You're going to die! Listen to him!" he screamed at the top of his lungs, but no one on the runway took notice.

"Don't let that plane pass!" Creighton barked down the runway.

Bridger turned his eyes to southeast corner of the field, spotting for the first time an airplane on the move with half-dozen men now approaching it head-on.

"Yeah, move them out of the way!" Bridger yelled, the taxing plane giving him his first glimmer of hope.

"What'd you say?" a militiaman yelled up to Bridger as he walked from the terminal further out on the pavement below. "And what happened to the window?"

"Oh, this..." Bridger's heart raced. "Yeah, we had a bit of skirmish up here, but it's all under control now." He swallowed hard. "And, uh... that plane out there's going to screw everything up if we don't get it out of the way! Rivard wants you and some men from down there to hustle on out and stop it, okay?"

"Okay, then!" The militiaman dashed back toward the underside of the building, shouting to his comrades. "Hey, guys! We've got to go stop that plane!"

After a few seconds of commotion from below, a group of men scrambled out and dashed down the taxiway, heading for where the plane still rolled along the distant tarmac. With the threat removed, Bridger took a deep breath before resuming his frantic search for a way to escape. Standing up, he glanced around until his eyes fell upon what remained of the ropes he'd cut away from himself.

"Are you yelling at someone in there?" a voice asked from outside the door. "What's going on?"

"Uh, everything's fine," Bridger answered as he grabbed the rope and started tying the cut pieces back together.

The doorknob turned and the door jarred as it caught against the door jam. "Hey, something's blocking the door."

Bridger's heart dropped to his stomach. Dropping the rope, he glanced down the two-story drop at his last remaining hope for escape.

The door rattled. "Dude, let us in!" the voice barked from the other side.

Bridger kicked at the Plexiglas, knowing the hole had to be bigger.

"Bridger?" Rivard said from outside the door. "What're you doing?" The door rattled more, the jam still holding but not for long.

Bridger beat the Plexiglas with his foot, more ice-sized pieces chipping away bit by bit. "Come – on – come – on!" He ranted with each kick.

"Get that door open!" Rivard demanded on the other side.

A shot rang out, blowing a hole through the door and sending Bridger diving for the floor.

"No gunfire!" Rivard barked. "You can't scare those people!"

"This'll work!" a voice yelled, followed by the heavy thumping of something beating against the door.

With more whacks, Bridger saw the door inch open, and so he responded in kind; scrambling to his feet, he picked up a chair and threw it at the Plexiglas, shattering away the entire pane.

"Get in there!" Rivard barked. "And somebody go down below!"

Bridger knew he was out of time and out of options, so without hesitation, he leapt from the window, hurdling himself onto the pavement below.

❧

Chapter 66

The sound of breaking glass caught Neon's attention, his eyes searching the outside of the terminal until he found the darkened room with the broken window, heading toward it just as someone leapt from the open frame.

"Holy crap!" he cried out, running full tilt toward the person who fell hard, tumbling across the tarmac.

"What was that?" a militiaman yelled from inside as he rushed out with two others at his side.

"Who is that?" Dylan yelled as he and J Paul ran behind Neon, Chepi and Penne coming up steadily in the rear.

Neon noticed Benedict's jacket on the man lying face down. "Bridger!" he yelled, dashing over to kneel at his side. "That was crazy! Where are you hurt?"

Bridger rolled sideways, grabbing Neon by the shirt to pull him downward. "You've got to... stop them!"

"Yeah, we'll do that! But what about you?"

He grimaced, hugging his arm as he struggled to sit up. "Got to — stop bomb!"

"What?"

"Is he okay?" J Paul shouted as everyone converged on him.

"Yeah," Neon answered, shoving his arms under his friend and lifting him. "I just need to get him—"

"Where'd you think you're going?" a winded militiaman shouted, running toward them from the building.

"Stop him!" Rivard yelled from the broken window above. "He's trying to stop our operation!"

"I'm taking an injured man for help!" Neon yelled back at him, then looking to the militiamen around him. "I know you want to fight the good fight here, but you won't deny a man medical attention, will you?"

"Yes, we will!" the winded man said, drawing his gun. "He stays here!"

"Whoa, dude!" J Paul held up his hands. "Hey, we're on your side! Let us take the guy just over to the ambulance at the fence."

"You're going to put him down *now!*" the winded man demanded.

"They won't... shoot," Bridger sputtered to Neon. "Just – go!"

Neon started to back away.

"Hold it!" the gunman said.

"No, you hold it, man!" a militiaman said. "Let the guy go get some help!"

"You need to stand down, man! Dylan added, shaking his head. "If you shoot, you'll trigger more gunfire and scare the shit out of the protestors."

"He's right," Rivard agreed from above. "Let him go for now."

The winded man caught his breath. "But–"

"I said, stand down!" Rivard yelled.

As the man lowered his weapon, Neon turned and hurried off along the side of the terminal, carrying Bridger toward the ambulance.

"Put me... down!" Bridger demanded, wriggling from his arms. "I've got to... warn them!"

"You're hurt, dude, and we've got to keep you away from the crazies!" he insisted as he struggled to lower Bridger to his feet.

"Ouch!" Bridger stumbled, struggling to stand.

"You probably broke something. Can you lean on me?"

"We can get him," J Paul offered as he ran to Bridger, grabbing his arm as Dylan dashed to his other side.

"No! No!" Bridger pushed them away, hobbling in the direction of the runway. "We've got to move them! That plane's got a bomb!" he shouted, pointing toward the incoming jet.

Chepi caught up, her eyes wide. "A bomb?"

"It's napalm, from the bat bombs!" Bridger added.

"Oh, my God!" Penne yelled out. "Benedict..."

"Dad?" Bridger looked back at her. "Where is he?"

"In that plane!" she shouted, pointing at the Cessna now confronting the group of militiamen at the end of the runway.

"No!" Bridger screamed as he stumbled onward, tripping on his bad leg and falling to the ground.

"Help him!" Neon yelled to the bystanders, throwing caution to the wind as he dashed like a madman past them all.

"But the jet!" Chepi yelled, trying to hurry after him. "You're going to get killed!"

Neon kept running, his fists pumping at his sides. "They're all going to get killed if we don't get them out of the way!"

⚜

Chapter 67

"**T**his is it — the show we've been waiting for!" Creighton announced on the bullhorn as the jet came closer, bearing down on them from the sky.

"I don't know about this, Gus!" Dixie blurted from behind his wheelchair.

"I don't either," Sonny told Kodak. "We should back up... for a better angle. Don't you think?" she asked, already backing away.

"No, hold your ground! Hold your ground!" Creighton barked. "You can do this folks! It's what we've waited for!"

"Hey, they haven't stopped *that* plane," John Paul noted, pointing down the runway to where the Cessna plowed through the militiamen.

"It's okay — it's okay!" Creighton insisted as he stared at the Cessna now approaching. "He won't hurt us, either, folks. I can—"

"Get out of here!" Neon yelled as he ran toward the crowd. "It's a bomb! It's a bomb!"

"A bomb?" Millie shrieked, looking with frightened eyes at her husband John Paul as others muttered the same, a couple scurrying off the runway.

"That's nonsense!" Creighton bellowed in the bullhorn. "It's another decoy sent to scare us, but it won't work! Hold your ground!"

"No, it's really a bomb on that jet!" Neon continued, pointing to the plane in the sky as it grew closer. "Like the ones that caused all the fires — it's napalm!"

"Napalm?" Creighton was taken aback as the possibility that Rivard was willing to kill him, too, suddenly struck him.

"Rivard did it!" Neon yelled at Creighton. "There're bat bombs on that plane!" He stopped, pointing at the jet now descending on its final approach.

"Oh, my God!" Creighton muttered to himself, stepping down from his ladder and backing away from what he feared to be true.

Chapter 68

"He's telling the truth!" Bridger yelled as J Paul and Dylan helped him limp toward where Neon stood. "That thing's going to blow up when it hits!"

"You've got to stay back!" Neon yelled toward Bridger, holding up his arms to motion for the two men to keep him away from the area.

"No! I've got to stop my dad!" he insisted, fighting off the two gripping his arms and stammering toward where the Cessna now taxied along the main runway.

Glancing across the field, Bridger spotted Penne hiking toward the end of the runway. "Stop, Ben!" she yelled from the distance as she, too, gave what little she had left to hurry toward the Cessna.

"You've got to stay back, Penne!" Chepi yelled as she awkwardly jogged with her arm still in its sling, catching up with Penne and pushing her off her feet to stop her from getting too close.

"We've got to stop my dad!" Bridger persisted, limping and hopping toward the Cessna as the military jet loomed close to the field.

"And we've got to get these people out of the way!" Neon yelled after him.

"I'll help!" J Paul shouted as he dashed past Bridger, suddenly taking note of a woman emerging from the fleeing crowd. "Mom?"

"Get your mother out of here!" John Paul yelled as he hurried with his wife and son past Bridger.

"Bridger, help us!" Dixie cried out to him as he staggered past where she stood with Gus, unable to push his wheelchair beyond the pavement.

Torn over helping his father, Bridger hobbled toward the couple to help them first. "The runways cross — we'll get you... out there!"

"I've got them!" Dylan yelled, running past him and racing Gus' chair out of the way. "Run for it, Dixie!" he shouted back to her.

"Oh, my Lord!" Dixie shrieked as she hurried off the runway, heading for the distant fence.

Despite the resolute few still on the runway, Bridger hadn't given up on the Cessna. Gimping along the side of the runway, he suddenly heard a gunshot, sending him tumbling to the grass. "Dad!" he yelled out as he looked up, fearing they had shot his father.

"No, it was me!" Neon said as he ran up behind his friend. "Warning shot to scare off the rest," he explained, lifting Bridger from the ground. "Including you!" he insisted, dragging Bridger away from the runway's edge.

"I've got to stop him!" Bridger insisted as the last of the protestors scattered, running in all directions to get as far away as they could. "He's speeding up!" Bridger noted, waving his arms at the Cessna as it now hurried down the runway.

In Bridger's weakened state, it took little for Neon to strong-arm him into submission, dragging him kicking and screaming away from the imminent danger.

"He's trying to get out of the way," Neon told him. "There's nothing else we can do!"

"He doesn't know there's a bomb!" Bridger cried out, struggling against Neon's tight grip.

"Get out of the way, Ben!" Penne cried out from nearby.

Her shriek echoed across the brightly lit runway where Benedict's plane picked up speed, but not enough to beat the oncoming jet. With its landing gear still retracted, the jet jerked slightly as if the pilot realized the wheels hadn't touched; but it was too late. Something below the jet caught against the tarmac, sparks flying as the jet skidded and rolled and then, in a split second, plowed into the Cessna, both planes igniting into a giant fireball that lit up the night sky.

⚜

Chapter 69

This was not the first time Bridger had lost his father in a fiery crash. It was, however, the first time he had witnessed it, the reality of it pushing so deep into his being that it aggrieved him more now than it ever had when he was just a small boy.

"No! This can't be!" he cried out as he clambered to his feet. "Not now..." With tears blurring his eyes, he wandered toward the blinding brightness that no longer intimidated him, holding up his bloodied hands and his father's leather jacket as protection against the scorching inferno.

"You can't go there!" Neon insisted, pulling Bridger back from the fire. "It's too late, Bridge... I'm sorry, but it's too late."

"I just wanted to..." Bridger began to argue but then stopped with a heavy sigh, reluctantly accepting that Neon was right. "I wanted to see him... one last time." Relenting to Neon, Bridger turned his back on the fire just as the military and emergency vehicles breached the perimeter fencing.

"Come on!" Neon grabbed Bridger by the arm and hurried him away from the center of the field. "No time to see how this goes down between factions," he insisted, helping Bridger toward the nearest ambulance that came to a stop nearby. "Let's get you some help — far away from this mess!"

"But where're the others?" Bridger scanned the field as he hobbled toward the back of the ambulance. "Chepi and Penne... are they okay?"

"They're coming," Neon answered as he helped Bridger over to a stocky EMT, then turning to point toward the two women walking arm in arm out of the darkness of the night.

"You better go help them," Bridger said, nearly passing out as the stocky EMT guided him to a seat on the cool, damp grass.

Neon jogged a few yards out to meet them, grabbing Penne at the waist and lifting her into his arms as she went limp. "Hey, we need help with this one!" he shouted as he hustled toward a slimmer EMT who came out to meet them.

"I think she's in shock," Chepi told the slim one as she took a step back. "And I'm sure she's already got a concussion from earlier today."

"How much earlier?" Slim asked as he reclined Penne on the ground. "What happened to her?"

"Probably a pistol-whipping, maybe five hours ago at most," Neon answered.

Chepi went to Bridger, gazing at him with wide, frightened eyes. "Oh, my God! What did they do to you now?"

"Did a lot of it... myself," he had to admit as the stocky EMT dabbed at his hands with gauze. "Broke the glass to get away. Ouch!" He hissed.

"Pretty deep cut here," Stocky told him.

"Yeah," Bridger agreed. "And I've got more... even deeper, on my back."

The slim EMT went to the back of the ambulance, wheeling out the gurney. "Definitely need to take the girl to ER," Slim told his partner.

"Yeah, let's send this one along," Stocky replied. "He's definitely going to need stitches."

"Your dad, Bridger..." Chepi said, reaching around the EMT to gently hug him. "I'm so, so sorry."

Bridger nodded with appreciation but couldn't say a word.

"And Penne's hysterical," she added. "They must've been very close."

"Yeah, I think so." Bridger looked to where they lifted Penne onto the gurney, relieved to see her eyes open as she gazed back at him.

"There for a minute, I thought your dad was going to make it," Chepi told Bridger. "But that jet came in so fast... There's no doubt a lot of people would've been killed if it weren't for him."

She bit her lip, tears falling from her eyelashes. "He was a very brave man."

"So they say," Bridger nodded, his chin quivering as he looked away from her to glance about the chaotic scene unfolding before them. In the glow still emanating from the raging fire, he could see militia, protestors, officers, firemen, and Guardsmen all scuttling about one another without coming to blows. Instead, they all worked side by side, rivals helping foes, neighbors helping strangers, the uninjured comforting the frightened and aiding the walking wounded in anyway they possibly could.

Holly drove her police Cherokee next to the ambulance, leaning out the window toward Bridger. "You're a train wreck, Klein! Glad your friends found you — are you okay?"

"Will be, with some stitches," he answered, pointing toward the terminal. "There're bad guys... in there, too. One's Dawson Rivard."

"Rivard... haven't heard that name." Holly looked down to write in her notes. "They're rounding up people in there so I'll check on it. He did this to you?" she asked, pointing at his injuries.

"He and his men attacked us at the TV studio," Chepi explained. "They tied us all up and beat up Neon and his boss Al, and then they took Bridger at gunpoint."

"And they dragged you here," Holly added as she continued making notes. "Okay, I'll check on that. And we're also looking for that Creighton guy who was on the bullhorn, so best get to it — I'll catch up with you at the hospital," she told him as she drove off across the grass.

"Hang in there, boss," Neon said to Penne as he helped Slim wheel her to the back of the ambulance. "Now I'm sending Klein with you, so you need to keep an eye on him until I find you at the hospital. You got that?"

Penne stared up at the sky, unresponsive, as they loaded her into the ambulance.

"You need to go with them and get those cuts stitched up," Chepi told Bridger.

"Yeah, this is your ride, too," Neon added as he helped Bridger up off the ground. "And I'm thinking maybe I should ride with you two."

"Not enough room for you, buddy," Stocky told him as he climbed into the back of the ambulance. "But let's get your friend in."

"Hey, Bridger! You okay, dude?" a familiar voice asked from behind them.

Bridger turned around to find Kodak standing with his camera under his arm. "Yeah, I'll be all right," Bridger told him.

"Good deal, because I've got some crazy footage that me and my man, Neon here, need to put together for the eleven o'clock. But I lost my reporter – she's busy helping out the people, you know," he added, pointing to Sonny Dais who was helping an elderly lady to another nearby ambulance.

"Yeah, that's not going to happen," Neon replied as he held the door, offering an arm up to Bridger.

"And you're not done here," Bridger told Kodak as he climbed into the ambulance and pointed back at the field filled with people helping others. "Tape all this – it's what's important."

"What? You mean all this helping stuff?" Kodak scratched his head.

"In all this mess, it's what matters most, isn't it?" Bridger said as Stocky helped him sit down beside Penne's gurney. "Show people... the surprising part."

"You mean the part where the planes blow up?" Kodak asked.

"No..." Swallowing hard, Bridger looked beyond where firefighters battled the smoldering remains of the crash that had taken his father's life, discerning the broader image of countless people whose lives had been spared and their faith in one another restored by the tragic sacrifice of one. "Devastation is... an easy story," Bridger choked on his words, fighting back tears. "Tell people something... they never would've imagined."

"Um... guess I'm kind of slow with this." Kodak shook his head. "I'm not sure what you mean."

"He means the good stuff, dude!" Neon said as he closed one of the ambulance doors. "Don't just tell them about a bunch of fires and shootings and..." Neon paused, gazing at Bridger. "He's saying you shouldn't give the bad guys what they wanted by scaring people with the carnage. Instead, you should show them the sacrifices people made and how this disaster brought people back together."

"Oh, like they did with the 9/11 coverage?" Kodak nodded. "Yeah, that's a good idea. Thanks, guys!" Shouldering his camera, he headed off into the night.

Neon grabbed the other ambulance door. "See you two at the hospital, then."

"Yeah..." Bridger nodded.

"We'll watch the eleven o'clock while they stitch you up — see if Kodak can get that video on by then," Neon added as he began to close the door.

"Yeah, hope he can," Bridger dragged his leg back from the doorway and slumped in his seat, gazing down to find himself covered in blood. "I'd like to see... the good guys win."

Chapter 70

Upon the breach of the airport's perimeter, Thoreau had directed his handful of Cadre operatives to scatter among the panicked protestors, figuring that to be their best chance for escape. Lifting a set of keys for himself from the Hertz counter, he managed to commandeer a Toyota Camry from the rental lot and flee the chaotic scene unnoticed by the overwhelmed police force. Then taking the highway northward, he picked up I-75 and continued to the tip of Michigan's Lower Peninsula where he could see the Mackinac Bridge suspended for the next five miles ahead of him, its illuminated towers and suspension cables marking the gateway to the next leg of his journey toward Canada.

As he passed the bridge's southern tower, Thoreau decided he shouldn't wait any longer to hear from his other men. Grabbing his cell phone from the passenger seat, he scrolled through his business contacts to select the one marked *Macro Alliance* and pressed call.

"Yes," a deep voice answered.

"It's Thoreau. Put Rue on the line."

"Just a minute," the person said, putting him on hold.

Thoreau turned on the speaker option and set the phone aside, freeing both hands to grip the steering wheel as the Camry jerked about in the wind blowing across the Straits and up through the open grate surface beneath him. Coming up on a slow-moving semi with its flashers blinking, the eighteen-wheeler's high profile further amplified the winds effect, rocking Thoreau's car as he made his way past the trucker.

"We've been waiting to hear from you," a woman said on speaker. "I was just beginning to wonder if you got out clean."

"Well, I'm as far as the Mac Bridge, so I'm probably good. But my team hasn't checked in yet, so I'm concerned they may have been captured. Most of them should be able to play it up as militia, though, so I'm hoping they'll all eventually make it to the rendezvous."

"Okay, let's sit on it for the night and see where we're at come dawn," she told him. "We're assessing the media coverage online now and waiting to catch network broadcasts as they come in. So far, we're hearing mixed reviews."

"Yeah, we had people pretty riled up, but things didn't end as we'd hoped," Thoreau told her. "The missionary came through for us with his pilot – got the guy to come in hot with the explosives on board, so we definitely got the big bang we were looking for. Unfortunately, though, all the protestors cleared the area before he came in, so we only got minor injuries along with one added fatality – your man, Benedict."

The woman gasped. "You killed him?"

"*I* didn't kill him, Rue! The pilot did – smashed into a plane the guy was driving around on the runway to scare all the people out of the way."

"But that's not possible," Rue sighed. "After all these years, I just… can't believe he's gone."

"Well, that's not the reaction I expected. I figured you'd be angry, but you sound… upset."

"Of course, I'm upset!" she snapped. "We needed him, you fool! He carried a wealth of information we could've used to put an end to this DIG nonsense, once and for all!"

"Okay, okay!" Thoreau replied as he passed the north tower, now approaching the tollgate on the opposite shore of the Straits. "Well, he's gone now, so there's not much we can do about it."

"Apparently… but I still want it confirmed. We'll do some extra digging after the crash report comes back so we can make sure it's really Benedict who's gone and not another ploy like he pulled before."

"You mean the one with the Klein kid."

"Yes," she answered. "And now that you mention it, what did you do with our young news reporter?"

"Not much!" he retorted. "He got away from us just before the explosion, and at that point I figured it better to let him go before he screwed up everything."

"Hmm... I see."

"But I suppose it doesn't matter now that dear old dad's dead – guess you won't be needing him anymore for anything."

"Not necessarily," Rue remarked. "There are others that maybe he could be used against, so he might prove useful again another day."

"Well, let's cross that bridge when we come to it," Thoreau remarked as he completed his own crossing of the Mackinac Bridge, driving up to a tollbooth and handing over a couple of dollars. "Keep the change," he said, pulling away as the toll collector nodded with thanks.

"I take it you've made it to the Upper Peninsula," Rue remarked. "Less than an hour and you'll be across the International Bridge on the Canadian side of Sault Ste Marie, so how about we meet you at the rendezvous around eleven.

"That'll work," he answered. "Then I can fill you all in on the rest."

"We'll look forward to it," Rue said. "In the meantime, don't dwell on today's final outcome. I know we didn't get as far as we'd hoped this time, but you still struck a major blow, Thoreau. You planted more seeds of doubt in the American psyche – seeds that we can bring to fruition soon if we just keep tending to them... and we will."

"I know." He nodded. "We just need some time to regroup."

"Yes, we do," Rue agreed. "So, hurry back and we'll get started on our newest plan – one that, next time, they won't be able to stop."

⚜

Chapter 71

"Is this what I'm wearing home?" Bridger asked as he sat up on the ER rooms examining table and looked down at the blue paisley pattern covering his hospital gown.

"Well, you won't be wearing these," the nurse replied as she held up what was left of the blood-splotched jeans they had cut off from him. "And your shirt was worse on the back, so I guess you're stuck." She pushed his jeans into the garbage liner, releasing the pedal to let the lid drop back into place. "I do have patient pants, though, so you won't have to travel bare-butt."

"I suppose that'd be better," he said as he looked at the multiple Band-aids on his bare legs and the ace wrap around his sprained ankle. "It might be good to cover up all these little nicks and bandages, too."

The nurse reached into the cabinet. "Everything's got to be better now that the doctor got all of those tiny shards of glass out of yours legs; and I have to tell you, he did a nice job stitching up your back, as well."

"So, my scar's not going to be any worse than it was?"

"Well... I'd see what the plastic surgeon has to say when you see her next week." Digging deeper into the cabinet, she pulled out a pair of tie pants speckled with tiny pansies and held them up by the waist so the legs dangled. "These should work, and I bet they'll fit over your ankle bandage, too. So, you've just got to remember to bring them back when you're done with them."

Bridger raised his eyebrows. "Don't worry — they're not really my style."

The nurse laughed. "Yeah, but what's even more embarrassing is that I'll have to help you put them on since your hands are bandaged up," she said, holding them low so Bridger could slip his legs into them.

"You've got me there," he replied as he slid his legs into the pansy pants and stood up on his good leg long enough for her to tie them at his waist, then sitting back down on the table.

"Now I've got to go fill out your release papers and bring them back for you. Is there anything else you need?"

"My dad's jacket?" he asked, concerned about what had come of it.

"The leather one," she replied, reaching over and pulling it off the back of the chair behind him. "We saved that, but it'll definitely need the dried blood stains cleaned off the inside. Did you want it on now? It might keep you warmer than just that open-backed gown."

"Yeah, thanks," Bridger said as the nurse helped him carefully slip his wrapped hands through the arms of the coat, gently hiking it up unto his shoulders.

"You've got friends biting at the bit to see you," she told him. "Do you feel up to seeing them yet?"

"Yeah, you can send them in."

She walked out the door just far enough to wave down the hallway. "You can come back now." Then she glanced back at Bridger. "I'll be right back," she told him, walking away just as Neon stepped to the doorway.

"Has the doc got you stitched up, dude?" Neon asked as he held up his fist to Bridger, looking for a bump instead of a shake.

Bridger held up both of his gauze-wrapped hands. "No fist-bumps for a while."

"Thank God, you're okay!" Kelli Sue said as she came in behind Neon, stepping to Bridger's side with her hands out-stretched. "Can I hug you?"

"If you're careful," he answered, allowing her to press her arms against his shoulders. "But where did you come from, and where's Chepi?"

"Oh, I've been here a while," Kelli Sue answered. "I brought Al in after the troopers came and hauled that one bad guy out of the station. But don't worry — I locked the station doors when

I left, and Kodak was bringing Sonny in shortly to put together something for the eleven o'clock."

"I see," Bridger said.

"And I dropped Chepi at the hotel so she could find her dad and maybe get a little rest before checking on you," Neon added, glancing at his watch. "But that probably won't happen now, since the governor's doing another presser shortly."

"She is?" Bridger questioned. "Man, hasn't she done enough damage already? What's she going to say now?"

"I don't know, and I promise we won't be there to find out," Neon answered. "I think we've earned ourselves a vacation from all of this. Don't you?"

"Yeah... I suppose we have." Bridger took a deep breath, sighing. "So, what's the deal with Al, K-Sue? Is he doing okay?"

"They're keeping him overnight for observation, but he's doing pretty well... considering," Kelli Sue added, lowering her head. "He's pretty upset over all of this, and he's still very worried about you."

"I'm fine." Bridger nodded. "But they still won't tell me anything about Penne, and it's got me really worried about her. Do you guys know anything yet?"

"Yeah, I actually went in to see her," Neon told him. "She's definitely got a concussion but I overheard that the CAT scan looked good — no signs of fractures or hemorrhaging. She's just still in shock — isn't talking yet, but I'm sure she will."

"I hope so," Bridger replied. "There's still so much... I want to know." He bit his lip, struggling against his overwhelming desire to cry.

"There's a detective here who wants to talk to you, Bridger," the nurse said from the doorway. "Are you up to seeing her, too, or should I have her wait."

"It's fine. I think I know who she is."

As the nurse stepped away, Holly entered the room. "Well, you look better," Holly told him.

"Thanks."

"I didn't say you look good — just better," she added with a smile. "So, are you up to a couple of questions while it's all still fresh in your mind?"

"Can't promise anything fresh — they've got pretty good drugs, you know, so it feels a bit cloudy in here," Bridger said, tapping on his head.

"Well, let's give it a try, and maybe these two can fill in some blanks if you can't," Holly said, pulling out her notepad. "So, that J Paul kid who was accused of taking the shot at the casino... he's good friends with the Granger boy who lost his grandpa at the gourd farm today, and so the two of them caught up with this Creighton guy out on the field. Guess they did a number on the old Pastor before they hauled him in for the police to deal with, so the guy's pretty banged up."

Neon tightened his jaw. "Good for them!"

"Not sure about that, but we'll see what comes of it," Holly replied. "So, this Creighton was running this militia operation, but you're all still telling me that he wasn't the guy at the top. Is that right?"

"Yeah, that's right," Bridger answered. "This Dawson Rivard guy who claimed he worked for the state parks as some kind of historian ended up being the one who was pushing all the buttons. He even told me he had someone on the inside at the Alpena Air Guard Base who loaded the last of all that napalm on that military jet without Creighton or the pilot even know-ing about it as it flew in and..." He stopped, unwilling to speak anymore of the horror he'd witnessed.

"I got it." Holly made some notes. "So, this Rivard seemed to be the brains behind this, and he had an inside affiliation with the one bad guy we brought in from the TV station and at least one other man we may now have in custody."

"Gomez and Finland?" Kelli Sue offered. "Well, that's what their Guard uniforms said, so we called them that."

"So, you think you've got Gomez and Finland?" Bridger asked Holly. "But what about Rivard?"

"Still working on that from some details we got at the scene."

"Well, I'll tell you something about that Rivard guy!" Kelli Sue interjected. "He was going to shoot Neon, and then he took Bridger and... look what he did to him! The man's a real son of a bitch!"

"Kell – E – Sue!" Neon exclaimed. "Yeah, he is, but your language!"

Holly flipped through her notes, looking to Kelli Sue. "And you must be Miss Llewellyn, the one our trooper didn't get a statement from because you had to take your boss Al to the hospital while they dealt with the suspects." She scribbled something. "Yeah, I need your descriptions of these guys, too, so maybe I'll start with you while Klein gets dressed to get out of here."

"Uh... this is it," Bridger said, pointing down at his mixed attire.

"And I love it!" Neon mocked, pressing his index finger against his cheek. "Is it a part of the hospital's new autumn collection? I mean, nothing says fall like paisley and pansies!"

"Don't knock it until you've tried it," the nurse told Neon as she entered the room, holding up a clipboard with attached papers. "I know it'll be hard to sign with those bandages, Bridger, so is anybody here next of kin?"

All eyes fell on Bridger as he gazed back at them and then looked down.

Neon grabbed the pen from the nurse. "Brother here – adopted late in life. Where do I sign?"

The nurse pointed to the lines on the paper. "Here and here," she said, holding the board as Neon signed, then handing him Bridger's prescriptions. "Fill these scripts and make sure he takes them so I don't see him back here tomorrow."

"But what if we *want* to see you again tomorrow?"

Bridger tapped with his gauze-wrapped hands at the front of his paisley gown. "Then you can bring her back this lovely attire from the fall collection."

"I can do that," Neon said, smiling at the nurse. "And one last thing – I need a wheelchair so I can take Bridger to see the rest of the family – people who've got to stay overnight, you know."

"He'll need to rent one, but you can borrow the one outside the door just as long as you make sure it ends up back in the ER when you leave tonight."

"Wouldn't dream of leaving it anywhere else," Neon told her as she left the room.

"And where do you think you're going?" Holly asked.

Neon looked at her. "I thought it'd be good for BK to see how Al and Penne are doing before we leave."

"But I told you I've got some questions to ask Bridger, and you, too."

"And you said you could start with darling Kelli Sue here, so let's do that."

"Yeah, we'll go talk in the waiting room," Kelli Sue said. "Meet us there when you're done, and tell Al and Penne I hope they're feeling better, will you?" she added as she left the room.

"We will." Bridger eased himself off the table.

"Okay, but you two need to hurry along," Holly insisted as she stepped into the hallway. "I've still got a lot of ground to cover tonight," she added, hurrying off to the waiting room.

"And you need your rest, dude, so we need to get going," Neon added as he helped Bridger through the doorway and over to the wheelchair, then easing him into it.

"Thanks," Bridger said to Neon as he sat down, managing to get both feet onto the footrests. "I can't thank you enough for... being here for me." He blinked, the tears welling up again.

"Well, what else am I going to do?" Neon smirked.

"No, really," Bridger asserted. "You've always been there for me, and now... you're all I've got left to–" He choked up, unable to finish.

"Hey, now cut that out," Neon said, kneeling at his side. "Yeah, we lost Silas, and that's awful. And it's terrible that we lost your dad, too. But you were doing okay all of this time when you thought he was already gone... and that's because you've got plenty of other people who care about you, and you know that."

He stood up, stepping to the back of the wheelchair and pushing Bridger toward the elevator.

Bridger bit at his lip, wiping at his eyes. "I suppose you're right."

"Damn straight, I'm right!" Neon answered as he pushed the up button to page the elevator. "First you've got problems with too many people worrying about you, and now you don't think there're enough? I don't think so! You can never have too many friends, but believe me, you've got plenty watching over you!"

"Yeah, I guess I do," Bridger had to smirk. "So, I suppose it's about time we go watch over them for a little while."

⚜

Chapter 72

Gazing at the still body reclining in the hospital bed below dimmed lights, Bridger kept his voice to a whisper as Neon wheeled him into Al's room. "I think he's asleep," he said.

"No I'm not." Al rolled his head to the side, looking at them as Neon parked the wheelchair right next to the bed. "And what're you two doing here?"

"Visiting you," Neon answered, stepping over to a vinyl recliner and plopping himself into it. "Thought you might like company."

"At 10:30 at night?" Al rolled back, grimacing as he moved. "Not usually, but for you two, I'll make an exception."

"Looks like you're really hurting," Bridger commented.

"Just some bruises and a couple of cracked ribs, I guess." Al hissed as he tried to straighten his bed sheets around his chest. "Nothing a little time won't heal."

"I'm really sorry, Al. I feel awful about you getting beat up like that."

"No need to be sorry — it wasn't your fault."

"But you were trying to protect me."

"And obviously not doing a very good job of it," Al said back. "I'm the one who should be apologizing, for not keeping you safe... or Silas, or your dad."

"Actually, I think we've all done enough apologizing for one day." Neon shifted in his seat. "I mean, you've got to remember that there were some pretty bad actors at work here, too, so maybe they're the ones we should be blaming for what happened."

"Well, you're right about that," Al agreed with Neon, then glancing at Bridger. "But I still feel badly for having kept all of this from you. I just hope you can understand that we did all of this hoping we could protect you."

Bridger nodded. "Yeah, I know that now — and I guess I need to thank you."

"No, there's no reason to thank me, son. Everything I've done I have *chosen* to do — no regrets."

"Well, I appreciate that." Bridger smiled at him. "So... when do you get out of here?"

"They say tomorrow," Al answered.

"Then right back to the old grindstone, huh?" Neon asked.

"Not quite that fast." Al grimaced, grabbing at his side as he turned to look again to Bridger. "But you'll be back at it now that this is over; probably putting together some laudable exposé that'll finally land you that national gig."

"I don't know about that," Bridger replied.

"You're kidding, right?" Al chuckled, gritting his teeth at the pain it caused him. "But that's what you always wanted, isn't it? And now there's nothing holding you back, so I figured you'd be ready to fly."

Neon stood up from his seat. "I think he just needs some time to think things through, Al."

"Yeah, I want to sort this out before I decide where I go from here."

"Fair enough," Al responded. "And I can't think of a better place to do that than Mission Point."

"Hadn't thought of that idea, and it's not a bad one," Neon nodded as he stepped to Bridger's wheelchair. "What do you think, dude?"

Bridger sighed. "Well, I suppose it'd be a chance to go through, you know... personal effects or whatever remnants there are that I should probably deal with."

Al nodded. "You won't have to do that alone, Bridger. You know we'll help you with that."

"Yeah, and I appreciate that Al."

"And now we've got to go see Penne before we leave," Neon told Al as he backed Bridger into the hallway. "Guess we'll see you tomorrow, boss man."

"I'll plan on it."

"We will, and get your beauty rest," Neon added as he pushed Bridger away. "Looks like you could use some."

Chapter 73

The wall-mounted television was on but muted when Bridger entered Penne's room, Neon pushing his wheelchair from behind. All the room lights were on, too, as a nurse leaned over Penne, flicking a pen light in her eyes and making notes on her medical chart.

"How's she doing?" Bridger asked as Neon pressed down the brake lock on the wheelchair.

"Uh, okay," the nurse answered, looking a bit startled. "It's past visiting hours, you know."

"It's family," Neon mumbled. "These two went through a lot together today, so I figured a visit would do them both good."

"A short one," the nurse insisted as she flicked off the overhead light and headed out of the room. "You've got five minutes."

"Hmm..." Neon curled his lip. "So, what's got her wound up tighter than a pair of Speedo swim trunks?"

"Hey, Penne — It's me, Bridger." He lifted his wrapped hands, resting them next to her on the side of the bed. "I don't think you'd want me to touch you with these mitts." He lifted one hand near her face, but she didn't look toward it, her eyes remaining fixed on the ceiling. "So, I guess I won't try holding your hand."

"Do you think she hears you?" Neon asked as he took a seat on the opposite side of her bed.

"Yeah... I do."

As they sat for at least a minute in silence, Bridger studied the physical intricacies of the woman he had come to know quite well in such a short time. He gazed at the tiny lines of age creasing the edges of her eyes and her lips, the gentle slope of her rounded nose, the hints of silver feathered through the light tones of blonde about her forehead and cheeks, and her long lashes brushed deep brown with mascara that fluttered with each blink of her vacant eyes. And as he watched her, he wondered more about who she really was, remaining most curious about her relationship with the father he knew so little about.

"Who was my father to you?" he asked her. "Were you... in love with him?"

"Bridger," Neon said from across the bed. "She's not going to answer you right now. All of that'll have to wait until later."

Bridger sighed. "But there's so much... I just want to know."

"It'll come," Neon told him. "And since we're staying at Mission Point where she'll end up, too, once she's doing better, then you'll have plenty of time to talk there."

"Yeah, and then maybe I can find out how I came to see her so long ago when I..." His voice trailed off.

"We'll get to it, dude," Neon said as he grabbed the remote control. "Hey, it's the governor. Let's hear what she's got to say for herself." He pushed the volume button. "Bet Penne would like to hear her sorry story, too."

"Just for a minute, and keep it down," Bridger insisted as the volume came up just loud enough to be heard.

"...and from our base of operation, we've been carefully monitoring events as they've unfolded this evening," the baggy-eyed governor said into the bouquet of microphones, the stark glare of camera lights bleaching her white as a sheet. "And I want to assure the public that the situation has been and still remains under control as the many dedicated members of our outstanding emergency forces continue to tackle the multiple crime scenes we've confronted over the past forty-eight hours."

"Under control..." Neon scoffed. "Yeah, but under *whose* control?"

"But as we've faced a multitude of tragedies today, people should take note of the many triumphs we've seen, as well, paying particular attention to the countless acts of goodwill witnessed at the airport when one of our National Guard aircraft accidentally collided with a private pilot mistakenly taxing on the runway."

"Mistakenly?" Bridger sat upright, still keeping his voice down. "What's she saying?"

Neon leaned forward. "Well, sounds like she's flipping the blame – probably trying to cover the Guard as well as her ass."

"We unfortunately lost two people in the accident," the governor noted. "However, we could have lost countless more were it not for the heroic deeds of everyday citizens who helped their fellowman flee to safety. These are the selfless acts of valor that prevailed in the face of evil. They are the kind gestures that today won over the hearts of those who stand here with me tonight." She motioned toward those standing just behind her shoulders as the camera slowly backed out to take in the bystanders. "They are representatives from factions who were previously at odds but now understand the need to find common ground."

"Is that Chepi there with her dad?" Bridger lifted his hand toward the screen.

"Yeah, and that's Dixie with just the top of Gus' balding head in front of her."

"I know you in the media would like to hear these people's stories, but first I'd just like to say how pleased I am to have witnessed the smooth execution of our emergency procedures. The effective cooperation between multiple divisions has proven exemplary, demonstrating that our vigilance in developing these strategic plans of operation have paid off. And so, with that, who here would like to tell their recollections of the great courage they witnessed today?"

"I'd just like to say something," Chepi said, moving to the podium as the governor stepped out of her way.

"Wonder what she's got to say," Neon whispered, leaning back.

"I'd like to tell you about the Cessna pilot who died today, because I know for a fact that his presence on the runway was no accident," she said. "That man took a plane out on the runway to scare away the protestors so they wouldn't get hit by a plane that had been stolen from a nearby air base."

With a sudden flurry of camera shutters clicking and flashes popping, the governor tried to cut in. "This is highly speculative and there are others wanting to speak who—"

"How do you know this?" a reporter questioned as the flashes continued to fire away at Chepi.

"I suppose I can't prove the plane was stolen, but I heard about it from people right there on the ground. And as for the Cessna pilot, I was right there on the field and witnessed the whole thing. So, I can tell you for a fact that the pilot of that small plane was the biggest hero of them all."

"Yes, he was," Dixie chimed in, nodding in the background.

"And let me add to the media that I suggest you wait to get the final report on what really happened before you go spreading any myths," Chepi said as she glanced at the governor. "I think you'll find that a further investigation will reveal many more truths than you might find here at this podium, and so I guess that's all I've got to say." She ended, walking away from the media's barrage of questions.

"Thanks, Chepi," Bridger said to the television.

"Man, our governor is something else," Neon whispered as he turned off the television. "Do you think she actually believes her own bullshit?"

"Yes, I do," Penne said.

"Penne!" Bridger turned to her. "Are you all right."

"Yes..." she said, her chest rising with a heavy sigh. "No... I don't." Her lips quivered, curling into a frown. "How could this happen?" Tears ran down her cheeks as her chest heaved. "He shouldn't have died!"

"I know, I know!" Bridger reached toward her with his wrapped hands. "I'm so sorry, Penne."

"And I'm sorry... for you!" she managed to tell him.

The nurse rushed into the room. "What's going on? Her heart rate's racing!"

"I'm okay," Penne told her, wiping her eyes with her arm.

"Oh, and you're coming around, which is good," the nurse said. "But these gentlemen must've upset you. Five minutes is up, guys, so time to leave."

"No, really... they're fine," Penne said, trying to tamp down her emotions. "I want them here."

The nurse scowled. "But honey, I need to check your vitals and do some—"

"They brought me around," Penne pointed out. "Please... just a couple minutes."

The nurse took a deep breath, looking at Neon. "Don't upset her again because I'll be right outside that door," she told him, marching out.

"What did I do?" Neon said.

"Speedo comment," Penne told him as she tried to sit up in her bed.

"You heard that?" Neon said as he leaned over and pushed the button to raise the back of Penne's bed for her. "So, you *were* listening, weren't you?"

She wiped her eyes, "Barely." Taking a deep breath, she looked to Bridger. "But I did hear you, and we do need to talk. I just... can't right now." She bit her lip.

"Hey, that's all right. It's going to be okay," Bridger tried to reassure her even though he felt like it wasn't. "We'll talk when you get out of here. There's a lot I'd like to know."

"I realize that," she nodded, reaching for a tissue from her side table. "I just want to say this..." She struggled, dabbing at her eyes with the tissue. "Your dad... he *never* wanted to leave you. But now that he's gone..." She caught her breath. "I know he'd be glad... that you're finally safe." Her shoulders shuddered with her sobs.

Bridger felt helpless in his wheelchair, unable to reach up to comfort her and, at that moment, incapable of comforting himself, as well.

"We're both so sorry for your loss," Neon told her as he placed his hand on her shoulder. "And we'll be around for you if you need anything, because you sure have been there for us."

Penne smiled up at him. "That's very kind, Neon. Thank you."

"But we should probably go before Nurse Annie from *Misery* comes back in here and hobbles one of us," Neon joked as he walked around the bed toward Bridger.

"Yes, I suppose you better." Penne sniffled, looking to Bridger. "And I suppose I can let you go now without chasing after you, although it could take some getting use to."

"I might need an adjustment period, myself," he said with a smirk.

"Just one last thing before you go," Penne said to him.

"Name it."

"Let me see your hands."

Bridger again placed his wrapped hands beside her. "They're still numb from the shots."

"Good," she said, taking one of his hands in hers. "I don't mind your mitts, if you don't mind mine."

"No, I don't mind at all." Turning his hand in hers, he held it as best as he could.

⚜

Chapter 74

After spending most of the week indoors at Mission Point sorting out the estates of Silas and Benedict, Bridger welcomed the afternoon carriage ride despite the blustery winds beginning to blow across the Straits, the gusts stripping the island of what little color remained on the autumn trees. He sat next to Penne with Neon across from them, the three swaying along with the steady clip-clop of the Brabant draft horses pulling their carriage up the hill, heading toward the island cemeteries.

"I still can't get over how many people came to Silas' memorial service," Bridger commented. "I guess I hadn't realized how many lives he'd touched here on the island, including the handful of students who showed up."

"And I thought Neon's eulogy was very touching," Penne added, looking to him. "You really captured Silas' inquisitive spirit — apparently something he'd shared with you two."

"Yeah, he was always trying to teach us something," Neon replied. "That's probably why his students liked him so much."

Bridger nodded. "Now I just wish we could do the same kind of memorial for my dad... but I suppose nobody would show up, would they?"

"The people who mattered most to him would," Penne replied, caressing the top of the urn she carried in her lap. "That's why we're doing this today."

"Yeah, of course we'd be there, but I mean all the other people who owe him so much," Bridger gently rubbed his bandaged hands together, careful not to reopen any of his wounds. "And I'm not just talking about the lives he saved last week, but all the sacrifices he made to help so many people over the years."

"Your dad knew there'd be no glory in his deeds, but he did them anyway because he wanted to make a difference," Penne told him.

"It's like those CIA guys who end up as a star on a wall, or the remains of those in the Tomb of the Unknown Soldier," Neon suggested.

"The Bravest Soldier crumbles in mother earth, unburied and unknown," Penne added. "It's from Walt Whitman." She looked down at the urn. "But we'll do one better than that today."

As the pair of draft horses pulled them past the Post Cemetery, Bridger leaned his head back to see the flag flapping in the wind at half-staff. "I think I came here with Silas a long time ago," he recalled, looking back to Neon. "Were you with us?"

"I don't think so," he answered.

"I remember him telling me that this was one of only four cemeteries in all of the United States where the flag's always kept at half-staff; the other three would be in Honolulu, Gettysburg, and Arlington."

"Silas told you that..." Neon said with an undertone of surprise. "...and you remember it?"

"Yeah, maybe my memory's not as shoddy as it used to be," he said as he looked back at the precise rows of upright headstones, recollecting a childhood stroll when he had walked hand-in-hand with Silas past multiple markers that simply read *U.S. Soldier*. "There're more than a hundred old gravesites in there with less than half of them marked with names, and I seem to recall that bothering me a lot," Bridger told them as he summoned up a much younger visage of Silas, one seen from waist-high through the eyes of a child. "I think I asked Silas how people would know which soldier was which, and he said..." He paused, finding himself suddenly enveloped in the comfort he'd found so often in the simple words and gentle embrace of Silas. "He said God would know, and that's all that mattered."

"He was a wise man," Penne said. "So, I take it you're still okay that we honored his wishes by spreading his ashes on Lake Huron."

"I'm at peace with that," Bridger replied as the carriage passed the Post Cemetery, making its way now between the Catholic and protestant burial grounds.

"Whoa," the carriage driver commanded, the horses coming to a stop.

"Let me help you out," Neon said to Penne as he climbed out first, offering a hand to her.

She climbed out with the urn held tightly in her other hand, then looking up to the driver who sat on the high bench in front of the carriage. "We won't be long."

"Got nowhere to be anyway," the old gentleman replied with a nod.

Bridger climbed down with help from Neon and then gently fisted the soft cotton wrapped around the top of the walking stick that Chepi had given him. Favoring his good leg, he limped along ahead of the others into the protestant cemetery.

"I'm embarrassed to say I don't know where the gravesite is," Penne said.

"So, you didn't help my dad set this up?" Bridger replied as he followed the path to the right, staying close to the inside wall.

"Yes, I did, but it was so long ago, I don't remember what lot we picked."

"It's over here," Bridger said, continuing to lead the way. "I never forgot how to find it, even as a kid. I needed to know so I always felt I could still find my mom and dad." Making his way past an old maple now blown barren by the wind, he hobbled through the dry leaves for a few feet, stopping to look down at the granite stone that read *Elliott Bridger Klein*. "I use to visit him here," Bridger said. "Guess it'll be good that I still can."

Penne stepped forward, uncapping the urn as she looked to Bridger. "You said you had a passage you wanted to read."

"Yeah," he said, opening up his father's leather jacket that he was wearing. "Neon, could you help me get it out of this inside pocket?"

"Sure." He reached inside and removed a pocket-sized New Testament, opening it at the bookmark and holding it close so Bridger could read from it.

"From John 16, verses 32 and 33," Bridger said. "Behold, an hour is coming, and has already come, for you to be scattered, each to his own home, and to leave Me alone; and yet I am not alone, because the Father is with Me. These things I have spoken to you, so that in Me you may have peace. In the world you have tribulation, but take courage; I have overcome the world... Amen."

"I don't want the wind to carry him away," Penne told them as she knelt by the headstone, tipping the urn close to the ground to pour out what few remnants they'd been able to retrieve after the fire. "Let's just make sure he stays put," she added, brushing her hand back and forth across the grass and then dusting them off as she stood up.

Bridger took a deep breath. "And you're sure we're not going to find any old records of his real name – the one he had before he first went undercover with that violent Trotskyists faction at U of M?"

"The whole idea with these identity changes is to bury them so deep that nobody can find them. Unfortunately, that means us, too."

"So, this is the best we can do," Bridger replied, pointing toward his father's headstone and then glancing at the one right next to it. "And Roslyn Klein..." He looked at Penne. "My mom's not here, is she?"

Penne looked down. "No, she's not."

"And since you don't know who my father was way before all of this..." He paused, looking down at his mother's plot. "You don't know where she is, do you?"

"No, I don't." Penne shook her head. "But I promise I'll do my best to find her."

"And you know I will, too," Neon added, patting him on his good shoulder.

Bridger nodded. "Thank you." He backed away, cautiously leaning against his stick as he headed back toward the carriage.

"Hey, here's your Bible," Neon said as he walked up to his friend and pulled open his jacket, trying to shove the New Testament back into the pocket. "Why won't it go back in?" He withdrew the book. "It's like something's in the way." Reaching into the pocket, Neon withdrew what looked to be a tarnished medal in the shape of a maltese cross attached to a faded red, white, and blue ribbon. "What's this?" he asked, handing it toward Bridger.

"I'm not sure," Bridger took the piece in his wrapped hand, turning it over to discover a brooch pin attached to the back of the ribbon. "It looks military," he said as he examined the fine print encircling an eagle in the center of the cross. "*Lex Regit Arma Tuentur* - don't know what that means." Managing to flip the medal once more, he found another circular inscription around crossed swords. "And this says *M.O. Loyal Legion U.S.*, then *MDCCCLXV*, which must be...1865?"

"The year the Civil War ended and the Military Order of the Loyal Legion began," Penne added. "That group was formed by Union soldiers determined to keep the nation together after Lincoln's assassinated." She gazed at the medal. "That must've been Benedict's membership medal..." Looking up, she grinned at Bridger. "...and now it's yours."

He looked back at her. "You don't mind if I keep it?"

"I think it came with the coat," she replied, the wind whipping at her tufts of hair. "Besides, it's a men's group so it won't get me anywhere, but maybe you can look into it." She stepped away, walking ahead of them toward the carriage.

Neon took the badge from Bridger's hand and tucked it deep in the outside pocket of his jacket. "Don't want to lose that." Reaching inside the jacket, Neon slid the New Testament back in place, then straightening Bridger's collar. "Now, we better get going, dude."

"No rush, is there?" Bridger started limping forward. "It's not like we have a date or something."

"Actually, we do," Neon replied. "We've got one more stop before we head back to Mission Point."

"Oh, come on," Bridger complained. "I'm really not in the mood for doing anything right now. Can't we just go back?"

"Nope," Neon answered as he helped Bridger along. "You may think you don't want to stop, but trust me — I've got something for you to see that I think you're going to like."

✠

Chapter 75

Gazing out the carriage at the familiar Victorian storefronts along the island's main street, Bridger looked ahead to where he could see Marquette Park on the left with the Indian Dormitory just beyond it. With a lump in his throat, he warded off recollections of the seagulls hovering over the corpse of Silas, choosing to summon up happier times when they had walked the beach or ridden bikes or watched the stars at night.

"Looks like more than the usual crowd finishing up the excavation behind the dorm," Bridger noticed, pointing at the people mingling in the distance.

"That's what I wanted you to see," Neon replied.

"What?" Bridger jerked up his head. "No, that's the last place I want to go today."

Penne looked at him. "Once you get over there, I think you'll change your mind."

"You mean, you knew about this, too?" Bridger asked her.

"I just heard about it today," she replied. "And it's something you're going to want to see."

"Really? And you, too?" he asked Neon.

"Yep."

"Whoa," the carriage driver commanded, the horses coming to a stop.

"It's going to be good," Neon added as he opened the carriage door. "I promise." He climbed out, helping Penne out, too.

Bridger stayed in his seat, staring at the façade of the building where Silas' life had ended. "I really don't want to go in there."

"We're not going inside," a familiar voice said from outside the carriage.

Bridger turned to see Chepi approaching the carriage. "Hey, what're you doing here?"

"Wouldn't miss this," she said, holding out her good hand to him. "Can I help you out of there?"

"Uh… yeah, I suppose I could use a hand." He climbed through the carriage doorway, making his way down to the pavement with his walking stick. "This thing sure has come in handy, so thanks again," he told her as he used the stick to walk with the rest of the group across the road toward the dorm.

"My pleasure," she told him. "Now, we just need to go around the side of the building toward the back."

Bridger stopped at the curb. "I'm not going back there."

"Yes, you are," Neon insisted, taking him by the arm. "And I am, too, because we need to see this."

Bridger reluctantly walked along with the group. "I just don't see what good it's going to do to drum up all the old memories."

"That's not what we're doing," Chepi said. "We're creating new memories today — memories of those who should be remembered." She pointed ahead to where her father stood near the back of the building. "I'll let Dad explain; he can do so best."

Bridger continued with the group, walking up to meet Takota. "Good to see you, sir," he said with a nod, extending his bandaged hand.

"And you, Bridger," Takota replied, hardly touching Bridger's bandaged hand as he gently shook it. "Sorry we couldn't get all the soil put back and the excavation equipment out of the way since they're still unearthing a couple spots. But that's okay since they were still gracious enough to let us go ahead with our plans."

"What plans?" Bridger asked.

"Well, let me show you," Takota replied, guiding the group around piles of dirt lining the peripheral of the dig site to where others stood in a large but incomplete circle.

Looking around at the faces of those gathered, Bridger noticed Al and Kelli Sue standing where the circle still stood open. "And what're you two doing here?" he asked them.

"We were invited, just like you and everyone else," Al answered.

"Come stand with me." Kelli Sue motioned with a smile. "Just look at what they've done!"

Limping with the others to Kelli Sue's side, Bridger finally took notice of the circle of ground in front of the many gathered around it. As the others filled in the remaining gap to complete the circle, Bridger stood with his mouth gaping open as he gazed upon the place where he had found his uncle dead only a week ago, now finding there an elaborate labyrinth with four quadrants sculpted of sod and stone. "It looks like a medicine wheel."

"Do you like it?" Takota asked.

"Yes, it's amazing!" Bridger nodded as he pondered the meticulous efforts put forth by so many to create the intricate shrine in such a limited amount of time. "How did you get this done?"

"We helped," a voice from the circle said, others chiming in with the same.

"Wow!" Bridger shook his head. "First the memorial service for Silas, and then this. He'd be really pleased, don't you think?" He said to Neon.

"He would be," he answered with a grin.

"But I think you need to take a closer look," Takota said as he entered the circle, motioning for Bridger to join him.

Leaning against his walking stick, Bridger followed Takota to the center of the circle, gazing at the familiar faces of those around him — people he recognized from the events of a week ago. "Thank you all for doing this," he told them. "It's incredible."

"As you already noticed, this labyrinth was designed to resemble a medicine wheel," Takota told him. "And just as a medicine wheel's divided into four seasons, we have divided this sacred ground into four places of remembrance for those who have gone before us. To the east and west, we pay tribute to those of our people who have left us too soon."

Chepi moved to the western edge of the circle, pointing to an engraved stone embedded there. "This marker is in memory of Naomi Drummond."

Directly across from her, Dylan Granger stood before the eastern stone. "This marker is engraved with the name William Granger, and I put it here in memory of my grandfather."

Takota held out his arms toward the two stones, then turning ninety degrees. "To the north and south, we remember those who helped our people – the ones who were *your* people who have now left *you*," he added, holding his hands out toward Bridger.

Then Al stepped from the circle, walking stiffly through the pain of his cracked ribs to where he stopped at the southern most point of the circle. "We've placed a marker here engraved with the name Silas Klein so that we will remember this great man who meant so much to us, and who did so much for us," he said, motioning toward the marker at his feet.

With the crowd silent, no one moved for a moment; but then Neon stepped forward, walking to the northern point that marked both the entrance to and the exit from the labyrinth. "And finally..." he began. "It is fitting that we placed the marker engraved with the name of Elliott Klein at the north of the circle where the path begins and ends, because he was there when we began this journey..." He paused, biting his lip. "...and he was there to save us at the end." He took a deep breath. "So, for all of us who walk this labyrinth in meditation, we will be able to think of him when we first begin as well as when we end."

Bridger raised his wrapped hands to his mouth, tears streaming down his cheeks as he looked to his dearest friend, unable to speak.

With not a dry eye in the circle, Neon walked to Bridger in the center and took him by the arm back to their places, telling him, "You know, autumn is the worst time for allergies. We'll hit the Benadryl hard after this is over."

Bridger snickered, grateful for the comic relief.

"How lovely," Penne commented, her chin quivering and eyes blotchy.

"Yeah, it is," Bridger agreed, rubbing her shoulder.

"To conclude our gathering, I understand we have one more tribute," Takota announced as he walked back to his place in the circle.

"Yeah, it's something from the fort," J Paul spoke up from beside Dylan, his parents standing to his other side. "We militia guys wanted to show our thanks, too, so we got a couple of our friends who work at the fort to put together a gun salute, and so if you'd all turn and look up that way..." Pointing up the steep bluff toward Fort Mackinac's white stone walls just off to the west, J Paul tucked his fingers in his mouth and blew an ear-piercing whistle. "Now, some of you might want to cover your ears."

"Wish he'd said that before the whistle!" Neon rattled his head but left his hands at his side. "I can take it — how about you?" he asked Bridger, taking his stick from him so he could cover his ears.

"I'm all set," he replied just in time for the seven men standing along the lengthy fort ramp to fire off a round, reload and fire again, and then repeat the process one last time to finish off their twenty-one gun salute.

"So, that completes our ceremony," Takota said to the group. "Some of you wanted to get together somewhere warmer afterward, so I guess we're gathering at the Yankee Rebel for any of you who want to join in."

"Oh, I love that tavern!" Kelli Sue said to Bridger. "Are you going?"

"I hate to be a party-pooper, K, but I'm just not up to it right now," Bridger told her.

"Oh, my gosh, I totally understand. You should go get some rest because tomorrow's your big day back to work! See you then," she said, giving him a gentle hug before heading off with the younger crowd.

"Told you you'd be glad you came," Neon said to Bridger.

"Yes, you did," he nodded. "And you were right."

"As usual," he added with a smile. "So, ready to get going?"

"I am," Penne said, looking worn out. "This has all been so nice, but I really need to get back now — got a few things to go over with Al before he heads back. We still have many decisions to make as we reorganize, *and* as we wait for you to make up your mind about our offer to expand your work for us," she added, tipping her head toward Bridger as if she expected his answer that very moment.

"Still as *de*-manding and *co*-mmanding as ever," Bridger replied. "Yeah, I think that's what I'm going to do, as long as I'll have more latitude in what I'm covering for the local *and* for ONUS."

"Hmm. Making counter-demands?" Penne's hand went to her hip. "What do you think, Al?"

"I suppose, but don't be expecting me to go easy on you," Al replied while pressing his arm against his chest. "You two need to hit the ground running, or at least limping in your case, Klein."

"We wouldn't have it any other way," Bridger said with a smirk. "Now I just need to do one more thing before we leave here, so could you guys spot me a couple minutes before we head back?"

"Sure," Penne answered. "What do you need?"

"My stick," he said, pointing to where Neon still held it in his grasp.

"Oh!" Neon handed it back to him. "That's it, dude?"

"Nope," he answered, making his way to the northern-most point of the circle. "I just need a brief moment of meditation — enough time to think about how this all began... about where I've been." Turning, he started to walk the labyrinth's narrow path heading toward the center. "After that, then maybe I'll have a better idea of where to go from here."

⚜

AN EXCERPT FROM THE NOVEL

"If I Should Never Wake"

"WHAT CAN'T I LIVE WITHOUT?" Helena Moore pondered while studying her few meager belongings. She knew exactly how much time she had left to decide what few things to take with her, and she was determined to use each minute wisely.

Her motherly instincts drew her to a recent picture of her only child, Kiki. She picked up the framed photo and studied her six-year-old's chocolate eyes, ebony cheeks, toothless grin, and, of course, her beautiful braids of pitch-black hair. How Helena loved her daughter's hair — so satiny soft, not wiry like her own.

Helena thought of bedtime, when her daughter would climb under her covers with those braids still tied in her hair and insist on hearing a story before untying them. So, Helena would tell her daughter about their life before coming to Windemere Island — about the warmth and sunshine they'd left behind in the Caribbean to move to the cool breezes of Northern Lake Huron. While she spoke, Helena would remove Kiki's ribbons and gently weave her fingers through her daughter's hair, untangling the braids until her hair fell softly once more. That was Helena's favorite time with Kiki, and she knew she would miss it terribly.

Helena set the portrait back on the shelf, knowing she would have to leave behind what she valued most.

Running through her mental list, she turned to her dresser, pulled open a drawer, and gazed at the few items of clothing she owned. Helena knew she could take very little with her or else someone would realize things were missing.

"If anyone suspects that you've packed, the deal is off," Helena had been told. She'd been reassured that everything she might need would be provided for her, but she still felt the need to bring some personal belongings.

Rummaging through her top dresser drawer, Helena pulled out a couple of panties and a sports bra. Other than the clothes on her back, this was all she dared to take. She placed the undergarments in the burlap book bag she'd been given to carry her things.

"Don't put too much in the bag," her contact had warned. "People might get suspicious if they see you hauling around a lot of stuff. If you want to get the money, then no one can suspect you planned to leave."

All this secrecy unnerved Helena, but she was willing to endure it for the promise of a very lucrative payday. With all of that money, she would no longer have to work such long hours as a hotel maid, cleaning up after other people's messes — just as her mother had before her.

Helena's mother, Ms. Maya Moore, was a hard-working woman. After Mr. Moore passed away years ago, Ms. Maya started coming to Windemere every summer to earn a better wage than she ever could on St. Croix. Whenever possible, she would work extra hours and set aside the money in the hope that one day Helena would go to college. But then Ms. Maya had fallen down the steps of their apartment house, suffering a permanent injury to her back. There would be no worker's compensation, and their medical benefits were meager. Helena had to face reality: she would have to work to take care of her mother, and her dreams of a better life would just have to wait.

By instinct, Helena picked up Kiki's dirty socks and placed them in the corner hamper. She never minded tidying up after her own family, but resented cleaning hotel rooms for strangers. Helena wanted a better life for her daughter — never wanted her to be stuck cleaning up after others – so for Kiki's sake, she was willing to take this chance.

The hardest part for Helena was knowing she would cause both her mother and daughter great anguish when she left them wondering what had happened to her. It was all supposed to look so sudden, so unplanned, as if she had gone unwillingly. Ms. Maya would fret that Helena might be hurt or even dead, and Kiki would wonder whether she would ever see her mother again.

Helena grabbed a pen and looked for paper to write a brief note telling them that she was okay. She wondered how to reassure them without giving away too much. When she found paper, she considered writing, "Trust no one – Tell no one," but these words sounded so ominous that they might frighten them more than if she said nothing at all. Besides, it would be too difficult for Ms. Maya and Kiki to pretend that Helena had disappeared without a clue when they actually knew something more. Out of their concern, they would be torn over what to tell and what not to tell the authorities. No, it would be best to leave them in the dark.

She set down the pen and blank paper. Her mother and daughter would know the truth soon enough, and then all would be happy when the three of them were reunited back at their true home of warmth and sunshine.

Helena stepped to the bookshelf below her window and removed the novel she had recently signed out at the island library. At the start of chapter three, she found a worn photo she had been using for a bookmark. With her index finger, she caressed the picture's surface, lightly tracing the outline of Ms. Maya embracing Kiki. Helena took comfort in knowing they would have each other.

It seemed likely that no one would notice the book and picture were missing, and even if they did, no one would think much of it. Helena figured people would assume she'd been heading someplace to read, and this would further support the notion that she had not planned to disappear. Besides, she might be bored at this "mystery place" and the book might prove a pleasant distraction — plus this way she had an excuse to take the photo. With this justification, Helena tucked the picture back at chapter three and placed the book in her burlap bag.

With little time left before her escort would meet her at the dock, Helena knew she had to hurry. Besides, her daughter and mother would be returning soon from the movie she had sent them to see. She reached in the closet for a jacket to protect from the late spring chill blowing across the open Mackinac Straits. With a glance at the clock reading 8:30, she knew the time had come for her to go.

Under the glare of the building's security light, Helena took the rickety fire escape stairs off the backside of the house, hoping she would avoid feeling the need to say farewell to the other tenants. As she walked down the steps, Helena glanced for one last time at the unsightly view of the backyard dumpster. This was what she had seen and smelled out her window each day, an impression she was glad to leave behind.

As she crossed the street and walked into the darkness, Helena slowed to consider one last time the magnitude of the choice she was making. She felt so torn over leaving Kiki, but reminded herself that she was doing this for Kiki's sake. Resolute, she regained her determined stride.

Upon approaching the desolate dock, Helena noticed a caustic odor that seemed to be coming from the water. She pressed onward, noting that the smell was growing stronger as she stepped up a small ramp and onto the dock. Glancing down toward the water as it slapped the shore, Helena searched for some sign of what must have been a chemical floating on the surface. In the moonless night, she saw nothing.

Suddenly, a shoe scuffed directly behind her. She spun around to see a figure standing on the ramp.

"You scared me!" Helena released her breath.

"Time to go."

"You're not who I expected." She hugged her burlap bag tightly to her chest.

He lunged at her, his arms grabbing her about the waist. She gagged as he clamped a foul-smelling rag across her mouth. As Helena felt her body go limp, the stranger whispered in her ear.

"I never am."

❧

SOLI DEO GLORIA

❧

Acknowledgements

The kindhearted contributions of many made this novel possible.

Thank you, Kelly, for keeping me on course with your early insights and opinions, and for your continued, unwavering support.

Thank you, Janna, for listening while you walked and for encouraging me throughout the journey.

Thank you, Heidi, for dotting my I's, crossing my T's, and reminding me about the cell phone dead zones.

Thank you, Wendy, for morning wake-up visits, continued encouragement, and for never letting me go hungry.

Thank you, Michele, for your perceptive observations, for suggesting 24, and for always believing in me.

Thank you, Maggie, for never holding back when teaching me what I need to know to make the story work.

Thank you, Mickey, for bringing your legal and tribal insights to the table when talking storylines over coffee.

Thank you, Levi, for sharing your historical and personal insights into the ways of northern Michigan's First People.

Thank you, Raleigh, for speed-reading your way through the manuscript and offering your own special brand of critique.

Thank you, Ron and Jackie, for your guiding ideas for distribution, encouraging me to reach higher and farther than I'd ever imagined.

Thank you, Dale and Ron, for your insights on the challenging realities of law enforcement.

Thank you, Cliff, for trusting me with your arsenal and for teaching me how to shoot straight enough to hit a melon.

Thank you, Paul, for sharing your wealth of knowledge on every handgun known to mankind.

And thank you, dear friends, for so often asking about the next book; your anticipation and eagerness have inspired me to never surrender...

⚜

about the author of
REMNANTS OF THE FIRE

Jeanene Cooper was born and raised in the southern region of Michigan, growing up in the historical community of Marshall and then completing her bachelor's degree in English and Communication at the University of Michigan in Ann Arbor. Upon relocating to Cheboygan in the northern Michigan region, she taught secondary education for over twenty years before leaving the profession to pursue a career in writing. Her first novel, *If I Should Never Wake*, was published in 2008, and was recognized in 2009 with Independent Publisher's Bronze IPPY medal for the Great Lakes Best Regional Fiction. Jeanene still resides in northern Michigan with her husband and two sons.

⚜